If You Ever Tell

CARLENE THOMPSON

St. Martin's Paperbacks

This is a work of fiction. All of the characters, organizations, and events portrayed in this novel are either products of the author's imagination or are used fictitiously.

IF YOU EVER TELL

ISBN: 0-312-37285-X
EAN: 978-0-312-37285-9

Printed in the United States of America

St. Martin's Paperbacks edition / April 2008

St. Martin's Paperbacks are published by St. Martin's Press, 175 Fifth Avenue, New York, NY 10010.

10 9 8 7 6 5 4 3 2 1

With love to April Blankenship

and her faithful companion, Promise

Thanks to Jennifer Meadows

Special thanks to Bridget, Rebekah, and Laurah Bush

PROLOGUE

TERESA FARR NEVER KNEW exactly what awakened her that warm late April night. Her eyes simply snapped open, a gentle breeze blew across her face from the partially raised window, the glowing red numbers of the digital clock on her bedside table flashed from 2:57 to 2:58, and she knew something was wrong.

For a few moments, Teresa lay still with her eyes wide open, making certain she wasn't just waking from a nightmare. Time did not ease her mind, though. Finally, she realized she was already fully awake and caught in an atmosphere vibrating with palpable tension—tension and danger.

She wanted to cry out, just as she'd done when she was a child frightened in the middle of the night and her mother would rush to reassure her all was well. But she wasn't little anymore. Teresa was seventeen, her mother was sick—barely functioning because of lifelong depression made worse by a humiliating divorce—and Teresa's father, Hugh, was remarried to his former secretary Wendy, a greedy doll of a woman just shy of thirty.

Everyone except Hugh seemed to know Wendy had divorced her young husband, Jason, and married a man nineteen years her senior because he was the major stockholder and president of Farr Coal Company, an enterprise worth at least $30 million. Teresa and her brother, Kent, hated Wendy, yet somehow the shallow woman had produced a smart, sweet, delightful eight-year-old child named Celeste whom Teresa couldn't help loving.

Considering her feeling that something wasn't right in the house, Teresa knew she should leap from her bed, burst into the hall, and flash on the bright overhead light. But she had already caught hell from her father for coming in late. Furious, he'd raged at her, demanding to know where she'd been, what she'd been doing, with whom she'd been doing it, for God's sake! When he met with only stony silence from her, he'd continued to yell for ten minutes, then run out of steam and told her to get upstairs to her room. Teresa could imagine his reignited rage if she woke up the household over what was probably nothing.

Still, she hadn't been able to close her eyes and pretend everything was all right. Although Teresa was exhausted, livid with her father, and afraid of the *wrongness* in her home, a visceral instinct had pushed her to find the threat she felt lurking in the Farr house that night.

She'd thrown back her light blanket, swung her bare feet to the floor, and slowly begun walking. She hadn't closed her curtains, and moonlight cast an eerie silvery glow throughout the room. She hesitated, then opened her bedroom door.

At first, nothing had struck her as odd. The house was quiet. The small Tiffany-style lamp Teresa loved burned on a table near the bathroom, a guide down the hall for little

Celeste, whose bedroom faced the front of the house. Hugh Farr and his new wife, Wendy, used the master bedroom right across from Teresa's room.

And that's when she realized what wasn't right. At night, Hugh and Wendy's bedroom door was always shut.

Except for now.

For a moment, unease tingled through Teresa. Then she walked to the Tiffany-style lamp that her mother had bought and cherished. Looking at one of her favorite possessions, the low-watt bulbs glowing softly through the glass shade of delicate blue and purple honey locust flowers, gave Teresa a small sense of comfort. Touching it felt almost like touching a rabbit's foot or some other good-luck totem. Silly, but reassuring.

While Teresa stood by the lamp, she looked at Hugh and Wendy's partially open bedroom door. Beyond it, Teresa could see nothing. She drew a deep breath, then walked purposefully through the open doorway and stepped into the master bedroom, as always surprised by the feel of thick carpet beneath her feet.

Teresa's mother had prized the room's highly varnished mahogany floors decorated here and there with lovely, soft-toned Aubusson rugs. Wendy had complained that the floor was cold against her bare feet, and Hugh promptly had the room carpeted in the hot pink Wendy chose along with cerise draperies trimmed with fringe and tassels. Even Teri's older brother, Kent, who didn't know a thing about interior design, couldn't look at the room without cringing.

Tonight Teresa couldn't have cared less about the violated bedroom décor, though. She thought about not hearing Wendy's sleep-blurred muttering or the occasional peeps and whistles that sometimes crept past the device Hugh had bought recently to stifle his stentorian snoring. It's a big bedroom and I'm just too far away from the bed to hear anything, Teresa had told herself.

She hadn't turned on the overhead light for fear of waking them, but she took several steps closer to the king-sized bed she knew lay right in front of her. Then she'd stopped and listened again.

Not one sound had come from the bed. Not the sound of someone shifting in their sleep, not the sound of Wendy mumbling or Hugh spluttering and snorting, not even the deep and easy sound of breathing from two people sleeping peacefully. Teresa had heard absolutely nothing.

But she had smelled something—something fresh, strong, and coppery. Coppery. She'd smelled blood before and now she smelled it around the bed. It's not blood, she had told herself sternly. You're just scaring yourself.

Using all of her willpower, she'd walked to the end of the bed, then veered right toward Wendy's side. Teresa had decided she'd rather wake up Wendy than Hugh, who would start yelling at her again, so she'd put out her left hand, gently touching Wendy's leg beneath the blanket. Wendy didn't move.

Downstairs, the big grandfather clock tolled three times. The clock also belonged to Teresa's mother, and Teresa had always loved its exquisite workmanship and the unusually deep timbre of its chimes, but that night they'd sounded strangely ominous. She'd taken a deep breath and forced herself to step forward, her foot squishing into a wet spot in the carpet just as her hand brushed over Wendy's slick abdomen, almost sliding into a deep slit.

At last, Teresa had screamed. She'd jerked her hand away from Wendy's stomach, slapped it over her mouth, realized it dripped blood, let it drop, and screamed again. Then, without thought, she had run toward the wall and groped for the overhead light switch. Wendy had chosen one of the largest chandeliers she could find for her boudoir, and Teresa might as well have turned on a floodlight. The room had flashed into dazzling view, temporarily blinding Teresa. She'd closed her eyes for a moment, then opened them to see the bed and the people in it garishly splashed with rich, shimmering red.

Teresa was unaware of her own voice tearing open the silence of night. She'd felt oddly removed from the whole gory scene as she'd run to her father's side of the bed to find him splayed like an insect ready for mounting, his throat slashed, his abdomen oozing blood. His left arm seemed to reach for Wendy, whose once-pretty face had been reduced to an unrecognizable mass of rips and gouges. Her blond hair snaked across the white satin pillowcase in wet, red strands.

Teresa had backed away, heaving as she tried not to throw up, and slowly realized she was shrieking. She could hear the next-door neighbors' Great Dane begin to bark and howl frantically. Teresa glanced up, and through one of the bedroom windows, she saw bright lights flashing on in the house next door, lights in what she knew was the master bedroom directly across from Hugh and Wendy's bedroom. Her screaming and the dog's barking had awakened the neighbors, she thought in relief. She had forced herself to stop screaming long enough to take a deep breath and fill her air-starved lungs. Then the image of eight-year-old Celeste had burst in her mind like a firework.

Without thought, Teresa had turned off the overhead light as if it might disturb someone and dashed from her father's bedroom, running down the hall and banging into a small antique table in the darkness. She'd cried out and stumbled sideways against the sturdy, erect body of an adult.

"No. Please," Teresa had managed before pain coursed down her left arm, the razor-sharp pain of a knife blade slashing flesh. Oh, God, now it's my turn to die, she'd thought wildly.

As Teresa clutched at the gash in her arm, the person pressed closer to her and she'd caught a familiar scent. Sandalwood. Her mother always wore a perfume containing sandalwood, Teresa had thought distantly as she squinted at the shadowy form beside her—the form of someone taller than she, of someone wearing a coat slick like plastic or vinyl, of someone whose head was covered with what seemed to be a large hood and the face turned downward.

Gripped by terror, Teresa had gone motionless like an animal waiting for the inevitable, fatal attack. She'd even stopped breathing, but her gaze slid sideways. She saw a latex-gloved hand move to the area beneath the hood and two fingers rise to hidden lips from which emerged a gentle, prolonged "Shhhh." The soothing sound echoing eerily in Teri's mind, she watched as the figure drifted away like an image in a dream—away, down the stairs, and out of the house.

Teresa had stood still for a moment, too surprised to move, too shocked to be anything but vaguely aware of the pain in her arm. Then several drops of warm blood had fallen onto her bare foot, startling her back to life. The figure had been coming from the front of the house—Celeste's room.

"Celeste," Teresa had murmured, her voice thin as it squeezed through her tightened throat. She'd swallowed, flying down the hallway now, and finally managed to scream, "Celeste!"

When Teresa reached the child's bedroom, she had stopped abruptly. She'd begun to hyperventilate and her heart had seemed to be crashing hard enough to crack her ribs. The pain in her slashed arm had dulled to nothingness. I can't do this, she'd thought for a frozen moment. I cannot go into this room.

Her body had not listened to her mind, though, and she'd tiptoed in, although she couldn't make herself turn on the overhead light. Moonlight had shown her the rumpled bed. Slowly, filled with dread, Teresa had followed the subdued radiance of Celeste's bedroom night-light—the light shaped like a white horse Teresa had given her at

Christmas, a light the child had loved and had named Snowflake.

Teresa moved to the bed. She murmured, "Celeste." Silence. But the night-light revealed no spots of blood. Teresa put her hands on the tumble of sheet and blanket. Nothing. The bed was empty.

She'd looked up and beside the glow of the night-light Teresa spotted Celeste's nearly empty toy chest. Finally beginning to tremble almost uncontrollably, Teresa had forced herself to walk straight to the box, lift the lid, then look to see Celeste curled into a motionless ball in the bottom of the toy chest. Teresa also had caught sight of the blood splotches she'd expected to see on the bed. The child had tried to hide—tried and apparently failed.

"No," Teresa had moaned, desolation washing through her like a cold wave as she lifted the little girl's rigid body from the coffinlike box. "Celeste," she'd muttered raggedly. "Don't be dead. Oh, God, sweetie, *please* don't be dead!"

"I'm not," the child had rasped in a flat, gritty voice. "I'm . . . not . . . dead."

Teresa, shaking violently, had burst into a torrent of relieved tears, unaware that Celeste would not speak again for the next eight years.

CHAPTER ONE

Eight Years Later

1

"DID YOU LEAVE ROOM for dessert?"

The pretty waitress at Bennigan's smiled into the face of Celeste Warner. Celeste looked back placidly, her aqua eyes wide, her perfect lips almost smiling, her long blond hair held back from her smooth forehead by a narrow pink velvet ribbon.

"I think we're full, aren't we?" Jason Warner asked brightly, looking at his sixteen-year-old daughter as if he expected an answer. He didn't. She hadn't spoken since her mother had been murdered and Celeste had been stabbed in the abdomen eight years ago when she lived in the Farr home. Jason glanced back at the waitress, who gave no sign she noticed Celeste's silence or immobility. She'd waited on Jason and his daughter before. "I guess we'll just take the check," he said. "The food was great, by the way."

"Thanks!" The waitress sounded as pleased as if she'd prepared the meal herself. "I'll leave the check here and pick it up in a couple of minutes. You two take your time."

Jason couldn't help noticing the hard stare the manager threw the waitress. It was 12:55 at Bennigan's on Saturday and the place was jammed. Jason knew the manager didn't want the help urging customers to take their time. He quickly opened the discreet black vinyl envelope, glanced at the check, slipped in a twenty and a ten, then looked back at his daughter. "I left enough for the food *and* a tip so our waitress won't have to waste time bringing back change," he explained.

Celeste merely blinked. What I'd give to see her smile, Jason thought. Hell, I wouldn't even care if she threw a temper tantrum. He'd once overheard someone describe Celeste's expression as "bovine" and he'd been furious, both because of the insult and because the person had spoken the truth. Although beautiful, Celeste showed no more emotion than a contented cow.

Jason glanced around, trying to look lively to hide his dark thoughts. "Boy, this place is even more crowded than usual, isn't it, honey?" Nothing. A group of people passed them, all laughing and chattering, their animation striking Jason as almost cruel compared to his daughter's eerie self-containment. Determined not to give in to depression, though, Jason patted his slim abdomen and smiled. "I ate too much, Celeste. How about you?" Nothing. "Well, ready to go to the park?"

Jason waited until several people passed their booth, then stood up. Instead of getting up, and walking slightly behind him with her head down as she usually did, Celeste sat perfectly still. Jason was so used to her immediately rising from the table, he'd already begun striding toward the door before he noticed Celeste was still in the booth. He rushed back to her. She sat uncannily motionless, her forehead furrowed. Then she tilted back her head and her nose twitched slightly, as if she was sniffing something. Surprised by the slightest sign of reaction from her, Jason abruptly scooted into the booth and looked closely at Celeste.

"Is something wrong, honey?"

Celeste frowned harder as she drew in a deep breath and held it. He hadn't seen her frown for eight years. Jason sat mesmerized. Then annoyance flowed over him. Bennigan's was always busy on Saturdays, but today it felt as if half of Point Pleasant had come for lunch. The place was noisy and people jostled beside their booth. I should have taken Celeste somewhere quieter, less crowded, he thought. "You push her too hard," his mother sometimes told him, making his teeth grind.

At such times, though, Jason reminded himself that what his mother, Fay, lacked in tact, she made up for in love and ever-vigilant care. Without hesitation, she'd taken in Celeste after Wendy's murder. "You can't care for her— you have to work," she'd told Jason reasonably when Celeste had been released from the hospital and rehabilitation after her stabbing.

Celeste had made a full physical recovery, but her emotional wounds had not seemed to heal. Two psychiatrists and two psychologists agreed that her silence and emotional withdrawal were the result of shock. Two years later, they said they were almost certain her muteness had become voluntary and she was now feigning a lack of emotion. "Celeste suffered no brain damage. She is choosing to be silent and to act detached," one of them had told Jason. "I'm not certain why—maybe she simply doesn't want to discuss the murders and the attack on her. She won't continue this behavior forever, though. Be patient, Mr. Warner. Celeste will talk when she's ready." So Jason had taken Celeste home to Fay, who'd abruptly begun quashing his arguments that caring for Celeste by herself would be too much of a strain and that they needed professional help.

"Don't be silly," she'd stated. "Those so-called professionals haven't helped Celeste one bit. Besides, you'd be doing me a favor to let me look after her. *And* you. I'm home alone all day now that your daddy's dead and I'm going stir-crazy. I'm strong as a horse and I want to be useful. You both need me and I need you. Mark my words—the situation will work out fine."

And it had, except that right now, Fay Warner would be unhappy with him, Jason thought morosely. She would point out that he should have known the restaurant was packed because of the full parking lot. She would tell him he shouldn't have gone there just because *he* liked the cheerful atmosphere. She would—

Suddenly Celeste leaned toward Jason, fixed him with a penetrating stare, and said in a voice rusty from disuse, "The moon was bright that night but I turned on my nightlight anyway—my horse nightlight Snowflake that Teri gave me. I loved that light, partly 'cause it was a horse and partly 'cause it was a gift from *Teri*."

Jason stared at his daughter, his gray eyes wide, his mouth slightly open. At first, he was stunned only by the fact that after eight long years she'd finally spoken. Then, he felt a brief wave of joy that the doctors had been right— the moment had come when she had finally decided to speak. Finally, with an unpleasant jolt, Jason realized Celeste was describing the night her mother had been murdered.

Celeste's frown deepened, her eyes narrowed, and she went on unemotionally in a flinty voice, "I was comin' out of the bathroom when someone opened Mommy's bedroom door, all soft and sneaky."

Jason's tongue touched his dry lips, and after a moment he managed to ask, "Who was coming out of Mommy's bedroom?"

Celeste looked puzzled. "All I could see was somethin' in a hood."

"A hood?" Celeste nodded. "You couldn't tell *anything* about the person?"

"It wore somethin' long and black—it seemed like a cape but maybe it was just a big coat. And its eyes . . . they were big with dark shadows all around 'em." Celeste shivered. "I couldn't move. I just held on to Yogi." Yogi, Jason remembered, was her big stuffed bear. "It made a loud, surprised noise. It didn't know I was there. Then it jabbed at me with a knife so fast I didn't know what was goin' on. The knife went through Yogi. I know I got stabbed, too, but I didn't feel it. Lots of my blood ran into Yogi. A nurse told me that's why he had to get thrown away." Celeste's eyes filled with tears. "I *loved* Yogi and he just got thrown away!"

Damn babbling nurse, Jason thought furiously. Hadn't she realized she was dealing with a traumatized child?

Celeste wiped at a tear running down her face. "After we got stabbed, I held Yogi tight and ran back to my room."

Jason forced himself to shut his mouth. His daughter was looking at him with big eyes suddenly filled with both horror and hurt, the first expression he'd seen in them for what seemed like an eternity. He reached across, touched her hand, and her fingers curled around his as a baby's would. He said softly, "I'm sorry about Yogi, but he probably saved your life. That would have made him happy." Another tear trickled over Celeste's cheek. "Honey, did the person stab you in your room?"

"No. I told you I got stabbed in the hall. Then I ran to my room."

Police had assumed Celeste had heard someone in the house, and hidden in her toy chest where the killer stabbed her. They thought Celeste's blood in the hall had dripped from the killer's knife as he'd made his way to the Farrs' bedroom from Celeste's. Now it seemed that the blood had actually come directly from Celeste when she'd run back to her own room.

"But it was gonna stab me some more. It came after

me," Celeste went on urgently, her voice rising, as if she might suddenly lose the ability to talk again. "One time Teri and me were playing and she told me my toy chest was a good hidin' place 'cause I didn't have that many toys in there. I got in to hide.

"But when I was closin' the lid, I heard somethin' comin' to my room. I knew I was gonna get killed this time. Then I heard screamin'. And the big dog next door was barkin' and snarlin' and it woke up other dogs 'cause they were all barkin'." Celeste stopped as if the air had run out of her and said in an exhausted voice, "And I didn't get killed."

Jason knew he shouldn't keep questioning Celeste in a restaurant full of people, but he was afraid if he made her leave, the break in her concentration would cause her to stop talking again. Maybe for months or even years. He took a sip of water, cleared his throat, and asked barely above a whisper, "Sweetie, are you sure you don't know who stabbed you?"

"I don't think so . . ." Her lips trembled. "*No.*"

Jason's eyes narrowed. "You meant what you said first. *I don't think so.* Celeste, who did you see?"

"No one," Celeste said obstinately. "But I smelled something kind of sweet." She rushed on as if she wanted to stop further questions. "I smelled it a few minutes ago."

"In here?" Jason gasped.

Celeste nodded reluctantly. Jason's head snapped around, then jerked back to his daughter as he prayed no one had heard Celeste or noticed his quick scrutiny of the patrons.

"Celeste, *why* did you start talking right now?"

The girl looked as if the words were being dragged from her. "The smell. And a noise. And a voice. All at once I felt like it was that night again and the words just came out even though I didn't mean to talk. I was just real surprised. And scared," Celeste finished meekly.

"I see." Jason spoke to her gently. "Honey, you've been able to speak for quite a while, haven't you?"

Celeste looked defeated. "Yeah. I really *couldn't* talk after I got stabbed and Mommy got killed. I don't know why I couldn't talk. And I was scared all the time, really, *really* scared. And I was so . . ."

She was obviously floundering for a word. "Shocked?" Jason supplied. "Horrified by what had happened to you and Mommy?"

"Yeah. Shocked. Horrified. I wanted to be in a dark, secret place where no one could hurt me, so I went there. In my head, not to a real place. Later I came out of the secret place, but I just tried to think of nothing. I tried to look like I wasn't thinking of anything. And I *wouldn't* talk because I didn't want to talk." Celeste gave her father a small smile. "I can write, too, Daddy. I could already write when I got hurt and I've been practicin' ever since I came out of my secret place. When I took classes in the hospital and when you had teachers come to give me lessons at home, I'd write a little bit, but I never showed how good I could write because I knew people would ask questions about that awful night and want me to write the answers. That was just as bad as talkin' about what happened.

"I don't want to talk about what happened, Daddy. Please don't make me talk about it," Celeste beseeched Jason. "If you ask lots of questions, I'll go back into my secret place where I'm safe. Maybe I won't come out again because I'm still *so* scared, Daddy. Maybe I'll always be scared. It was so awful . . . *so* awful . . ."

Celeste began to shake all over. Jason squeezed her delicate hand, but she pulled it away, grabbing at her other hand and beginning to twist them together nervously. She turned slightly and glanced around the room. Jason watched closely as her gaze seemed to grow far away. Either that, or it had turned in upon itself, remembering. He thought he had lost her again, that she wasn't going to utter another word. Finally, though, her expression seemed to harden, to morph into one of impish malice. She looked at him with an amused, almost cocky gaze before she tilted her head and began to chant loudly:

> *"The clock struck three,*
> *And Death came for me.*
> *When I opened my eyes,*
> *There was Teri!"*

People around them had begun to stop talking, everyone turning to stare at the lovely teenager. Somewhere a glass crashed to the floor. To Jason's horror, Celeste repeated piercingly, "The clock struck three, and Death came for me. When I opened my eyes, there was *Teri!*" As complete silence fell all around them, the color drained from Jason's slender face and he realized he was gawking at his daughter just like the other patrons of the restaurant. At last, Celeste took a deep breath, leaned back, gave her father a wide, charming smile, and said sweetly, "I'm a *very* lucky girl."

2

"Frozen margarita, piña colada, brandy Alexander," the waiter repeated to the three women sitting near the stage at Club Rendezvous.

"And I want *three* cherries with the piña colada," Teresa Farr said, raising her voice above the music of the live band.

The waiter looked at her in feigned shock. "An extra cherry? Miss Farr, do you want to break the club's budget this month?"

"I'll pay for the third cherry."

"Okay, it's your money," the waiter sighed as if in despair. Then he winked at Teresa. "Be right back, ladies."

The woman with layered strawberry blond hair sitting next to Teresa gave her a nudge. "He winked at you, Teri. And he's *cute*."

"He's also barely old enough to be working here, Sharon." Teresa laughed at her sister-in-law. Teri tucked long, silky black hair behind her ears to expose large silver hoops and adjusted a shimmering silver tank top she wore with black slacks. "He took three lessons right after I started the riding school, but he was too scared to continue. I never date guys who are afraid of horses."

"You never date at all anymore," said the third woman at the table, Carmen, the eldest. She had high cheekbones, a narrow nose, smoky blue-gray eyes, and shoulder-length brown hair enhanced by bronze highlights. Teresa knew that in Carmen's late teens and early twenties she had modeled. "Just catalogue stuff," she always said dismissively. "I never made it in the couture lines—I was a couple of inches too short for industry standards." "We're celebrating your twenty-sixth birthday, Teri," she now teased. "Have you already sworn off men?"

"No, Carmen, I've just been busy getting the riding school started, but I could ask you the same question. Have *you* sworn off men?"

Carmen laughed. "I'm twenty years older than you."

"And you look about ten years older."

Carmen rolled her eyes. "I wish. Anyway, I get credit for having been married. I'm a widow and I'm expected to spend the rest of my life alone, being the sedate woman I am."

"*Sedate!*" Teri laughed. "Good heavens, you're anything except sedate, Carmen. You're lively, upbeat, fun—that's why you were such a wonderful friend for my mother. And if you don't realize you *are* still quite the stunner, then you didn't notice how many men were looking at you with lust in their eyes when you walked in."

Carmen grinned. "I think you need glasses."

"I have twenty-twenty vision. Seriously, though, you've been a widow for nine years and you've hardly dated anyone, at least that I know of."

"Anyone that you *know* of." Carmen's eyes twinkled. "Besides, I like being strong and independent, like you, Teri."

"Don't count Teresa out of the game so soon, Carmen," interrupted Sharon, who always seemed preoccupied with finding a husband for Teresa. Her own life revolved around her husband—Teresa's brother, Kent—and their son, Daniel, who had Sharon's heart-shaped face, short nose, velvety brown eyes, and spattering of freckles. "And Teri, you can't possibly believe Carmen has given up on men. I'm sure there's *someone*. In fact, I know there is."

Carmen raised a perfectly arched eyebrow at Sharon. "Oh really? And who is this mystery man?"

"Does the name Herman Riggs ring a bell?"

"Oh, God," Carmen moaned. "*Him?* He's history."

Teresa pretended to look horrified. "Carmen, you only had a few dates with him and you've already dumped him like a hot potato? You didn't even give the poor guy a chance!"

"That's because the 'poor guy' still lives with his mother, talks about her constantly, and on our third date was terribly excited because she'd promised to teach him how to knit a sweater." Teri and Sharon burst into laughter. "If I ever say the marriage vows again, I think I can do better than Herman."

Teresa looked regretful. "I guess Herman will have to look elsewhere for his true love."

"He's already found her," Carmen said dourly. "His mother."

The three women were laughing as the waiter came back with their drinks, pointing out to Teresa that he'd given her *four* cherries, but she was forbidden to mention this largesse to his boss or he'd be fired immediately. "I don't think you'll get in trouble if the extra cherries are for Teresa," Carmen assured him. "The owner of Club Rendezvous used to be engaged to Teri until she ended things and broke his heart. He's still pining for her."

"No kidding!" the young waiter burst out. "Mr. MacKenzie is in love with Miss Farr?"

Teresa's slender face reddened beneath the tawny skin she owed to her Shawnee heritage. "No, he is not. We were involved a *long* time ago." She glared at Carmen. "I'd appreciate you lowering your voice. Half of the people in here now know Mac and I were engaged."

"Half of the people in here already knew it." Carmen grinned as their waiter hurried away, clearly eager to spread the hot news flash to other young waiters and waitresses rushing back and forth to the bar.

Teresa watched the quick verbal exchanges, then the furtive glances thrown her way. "Now look what you've done!"

"I'm only telling the truth," Carmen said innocently, winking at Sharon. "Aren't I?"

"Yes." Sharon was smiling and looking uncomfortable at the same time. Her posture had stiffened and the lightness left her voice. "Kent doesn't like people talking about it, though."

"Well, they were engaged and even if Teri gave *him* the heave-ho, I don't think she's as blasé about Mac as she pretends to be."

"You really should write a column for the lovelorn, Carmen." Teresa picked up her cherry-laden drink. "I'll speak to the newspaper editor on Monday morning about hiring you."

"Good," Carmen replied jauntily. "I'm sick of working at Trinkets and Treasures. As you pointed out, I'm not at all sedate. I'm *far* too lively to own and manage a gift shop. It's boring."

"Mac and I were engaged *ages* ago," Teri went on relentlessly, taking a gulp of her drink. "I was twenty. Just a kid, really, and extremely romantic and impressionable. It was a passing fancy. A crush. I never even think about Mac anymore. Not at *all*. And I'm absolutely sure he never thinks about me."

"Is that so?" Carmen slanted a look at Mac. "Well, for someone who never thinks about you, he certainly has his gaze locked on you tonight."

"Don't be ridiculous, Carmen."

"I'm telling you, he's been wandering around the bar, ostensibly talking to customers but really staring at you all evening," Carmen went on, then smiled in satisfaction. "And now he's finally headed this way."

"Oh no!" Teri exclaimed.

"Oh *yes*!" Carmen touched Teresa's hand. "Put your drink down. You've drained the glass dry. And don't look so flustered."

"I'm *not* flustered." Teresa banged down the glass on the table. "Why would I be flustered? I'm just—"

"Good evening, ladies." The man stood casually beside them. He looked about thirty, with sun-warmed skin, a dimple in his chin, and a few horizontal lines in the forehead below his slightly wavy mahogany brown hair. His drop-dead grin flashed over all three while his hazel eyes with their intriguing flecks of gold fastened on Teresa. "Enjoying yourselves?"

"It's my birthday," Teresa blurted out.

"And you're not having a traditional party with your relatives and close friends?"

"We did the traditional stuff earlier," Carmen told him. "Then we got rid of everyone, left Kent to babysit his son, and came out to have some real fun."

"I'm glad you think coming to Club Rendezvous is fun, Ms. Norris," Mac said.

"Please, it's Carmen. And I—we—love this place. Don't we, Teri?"

"Uh, yes. It's . . . nice." Teresa felt color warming her

face and she almost knocked over her near-empty glass. Damn, she thought as she caught it just in time. Why was she acting like a teenager? And why did Mac still have that devastating dimpled smile that used to set her heart pounding? "The club is quite pleasant," she added.

"That's a ringing endorsement, Teri," Mac said dryly. He looked at Sharon. "I haven't seen you for ages. The club opened eight months ago and you and Kent have never been here."

"Kent's always busy in the evenings." Sharon sounded impatient. "Paperwork, phone calls. Always off in his study like his child and I don't even exist. Besides, he says he isn't the club type. I think he believes he should behave like a pillar of the community. He even belongs to all those do-gooder clubs his father did."

"The ones he used to make fun of?" Mac laughed. "Well, I believe the part owner and president of Farr Coal Company is still allowed to go clubbing, especially with his wife."

"So I tell him, but he doesn't pay any attention to me." Sharon forced her lips into the semblance of a good-natured smile, although Teri knew Kent's preoccupation with work and community activities was getting on Sharon's nerves. "I guess he's trying to set a good example for our son."

"Can't blame a guy for that. I wish my father had done the same." Mac looked at Teri and gave her that maddeningly sexy grin. "You need another drink, young lady."

"No, I—"

"Yes, you do." He motioned to her waiter, then glanced at the band onstage that had just finished a number. He nodded to the blond lead singer. "I hope you don't mind, Teri, but I took the liberty of requesting a song for your birthday. Will you do me the honor of dancing with me?"

Teresa suddenly felt angry with him and panicked at the same time. "You *shouldn't* have taken the liberty," she answered stiffly. He held out his hand to her. "Mac, no. It was a nice gesture, but I haven't danced for years and—"

Seeming not to hear a word she said, Mac took Teresa's hand. In spite of her determination not to dance with him, she rose from her chair and followed him to the dance floor as if mesmerized. The blond singer smiled and spoke into the microphone. "This song is for Teresa Farr from Mac MacKenzie. Happy birthday, Teresa."

Many people clapped; a few men whistled and yelled, "Happy birthday, Teresa!" Other dancers cleared a circle for them as Mac's arm closed around Teresa's shoulder and he pulled her close to him. He was strong and warm, she thought, just like in the days when they were in love, and almost against her will she felt herself melting into his embrace. The first notes of "Take My Breath Away" began. It had been their song, hers and Mac's.

"You remembered," she said.

"Did you think I'd ever forget? We danced to it for the first time one summer evening in your backyard," Mac said, his voice tantalizingly warm on her neck. "I'd just finished mowing your lawn and you and your mother were sitting on the porch with the music playing. You were only sixteen, but you looked so carried away by the song, I couldn't help asking if you'd dance with me."

"I think I remember that evening," Teresa said casually. Actually, she'd had a mad crush on the "much" older Mac and had felt almost dizzy being so close to him.

"Your mother watched us. At the end, she clapped and said we danced beautifully. She looked genuinely happy."

"And she so rarely looked happy. Poor Mom." Teresa felt tears stinging in her eyes, resulting from painful old memories—memories of her first love, memories of what had seemed a magic evening a lifetime ago, memories of a mother who'd simply vanished one day. Teri didn't even know if the woman was alive. With a catch in her voice, she said, "Mom was fond of you, Mac."

"As opposed to your father. I was the son of the Farrs' housekeeper, the guy with no prospects who mowed his grass. Hubert W. Farr. What a jerk he was." Mac almost stopped dancing. "I'm sorry."

"Just because he was murdered doesn't mean he became a saint. He *was* a jerk." Mac's body had tightened and Teri had an impulse to hold him closer, to make him forget how horrible her father had been to Mac and to his mother, but she caught herself in time. She knew she must always watch her step with Mac. He still held so much attraction for her that she dared never to sound warm, tender, vulnerable. "Let's change the subject," she forced herself to say lightly.

"I think that would be a great idea."

"My riding school is coming along slowly but surely." Teri knew she sounded falsely cheerful. "It's doing surprisingly well, actually, considering how new it is."

"Great. Farr Fields? Isn't that what you named it?"

"You know I did."

"I'm glad you're doing something you love. You always were crazy about horses and you were an excellent rider, or so everyone told me. I wasn't much of an equestrian, if you remember."

"You did take a few spills when I bullied you into getting on my horse." Teresa couldn't help giggling. "Remember when that bee stung the horse's nose and it took off like a rocket? You were yelling your head off, scaring the horse even more, as you slid off the right side and hung on for dear life about two feet above the ground."

Mac grimaced. "Don't laugh. My life was flashing through my eyes."

"But you lived to tell the tale." Teresa shook her head. "I wish I had a video of that incident."

"Thank God you don't. You'd show it to everyone and make a laughingstock of me."

"No, I'd use it as an instructional video of what *not* to do if your horse panics."

Mac's arms tightened slightly around her, and Teresa's heart beat a bit faster as the singer poured out the romantic words of the song with an intense, seemingly heartfelt passion. Teresa briefly closed her eyes, drinking in the soap and water smell of Mac, masculine and fresh, unmarred by cloying cologne. His warm hand on her back felt as if it were burning through the thin fabric of her top. She felt herself slowly slipping deeper into his embrace that felt so natural, so comforting, so seductive, then caught herself and almost jerked away from him. His arms tensed, as if he was determined to hold on to her, which was exactly what she wanted and exactly what she wouldn't let happen.

"Daniel is going to start taking lessons tomorrow," Teresa blurted loudly, trying to cover her physical response that had been a dead giveaway of her emotions. "He's almost eight now."

Mac drew back, looking at her with a mixture of rue and humor. He'd felt her desire and he wasn't going to make a pretense of not noticing it. The man had always refused to act as if they had no past, no matter what Teresa wanted. "Who's Daniel?" he asked casually.

"My nephew! For heaven's sake, Mac, don't you even know the name of Kent's son?"

"Kent and I aren't the best of friends anymore. He barely speaks to me on the street. I'm sure he didn't want his wife or you to come here. He seems more like your father every day."

"I think Kent is trying to make everyone forget the scandal caused by the murders. Maybe he's overcompensating a little." Teresa's defense sounded weak because she also guiltily thought her brother was turning into a sanctimonious stuffed shirt. "He's a very good husband and father."

"I don't know how he is as a father, but Sharon doesn't seem thrilled with her marriage."

"Oh, I don't know about that. . . ." Teresa trailed off because, once again, she had to agree with Mac, although she'd never let him know it. "What makes you think she's unhappy?"

"Her expression. She used to laugh a lot and always seemed to be having a good time. Now—"

"Now she is a wife and mother with important responsibilities." Teresa realized she sounded prim and unnatural. She told herself she must act relaxed even if she didn't feel it. "Listen, Mac, I was stiff as a board back at the table," she said quickly. "I'm sorry. Your nightclub isn't just *quite pleasant*—it's beautiful."

Mac leaned back and raised his eyebrows. "Well, thanks, Teri! I admit I was a little disappointed by your earlier glowing remarks." Mac's face slowly relaxed and he smiled into her eyes. "Remember when I used to talk about building it? A lot of people laughed at me. They said I'd never settle down and probably end up jobless and homeless. You never doubted that I could do it, though. You even helped me plan this place."

"I offered a few ideas," Teresa said casually, although she vividly recalled sitting huddled over Mac's sketches of the proposed club and making many suggestions about lighting and color palettes.

"I was going for a disco theme, but you insisted the place should be classier, more timeless," Mac went on. "You're the one who suggested the Art Deco look. I didn't even know what Art Deco was."

Teresa glanced around at the interior of Mac's club—the stark lines, generous use of glass and chrome, the predominantly ivory color scheme dramatized with touches of black and vibrant azure. High on the walls were large mosaic tiles, each done in an intricate Middle Eastern pattern of sea blue, lavender, and willow green ceramic squares. The place was striking and elegant. "You thought my ideas were strange."

"I wasn't exactly an interior design expert," Mac laughed. "It took me a while to give up my dream of miles of bright red shag carpet and strobe lights."

Teresa grinned. "I think you'd seen *Saturday Night Fever* a few too many times."

"Exactly. It was Mom's favorite movie. A long time ago, she and my dad won a dance contest in a disco club. I think Dad wore a white polyester suit like Travolta's. That's why she watched the movie over and over, remembering happier times before Dad left and she had to support all three of us kids."

"I can't imagine Emma MacKenzie dancing in a disco club." Teresa laughed. "I'm sure back then she never dreamed she'd end up as the Farr housekeeper. What an awful fate."

"She liked her job when your mother was there. Mom thought the world of her." He paused. "And then Wendy came along."

"Well, now your mother doesn't have to work as anyone's housekeeper, thanks to you." Teresa hated the rush of tenderness she felt toward Mac when she remembered how much he used to talk about wanting to give his mother and two younger twin sisters a better life. "How are those siblings of yours?"

"They're seniors at Marshall, both education majors and taking summer classes so they can graduate early."

"Wonderful! And your mother?"

"She has a small apartment downtown. She also *finally* let me teach her to drive and I bought her a car. A *used* car—she wouldn't stand for me buying a new one. And after all those years of her refusing to drive, I now have a hard time keeping her out of the car and under the speed limit." Mac laughed. "She bakes muffins, cookies, brownies, and she's developed quite a little business for herself supplying local restaurants. You could never turn Emma MacKenzie into a lady of leisure."

"Mac, what you've done for your family is fantastic." Teresa was aware of the tiny quiver in her voice, the quiver of proud, unshed tears.

Mac's tone grew soft and warm. "I've had a lot of luck and I never forget for an instant the part you played in causing that luck. I remember our early times together like they were—"

"Yesterday?" Teri interrupted crisply, furiously blinking away a slight sheen of tears, maddeningly aware of treacherous old feelings beginning to resurface.

"Too long ago, Teri," Mac said with husky emotion.

Teresa looked up into his face, had only gotten more handsome as time sharpened its planes and strengthened his chin. And those eyes . . .

"What is it?" Mac asked, gazing deep into her own ebony gaze. "Thinking about what it was like when we used to be a couple?"

The singer's beautiful voice seemed to fill Teresa's mind and heart. Then a picture flashed in front of her—an old picture of a younger Mac working as a bartender, and the bar's stunning redheaded owner Teresa had been so jealous of even though Mac had reassured her repeatedly that he didn't even like the woman. Then had come the crushing day Teresa had walked into a storage room and found Mac holding the redhead tightly as he deeply kissed her. Teresa would forget neither the redhead's glance of glinting-eyed triumph nor the guilt and embarrassment of Mac's expression when he'd caught sight of Teresa. Now, on the dance floor, Teresa abruptly stiffened and moved away from him.

"I know what you just remembered, Teri," Mac said mildly.

"Oh? Are you a mind reader as well as a businessman now?"

"Not at all. I just know you. I know your body language and your expressions. You were remembering—"

"The song's coming to an end." Teresa took her arm off his shoulder and gave him a polite smile. "Thank you for requesting this number," she said woodenly. "It was very considerate of you."

"Yes, ma'am. Thank you." Mac had immediately switched

his demeanor. He's making fun of me by tossing my discomfort in my face, Teresa thought angrily. "We try to please here at Club Rendezvous, ma'am."

Teresa ignored his jibe at her formality. "I believe I have a fresh drink waiting for me at the table."

"You do indeed, with four cherries in it. The two extra cherries are on the house in honor of your birthday." He gave her that maddeningly dazzling smile and made a slight movement that resembled a bow. "Thank you kindly for the dance. Shall I walk you to your table?"

"It's only a few feet away. I think I can make it by myself."

She fled back to the safety of the table and immediately turned on Carmen. "You told him we were coming tonight and it's my birthday!"

"I told him we were coming. He already remembered your birthday." Carmen propped her elbows on the table, cupping her chin in her hands, and grinned. "For a while you two looked pretty cozy out there."

"We were just dancing," Teresa snapped, grabbing her fresh drink.

"Barely. Mostly you were clinging, gazing romantically into each other's eyes."

"Oh, Carmen, don't be absurd!"

"You were. Not that I blame you. God, they invented the word 'rakish' to describe Mac MacKenzie's smile. It could stop a heart. And those dimples . . ." She sighed and closed her eyes for a moment. "I thought for certain there would be a lingering kiss at the end of the song."

Teresa glowered at Carmen, then stared straight ahead, embarrassed although she knew Carmen was only teasing.

Sharon, obviously realizing Teresa was in no mood for what could be considered mockery, tossed a hard look at Carmen. Teresa knew that although her sister-in-law tolerated Carmen, she thought the older woman tactless, even brash. "I can't imagine that Carmen was your mother's best friend. My mother would have had *nothing* to do with her," Sharon had huffed once to Teresa, and remembering that Sharon considered her deceased mother the perfect woman, Teresa had merely smiled.

"I know that's your favorite song, Teri. It was nice of Mac to request it for you on your birthday, but you didn't look to *me* as if he were sweeping you off your feet. I'm sure not to anyone else, either. Some people just enjoy making others feel uncomfortable." Sharon flung the words defiantly at Carmen.

Although Carmen clearly had gotten Sharon's message, she relaxed in her chair and said casually, "I love that song, too. I used to have a cassette tape of it, but the tape snapped. I think I'll order a CD tomorrow." She paused, grinning without malice at Sharon. "When it comes in, I'll ask Herman over to dance to it with me if he isn't too busy with his knitting. Would you and Kent like to join us?"

Teri laughed and even Sharon smiled, breaking the strain at the table. A couple of minutes later, Sharon had begun talking about getting her son, Daniel, started on his riding lessons at Teresa's school, reminding her of the family's planned tour tomorrow afternoon, although the child had been to Farr Fields many times. "Teri, you do have a nice, gentle horse for him to train on, don't you?" Sharon anxiously asked.

"I have one that's perfect for him." Teresa pictured the pony she'd chosen for the little boy who was becoming skittish because of Sharon's constant hovering.

"I want your *most* gentle one," Sharon ordered.

Carmen frowned in barely concealed annoyance. "Sharon, you act like Teri's going to put Daniel on a raging stallion."

Sharon's cheeks grew scarlet under her freckles. "Horses can be dangerous, Carmen, or didn't you know that?"

"Hey, girls, let's not have a chick fight here in front of

everyone," Teresa said with artificial ease, trying to cut the sudden flashing hostility between the two women. "Sharon, I have students even younger than Daniel. I know how to train children and so do my employees, Gus and Josh." She patted Sharon's hand. "We'll be extra careful with him. After all, he's my nephew!"

Sharon gave Teri a weak smile, said nothing else, took two sips of her drink, and after ten minutes glanced at her watch. "It's almost eleven," she announced. "Time for me to go home."

"But the party's just beginning," Carmen protested.

"I've been gone for hours. I need to check on Daniel. Teri, you and Carmen stay. Don't let me interrupt your evening."

"I think I should be leaving, too," Teresa said in support of her sister-in-law, whose tension she saw growing. Sharon really just wanted to escape Carmen's company. "I have to get up early in the morning."

"Me, too." Carmen was suddenly taking a last sip of her drink and reaching for her purse. "None of us need to be driving after more than two drinks anyway."

Out in the parking lot, Sharon rushed for her car, but Carmen lingered near Teri's. "I hope I didn't offend you tonight, teasing you about Mac."

Carmen's tendency to tease about sensitive matters often irritated Teresa, but she always reminded herself what a good friend the woman had been to her mother. Carmen had befriended the lonely Marielle when Teri was thirteen and she'd been able to lift Marielle's spirits like no one else could. After the murders, Carmen had taken in Teri and offered her reassurance and safe haven during that nightmare time, fending off reporters like a pit bull. Carmen had comforted her and never said, "I told you so," after Teri's breakup with Mac. Carmen still offered Teri emotional support and friendship without trying to act like a mother.

Suddenly, Teresa hugged Carmen. "You didn't offend me with your teasing about Mac. I'm used to you."

"Well there's a compliment for you." Carmen laughed. "I really did want you to see the club, Teri. It turned out beautifully. But I wasn't trying to make history repeat itself. I can't forget how you came crying to *me* when you caught him with that other woman."

"I never told anyone except you why I ended our engagement," Teri said.

"And I kept the secret, too. So, Mac aside, did you have a good time?"

"Mac aside, I had a great time except for you digging at Sharon."

"Sharon needs a stern talking-to about her absurd overprotectiveness."

"She's the same way about Kent and about her father now that he's a widower. I think the protectiveness is really a mask for possessiveness."

"Goodness, my Teri is a psychologist now!" Carmen laughed. "Well, whatever it is, I chose the wrong time to call her on it, although there's no good time to criticize Sharon. She doesn't like criticism."

"Who does?"

"You're right. Anyway, I'm sorry. I'll apologize to Sharon if it'll make you happy."

"It will." Teri smiled in relief. "I'm glad you suggested we come to the club."

"I thought a visit was due because you've never been here and you did the lion's share of designing it. I wanted you to see the finished product. Sure you're all right to drive?"

"My drinks were mostly cherries, so I think there's very little alcohol in my system."

Carmen laughed. "You and sweets. I'll never know how you can eat so many of them and stay so thin. You have your mother's slender frame. And her beauty. Except for your dark eyes, you look so much like Marielle, it's almost uncanny." Sadness shone in Carmen's gaze for a moment. Then she smiled and began walking away, throwing a cheerful, "Happy birthday, kiddo," over her shoulder.

The club had been busy and the parking lot was still almost full. Teresa glanced at all the cars, thinking that most of them wouldn't be leaving for another hour, then opened the door of her white Buick Lucerne. As soon as the interior lights came on, she saw papers lying on the driver's seat. She wondered if Mac had left a note in her car until she saw that the top sheet was a newspaper clipping dating from eight years ago. The headline seemed to scream at her:

OWNER OF FARR COAL COMPANY AND WIFE MURDERED

"Oh no," Teresa murmured, a chill running over her in spite of the warmth of the June night. She picked up the papers and glanced at the article, a few phrases jumping out at her about Hugh's and Wendy's deaths by stabbing and the injury of little Celeste, who according to the newspaper was in stable condition in spite of a knife wound to her abdomen. The paper also emphasized that Teresa had sustained only "a superficial wound to the left arm," a fact that had fueled some people's belief that Teresa had wielded the knife the night of the murders.

Feeling slightly dizzy, Teri let the newspaper clipping flutter to the asphalt. Then she read the computer-printed note:

Dear Teresa,
 Roscoe Lee Byrnes meets his maker this week. Will you finally feel safe? I don't think so now that Celeste Warner is talking again. Or have you been too busy

celebrating your birthday to hear the latest breaking news? It seems she remembers the night you murdered her mother and tried to kill her too. She's scared now— not telling everything—but she will soon and then your nightmare will really begin.

CHAPTER TWO

1

TERESA AWAKENED HEAVY EYED and sluggish. She wondered what was wrong. She'd only had two drinks at Club Rendezvous last night and been in bed before midnight. Then the memory of the parking lot flooded back to her. Finding the newspaper clipping and the note. No wonder she hadn't slept well, Teresa thought.

She groaned and rolled onto her side. At the bottom of the bed slept her dog, Sierra, a fifty-pound mixed breed with short, gleaming chocolate brown hair, white hind paws, and pointed ears a bit too large for her delicate face. Teri smiled as she looked at the dog deep in sleep, untroubled by old tragedies and frightening new threats.

Teresa's gaze slowly drifted away from the peaceful dog to the rest of her bedroom. Sunlight poured through the window facing east, highlighting her pale buttercup walls and shining on the simple engraved pine furniture she'd placed throughout the large bedroom. Some people told her the room looked almost Spartan—she needed more than a dresser, a nightstand, a cedar chest, and an overstuffed chair covered in ivory linen striped with moss green.

Teresa loved the room, though. The unfussy furnishings did not detract from the fireplace across from her bed with its creamy tiles hand-painted with green ferns and a few small butterflies and hummingbirds. She especially liked the décor so radically different from the garish pink and cerise room in which her father and Wendy had been murdered, a room that still appeared in Teri's recurring nightmare.

She'd had it last night—the same nightmare she'd had a hundred times of walking into her father's darkened room, of slowly approaching Wendy's side of the bed and stepping on soaking-wet carpet, of turning on the light and seeing her father's and Wendy's dead bodies, their many stab wounds oozing blood. Her screams. That's where the nightmare mercifully ended. For years she'd become accustomed to having the nightmare at least once a week. Then, when she was twenty-two, it had abruptly stopped. She was disheartened by its return.

Teresa realized the note had prompted the dream. Almost against her will, she rolled over, opened the drawer of her bedside table, and withdrew the half page of typing paper left in her car last night. The words seemed to jump out at her in the bright morning light:

> Dear Teresa,
>   Roscoe Lee Byrnes meets his maker this week. Will you finally feel safe? . . .

Teri laid down the paper and stared across the room into the fireplace. Roscoe Lee Byrnes. The serial killer the police had apprehended attempting to escape a grisly crime scene in Pennsylvania just two weeks after the Farr murders. The man scheduled for lethal injection in a few days who had confessed to killing Hugh and Wendy Farr and twenty other people. Teresa thought of how easily Byrnes could have added two more victims to his list if he'd murdered her and Celeste.

But he couldn't possibly have been trying to kill me, Teresa admitted reluctantly to herself as she had hundreds of times. That awful night, amid all the carnage he'd wrought, why had he been content just to cut her arm? Teresa glanced down at the narrow nine-inch scar stretching from her bicep almost to her wrist. The wound had been so shallow the scar now was barely visible. Her attacker's action didn't make sense, and for eight years Teresa had obsessed over why her life had been spared when the other people in the household had been so viciously torn and gashed.

After Byrnes's confession, local police and the FBI decided Teresa's screaming had saved her life that night. The neighbors said that through their open bedroom windows facing the Farr home, they had heard her wild shrieks. The husband had immediately turned on a bright bedside light and called 911. Meanwhile their Great Dane, spending the night on the porch, had begun howling and set off every other dog near the Farr house.

From the Farr bedroom, the police reasoned, Byrnes must have seen the neighbor's glaring bedside light and guessed someone was reaching for a phone. He had also heard the strident howls of at least five dogs and he'd been frantic to escape the house. He'd probably thought police would answer alarm calls quicker or that maybe they even made routine passes around the homes of the affluent. That was the answer, most of them decided. Byrnes had been too intent on flight to waste time killing Teresa. He'd merely slashed at this unexpected impediment between him and escape.

Still, the Farr house security alarm hadn't gone off and none of the locks had been picked. That fact the police couldn't understand until Teresa told them that her father had been "upset" with her when she'd come in late. He'd lectured her, sent her to bed, and almost immediately she'd heard his heavy footsteps climbing the stairs. He often forgot to turn on the alarm when he was distracted, she'd told them, and had no qualms about giving the police this expurgated version of the scene that night because her conscience was clear when it came to Hugh's death. Actually, she'd been terrified that if the police knew about the violence between her and Hugh that day, both before and after her night excursion, she'd be an even more likely murder suspect.

After his apprehension in a small Pennsylvania town, police had presented a scenario of the Farr murders to Byrnes, one in which he'd perhaps seen a pretty girl, followed her home, waited a couple of hours, decided to go in after her and whomever else he could find, and luckily discovered the front door unlocked. They went on to add that because of all the noise and the lights next door, he'd been in such a hurry to escape, he hadn't taken time to kill a teenage girl who might put up a struggle.

Later the cops had allowed Teresa to see a video of them presenting Byrnes with their theory of the crime, then waiting anxiously for his reaction. Byrnes had stared expressionlessly at them for almost a full minute with his pale, yellow-tinged blue eyes, then nodded his unusually big head with its sparse hair, fat red cheeks, and receding chin. Finally, he'd said, "Yeah, that's what happened," in the rumbling monotone that was his voice. The police had been satisfied. Teresa hadn't. They had not seen the killer calmly descend the stairs, open the front door, and close it behind him. To her, that escape didn't seem to be one of a man frantic with fear, frenziedly trying to flee.

She had never described the killer's unhurried "get-away" to anyone, though, because too many people already believed her unstable mother had killed her callous ex-husband and his new, pregnant wife. Nor had Teresa mentioned the whiff of sandalwood she'd caught that night when the killer bumped against her. She'd read that sandalwood was used in both women's and men's colognes, but she was certain someone would mention that Marielle Farr always wore the scent of sandalwood, pointing toward her as the possible murderer.

Teresa sighed and muttered in frustration, "It was eight years and two months ago. Enough of the tragic replay."

She climbed out of bed, managing not to disturb a snoring Sierra. Teresa went into the bathroom and looked at herself in the mirror. Her complexion was paler than usual and she had dark shadows beneath her eyes. "You have one birthday and you look ten years older," she told her reflection, but she knew she didn't look tired because she was officially a year older than the day before yesterday. She'd had a bad night because of the chilling note left on her car, a night torn with nightmares of the murders, and a heartbreaking dream about her lost mother.

Teresa turned on the radio she kept in the bathroom. Steve Winwood's "Back in the High Life Again" came on, an upbeat song that for once did nothing for Teri's downbeat mood. She couldn't stop thinking about her mother, Marielle. After a breakdown and stint in a psychiatric clinic precipitated by the divorce, Marielle had gone to stay with her Aunt Beulah who lived just north of town. Doctors had pronounced Marielle unfit to care for a teenage girl, causing her to lose not only Hugh but also custody of Teresa.

Marielle's aunt told police that on the day of the Farr deaths Marielle had seemed calm, even somewhat cheerful, and said she was going for an afternoon walk on her favorite path in the woods. Encouraged by her improved mood and unusual energy, Beulah claimed that for the first time since Marielle's release from the hospital, she had let the younger woman go out of the house alone.

Teresa's eyes filled with tears. Her beautiful, gentle mother had never returned to Beulah's house. There had been a massive police search for Marielle, especially because of the murders, but the investigation had revealed absolutely nothing. As far as Teresa knew, no one had seen or heard from her mother for eight years. Marielle Farr simply seemed to have fallen off the face of the earth the beautiful day in April that had ended so grotesquely for Hugh, Wendy, and Celeste.

Teri impatiently wiped at her tears, then splashed cold water on her face, hoping she could whisk herself away from the ghastly trip down memory lane, but it didn't work. As she briskly tried to rub some color into her wet skin with a towel, she remembered the day after the murders when her bewilderment over her mother's disappearance, along with her horror over the brutal killings, was suddenly magnified when she realized the police thought that if Marielle hadn't stabbed Hugh and Wendy to death, then Teresa had. Her father and stepmother, both of whom everyone knew Teresa hated, had been murdered. Celeste, whom people mistakenly assumed Teresa also hated, had been stabbed in the abdomen. Teresa, however, had suffered only a shallow cut on the arm.

She hadn't been arrested, but not because local law enforcement believed her innocent. She'd remained free simply because of lack of evidence—the police never found the murder weapon, which according to the medical examiner was a long, razor-sharp serrated knife—and while Teresa's nightgown bore some blood from the victims, the gown would have been soaked if she'd violently stabbed three people. No other bloody clothes had been found in the house, nor had blood been found in the drains as it would have been if Teresa had stripped naked to stab her victims, showered, then put on a nightgown merely smeared with blood.

In addition, Teresa had also agreed to take a lie detector test, which she had passed. Some local students of crime remained unconvinced, though, ominously pointing out that "certain kinds" of people were capable of beating the machine. That, they added triumphantly, was why lie detector results were not allowed as evidence in court.

Most people, though, didn't care to look at evidence appearing to rule out Teresa. They seemed to find the idea of a seventeen-year-old girl going on a killing spree much more entertaining. During the next two weeks, the looks of alarm and disgust Teresa saw in people's eyes, and the long, intense police interrogations she'd undergone had frightened her nearly senseless. Even eight years later, Teresa remembered back then only four people in the world loudly proclaiming her innocence—her brother, Kent; her mother's best friend, Carmen; the housekeeper, Emma MacKenzie; and especially Emma's son, Mac.

Sunlight poured into the bathroom on this glorious first day of July, but Teresa shivered as if a chilly breeze were washing over her when she remembered that unbelievable, terrifying time—a time when she'd kept hoping she was having a nightmare from which any minute she would awaken. "But I didn't wake up," she murmured to herself as she stripped off her nightgown and turned on the shower, making the water hotter than usual. She had spent seemingly endless days and nights in a haze of disbelief, knowing that almost everyone in town thought she'd killed two people and critically wounded a child.

Teresa was shaking as she stepped into the shower stall, letting the water stream over her hair, her face, and down her body that actually bore chill bumps. Teri hadn't experienced a bout of the old, recurring panic for a long time, but the note had brought it rushing back. Once again she felt as if she were a seventeen-year-old girl with a murdered father, a lost mother, and a town half-full of people who thought she was a deranged killer, a town half-full of people who felt they had to be sure to lock their doors at night because Teresa Farr was on the loose. It had seemed ludicrous, and at times she'd even laughed at the idea. Then she would realize that people really were afraid of her, and she'd choked on her laughter and burst into tears—tears of grief, disbelief, and overwhelming fear.

Two weeks later, what seemed to her a miracle happened—Roscoe Lee Byrnes confessed to the murders. Townspeople had been stunned. A few seemed disappointed. Many refused to believe him, tenaciously arguing that people sometimes confessed to crimes they hadn't committed. Everyone knew that was true—everyone who watched television and saw movies, that is. They dismissed law enforcement's reminder that people offering false confessions were usually harmless nuts seeking attention, men who'd probably never done anything more vicious than yell at the neighbor's cat. Imagining Teresa Farr stabbing three people in the deep, dark night was much more exciting.

Nevertheless, because of the certainty of the FBI that Byrnes's confession was genuine, the local population's distrust of Teresa gradually faded. After all, Byrnes was a *serial* killer, they said to one another in obsessive discussions of the case that had kept people preoccupied for months. Teresa had been out late that night and Byrnes probably was, too, hunting for victims. He'd also raped three of his female victims, girls in their teens. He'd probably seen Teresa, followed her home and waited—waited for that unlocked door, that sleeping family and the pretty teenager he'd planned to enjoy before he killed her, too. Also, newspaper articles and even a story about the crime in a national magazine informed the public that Roscoe Lee Byrnes always killed viciously at night and always used a serrated knife, repeatedly stabbing his victims.

Adding to evidence about Byrnes being the killer was a clerk at a convenience store two miles away from the Farr home who unequivocally identified Byrnes as being a customer the evening before the murders. The clerk said that after seeing pictures of the confessed murderer, he was certain he'd waited on the guy, claiming he'd never forget those weird, pale, bulging eyes and large, bullet-shaped head. The guy had bought barbecue potato chips and beer, the clerk had said in a news clip. Cheap beer, he'd added disdainfully in his two minutes of television fame, beer Byrnes had paid for in dirty, wadded-up dollar bills. The clerk's story had been backed up by a couple of unmistakable images of Byrnes caught on tape by the store's surveillance camera.

So, by summer's end most people had absolved Teresa, who'd gone to live with her missing mother's friend Carmen until she turned eighteen the last week of June, then went away to college in September. All the while, Teresa had tried fervently to believe in Byrnes's guilt. She'd even pretended to believe it, but because of the killer's leisurely departure from the home, not to mention his happening to be wearing a scent similar to her mother's perfume, Teresa had never felt certain Byrnes was really the murderer who had struck at the Farr house on Mourning Dove Lane. For eight years, she'd been waiting for the appearance of evidence that would erase her doubts.

Teresa stepped from the shower and reached for a big, fluffy bath towel, noting with a smile that Sierra had finally arisen and come in to supervise her morning routine. She bent down and petted the dog's head as she sat patiently about a foot away from the shower stall. "Hey, girl, afraid I'll go down the drain if you're not here to look after me? Or are you just wondering if I've gone crazy, hanging around in here talking to myself?"

Sierra emitted one of her habitual snorts and stood up. As she looked at the dog, cheerfully wagging her tail and gazing at Teresa with trusting amber eyes, she felt a strange but welcome sense of relief. The time for Byrnes's execution had finally come, she thought. His appeals had ended and so would the life of Byrnes in a matter of days. Everything pointed to him being the killer. He had even admitted to the murders. Her doubts were silly and she thought that as soon as he was executed, she'd feel as if that hideous chapter in her life was finally over.

Then another thought struck Teri as she bent at the waist and wrapped the towel around her length of wet hair. Through all the years, no one had revealed fresh evidence to absolve Byrnes of the Farr murders, so what did the note left in her car mean? Was someone asking her if after the execution, she'd feel safe from a psychopathic killer? Possibly. Probably. Especially because they'd said Celeste was talking again. If that was true, Teresa was thrilled. She had longed for the day when Celeste would speak once more, when she would become "normal" and emerge from her almost trancelike state.

But the note did not have a reassuring tone. It had sounded threatening in a sickly gleeful way, especially when it said Celeste would finally tell the truth. What truth? That she'd seen the murderer? A tiny, cold finger seemed to run down Teresa's spine as she realized why the note's tone had been triumphant. The writer was elated because he was telling her that Celeste would soon identify the real killer of her mommy and Hugh and that murderer would be Teresa.

I am not going to think about that stupid note, Teresa thought. It had ruined the end of what had been a great day—her realization that she had not only emerged from the trauma of the murders but also accomplished her dream to have her very own riding school. And then she'd found the note. But it was just a note. A note couldn't harm her, couldn't take away her peace of mind, unless she let it, and she didn't intend to be daunted so easily.

Feeling stronger, Teresa made herself smile at nothing, as if the old song lyrics "Put on a happy face" could make her uneasiness disappear. Just as she left her bedroom and headed for the stairs, her fax machine emitted an imperative beep alerting her to an incoming message. She walked into the small spare bedroom she used as an office, noting absently that she definitely needed to do some filing and general straightening, and went to the machine. Yesterday morning, she'd e-mailed a horse equipment company asking for their price list on particular tack items. She hadn't expected an answer early Sunday morning, but she couldn't think of who else might be sending her a fax.

Teri tapped her foot impatiently as the machine ground out the paper. Really, she needed a new one, she thought. She'd bought this machine when she started college, it had served her well for years, but now that she was in business and that business was nicely increasing, she really needed something faster, more updated—

Teresa's wandering thoughts slammed to a halt as she picked up the paper, still warm from the machine, and read the message:

> *Have you learned your lesson, Teresa? The guilty will be punished. Accept it.*
> *For you there is no escape. No Escape NO ESCAPE*
> ***NO ESCAPE***

The paper shook in Teri's hand, but she said aloud in a dry, unconcerned voice, "A prank. Just a stupid prank." Then she looked at the top of the fax. As her vision wavered, the paper slipped between her suddenly cold fingers and fell to the floor.

According to the header, the sender was Hubert Farr.

2

Celeste Warner daintily cut a piece of her blueberry pancake, popped it into her small mouth, and began chewing, her big eyes seeming to smile although her facial expression was serious. "You sure do like pancakes, don't you, darlin'?" her grandmother asked heartily. Fay had pulled her long light brown gray-streaked hair into a French twist decorated with three rhinestone-tipped hairpins, a style she usually saved for the few social events in her life. "You eat as many as you like. I made enough batter to feed the whole neighborhood!"

"Mom, you seem to think the more you feed her, the more she'll talk," Jason said half-jokingly. "You've been pushing food at her since we came home yesterday afternoon from Bennigan's."

"Well, food made her talk there. It only makes sense that food's the trigger," Fay answered as if with ultimate logic.

"She ate for years and she didn't speak," Jason returned patiently. "Why would food suddenly have been the trigger yesterday?"

Fay gave her son a deep look. "The mind is a mysterious thing, Jason Warner. It's way beyond our understanding."

"Yeah, I guess so," Jason answered mildly. Fay seemed satisfied with her explanation and he didn't care to mention Celeste's referral to a "smell" that set off her talking spree. After all, he'd have to explain that smell is the strongest of the five senses and his mother would probably start an argument claiming that he had no way of knowing such a thing about the mysterious mind. "I just wish she'd speak again, Mom."

"Celeste will talk when she has something to say, won't you, darlin'?" Fay swooped by with the frying pan and placed another pancake on the girl's plate almost like a bribe. "But you won't talk about that terrible night so long ago. And you won't say that awful rhyme again, will you? You'll say something nice and pretty and sweet."

Celeste raised her head and, smiling, looked into her grandmother's hopeful blue eyes.

> *"The clock struck three,*
> *And Death came for me.*
> *When I opened my eyes,*
> *There was* Teri!

> *"The clock struck three,*
> *And Death came for—"*

"Okay, honey, we heard you the first time." Jason's voice remained calm, but his mother stepped back, looking ready to drop the frying pan. After yesterday, he'd recovered from the shock of his daughter finally speaking and decided that he'd handle things more professionally this time instead of merely gaping at her. He began in a matter-of-fact voice. "In Bennigan's you said that on the night of the murders, you ran into someone coming out of your mommy's room and the person stabbed you." Celeste nodded serenely. "Are you absolutely sure it wasn't Teresa?"

"Jason!" Fay gasped, but for once Jason abruptly held up his hand and silenced his mother.

Meanwhile, Celeste stared blankly at him before saying, "I didn't see a face. The hood was in the way."

Fay couldn't remain silent. "So you're not sure that Teresa didn't hurt you."

Celeste put down her fork, then reluctantly nodded. "Well, Teri did hurt me."

"Teresa hurt you?" Jason asked in loud surprise. After Wendy's marriage to Hugh, Celeste had always spoken glowingly about Teri. When Jason had finally met Teresa Farr, he'd liked her, too, not just for her kindness and friendliness to him but also for her surprising warmth toward Celeste. He couldn't fathom the girl fooling him so profoundly. Jason leaned forward and demanded again, "Teresa *hurt* you?"

"Don't shout and her name is Teri," Celeste said irritably. "I was in the toy box. Teri hurt me when she lifted me out and put me on my bed."

"So she could stab you again?" Fay asked breathlessly.

"I got stabbed *one* time outside Mommy's door," Celeste said. "Teri hurt me *after* that when she put a pillow on my stomach and pressed hard!"

"To stop the blood loss," Jason murmured in relief.

"Or to smother her," Fay argued.

Celeste flung down her fork. "I'm not dumb! I know I don't breathe through my tummy, Grandma!" Celeste looked ferociously at her grandmother and father. "Grandma, you tell me not to talk about that night, but you keep askin' questions. And Daddy, I *keep* sayin' I didn't see who stabbed me, but you don't even *listen* to me!"

"I'm sorry, sugar pie." Fay's voice was weak and she backed away from the girl.

"Well, I'm done talkin' today," Celeste announced, and firmly shut her mouth. Jason felt sudden fury with his mother when Celeste pushed herself away from the kitchen table and stomped into the living room. In a moment, they heard the television turned up almost full volume.

"Satisfied?" he demanded of Fay.

"She's mad at you, too!" Fay shot back, tears glistening in her eyes, before he sat down on Celeste's abandoned seat. "I said I'm sorry. I guess I never did know when to be quiet."

Jason wanted to agree, but his mother was right—he'd been guilty of giving Celeste the third degree, too. Besides, Fay looked so ashamed he couldn't add to her misery, so he said nothing, but glanced away from her tremulous face. Otherwise, he wouldn't be able to continue the discussion he was determined to have with a

woman who'd decided never to even consider Teresa
Farr's innocence.

"Okay, I'm guilty, too. But what really gets to me,
Mom, is that you haven't accepted the fact that a serial
killer *confessed* to murdering the Farrs." She remained
stubbornly silent. "Aren't you paying attention to what Celeste is telling us? Why would Teresa stab her, then try to
save her life?"

"Celeste is in shock. She doesn't know what she's saying."

"She *was* in shock. She's obviously coming out of it and
beginning to talk about that night, but she'll stop if you
keep hammering on Teresa Farr."

"Well, maybe she *should* stop. Maybe Celeste should
never remember what happened on that godforsaken
night!"

Jason took a deep breath and closed his eyes. He believed that no matter what conflicts he might be holding
silently within himself, the right thing to do was not make
Celeste a prisoner of her memories. "Mom, for eight years,
when Celeste wasn't in some institute where they promised
to have her talking in two weeks, she's been with you, and
you've kept her wrapped up in a cocoon. I know you did it
to ensure her safety, but she hasn't led anything resembling
a normal life. Maybe that's why it took her so long to start
talking again. To her, the whole world has become dangerous."

"For her, the whole world is dangerous," Fay said defiantly. "Especially the world around here and *most* especially this town since Teresa Farr decided to come back
and settle here. I've made sure that woman hasn't even gotten a *glimpse* of Celeste. I've kept Celeste secluded from
her."

"You've kept Celeste secluded from just about everything." Jason looked at his mother tenderly. "Mom, I appreciate all you've done for Celeste and me the last few

years, but she's *my* daughter and I have to insist that you follow my wishes. For one, you have to stop making her a captive in this house. For another, I want you to *listen* to her. Don't contradict her and above all, don't force words into her mouth, especially about Teresa. If we let her talk about what she wants, when she wants, we might find out more about that night and about Byrnes."

Fay looked at Jason with rebellious eyes. "She remembers Teresa Farr. She doesn't know anything about Roscoe Byrnes."

"What makes you think Celeste knows nothing of Byrnes? She's not blind and deaf. She reads. She watches television. She took classes when she was in the hospital. We've hired tutors for her when she's home. She's not autistic—she was mute because of trauma. She can write almost as well as an adult when it suits her. You have to accept that Celeste didn't stop learning when she was eight years old and Byrnes killed her mother. The psychiatrists' tests for kids like Celeste show she's very bright *and* observant."

"They claim she's damaged," Fay said flatly.

"Mom, I know you don't have a high opinion of psychiatrists, but not one of them has called Celeste *damaged*. They've told me shock probably turned her involuntarily mute when she was younger, but they're certain she became *voluntarily* mute years ago. She just decided *not* to talk. Now, thank God, she's finally willing to talk. She might not sound like a regular sixteen-year-old because she's been so isolated from kids her own age, but that doesn't mean there's anything wrong with her intelligence *or* her memory. She *needs* to talk about that night. In her own way, in her own time, without interruptions."

Jason leaned toward his mother, who, since the murders, no longer looked younger than her age. In fact, Jason thought she looked a good deal older than sixty, even though she was still physically strong and full of energy. "Mom, I want to help Celeste return to full health—to the girl she would have been if Wendy hadn't taken her away from me." Fay's eyes flared at his last phrase. Her hatred of Wendy would never die, and he was a bit ashamed of himself for using his ex-wife's name to manipulate his mother, but he felt desperate. "Isn't that what you want—for your granddaughter to be completely normal and happy?"

"Yes, of course, but I'm afraid this isn't the way to do it . . ."

Jason took a deep breath. "For once I'm not going to listen to your advice. This is what *I* think is best, and you know how much I love my daughter. I wouldn't do anything I felt could harm her." Jason loved his mother and he respected her, but this was one time he knew that Celeste had to come first, no matter how much his course of action hurt Fay. "Mom, if you can't go along with what I want, I'll take Celeste away."

"You won't!" Fay nearly choked. "You wouldn't do that!"

"Yes, I will take her—not as a punishment to you, but as what I feel is the wisest move for Celeste." He paused as Fay looked at the table, her shoulders shaking, her mouth clamped shut so tightly her lips turned white. He knew she was trying to conquer the fiery words within her, something she'd rarely done in her life. "I realize how hard this is for you, Mom," Jason said patiently. "I'm not trying to be a bully—just a good father. Just as you've been a good mother to me and grandmother to Celeste. Please, Mom. Don't fight me—help me."

Fay remained silent, her gaze locked on to the checked tablecloth for a few moments. Then she sighed and looked at him with defeat in her gaze. "All right, Jason. I think you're doing exactly the wrong thing, but I won't fight you if it means I might lose Celeste. When the time comes that you've seen what a colossal mistake you've made, though—"

"It won't come to that," Jason cut her off with a confidence he didn't really feel. "I promise no harm will result from what I'm doing for my daughter."

Although he sounded completely confident, part of Jason was terrified he might drive Celeste so deep into herself that this time she wouldn't ever come out again.

3

Five minutes later, Teresa sat on her desk chair, staring at the fax lying in front of her. She knew obtaining her fax number was no hard task—she'd distributed business cards listing her telephone and fax number along with her e-mail address. She also knew how easy it was to change the header on a fax machine or to generate a fax from a computer, so she wasn't scared by the header reading that the fax had been sent by Hubert Farr. What worried her was the fact that someone was *trying* to scare her. Was this person just childishly malicious? Or were they a definite threat to her?

She knew the fax could be traced with the help of the police, and she spent another ten minutes trying to decide what to do. She'd reached for the phone three times, meaning to call local law enforcement, and three times she'd jerked her hand away from the receiver as if it were a snake.

Police. The word had struck fear in her ever since the murders, ever since she'd been questioned until she'd grown too hoarse to answer and finally allowed the lawyer Kent had hired to stop the police interrogation. Even after the capture and confession of Roscoe Lee Byrnes, she'd been subjected to "follow-ups," the FBI wanting to ask "just a few more questions, Miss Farr," until law enforcement in general terrified her as much as the thought of a monster would a child.

So, she would not call the police, Teresa decided. If the fax turned out to be anything important and she was later forced to show it to them, she would say she hadn't done so earlier because she thought they would dismiss it as a prank. And that's exactly what they *would* do, Teri told herself. Dismiss it. After all, the confessed killer of Hugh and Wendy Farr would be executed in less than a week. Everyone who followed the case knew about the execution of Byrnes. So the fax was nothing more than a sick joke, just like the note in her car—something to unnerve her during the last few days of Byrnes's life. So forget the fax, she thought. Forget the note. Forget all of it. Someone simply had a nasty sense of humor.

Determinedly cheerful, she turned to Sierra, who sat beside her chair. "I say we have some fun this morning; how about you, girl?" The dog's tail flew back and forth and she barked once. "Okay. Race you down the stairs!"

Teresa had set the timer on the coffeemaker and could already smell the aroma of a strong African blend as the two of them ran into the kitchen. Sierra led the way, as always, and Teresa announced, "You won!" She handed Sierra a dog biscuit before pouring her own mug of coffee. The dog looked at her reproachfully, biscuit clenched between her teeth. "I know you want a big breakfast, but until I've had at least one cup of coffee, that's the best I can manage. And quit glaring at me that way. I'd like to remind you that there are starving dogs all over the world who'd give *anything*—"

Like a child, Sierra began munching furiously as if trying to drown out the lecture she'd heard countless times. Satisfied, Teresa took two aspirins for the dull headache lingering behind her eyes and wandered out of the kitchen into her living room, enjoying the feel of cool varnished hardwood floors warmed here and there with thick flax rugs.

Her mother would have liked this room, Teresa thought. Her mother would have approved of Teresa having the ramshackle farmhouse torn down, and hiring an architect to design a modest home that looked like a graceful brick country house with a wide front porch, beamed wooden ceilings, and lots of windows. Although Marielle Farr had suffered from what Teresa now knew was chronic depression, she had never hidden herself in dark rooms with draperies pulled against the light. In fact, Teresa remembered her mother often standing in front of windows, her dark head leaned back, eyes closed, and a faint smile on her perfect lips as she seemed to soak in outside light, whether it was sunny or gray. She'd even loved thunderstorms, gathering her children, Teresa and Kent, close beside her and encouraging everyone to imitate the roars that sometimes shook the house. Whoever did the best imitation got an Eskimo Pie, and the kids had begun looking forward to the contests instead of fearing the storms.

The phone rang and Teresa jumped, slopping hot coffee on her hand. She cursed under her breath, reluctantly admitting to herself that she was still deeply rattled by the note and the fax no matter how hard she pretended to dismiss them. She supposed what she felt was normal, though. After all, how could she dismiss the fact that someone out there wanted to remind her of the murders, wanted to hurt and to frighten her? Teri had always thought she had better than average self-control, but she realized she didn't have complete self-mastery. She couldn't shut out all anxiety and worry, especially when someone was trying so hard to roil those feelings in her, but she could try.

The phone rang again. Teri took a deep breath, determinedly crossed the room, picked up the cordless receiver, and managed a jaunty, "Hello?"

"Church will be out about noon, Sharon has a roast cooking for lunch, so we'll be eating immediately after we get home. We can make it to the farm around one thirty."

"Pardon me?" Teresa couldn't help grinning in spite of her rocky night and morning. "To whom am I speaking?"

"Kent, of course."

"Oh, of course. Tell me, Kent, is this your usual phone

manner or do you sometimes deign to greet people before you begin speaking at machine-gun rate?"

He paused, then asked sweetly, "Hello, Teresa; how are you on this beautiful morning?"

"Why, I'm fine; thank you for inquiring. How about Sharon? Not too hungover to go to church?"

Kent's voice had returned to its usual abrupt rate. "No, but I wish you hadn't taken her to Club Rendezvous."

"I didn't. She went of her own free will. Carmen and I didn't kidnap her. And what's wrong with Club Rendezvous?"

"Don't be ingenuous. You know *who* is wrong with that place."

"Mac MacKenzie."

"Good guess. I'm surprised *you* went there."

Teresa had never told either Kent or Sharon about seeing Mac clutching and kissing a redhead while he was engaged to her. She had confided only in Carmen. Teresa had told Kent she'd decided she was simply too young to get married, she really didn't know what she wanted out of life, she couldn't see herself tied down to one person until she died . . . And Kent hadn't believed one word of it.

"I went because I was curious, Kent." Teresa congratulated herself on the casual tone of her voice. "I did help Mac design the place, if you remember."

"I remember," Kent said dourly.

"Well, we all had a good time. Even Sharon."

"I guess that's why she didn't mention earlier she was going there."

"She didn't mention it because she knew you wouldn't approve. For heaven's sake, Kent," Teresa said in exasperation. "You used to be fun."

"I'm still fun."

"Yeah, you sound like a barrel of laughs."

"I'm just so busy at work, I forget there's anything but keeping Farr Coal Company up to speed."

"That's what happened to Dad, and you sure don't want to turn out like him, even though he did make time for Wendy in his busy schedule."

"Well, Sharon doesn't have to worry about other women. We've been sweethearts since high school."

"And married with a child while you were still in college," Teresa said. A child who arrived only six months after their wedding, which had been a quick, unemotional ceremony held in a judge's chambers three weeks after the deaths of Hugh and Wendy and a week after the arrest of Roscoe Lee Byrnes. It had been a bleak affair, but Sharon and her only living parent, her father, Gabriel, had looked immensely relieved—and six months later Teri had realized why. But those times were best forgotten, she reminded herself, especially because Kent was so touchy about the early birth of his son. "Is Daniel excited about meeting his horse today?" she asked quickly.

"He's ecstatic. I don't know how we'll hold him still through Sunday school and church." Kent paused. "Sorry I was so curt earlier, but frankly I am a little on edge. Sharon is worried about him taking riding lessons. She's worried about him doing anything—swimming, playing soccer, you name it—and she's making *him* nervous and unhappy because she usually keeps him from doing the things his friends do."

Sharon was a wonderful mother but increasingly overprotective, just as Carmen had pointed out last night. But Carmen was not one of Kent's favorite people, either, so Teresa dared not mention having discussed the problem with her. Unfortunately, Teri had no advice of her own except for Kent to put his foot down and insist that Daniel be allowed to participate in sports, which she knew would cause trouble in what she'd once considered almost the perfect marriage. "Maybe you should talk to a professional, Kent," she said carefully. "I'm childless. I don't have much experience with children except for Celeste, and that was a long time ago."

"Yeah, Celeste," Kent said softly. "Poor kid. I guess you heard that she started talking again."

"Yes." Instinct told Teresa not to mention that she'd learned the news by a threatening note left in her car last night. "I don't know where Celeste was or what she said, though."

"I've gotten about five different versions, but it seems Jason had taken her to lunch at Bennigan's yesterday and all at once she just started babbling about the night of the murders."

"The night of the murders!" Teresa tried to sound surprised, although she'd already learned that information from the note. "What did she say?"

"I don't know. It seems she suddenly stopped talking and started shouting some kind of chant."

"A chant?"

"I know it sounds crazy." Kent paused. "You might as well know, she mentioned you in the chant. You and death. We must have gotten twenty calls last night about it. People giving garbled accounts of the incident and wanting more information. I just said I had no idea what people were talking about and hung up."

"A chant about me and death?" Teri repeated. "What about me and death?"

"I wasn't lying to those people. I really don't know. Listen, I shouldn't have said anything." Teresa could hear Kent's regret for bringing up the subject. "Besides, I don't have the story straight. I'm sure we'll get all the details at church today, though, and Sharon can tell you about it this afternoon. Unless you want to call Jason. I know you two were friends."

"We were acquaintances, not friends. He was always nice to me because Celeste told him I treated her well."

"You treated her like she was your real sister. I liked the kid, but you really loved her."

"I felt sorry for her," Teresa said abruptly, feeling ridiculously guilty for admitting to her brother that she'd loved Wendy's child. "I don't think I should call Jason, though. I haven't heard a word from him since she was taken to the hospital the night of the murders. Fay Warner lives less than a mile from here, but she's kept Celeste safely away from me—I haven't even *seen* the girl for eight years, which is no surprise considering that everyone thought I'd tried to kill her." Teri realized her heart was pounding.

So Celeste was talking again. Not just talking—chanting about Teri and death. Was that why she'd gotten both the note and the fax? For a moment, Teresa felt like telling Kent about the hateful messages she'd received. Then she remembered that he was already on edge about Sharon. Teresa didn't want to ruin the day, especially for Daniel, and if Kent told Sharon about the harassment Teresa was enduring, she knew Sharon would use it as an excuse to cancel Daniel's visit to the horses—she might even declare that the child couldn't take lessons. Keeping in mind how disappointed Daniel would be if everything went wrong, Teri forced herself to breathe deeply and keep her mouth shut about the notes.

Kent was saying, "Teri, not everyone believed you tried to kill—"

"It doesn't matter now." The subject was still painful for Teresa and she didn't want Kent wasting his breath trying to comfort her. "Even if Sharon hears *everything* at church, she probably won't tell me. She'll want to spare my feelings. Someone else will give me the details about Celeste later," Teresa rushed on, trying to sound unconcerned. "Carmen, probably. She has an uncanny way of knowing everything that's going on in town."

"That's because she's a gossip who loves to spread bad news."

"Oh, Kent, she is not," Teri said in annoyance. "If so, she would have mentioned Celeste last night so she could spoil my birthday. You just don't like her."

"I don't like loud, pushy women," Kent pronounced.

Teresa rolled her eyes. God, he was starting to sound downright prim. "Carmen is not a shrinking violet, if that's what you mean by 'pushy.' And she is *not* loud. She's just not soft-spoken."

"She's not soft-spoken. That's an understatement," Kent said derisively. "Teri, I don't see why you can't find a friend your own age. Carmen is old enough to be your mother."

"She doesn't look or act like it. And I do have friends my age."

"Who?"

"Well . . ." Teresa suddenly realized she wasn't close to any woman near her own age except for Sharon. The friends Teresa had in high school were busy young mothers or always had an excuse for not dining out or going shopping with her. In other words, she had never been completely accepted back into the fold of her hometown. That fact hurt, too, but she'd never let Kent know it. "I'm good friends with some women I meet at the horse shows and auctions." Actually, she'd only had lunch with two of them a couple of times. "You wouldn't know them."

"I hope they aren't wildcats or weird. You were always attracted to the wrong sort of people, just like Mom."

"And what does that mean?"

"Just that both of you could be incredibly naive."

"That is—"

"Ridiculous. Insulting. I don't know what I'm talking about." Furious, Teresa tightened her lips to prevent getting into a useless argument with him. "Well, I'm in a hurry, Sis. Bye for now."

"Good-bye, Mr. Self-Righteous," Teri snapped, but Kent had already hung up.

Angry yet nevertheless half-amused by her brother's increasingly foolish certainty of his own good judgment, Teresa smiled ruefully, knowing that life had a way of taking down those people who thought they had all the answers.

She didn't need to say a word to Kent—he'd find out on his own someday that he didn't know everything. She just hoped the lesson wasn't too hard—certainly not as hard as it had been on her father, much as she'd hated the man.

Teresa stared out the big front window over the twenty acres of her land that were visible from her front window. At one time people had farmed that land. When Teri had been looking for a home, she was told the former owners hadn't kept up the land, not that it had been prime farming land anyway—too much clay, not enough topsoil—and she'd been able to buy the one hundred acres comprising the whole farm along with the house for a ridiculously low price.

Teresa immediately had hired a crew to clear the land, then a construction crew. After two years, when their jobs were finished, she had a beautiful house sitting on a knoll rolling down to a field covered with kelly-green grass, thanks to what seemed like tons of fertilizer spread over the ground time after time. Pristine white fences lined the field that boasted two riding rings and two large paddocks. There was also a jumping course for those students further along in their riding expertise and the people who were already good riders and merely boarded their horses at Farr Fields.

The other eighty acres of her land spreading beyond the view from the house included a large, beautiful pond and riding paths carved out of the sycamore and honeysuckle jungle the land had become during the twenty years it had been neglected. Her two employees, father and son Gus and Josh Gibbs, were already at work this morning: Gus exercising Kent's palomino, Conquistador, whose coat shone like burnished gold in the sunlight, while Josh brushed the ebony mane of Teresa's Arabian, Eclipse. If the truth were known, Teri thought, she was really closer to Josh and his father Gus than to any female friend Kent would have deemed suitable. She would trust either man with her life.

Absently, Teresa rubbed her left arm with its long, thin scar left from the killer's knife. The vista stretching beyond her was beautiful, but she looked at it with vague eyes, not really seeing the rolling fields of rich grass, the horses, the hyacinth blue sky.

Her vision had turned inward to the house on Mourning Dove Lane—the house where she'd walked in terror one night, knowing something dark and evil had invaded the once-peaceful walls; the house where she'd found her father and his wife dead and mutilated in the warmth of their own bed; the house where someone had stabbed little Celeste and seemed to kill her psychologically if not physically, leaving her mute from shock and fear, nothing more than a consciousness trapped in a silent body.

But the attacker had failed with the child, Teresa thought. Celeste, the spirited little girl Teri once knew, had been too strong and smart even for a vicious killer. She had survived her knife wound, and after eight long years, when everyone had given up hope of her bouncing back emotionally, she'd finally begun talking again.

To Teri, the news was a miracle, a reason not only for amazement but also for joy. Unfortunately, she knew that for some people, the most fascinating thing now about Celeste Warner would be what she had to say.

CHAPTER THREE

1

CARMEN NORRIS STRETCHED LANGUIDLY, pulled the sheet higher over her slender body, kept taut by tri-weekly workouts, and scooted closer to Gabriel O'Brien. She asked softly, "Gabe, how much longer are we going to keep this relationship a secret?"

"Not long," Gabriel answered in his deep, resonant voice. "You know I've just been giving Sharon enough time to get over her mother's death before I tell her I'm planning to marry again."

Carmen tried not to betray the growing irritation she felt about keeping Sharon happy at the expense of everyone else's feelings. "Gabe, Sharon's mother has been dead for four years. Sharon will always miss her, but you're still alive and you have a right to happiness. Sharon will never be delighted about you even dating another woman, much less marrying her, though."

Gabriel drew in a deep breath and let it out slowly. "I know," he said finally. "I thought if I gave her enough time, she'd eventually adjust and accept the idea of me being with someone else."

"Adjust and accept!" Carmen laughed gently. "Gabe, if anything, you're causing Sharon to do just the opposite. You're giving her time to think of you as someone who will *never* remarry."

Carmen stared at the man beside her. The bright morning sun shone on his thick, curly hair, the same strawberry blond as Sharon's before Gabe's became laced with gray. Except for the hair, father and daughter bore no resemblance, though. While Sharon's face was porcelain-skinned and softly curved, Gabriel's was all strong planes with a slightly aquiline nose, and skin lined and leathery from the years he'd spent working the customary month on/month off schedule on excursion boats, starting as a deckhand and continuing to the position of pilot, and finally to captain.

Carmen felt a wave of desperation rush over her. She hadn't felt romantic love for years, and she'd never experienced the ardency she did for this man. The men in her past paled in comparison to Gabriel O'Brien. She couldn't bear the thought of losing him because he had a spoiled, selfish daughter who didn't want him to be happy. Then he smiled at Carmen and she relaxed slightly. "You're right, Carmen. Sharon does expect to be the only woman in my life. Maybe I've babied her too much."

"Maybe you have," Carmen said carefully. She always felt as if she were walking on eggs with Gabe when it came to the subject of Sharon. "I certainly mean no criticism—I know your wife had trouble getting pregnant, how long you waited to have Sharon, how delicate her health was when she was a child. It's only natural you're protective. But Sharon is a healthy *adult* woman now. You should treat her like one. To do otherwise is almost insulting to her."

"I never thought of it that way," Gabe said slowly.

"Besides, we're acting as if we're doing something wrong and I'm really uncomfortable with that feeling. Aren't you?" Carmen ventured.

"Well, yes, I guess I am."

"After all, neither of us is married. There is *nothing* wrong about our love for each other." She paused, feeling it was time for a lighter note. "Besides, I can't even wear my beautiful engagement ring!"

"You're right," Gabe said with the beginning of a smile. "Although I wish I could have bought a bigger diamond."

"Oh no, Gabe. What you got me is perfect! I love it," Carmen said truthfully. She opened her bedside table drawer, withdrew and opened a jewelry box. She slipped on the engagement ring and held it up toward the window, allowing sunlight to set the one-carat diamond sparkling. "It's absolutely beautiful, Gabe."

"If you say so. But if it had been two carats . . ."

"It would have been too big for my taste." Carmen wiggled her finger, making the diamond twinkle. "I want everyone to know we're engaged, Gabe. I hope you do, too."

"I do."

"Then let's go public."

"Go public?" Gabriel looked startled.

"Tell people. See each other openly." For a fleeting moment, Gabe looked trapped. "We need to do it soon, Gabe," Carmen said rather urgently, then eased her tone. She didn't want to sound frantic. "It's just that we must be fair to everyone and tell them within the next couple of weeks if we're going to marry in early September like we planned. We don't want to spring this on the families."

"The families?" Gabriel asked.

"Yes, Gabe. Well, Sharon and Kent and Daniel for you, of course. And I've always thought of Teresa as family—the daughter I was never lucky enough to have. I'm sure she'll be flabbergasted about our plans. For once in my life, I've managed to keep a secret."

"Congratulations. Just don't keep secrets from me. As for telling everyone soon . . ." Gabe seemed to waver for a moment. Then Carmen saw resolution slowly harden his expression. "You're right. We should tell people we're getting married. After all, September isn't far away."

Inwardly, Carmen felt an almost dizzying euphoria, but she was careful to seem no more than pleased. "September will be here before we know it, and we do want to give Sharon some time to get used to the idea." Carmen pretended to think, although she'd already come up with the idea weeks ago. "I say we make the announcement this week on the Fourth of July. Independence Day."

"This week?" Carmen watched as doubt flashed in Gabriel's eyes. "Well, if Fourth of July is really important to you . . ."

"Oh, it *is*!" Carmen's voice grew soft and wooing. "Maybe it sounds silly to you, Gabe, but to me it's symbolic. It signifies that we'd be free of sneaking, hiding, and actually *lying* to people. I love you. I don't want to hide it and I certainly don't want to *lie* about it."

Gabe looked at her warmly. "I love you, Carmen, and I don't want to lie about our relationship, either. In fact, we won't lie even one more time. We'll make the announcement this week."

"Wonderful!" Carmen burst out, kissing him on the cheek.

Gabe frowned and for a moment Carmen's high spirits wavered. Then he said, "But you know, sweetheart, you'll be breaking Herman Riggs's heart."

Carmen giggled in relief. "I still feel guilty about using Herman as a smokescreen even though I know he didn't feel anything except friendship for me."

"I wouldn't be too sure about that. If Herman were madly in love with you, he'd be afraid to tell you because of his mama. And with good reason. That woman is like a mother tiger about her little boy and she weighs a good two hundred pounds. If Herman wanted to spend more time with you than her, she'd rip you to shreds."

This time Carmen burst out laughing, as usual making Gabriel grin at the unexpectedly deep chortles that sometimes emerged from her slender, elegant frame. "You're right. Mrs. Riggs will never turn loose of that poor guy, and the sad thing is that I don't think he really *wants* his freedom."

Gabe laughed, then grew quiet, leaned toward the bedside table, pulled a cigarette from a pack, and lit it. He took a deep draw and stared at the ceiling.

"You usually only smoke when you're troubled," Carmen commented. "What's wrong?"

"I'm thinking about Sharon."

"Oh, Gabe, I thought we'd settled the matter of telling her."

"We did. I was thinking about why she's seemed so nervous and unhappy lately. I wonder if it's because of Kent."

"I thought you liked him."

"I do, but he seems to have changed." Gabe took another draw on his cigarette, then abruptly stubbed it out and turned on his side, propping his head on his hand and looking intensely at Carmen. "I think he's acting more and more like his father did, and I couldn't stand Hugh Farr."

"I met Kent when I became friends with Marielle. He was always friendly but not charming like Teri. I'm not around him much now, but when I do see him, he's different. Almost rigid, humorless. I don't think Teri is as close to him as she used to be, although she's never said anything about their relationship. Now that you mention it, though, Kent does seem more like his father than he used to, and Hugh didn't make a lot of friends with his superior manner."

"He was arrogant as hell! Acted like he was royalty, him with all his money and what he thought was his devastating way with the ladies. It never occurred to him girls just liked him for his money."

"Not Marielle," Carmen said definitely.

"No. Poor thing. Everyone knew her parents pushed her into that marriage—a marriage that never stopped Hugh from having affairs. Wendy certainly wasn't the first." Gabriel looked at Carmen. "Marielle must have known about Hugh's other women."

"Yes, she knew," Carmen said reluctantly.

"Then why didn't she leave him?"

"She only mentioned his affairs a couple of times—the subject was fairly much off-limits. I feel like I'm betraying her by talking about them even with you. She was so hurt and embarrassed by them, but she was afraid if she left Hugh, he'd find a way to get custody of the children." Carmen looked up and smiled bitterly. "Her fear wasn't unfounded, Gabe. After all, when they finally did split up, Hugh got full custody of Teri."

"The bastard! He used Marielle's mental troubles against her—troubles he caused." Carmen looked at Gabe warily, her body tensing. He'd suddenly become furious at a time when he should be happy that they were finally going to announce their engagement. His mood frightened her, made her doubt his true joy over their upcoming marriage.

No, Carmen thought firmly, trying to calm herself. He'd gotten furious when he was talking about Kent and Sharon and about how he feared Kent was becoming like his father. He's not unhappy at the thought of getting married, she told herself. He's simply worried about Sharon. Gabe is *always* worried about Sharon. After we're married, though, his preoccupation with her will weaken. It has to, or we'll never make it, because Sharon doesn't like me and she'll never stop interfering in our relationship.

"I never liked Hugh, even when we were kids," Gabe went on, seemingly unaware of Carmen's inner turmoil.

"Then he tried to keep Kent from marrying Sharon because, as he had the nerve to tell my daughter right to her face, 'You're just not Kent's equal, intellectually or socially.' That's when I started hating him. Sharon was only nineteen and shy, insecure. She was devastated by what he'd said. Not only that, Hugh told his own son that if he married Sharon, he'd cut him off completely."

"You mean write him out of the will?"

"Didn't Marielle or Teresa tell you?"

"The months before Sharon and Kent got married, Marielle was in the sanitarium and then at her aunt's. I rarely saw her, and when I did, she never mentioned Kent's relationship with Sharon, and neither did Teri when she stayed with me after the murders."

"Well, Hugh not only threatened to write Kent out of the will if he married Sharon; he also said he wouldn't finish paying Kent's tuition for college. The old bastard even put a codicil in the will demanding that if Hugh died, at the time of the death Kent had to produce evidence he was not secretly married to Sharon or the entire estate would go to Teresa."

Gabriel's voice grew louder. "He said if Kent defied him, he wouldn't let him in the house again, much less give him a position at the coal company. Kent didn't have a job and had no money except for what Hugh gave him. And there was poor Sharon, so young and—" Gabriel cut off swiftly, snapping shut his mouth. Finally, he said, "Sharon was . . . committed to Kent."

Carmen gave Gabriel a soft, soothing kiss, but her mind was working feverishly and not about the announcement of her engagement. She had never been a fan of Kent's, even when she was close to his mother. Carmen had seen signs of weakness in him, and she couldn't stand weak men.

When Sharon gave birth to Daniel six months after her marriage to Kent, Carmen and everyone else knew Sharon had been pregnant when Kent married her. If Hugh had been serious about completely cutting Kent out of the will if he were even secretly married to Sharon at the time of Hugh's death, would Kent have had enough love for Sharon, enough strength of character, to marry her anyway? Carmen didn't think so. Maybe Sharon hadn't believed he would have, either.

If Kent had abandoned Sharon, she would have refused an abortion and everyone would have known Kent was the father of her child. Meanwhile, Gabriel would have wreaked havoc on the reputation of both Kent *and* Hugh for "shaming" his daughter, and this was a small community.

In light of those possibilities, Carmen thought, Hugh Farr's murder had been perfectly timed for Sharon and Kent.

2

As they walked toward the barn, Daniel informed Teri that he had a loose front tooth, which he hoped would fall out before night so the tooth fairy would visit, and then proclaimed, "I want to ride one of those big horses with the fuzzy feet."

Kent grinned at her, his wavy black hair shining almost as much as Teresa's long, straight locks. "He saw a Clydesdale in a book on horses the other day."

"Oh." Teresa looked at her seven-year-old nephew solemnly. "Daniel, I'm sorry, but I don't own any Clydesdales. They weigh about as much as a car and they eat over fifty pounds of food a day. Besides, they're even taller than your daddy."

Daniel's eyebrows drew together in disappointment. The sun shone on his strawberry blond hair and emphasized the freckles on his nose. He looked exactly like his mother, Sharon, who stood beside him clutching his shoulder as if she expected him to dash into the barn, mount a large stallion, and speed off into the wilderness. "But you have other big horses, Aunt Teri."

"Only three of the horses are mine. Some belong to other people. I run a sort of hotel for horses." Daniel laughed. "But because you've never even ridden a horse before, I don't think we should start with one of the big ones. I have one particularly in mind for you. In fact, I already told him about you and he's really looking forward to having you ride him. His name is Caesar."

"Caesar! That sounds good!" Daniel said enthusiastically.

"Just look at the horse, Daniel," Sharon ordered. "Don't touch him. He might bite you."

"Quit treating him like a baby," Kent snapped.

"Yeah, I'm *not* a baby!" Daniel burst out.

Teresa strode ahead of them into the barn, gritting her teeth. Did they have to start a family argument *now*? If so, she didn't want to get involved. "Right this way, folks," she called, forcing herself to sound pleasant. "And keep your voices down. You'll scare the horses."

Teresa led them into the coolness of the big white gabled barn. "Why do you have a rubber floor?" Sharon asked as her tennis shoes began squeaking.

"It's rubber matting over concrete," Teri said. "It cushions the horses' feet and has better traction. It's also easier to clean and keeps urine from sinking into wood or dirt."

"You and Gus and Josh designed this barn, Teri," Kent challenged. "I remember you telling me it would have a concrete floor, so you don't have to worry about urine sinking into wood or dirt."

"Did you hear the part about it cushioning the horses' feet?" Teri asked.

"Aunt Teri wants her horses to be happy," Daniel said stalwartly. "That's why she made such a pretty barn with soft floors."

"Thank you, Daniel," Teri answered. "I want the horses to be happy *and* comfortable."

She was aware of Sharon glancing around in obvious surprise. Teri guessed her sister-in-law, who had never set foot in the barn before today, had expected it to be dark, dank, and repellant. Instead, a dehumidifier kept the barn dry, and fiberglass windows and skylights cast diffused sunlight over the horses Teri's handlers, Gus and his son, Josh, kept beautifully groomed. They had just finished cleaning the building and it still smelled pleasantly fresh.

Sierra trotted along beside Teresa. The dog loved horses and most of them seemed to love her back. She pranced past Kent's palomino Conquistador; the bay-colored quarter horse Captain Jack; the brown thoroughbred Sir Lancelot; and touched noses with Teri's own solid black Arabian, Eclipse. Teresa stopped beside Eclipse and motioned to the horse in the next stall. "And here is Caesar," she announced grandly.

Daniel looked at the thirty-five-inch-tall chestnut Shetland pony. He frowned, then motioned for Teresa to lean down. He whispered in her ear, "I don't want to hurt his feelings, but he's *short!*"

"That's because he's a Shetland. Some are even shorter than he is. A few are taller, but not many." Daniel continued to study the horse critically. "Shetland ponies come from islands off the coast of Scotland, so far north they're near the Arctic Circle. The history of this pony dates back almost five *thousand* years!" Teresa made her voice dramatic, hoping to dazzle the doubtful Daniel. "The people of the Shetland Islands taught the ponies to carry heavy loads of seaweed from the ocean up to the fields to be used as fertilizer. The Shetland is a very strong breed, Daniel. It lived in conditions that would have killed most horses— terrible weather, little food—so it's very strong. Yet it has the kindest eyes of any horse I've ever seen. Can't you see what beautiful eyes Caesar has?"

Daniel took a step closer and peered at Caesar's gentle

gaze. "Yeah, they're pretty." Then he looked down. "He's got fuzzy feet like one of those Clyderails."

"Clydesdales. And yes, he does." Teresa had brought an apple sliced in quarters and stored in a plastic bag. "Hold out your hand." Daniel did as he was told and she dumped a piece of apple into his little hand. "Why don't you try feeding him? Just hold out your hand with the apple slice in the palm. Caesar will take the apple piece right into his mouth." She looked at Sharon, who already had her mouth open to protest. "Caesar is used to eating out of hands, even children's. He won't hurt you, Daniel."

The little boy stepped closer to the horse and held out the piece of apple. Caesar bent his head and delicately took the apple into his mouth. Daniel giggled. "His lips are so soft and they tickle!"

"I told you. Caesar knows his manners and he loves children."

Daniel reached for another quarter of the apple and this time chortled when the horse lifted the apple slice and began happily, if messily, munching. After Daniel had given the rest of the fruit to Caesar, he burst out "I want to give him another apple!"

"One is all he needs right now. We don't want him to get a tummy ache from eating too many snacks." Teresa smiled as Daniel reached out and stroked the horse's muzzle. Caesar snorted, then pushed his face more forcefully into Daniel's hand. "He likes you."

"And I like him!" Daniel beamed at his aunt. "We're already good buddies. Can I take my lessons on him?"

"I told you I'd picked him out especially for you. We'll start tomorrow," Teresa said. "This is Sunday, Caesar's day off, but he'll be waiting for you in the morning."

"But what if he's lonely out here all by himself?" Daniel asked plaintively.

Teri smiled. "He's not all by himself. Horses often make friends with their stablemates. Caesar is very good friends with my horse Eclipse, and the gray Connemara pony on the other side of him is his girlfriend. Her name is Cleopatra. In the meantime, why don't we go back up to the house and have something to drink? I even baked cookies this morning."

Ten minutes later, they sat around the kitchen table, the adults drinking coffee and everyone nibbling on the cookies. "These are good, Aunt Teri!" Daniel reached for another one. "You didn't burn them as bad as usual."

"Daniel!" Sharon reprimanded sharply.

"From the mouths of babes." Teresa laughed. "Thanks, Daniel. I know a lady who bakes cookies for a living." She didn't name Emma MacKenzie. "Maybe I'll take lessons from her and next time my cookies won't be burned at all."

Daniel shook his head. "Then they wouldn't taste a bit like your cookies." He began stuffing a fourth cookie in his mouth when Sharon told him that would be his last or he'd get sick.

Kent rolled his eyes at Teresa and murmured, "This kid could eat two dozen cookies and not get an upset stomach."

"I heard that," Sharon said reproachfully. "I wish you wouldn't undermine my authority in front of Daniel!"

"You wish he wouldn't do what?" Daniel managed around a mouthful of cookie.

"I'm taking my coffee and *one* cookie to the living room and the television," Kent said tightly. "It's time for the golf match to start."

"Don't get crumbs all over Teri's furniture," Sharon warned. Kent said nothing, but Teresa noticed his shoulders going rigid under his polo shirt. "And don't—"

"Spill my coffee, burn holes in the carpet with my cigarette, or get nose prints on the TV screen," Kent finished for her, his voice edgy. "I will be on my best behavior, Mrs. Farr."

After he'd left, Sharon looked at Teresa in bewilderment. "I don't know why he's so grumpy with me all the time lately."

Because lately you never stop carping at him, Teresa almost said, but she didn't want to say anything critical of Sharon in front of Daniel. She did intend to speak to Sharon about the matter soon, though, before her bossiness became a real problem between her and Kent. Teresa just hadn't figured out a tactful way to approach the issue yet. Sharon was extremely sensitive to any form of censure, even when she was acting normally, and her nervousness told Teri that Sharon was experiencing more than everyday tensions.

"Isn't this the most glorious day?" Teresa asked quickly, trying to divert Sharon's attention from Daniel. "Seventy-five degrees, hardly a cloud in the sky, and low humidity. It's usually much hotter and more humid at this time of year."

Sharon nodded vaguely, clearly not thinking about the weather. She twisted her diamond and gold engagement ring round and round her long, strong finger, then said out of the blue, "I inherited my father's hands. I used to be embarrassed about their size, but a long time ago Kent told me they had 'character.'"

"They're big like the Clyderdales' hoofs," Daniel volunteered cheerily.

Teri concentrated on not laughing at Daniel's comparison, but Sharon smiled, her eyes twinkling. "That's my boy—always the charmer." She looked fondly at her son, then at Teri. "Let's forget about my hands and get back to our former scintillating subject—the weather. You're right, as usual. It is beautiful, but I don't think it's going to hold through the Fourth of July."

"I think it will." Relieved by Sharon's change of mood, Teri asked, "Want to bet on it? Ten dollars says we'll be attending the Fourth of July concert and fireworks display on a perfect evening."

"Ten dollars says it will be pouring rain, and I always collect on bets, Teresa Farr." They shook hands, laughing.

"If it doesn't rain, we're going down to Tu-Endie-Wei Park to watch the fireworks display," Sharon added, referring to the beautiful park that sat on the point where the Ohio and Kanawha rivers met. "I hope you'll come with us."

"I go with you every year, Sharon. Why would I miss this one?"

Sharon looked at her with innocent eyes. "Oh, I thought you might be going with Mac."

"With Mac!" Teresa was shocked. "What on earth made you think I'd go *anywhere* with Mac?"

"You two looked so intimate last night."

"Intimate!" Teresa blurted.

"Well, yes. You were dancing *so* close and gazing into each other's eyes." Sharon's innocent expression dissolved as she broke into giggles. "I'm sorry. I just couldn't help teasing you, although a couple of times, when you weren't moving around the dance floor stiff as a board, I began to wonder—"

"Hey, Teri, come here!" Kent yelled from the living room.

"Don't tell me he wants me to watch someone sink a putt," Teresa groaned even though she was grateful for the change of subject. "I hate golf."

"Teri, now!" Kent shouted even louder. "Hurry!"

Teresa rose from the kitchen chair, leaving Sharon to make sure Daniel didn't eat the entire plateful of half-burned cookies, and walked quickly into the living room. Kent sat forward on one of her rust-colored plushy armchairs, looking almost fearfully at the television rattling on in front of him. "Kent, you know I don't like watching golf."

He waved a hand at her for silence. "The game was delayed, so I flipped over to a news channel. They said this story was coming up next. Be quiet and listen!"

Teresa didn't bother to sit down. She stood next to Kent as a perfectly groomed female broadcaster gazed at the television camera with practiced sincerity and began the story in her carefully unaccented voice:

"Roscoe Lee Byrnes, the forty-three-year-old man convicted of killing twenty-two people over a three-year-period, and scheduled for lethal injection in Pennsylvania on Friday, announced yesterday evening that in his confession eight years ago, he lied about murdering Hubert and Wendy Farr of Point Pleasant, West Virginia. Hubert Farr, forty-eight at the time of his murder, was the owner of Farr Coal Company, a large mining operation in Mason County, West Virginia. He and his wife, Wendy, twenty-nine, were savagely stabbed to death at night in their bed. Mrs. Farr's eight-year-old daughter by a previous marriage also suffered a serious knife injury but survived the attack. Mr. Farr's daughter, seventeen, received only a minor cut on the arm. When asked why he lied about the Farrs, Byrnes had this to say."

A video of Roscoe Lee Byrnes appeared on the screen. He sat motionless at a table. The camera drew closer to his face. His bulging eyes looked even eerily paler than Teresa remembered. His face was fuller and oddly shapeless, like a lump of clay. Neither his surprisingly high, thin voice nor his gaze bore the slightest emotion when he spoke:

"I know it don't make no difference whether I kilt twenty-two people or twenty—I'm still gonna die—but I wanna set the record straight." Byrnes finally blinked, rubbing together his chubby cuffed hands folded in front of him. "See, I always kilt people that didn't amount to much. I wanted credit for killin' someone rich and important like that Farr guy. But now that I've found Jesus Christ and know I'll be seein' him soon, I feel like I gotta tell the truth about them Farr people." Byrnes paused, blinked again, and ran his tongue over his puffy lips. "I've been to that town in West Virginia where they lived, Point somethin', but I never even heard of the Farrs till the police asked me if I kilt 'em. They got kilt the night after I was in that town.

That seemed real strange to me, kinda like somethin' that was meant to be. Anyway, them police seemed all excited over those Farrs gettin' offed, so since I'd been to that town and all, I got a notion to say I did it and impress ever'one. But I was lyin'. I want people to know it before I die. You hear that, God? I'm tellin' people I lied and I'm sorry. I don't want credit for killin' nobody I really didn't kill. But I also wanna say I *know* one day the person that did kill them people and stabbed that li'l girl will get what's comin' to 'em. The Bible says: 'An eye for an eye,' and God told me in a dream just a couple a nights ago that's what's gonna happen. He's gonna take his vengeance on whoever did kill them people, and it's gonna happen soon. *Real* soon."

CHAPTER FOUR

1

KENT LEAPED UP FROM the armchair and roared, "That's a lie, you fat son of a—"

"Kent!" Sharon stood in the doorway, her face chalk white, her right arm wrapped tightly around Daniel, who gazed at his father with huge frightened brown eyes. "Shut *up*!" she hissed at her husband in a venomous voice Teresa had never heard her use before. "Have you forgotten your son is here?"

"No, I haven't forgotten," Kent barked. "But that Byrnes bastard is claiming—"

"I heard." Sharon glared at Kent. "Daniel heard, too, and he's scared to death. Byrnes didn't scare him, though. *You* did. How does that make you feel?"

Kent sagged, his tone lowering. "Lousy, Sharon. I didn't know the two of you were standing there. I'm sorry, but I can't monitor what I say every minute."

"You should when you have a child!" Sharon's face had gone from the color of parchment to scarlet. "What kind of father *doesn't* always think about his child?"

"Dammit, Sharon, will you settle down?" Kent's voice rose again. "For God's sake!"

"If you can't get control of yourself and your language, Daniel and I are going home right this minute!" Sharon shouted just before Daniel, who'd been looking from Kent to Sharon with fear and bewilderment, suddenly broke into noisy sobs. "Now look what you've done!" Sharon flung at Kent.

"Okay, you two, that . . . is . . . enough," Teresa said loudly and firmly over the sound of Daniel's crying. "You're acting like a couple of brats yelling at each other and you're *both* frightening Daniel." Sharon gave her an injured look. "Yes, Sharon, you're as bad as Kent." Teresa looked at her nephew wiping the backs of his hands over his tear-streaked face and letting out one last wail before he began to hiccup. "Sharon, take Daniel back to the barn to visit Caesar while I talk to Kent."

"Me?" Sharon looked affronted. "I don't know anything about horses!"

"You don't have to be an equestrian to stand by Daniel while he pets Caesar," Teresa said sharply, losing patience. "You've already seen the pony isn't going to bite him."

"We'll go home," Sharon snapped.

Daniel hiccupped again, then whimpered, "Please take me to see Caesar, Mommy. I wanna pet him again and tell him I'm comin' back tomorrow. *Please!*"

Sharon sighed, shot murderous glances at both Kent and Teresa, then led Daniel out the front door, clutching his hand so hard he yelped, "Ouch!" As soon as the door closed behind them, Kent looked at Teresa. "Thanks, Teri. She's driving me crazy lately."

"And I'm sure she feels the same way about you. Look, Kent, I didn't ask her to leave so we could discuss your marriage. I asked her to leave because Daniel was so upset and because you and I need to talk about what we just heard on the news. Roscoe Lee Byrnes is saying he didn't kill Dad and Wendy."

Kent flopped back into the armchair as if he'd been punched in the abdomen. "He's lying."

"Why?"

"How should I know? Maybe he's making one last-ditch effort to save himself."

"He's a serial killer, Kent. He said it himself—he killed all those other people and he's going to be executed on Friday whether or not he killed Dad and Wendy."

"Then maybe he wants to generate a little last-minute publicity for himself. After all, he said he'd never killed anyone *important.* Dad and Wendy were hardly celebrities, but apparently their murders caused a bigger splash in the news than any of his other victims did."

Kent went silent, gazing past Teresa out the front window. Suddenly she noticed that her brother's eyes were bloodshot and the lines between his mouth and nose had deepened noticeably in the last few years. His black hair was also turning silver at the temples. She'd known he worked hard managing the coal mine, but he must be under a lot of strain to be aging so quickly—maybe more strain than his job caused. But now wasn't the time to ask questions about how his life was going. "Kent, you look like you're daydreaming. Are you listening to me?"

"Yes, I'm listening." He rubbed his hand across his forehead. "But I don't want to talk about Byrnes anymore. And I don't want you talking about his so-called confession with Sharon."

"I hadn't given a thought to talking about it with Sharon. She's nervous enough already, although I don't know why. She didn't used to be that way."

"I regularly beat her."

Teresa closed her eyes. "This is not the time for bad

jokes, Kent. Let's concentrate on the matter at hand, which is Roscoe Lee Byrnes denying that he killed Dad and Wendy and stabbed Celeste. We *have* to talk about it whether you want to or not."

Kent flung out his arms in exasperation. "Well, what is there to say? Do you expect me to do something about it?"

"I expect you to think about the effect what he said is going to have on us. Sure, Byrnes might be lying, but I don't know why. He knows it can't save him, and I don't buy your theory that he's seeking last-minute fame and glory. He's not the type."

Kent gave her a hard look. "Are you an expert on serial killers now, Teri?"

"I've read quite a bit about them the last few years. I'm no expert, but . . . well, some of them try to be flashy and make names for themselves."

"You think Roscoe Lee Byrnes is the flashy type?"

"No. I'm just offering a suggestion to explain what he's doing—a desperate and unprofessional suggestion, I admit." Teresa sighed. "I hate to say this, Kent, but though he's a psychopath, I think he's telling the truth because he believes he's going to see God soon and he wants to have a clear conscience, or whatever psychopaths have instead of consciences."

"Maybe so, but how can we stop him from making a show before he's executed?"

"We can't. He's already done it. We have to think about the fact that a lot of people will take him seriously—people here, where we live, where we do business. How will we handle that?"

Kent's expression turned to one of a furious little boy. "I don't think anyone will believe him," he said with childish bravado. "I don't think they'll believe him one little bit."

In spite of her misery, Teri burst out laughing. "Kent, you sound like you're about Daniel's age because you're afraid people *will* believe him and you feel helpless."

Kent glared at her, flushing. She knew she'd hit the nail on the head and she wished she could just drop the matter, pretend Byrnes had never recanted his confession. But he had, and she and her brother had to deal with the fallout, not hide from it.

"Kent, there's more going on than Byrnes altering his confession."

He closed his eyes. "Oh no. Please don't make this worse."

"Sorry, but I can't help it. You told me Celeste had started speaking yesterday in Bennigan's. What did she say?"

Kent's gaze darted away from Teresa. "It's just a lot of nonsense, Teri. Forget it."

"I will *not* forget it. You said you'd get all the details from the churchgoers this morning. If they didn't say much to you, I know they did to Sharon and she would have told you. Now you tell me or . . ."

Kent looked back at her and raised an eyebrow. "Or what? You'll beat me up?"

"Don't look so cocky. If you'll remember, I did a pretty good job of thumping you when you were eleven and tore up my Barbie doll."

"I accidentally set her hair on fire and all you did, tough girl, was kick me on the ankle. Big deal. It didn't even hurt."

"Oh yeah? Then why did you limp for two days?" Kent came close to grinning. "Tell me what Celeste said in Bennigan's or I'll kick you again and this time it won't be on the ankle!"

Kent shook his head. "You've always been a glutton for punishment, Teri; otherwise you wouldn't have settled in this town when you could have lived somewhere else. Okay, here's all I know. Apparently Celeste said that the night of the murders there was someone in the house wearing a hood."

Teri's stomach tightened as the image of a hooded figure flashed in her mind. "Go on."

"Celeste said she'd gotten up to go to the bathroom and just as she was going back to bed, the figure—obviously the killer—opened the door to Hugh and Wendy's bedroom, saw her, seemed surprised, and then stabbed her."

Teresa drew back, surprised. "So the killer stabbed her in a reflex action. Maybe the person didn't mean to kill *her*—only Dad and Wendy—but he thought Celeste had seen him so he went after her. My God, we never knew this. Did she see who it was?"

Kent looked uncomfortable. "I don't think so. Not that anyone heard, that is. She said after she was stabbed, she ran back to her room and someone came after her."

"*That* had to be the killer! The person I bumped into in the hall."

"Maybe."

"*Maybe?*"

"Well, she said something about the killer wanting to stab her some more."

"So she did know it wasn't me who came to her room first."

"I guess."

"She had to know it wasn't me!"

"Teri, I told you I wasn't sure I know exactly what she said. I don't know if *she's* sure of exactly what she thought or knew that night."

"I collided into that hooded figure when he was coming down the hall from Celeste's room and I was going *to* her room to see if she'd been murdered. That's when he cut my arm," Teresa said emphatically. "I've told you that a hundred times!"

"Okay, settle down. I'm not contradicting you—I'm telling you what Celeste said, and that's secondhand. I didn't hear her and I don't believe even the people in Bennigan's who did hear her either got straight what she was saying or aren't making it more dramatic."

Kent looked up at Teresa from his position in the

armchair, his tired gaze full of sympathy and trust. "*I* know you didn't go to Celeste's room to stab her. It had to be Byrnes, but he didn't find her and then there was all that ruckus and he thought he'd better get out of there in a hurry, just like the FBI said. God, Teri, do you think I believe you would have stabbed that little girl? Or Dad and Wendy, for that matter."

Teresa took a deep breath. "You didn't believe it, but the police did."

"Well, I'm not the police." Kent leaned forward and gently took her hand. "Now who's acting like an enraged little kid?"

Teresa forced her lips into a weak smile. "You're right. I'll try to act like a calm and rational adult." She took a deep breath. "Okay, what about this chant you said Celeste was repeating? A chant that mentioned me."

"Nobody could remember it exactly." Kent sounded reluctant, as if he'd rather be talking about anything else in the world. "There was something about a clock striking three."

The grandfather clock, Teri thought immediately. She remembered the grandfather clock chiming three times when she was going into Hugh and Wendy's bedroom. "Go on."

"Well, also something about death coming for her and something about you. She said it over and over."

"It was a rhyme," Teresa said with certainty. "Even when she was a child, she loved making up rhymes. She did it constantly."

"Okay, well that's all I know, Teri. Honestly. The crowd at Bennigan's said after she'd begun shouting this chant, or rhyme, or whatever you want to call it, her father rushed her out of the restaurant."

"I see." Teresa was amazed at how composed her voice sounded. She didn't feel at all composed—she felt shaken and slightly sick. "So Celeste starts talking after eight years, she mentions death and *me,* and then Roscoe Lee

Byrnes decides to tell the world he didn't kill Hugh and Wendy Farr. What fabulous timing."

Kent attempted a nonchalant shrug. "It's just a coincidence. We have to stop thinking about it."

"Stop thinking about it? Is that your answer?" Her brother looked away as Teresa went on relentlessly. "We *can't* stop thinking about it! Look, Kent, I don't want to dredge up all of this any more than you do, but who were the main suspects in the murder of Dad and Wendy? Me and Mom."

"Well, Mom's dead," Kent said dully.

"We don't know that."

"We just haven't seen or heard from her for eight years."

"No, we haven't, but that doesn't mean she's dead. But because we haven't seen her for eight years—and, as far as I know, no one around here has—that leaves two other people with a very strong motive for murdering Dad and Wendy. I know you had an alibi for that night, but not everyone was convinced it was true. Have you forgotten you and your friends being questioned, over and over, because a lot of people didn't believe you were really in Virginia at a party that night?"

Kent looked up at her, his dark eyes filled with misery. "Dear God, do you think I don't realize that, Teri? We're the ones whose mother was dumped like a bag of garbage by our father, and we're the ones who inherited his estate. Who wouldn't look at us as prime suspects?"

"Yes," Teresa said softly. "But I'm the only one of us who had absolutely no alibi, not even a shaky one. I was the one who'd let everyone know how much I hated Wendy, how much I resented Dad for what he did to Mom, how I hated being forced to live in that house with them. God, I had a big mouth!"

"You were seventeen and mad as hell."

"Yes. I was also the one in the house that night who wasn't seriously injured. If the police had found one scrap of evidence—the murder weapon, traces of blood in the shower, or blood-soaked clothes—I would have been locked up." Teresa, deciding to be completely honest, took a deep breath. "And I didn't tell you earlier, but based on a note I found in my car last night and a fax I received this morning, in spite of Byrnes's confession eight years ago, I'm also the one somebody has *always* believed is guilty."

2

J. A. MacKenzie wiped the bar of his empty club, leaned down, looked sideways at the black teak length gleaming with a coat of polyurethane, and smiled when he saw no smears, not even a fingerprint. His waiters and waitresses always cleaned up after the bar closed at night—a service for which they were well recompensed—but Mac was never happy until he'd cleaned Club Rendezvous himself on Sundays. Maybe it was because daylight exposed more spots, crumpled cocktail napkins, and peanut halves embedded in the carpet around the bar. Or maybe it was because his mother had always kept her own house and that of the Farrs immaculate. The "compulsive housecleaner" gene had been passed on to *him*, he mused ruefully. His twin sisters were satisfied if their apartment looked passable and thrilled if someone actually called it neat.

Although Mac would never have admitted it, he enjoyed being alone in the club during the day when he could simply stand and gaze at the elegant ivory, black, and azure expanse. It reminded him of all he'd accomplished since his father left Mac's mother with three children and no words of explanation or apology. It reminded him of his early teens when he'd risen at five o'clock on icy mornings to pedal his old bike on a paper route and later when he'd thought he'd die of heat exhaustion from frantically mowing as many lawns as possible, earning money to help his mother and sisters. It reminded him of those two pretty, intelligent sisters he was able to put through college. He sighed. Mostly, it reminded him of Teresa Farr.

She was sixteen when he'd first seen her. He was mowing her father's backyard and singing Billy Idol's "Sweet Sixteen." Mac had felt as if someone was watching him and looked up to see a girl with long hair like black satin and ebony eyes in an oval face just a shade lighter than tawny. She wore a tank top and looked at him calmly, her arms resting one over the other on the windowsill. He was almost twenty, but he'd blushed like a kid, let out a strangled laugh, and shouted in a voice that cracked, "Sorry. Got carried away."

"I liked it. You've got a great voice."

To his horror, Mac had felt his blush deepening and wondered why he didn't just give her a dismissive smile and get back to work. But he couldn't look away from that face or those eyes that twinkled down at him with a mixture of spontaneity, flirtation, and knowledge beyond her years. "I'm Teresa Farr," she called. "And you must be the Mac MacKenzie all the girls have a crush on."

"Yeah, I'm Mac." Snappy comeback, he'd thought. He tried again to sound cool and confident but failed, stumbling out an almost shy, "I don't think all the girls have a crush on me, though."

"You'll just have to take my word for it." Teresa had tilted her head, her hair falling like a silken veil to her right elbow. "It's funny that you were singing 'Sweet Sixteen' when I was sitting right up here in my room with the window open. Did you know I was here and that *I'm* sixteen?"

"No." That was a lie. At least partly a lie. He hadn't known she was in her room. But his mother, the housekeeper at this house, had told him last month that the Farrs' "sweet, shy little girl" was just turning sixteen and her mother, Marielle, was throwing a surprise party for her. Sweet and shy? Mac thought, feeling like laughing. Mothers could be easily fooled. "I mean I didn't know you were in your room. I didn't know where your room was. I didn't even think anything about where you were or what you were doing. I was busy—"

"Singing."

"Yeah. I mean no. Mowing grass. I wasn't slacking off." He'd wiped sweat off his forehead, decided the motion looked as if he were trying to indicate how hard he'd been working. "Really hot out here today. Humid. I don't mind heat, but humidity just kills me. Well, it doesn't make the job impossible, just harder. Not that it's *too* hard for me to do well." He'd paused as she smiled languidly, seeming to enjoy his clumsiness at witty repartee. "Did you know you have a lot of crabgrass in the backyard?" he'd ended miserably.

"No, I didn't. Should we do something about it?"

"There's stuff you can sprinkle on the ground that doesn't kill the regular grass, just the crabgrass. That should be done in early spring before the crabgrass germinates and again in midsummer." Mac had known he was talking too much. "I'd better get back to work," he'd said abruptly, wishing he could stop staring at this jailbait vixen leaning out the window, but he couldn't.

"Will you sing 'Sweet Sixteen' some more? Some of my friends are really into rap, but that's not for me. I like a lot of the older songs, even some from the *sixties*! I love it when Billy says he'd 'do *anything*' for his sweet sixteen-year-old girl." She'd grinned, flipped her hair, winked at him, then called, "Oops, I hear my father coming up the stairs! I have to go now, but I'll see you again, Mac MacKenzie."

She'd darted away from the window and left him standing, mower running, mouth slightly open, sweat pouring, heart beating fast. Then Hugh Farr's wide face appeared at the window, glowering, and Mac managed a cheerful wave, then had begun mowing with a vengeance as he tried to wipe the song "Sweet Sixteen" out of his mind.

Later that evening he'd laughed at himself. He must have been suffering some kind of heatstroke to have such a powerful reaction to a silly flirty little sixteen-year-old girl, he'd mused. If he saw her again, he probably wouldn't even give her a second look.

But over the next few years, he had seen her repeatedly and she always had the same effect on him—intense attraction and discomfort because she was too young for him. Still, Mac had never gotten tired of looking at her. Or talking to her. And later of kissing her and planning a life with her.

"And you are a sentimental dope wasting time thinking about the past, because she made it perfectly clear she doesn't want to have anything to do with you anymore," Mac told himself aloud in the empty club. "And who could blame her? I was young and stupid and I have no one except myself to blame for blowing my chance with Teri Farr a *long* time ago."

Half to take his mind off Teresa, half to fight off an impending wave of sadness for "the good old days," Mac snapped on the twenty-seven-inch-screen television on a shelf at the end of the bar. A lot of people told him he should get one of those sixty-two-inch high-definition televisions, but Mac always told them he didn't want to turn Club Rendezvous into a sports bar. At night, he wouldn't even allow his employees to turn on what they considered the pitifully dilapidated small television set on the shelf. Now a perky blond announcer whose smile looked strained repeated the news for what was probably the tenth time that morning.

Mac was on his way to retrieve a pale blue matchbook lying under a table on the ivory carpet when the name "Roscoe Lee Byrnes" pierced his preoccupation like a needle popping a balloon. He jerked upward, banging his head on the underside of the table, and swore loudly. Then, rubbing at the spot on his head that was already beginning to throb, he moved away from the table and stood to listen to the newscaster talking about Byrnes's execution this week.

Her glossy red-lipped smile of a few moments ago had vanished and her dark blue eyes hardened with the somberness of her current news subject:

"Roscoe Lee Byrnes, the man convicted of killing twenty-two people over a three-year period, announced last night that in his confession eight years ago when he was apprehended in Pennsylvania, he claimed two victims whom he now says he did not kill—Hubert and Wendy Farr of Point Pleasant, West Virginia. Hubert Farr, owner of Farr Coal Company, and his twenty-nine-year-old wife were stabbed to death in their bed. Mrs. Farr's eight-year-old daughter received a serious knife wound to the abdomen but survived. Mr. Farr's teenage daughter received only a shallow cut on the arm. Byrnes now says that although he had been in the Point Pleasant area near the time of the murders, he not only had never heard of the Farrs, he did not kill them."

Mac's mouth opened slightly in shock and he moved closer to the television although he could hear perfectly from where he stood. Nevertheless, he turned up the volume, then stood back and stared unflinchingly as the broad face of Roscoe Lee Byrnes appeared in a video clip. His head looked huge, as if it were going to overflow the television screen, and Mac had the feeling that behind those big pale blue eyes lay nothing—no conscience, no soul, nothing.

Byrnes twisted his beefy hands together as the tape picked up the sound of dry skin rubbing against dry skin. "I know it don't make no difference whether I kilt twenty-two people or twenty—I'm still gonna die—but I wanna set the record straight. . . ."

The man's rumbling, toneless voice set Mac's teeth on edge, and although he wouldn't like to admit it, Byrnes's hauntingly pale eyes made him feel cold. It was hard to believe this blundering, doughlike creature had killed again and again. It wasn't hard to believe he didn't seem to feel a shred of remorse.

"Them police seemed all excited over those Farrs get-

tin' offed, so since I'd been to that town and all, I got a notion to say I did it and impress ever'one. But I was lyin'. I
want people to know that before I die. You hear that, God?
I'm tellin' people I lied and I'm sorry. I don't want credit
for killin' nobody I didn't kill. But I also wanna say I *know*
one day the person that really did kill them people and
stabbed that li'l girl will get what's comin' to 'em."

The video ended and the blond newscaster reappeared.
"Roscoe Lee Byrnes will die by lethal injection in State
Correctional Institution–Greene in Waynesburg, Pennsylvania, on Friday." Her broad smile reappeared with startling immediacy. "And in other news . . ."

But Mac didn't hear her. His face grim, he clicked off
the television and headed for the door of the club.

3

The dark hall seemed endless, stretching in front of her like
a tunnel deep beneath a giant mountain. Someone was
screaming—shrilly, mechanically, deafeningly. The noise
came from all around her. She banged into something—a
table—then ricocheted into a warm, shadowy being swathed
in something slippery. The Being had no face that she could
see, but it had a scent—the scent of sandalwood. The Being
held up two cautionary fingers to what must have been its
mouth, and in spite of the screaming, Teresa heard a soft,
comforting, "Shhhh." She strained her hearing and there it
was again. "Shhhh," right before she felt pain slice her left
arm. She froze, the screaming that she now realized had
been her own stopping as she watched the Being drift down
the stairs and out the front door. Then she felt blood dripping
down her arm. She began to run and cry, "Celeste!

"Celeste! Celeste!"

Teresa sat bolt upright in bed as Sierra leaped onto her
lap, ears even more erect, a low growl rumbling in her

throat. Teri squeezed the shining brown dog, her gaze shooting all around her cheerful bedroom, still full of late-afternoon sunlight. It was a dream, she thought in relief.

The dog sensed the lessening of tension in Teri's body. After another scan around the room with her own sharp honey brown gaze, Sierra turned and placed a reassuring lick on Teri's nose. "Thank you," Teri said. "I feel much better." Sierra jumped up and whirled around, front legs flat, back end sticking up, ready for a frolic.

Teresa rubbed the top of the dog's head. "Sorry, but I'm not up to romping right now." She glanced at the bedside clock. It was five o'clock in the afternoon and she'd just awakened from a two-hour nap feeling worse than when, upset, depressed, and tired from lack of sleep the night before, she'd crawled into bed after Kent left. "Let's go downstairs and get a snack," she said. "Dog biscuits and ice cream are great for chasing away the dregs of bad dreams."

Once downstairs, Teresa put three scoops of ice cream in a bowl and dug out a large beef-basted biscuit from the "treat bin." Sierra looked hopefully at the bowl, but Teri shook her head. "Sorry, girl. This is double chocolate fudge and dogs aren't supposed to eat chocolate." She laid the biscuit on the vinyl floor and felt a twinge of guilt as Sierra looked at it with vast indifference. "I promise to get cherry swirl at the grocery store tomorrow, if you'll settle for a biscuit now," Teri cajoled as the dog slowly bent her head and picked up an unappetizing biscuit.

They ambled back to the living room, Sierra clenching the biscuit between her teeth as if it were a piece of dry wood, Teri holding the cold bowl of ice cream against her burning forehead. She glanced at the television, then, fearing she might see another announcement about Byrnes claiming he didn't kill Hugh and Wendy Farr, turned on the stereo instead. She flung herself onto the big, soft recliner that always felt as if it were lovingly holding her.

This was supposed to be a happy day, Teri thought, the

day when little Daniel got to meet the guy she hoped would become his best friend, Caesar. Instead, the afternoon had turned into a nightmare with Sharon and Kent falling into an argument, Daniel sobbing, and, worst of all, Roscoe Lee Byrnes proclaiming his innocence of the Farr murders at the expense of Teri's and Kent's peace of mind. By evening, the whole town would be rehashing the murders of Hugh and Wendy and speculating on the guilt or innocence of Teresa, the "wild, rebellious" teenager who'd survived the bloodbath with a cut while everyone else in her house had been slashed to death or seriously stabbed. No wonder I had to go to bed for a while after Kent and Sharon left, Teri thought. I haven't had a headache like that since—

Since right after the murders, before Byrnes had been caught and had confessed to killing Hugh and Wendy. Then Teri had a constant headache, an unrelenting upset stomach, and nights filled with gruesome dreams of mutilated bodies and massive pools of blood.

After Byrnes's confession eight years earlier, her stomach had calmed and her headaches had lessened. She'd still been plagued with nightmares about finding the bodies of Hugh and Wendy, but they'd always ended with her screaming. She'd never had a dream that took her beyond Hugh and Wendy's bedroom. She'd never felt herself walk down the hall, bump into the killer, and feel him slash her left arm quickly and deftly, almost absently.

And in the dream she'd never heard the killer emitting that soft, soothing, "Shhhh," right next to her ear, a soft, soothing, "Shhhh," she suddenly realized she'd heard long before that awful night eight years ago.

CHAPTER FIVE

MAC MACKENZIE COULDN'T MAKE himself stop clenching the steering wheel of his silver Lexus as he always did when he was angry or distressed, and this afternoon he was both. If only he hadn't turned on the television when he was cleaning the bar . . . if only, what? Roscoe Lee Byrnes wouldn't have claimed he didn't kill the Farrs? Mac and especially Teresa would no longer be objects of suspicion? Perhaps they wouldn't be subjects of another grueling police investigation? No, the earlier he'd found out about Byrnes, the better. Mac still had time to talk to his mother today.

Mac pulled up in front of her first-floor apartment and glanced in the rearview mirror at his face, slightly damp from anxiety and the fact that he'd forgotten to turn on the car air conditioner. He took a deep breath and closed his eyes for a moment, knowing that he must act calm. His mother's health was fine, but ever since the Farr murders, she'd been excitable, nervous, overreacting to any unexpected bad event, no matter how minor. Byrnes's announcement could hardly be considered minor. Mac needed to see if she was all right.

He tapped lightly on Emma's door and in a moment, the tall, slender woman wearing an apron appeared, every silver hair in place, a soft shade of pink lipstick brightening her pale face. She had a dab of flour on her cheek and she wiped her hands fervidly on a towel. "Hiya, Mom," Mac said easily. "How's it going?"

"Jedediah Abraham!" his mother cried in loud joy.

Mac cringed. He loved that his mother was always so glad to see him. He hated that she'd named him after his two grandfathers and all of his life had stubbornly insisted on calling him by both names, not just "Mac" as he'd christened himself. "I wasn't expecting you today, Son."

"So I see." Mac wiped at the flour on her cheek. "You're busy baking, aren't you? What's on the menu today?"

"An experiment. And come in out of the heat. My goodness, your cheeks are flushed red as roses and your hair is in ringlets. You look like you ran here."

"My hair is wavy, Mom, and my cheeks don't look anything like red roses. You make me sound like a Renaissance maiden." Mac stepped into the small apartment, tastefully decorated in shades of burgundy and blue. "I'm almost afraid to ask what kind of experiment you're conducting. Nothing that can blow a hole in the ozone layer, is it?"

Emma giggled, her facial skin crinkling like thin tissue paper, her green eyes dancing as she took his arm and pushed him toward the most uncomfortable chair in the room. She was remarkably strong for such a thin woman and she kept pushing him until he'd landed with a thud on a cushion hard as a church pew. "Oh, honey, you and your silliness! A hole in the ozone layer. That doesn't say much for my cooking, does it?" Emma chirped while Mac tried to absorb the shock to his lower back and attempted to arrange himself in a more comfortable position. "I'm working on a new muffin recipe."

"Mom, you're going to corner the market on baked goods in this town," Mac said. "You know you don't have to work this hard. You don't have to work at all."

"Well, what am I supposed to do? Sit in my robe and watch soap operas all afternoon like Mrs. Beemer down in Apartment Five? Or gossip on the phone half the day like that crabby old woman in Apartment Eight? She must pay people to talk to her, she's so disagreeable!"

"No, Mom, I know you aren't one for having idle hands. I'm just saying you don't have to work yourself to a frazzle. You're a lady of leisure, now."

"Lady of leisure, my foot," Emma pronounced as she set a glass of iced tea beside him. "What happens to us if that club of yours goes kaput?"

"I don't expect it to go kaput, but if it does fail, I'll do something else." Mac gratefully sipped the cold, sweet tea. "I refuse to ever let us be poor again, Mom."

"I've been poor most of my life and I've gotten used to it." Emma returned to the small kitchen divided from the living room only by a long Formica-topped counter. She picked up a large mixing bowl and began furiously whipping batter. "I never wanted my children to be poor, though, and you were for so long. And I certainly don't want my girls having to drop out of college! Wouldn't that be awful with them just months away from being seniors?" She set down the bowl with a clatter. "Oh my, it would be terrible!"

"Mom, don't get upset over something that isn't going to happen." Mac spoke soothingly. "We're not poor. The girls are going to finish college, I'm going to keep my club open, you're going to bake until you wear out that new oven, and we'll all live happily ever after." His mother still looked alarmed, lost in her sudden vision of the family abruptly falling into dire poverty. Now certainly wasn't the time to bring up Byrnes. Mac searched his mind for a topic of possible interest to her and said, "I see you got your hair done yesterday."

"My hair?" Emma's hands lifted from the bowl to her silver curls. "Yes, I did get my hair done. It's an extravagance—"

"No, it isn't. What's the latest gossip at the beauty shop?"

"Oh, nothing that would interest you. Anyway, the girl who did my hair was jabbering away about her boyfriend and not paying attention to what she was doing. She fixed my hair *completely* wrong this time!"

Mac stifled a smile. His mother's hair, which had turned pure silver over a course of six months after the disappearance of Marielle Farr, looked exactly as it always did. "I think it looks fine," Mac said heartily. "So many older women have wispy hair, but yours is as thick as it was in photos I've seen of you when you were twenty!"

Emma blushed and smiled, picking up the bowl and assaulting the batter again. "Do you think so? Your father always loved my hair." Her smile faded. "He just didn't love it enough."

"You mean he loved drinking and gambling more," Mac said bitterly. "He didn't have the brains to know a good woman is worth more than all the alcohol and gambling money in the world."

Emma stopped thrashing the muffin batter and looked into his eyes. "Just like Hugh Farr and all of his other women when he had Marielle." Her voice turned brittle. "I know why you're here. First Celeste started talking about the murders and saying something about Teresa; then that awful Byrnes person went on TV and said he didn't kill Hugh and that slut Wendy. Why can't this horror ever end? Will someone give me an answer?" Emma suddenly began to tremble. "Will *you* give me an answer?"

Mac rose and strode to his mother, taking her shaking body into his arms. "That's why I'm here, Mom. I was afraid you'd heard about Byrnes and you'd be upset."

"Well, I did and I am!" Emma's throat worked as she swallowed sobs. She jerked herself away from Mac, set down her mixing bowl on the kitchen counter again, then turned back to him. "That's why I started baking. Baking usually calms me down, but not today." She looked up at him, tears standing in her eyes. "Did you hear what Celeste said? She accused Teresa of the murders. How *could* she? Teresa loved that child so much!"

"Last night a few of my customers told me about the scene with Celeste in Bennigan's. I don't think Celeste accused Teri of anything. She just mentioned Teri."

"She *chanted*!" Emma sounded as if the girl had thrown fireballs from her bare hands. "She chanted like some kind of demon! I *never* thought she was any better than her mother, even if she was just a little girl when I knew her. The apple doesn't fall far from the tree, you know. Wendy was evil and maybe Celeste has turned out just like her!"

Mac always worried when his mother started using language that seemed more suited to Puritans than a modern woman. She'd always been highly religious, but her faith had begun leaning toward the extreme ever since Hugh Farr had divorced Marielle, and the Farr home had become a maelstrom of tension and unhappiness.

Even then Mac worried about it, although he'd been barely out of his teens and more concerned with plans for his future—plans he hoped would make him a success and better able to care for his family financially—than by the alteration he'd noticed in his mother's spirituality. She'd no longer talked of her belief in the goodness and gentleness of God. Instead, she'd begun to believe in a God of vengeance, and she no longer urged her children to "turn the other cheek" as she'd done throughout their lives.

"Mom, Celeste isn't evil," Mac said gently. "She endured a horrible ordeal when she was a kid, and as for what she said in Bennigan's . . . well, we don't really know exactly what she said, now do we? Can't we give her the benefit of the doubt?"

Emma still trembled in his arms. "I guess so, although like I said—"

" 'The apple doesn't fall far from the tree.' Does that mean I'm like my father?"

Emma looked appalled. "You are *nothing* like that man!"

"Then maybe Celeste isn't anything like Wendy. She's probably more like her father, Jason, and I've heard he's a pretty nice guy." Mac forced a smile although his mother's agitation upset him. "Why don't you try to calm down for now, Mom? We'll find what Celeste really said. And I can't think anyone would believe Roscoe Byrnes."

"They might. They just might, Son." She whirled away from him and picked up her bowl of muffin batter. "Eight years ago, so many people were determined to believe that Teresa killed her father and his paramour they didn't want to even consider some stranger did it!" With a shaking hand, Emma grabbed up a dipper, filled it with batter, and dumped too much into a muffin cup, making it overflow onto the spotless counter. "Now look what I've done!"

"I'll clean it up."

"No!" Emma attacked the spilled batter with paper towels. "I didn't mean to snap at you. I just can't stand that all of this has come up again just when Teresa has been making such a good life for herself. She calls me sometimes, you know," Emma went on. "She even came to see me twice. She told me not to tell you."

And she'd acted so innocently surprised at the club last night when he'd told her his mother was well and living in an apartment. So she hadn't lost interest in the MacKenzie family after all, Mac thought, pleased in spite of Teresa's secrecy. "So Teri's been to see you. That's nice," he said indifferently.

Emma tossed away the paper towels and took a deep breath. Relieved, he could almost feel the rush of fear and anger beginning to settle within her. She ran cold water over her hands, dried them endlessly on a dishcloth, then turned and looked at Mac cannily. "You have been smitten with Teresa since she was just a little girl."

"God, Mom, you make me sound like a pedophile. She was sixteen when I first met her."

"Don't take the Lord's name in vain, Jedediah Abraham! Teresa was too young for you even if she was sixteen."

"I know it. I knew it then. I didn't start seeing her until she was seventeen and then we just went for walks and talked. She seemed older than seventeen."

"And you fell in love with her. I knew it and Hugh Farr knew it, too."

"Yes, he knew and tried to keep us apart, but Teri would always sneak out to see me. Hugh thought we were . . . well, doing things we shouldn't—but as I said, we mostly just talked. We'd get Cokes or ice-cream cones and go sit in that little park about a block away from her house. After her mother was sent to the mental institution, then to her aunt Beulah's, and Hugh got the restraining order to keep Marielle away from Teri, she said I was the only one she could talk to who really understood her.

"She cried a lot about her mother and said as soon as she was eighteen she was leaving the Farr house and 'rescuing' her mother. Teri didn't like Marielle's aunt Beulah any more than she liked her father." A wave of sadness crossed over Mac's face. "But Teri never got the chance to rescue her mother. She didn't even get a chance to *see* her mother alone before Marielle disappeared."

Emma immediately began slopping batter into the muffin cups. Mac knew her nervousness was returning. "Mom, what's wrong?"

"Nothing, dear," she said with sweet vagueness.

"I know you. Something I just said upset you." Emma slopped more batter in the direction of the pan. "You know you can't keep a secret from me."

Emma's head whipped around. "Oh, all right! You never could mind your own business. Ever since you were a child, you had to know *everything* that was going on. You can be quite annoying."

"I enjoy being annoying," Mac said evenly, hoping to calm his agitated mother. "Now tell me why you're so upset."

Emma sighed gustily, gave up on the muffins, and led him back to the living room. She pushed him back onto the chair and seated herself primly on her chintz-covered couch. "Teresa *did* see her mother one last time before Marielle . . . went away."

Mac sat up straight on the rock-hard chair. "Teri saw her mother! She never told me!"

"It was a secret. Teresa knows how to keep a secret!"

"Yeah, I know. And so do you, apparently." Mac leaned forward and gently took his mother's heavily veined hand in his. "Now tell me how and when Teri saw her mother."

Emma looked resigned. "Marielle came to the Farr house the day after Wendy's big party announcing she was pregnant. Marielle thought Hugh and Wendy were gone. Hugh *was* gone and not supposed to be back until evening. Wendy was home, but her car was at a garage being fixed. Anyway, I heard this little tapping on the front door, and when I opened it, there was Marielle. I was so surprised I just stared at her."

"Marielle's aunt Beulah's house is three miles from the Farr house. Did someone drive her?"

"No. She'd walked all that way. She was so tired, poor thing. Her health was poor."

"Her mental health?"

"Her physical health. That Beulah!" Emma jerked her

hand out of Mac's and waved it angrily. "She didn't care anything about Marielle even if they were blood kin. She just took in Marielle because Hugh paid her. She never really looked after Marielle. I know because Beulah let me visit two or three times. Marielle was too thin—not being fed properly—and Beulah never even offered us a cup of coffee. One time I marched right into the kitchen and made a pot of coffee myself. I fixed a peanut butter and jelly sandwich for Marielle, too. Just about all Beulah had was junk food. At least peanuts have protein, and poor little Marielle certainly needed some healthy food."

"Good God!" Mac was genuinely surprised. "Did Teri know her mother wasn't getting enough food?"

"I'm sure she didn't. Marielle probably made some excuse for her weight loss or wore bulky clothes when Teresa visited. If that girl had known her mother wasn't getting enough to eat, she would have done something."

"She certainly would have, even if she was just seventeen." Mac couldn't keep the admiration out of his voice.

"Marielle told me Beulah spent most of her time reading or watching television up in her bedroom," Emma went on. "Beulah never kept an eye on her. She took a nap every afternoon as if she'd done something to make her tired. Couldn't have been housecleaning. That cramped little cottage looked like no one had dusted for weeks, and the kitchen—sticky floor, dirty counters. I saw a cockroach once walking around like he owned the place!"

Mac stared at his mother. "Mom, you never said anything to me about visiting Marielle."

"I promised Marielle I wouldn't tell *anyone* about my visits. She was so scared of Hugh, she thought if he found out, he'd fire her. She was also afraid he'd find out Teresa visited her more often than the judge had said she could. We didn't worry about Beulah telling—Hugh would have taken away Marielle and Beulah would have lost the money he gave her for Marielle's care."

"Hugh probably knew how Marielle was being treated, but he didn't do anything. He was a mean old bastard." Mac's mother gave him a steely, reproving glance and suddenly he felt like he was fourteen. "Sorry. I meant he was a mean old . . . man. Now tell me more about when Marielle came alone to the Farr house."

Emma immediately looked away again. "I shouldn't have let it happen, I guess, but for a mother not to be allowed to see her child . . . well, it was cruel! When Marielle turned up at the house, I told her she shouldn't have come—there would be trouble. But she begged to see Teresa. She had tears running down her face and she looked so pale and thin and miserable, I just couldn't stand it. I told her Wendy was home and she should stay outside, go to the side of the house where all the bushes were so she could hide, and I'd get Teresa.

"It was lucky that the girl was home and Wendy was watching television. Teresa sneaked outside. I was happy for those two, but I was a nervous wreck, scared Wendy would ask me where Teresa was—Hugh made her do that so he could keep tabs on Teresa—but she didn't ask me, thank the Lord. At least I thanked him at the time.

"Then something worse happened. Hugh Farr came home about ten minutes later! He *dragged* Marielle into the house and threw such a fit I thought my heart would stop. Teresa came in screaming at him and he slapped that poor girl on the face so hard she nearly fell down. Wendy *laughed*! While he was busy slapping his child around, poor Marielle ran out of the house and vanished.

"Then Hugh turned on me. Wendy *had* seen me talking at the door to Marielle, and instead of saying anything, she just let our plan play out while she called Hugh. She was a sneaky little twit, not fit to be a mother to that little girl she was going to send off to some boarding school so she wouldn't be bothered with her. Anyway, Hugh stood in front of me and nearly yelled the house down. I was so scared I dropped the glass bowl I was holding and he yelled even louder." Emma paused, looking puzzled. "Son, I thought I told you part of this—at least that Hugh had slapped Teresa and that he'd shouted at me."

"You told me he shouted at you when he fired you. That's all."

Emma's expression turned to one of bewilderment. "But you were so angry—are you sure I didn't say more to make you so mad?"

"Didn't I have a right to be mad as hell that he'd yelled at you and fired you? You also said he threatened he'd make sure no one in this town would hire you again."

Emma's gaze seemed to turn inward in concentration. "Yes . . . yes, he did say that. Not that many places would have had me anyway. I wasn't much good at anything by then."

"You were wonderful—smart and hardworking. You'd certainly done more than your duties for the Farrs, even after Hugh divorced Marielle. Go on with your story, Mom."

"Well, I begged him not to fire me and he came at me. I thought he was going to hit me, but Teresa grabbed his arm. The wicked man turned on her and slapped her across the face again! Celeste came into the room white-faced, but Hugh and Wendy didn't pay any attention to her. Hugh told me to get out and I ran for the door, but not before I told that vixen Wendy she *should* laugh now and be happy with that fiendish excuse for a man she married, because soon God would vent his wrath on *both* of them!"

Emma began to cry and Mac moved to the couch, sitting close to his mother and closing his arms around her slender body. "Don't cry, Mom. It was a long time ago."

Emma sobbed. "Hugh said he was going to the police about you and say you'd done something vile to his daughter. In spite of that, you wanted to confront Hugh, but I told you to stay away from the house. Hugh also said he was going to tell on Marielle for coming to the house and breaking the court order for her to stay away. He said they'd put her back in the institution."

Emma wiped at tears with the back of her hand like a child. "Hugh really hurt Teresa when he slapped her the second time—her face was fire red and her lip bled, all because she'd been trying to protect me. And nobody, not even Wendy, paid any attention to Celeste, who stood like a little stone statue. She didn't even blink."

"She must have been terrified."

"Maybe," Emma said slowly. "But she wasn't crying. She just stood and stared. It didn't seem natural, not natural at all."

"Okay, Mom. Don't think about it anymore. It was a long time ago."

"Yes, a long time ago." Emma let out one final, wrenching sob, then pulled herself up and looked into Mac's eyes with a fierceness he'd never seen. "All of that violence ended a long time ago because Hugh and Wendy were stopped," she ground out. "God forgive me, they *had* to be stopped before they ruined all of our lives!"

CHAPTER SIX

1

As HE HEADED BACK toward the club, Mac would find himself gripping the steering wheel of his car, relax his hands, and in a few moments discover he had a death grip on the wheel again. He turned up the music, turned down the music, and finally turned off the music. His mother's words tolled in his head: "*God forgive me, they* had *to be stopped before they ruined all of our lives!* When he asked her what she meant, she'd only said, "Some things shouldn't be discussed."

After he'd asked for the third time, she'd looked at him with dulled eyes, run her hand over his wavy hair, and said in a sad, tired voice, "I don't mean to be rude, Son, but I'd really like to be alone now. I'll talk to you again in a few days." When he left, she didn't even say good-bye. She'd simply gone back to the kitchen and begun absently stirring what was left of her muffin batter.

She's been hiding from her memories, Mac thought. That's why she'd thrown herself into her little pastry business. His mother had always tried to repress the dark parts of her life by keeping herself busy. Apparently, she's been doing a good job of it, he mused dolefully, until I made her dredge up the past, go over the details of one of the worst days of her life. Of course, he'd gone to her apartment with good intentions, but good intentions often led to disastrous outcomes.

"God forgive me, they had to be stopped . . . they had to be stopped . . . God forgive me . . ." Emma's words echoed in Mac's mind. What the hell had she meant? Did she think that Hugh's and Wendy's deaths were the result of divine intervention? Did she think God had sent someone else to the house that night to murder the couple she considered evil? Was she asking God to forgive her for thinking they'd gotten what they deserved? Or was she asking God to forgive her for something worse? For something she had done?

The last question sent a shock wave of apprehension through Mac. Quickly he lit a cigarette, although he'd promised himself he would stop smoking by the end of summer. When he was nervous or troubled, though, holding a cigarette in his hand seemed to comfort him, and he was troubled now. In fact, he was just about as troubled as he'd been eight years ago when he'd realized that the death of Hugh Farr hadn't set Teresa free, but instead had put her in serious jeopardy of being found guilty of murder.

At first Mac had planned to go back to his apartment above the club and try to relax, but he knew he was incapable of relaxing. Suddenly he knew there was one other woman he needed to see today. He drove past his club and headed north, and turned onto the narrow road leading to Farr Fields.

As he drove past the acres of emerald green grass covering the fields, he remembered what they had looked like four years ago—patchy, weed-filled, dry—and thought of the Herculean job Teresa had done turning this place into rich and beautiful land. Although he had not been in contact with her at the time, friends told him Teresa hadn't turned all of the work over to hired hands. She had been out here working just as hard as the men.

Mac had always admired Teri's tenacity, her industriousness, her willingness to get her hands dirty and sweat like crazy helping with jobs in any way she could. She didn't have a snobbish or lazy bone in her body. In that way, she reminded him of his mother. But there was a difference—Emma MacKenzie had always been timid and easily browbeaten.

Teresa Farr, on the other hand, was stubborn, impetuous, sometimes reckless, and probably emotionally the strongest woman he'd ever known. And right now, it was those very qualities, along with her refusal to admit she was as destructible as anyone else was, that frightened Mac. If she believed Roscoe Lee Byrnes was telling the truth, she'd start looking for who did kill Hugh and Wendy, not out of love for the dead couple, but out of need to clear her brother and herself. And Mac knew that digging for the truth could get her hurt or even worse.

He saw a pale face glance out the front window and the door opened before he'd even rung the bell. Teresa, standing tall and unsmiling, asked in a dull, tired voice, "Here to offer condolences?"

"No, I'm here to offer support," Mac said evenly. "May I come in?"

Teri motioned for him to enter. As soon as he stepped inside, a brown whirlwind circled him, growing and barking ferociously. Mac's hazel eyes widened and he moved back toward the door until Teresa said loudly, "Sierra, no! That's enough!" The dog stopped spinning around him but continued to stare fiercely, shining brown hair along her backbone raised, a low growl lingering in her throat. Teri stooped down and put her arms around the dog. "This is a friend. Understand?" Teri reached out and patted Mac on the calf of his leg. *"Friend."* The dog looked at Teri, then her hand on the stranger's leg, then sat down, although she continued to stare at Mac balefully.

"Good lord," Mac said in a mixture of surprise and relief. "Looks like you've got a pretty good watchdog there."

"Her name is Sierra and she *is* a good watchdog. Sometimes too good. The only problem is that while she sounds fierce, she's never bitten anyone in the three years I've had her." Teri paused. "Would you mind saying her name and patting her on the head or something so she'll know you don't mean me any harm?"

Mac, a long time dog lover, smiled at the glowering dog and said, "Hi, Sierra. You sure are a pretty girl." He then bent and put his hand, palm down, under her nose. "I'm Mac," he went on as the dog sniffed him assiduously. "I won't hurt Teri. I promise."

Somewhat appeased, Sierra stood up, took two steps back, and allowed Mac to enter the room. He flashed her one last smile, then glanced around him. He'd never seen Teri's house and he admired the gleaming oak hardwood floors, the beams on the high ceiling, and all the windows allowing sun to shine on the pale yellow walls and cream-colored furniture decorated with large rust and golden tapestry pillows. The room emanated a pleasant feeling of rustic coziness.

"Good heavens!" Mac exclaimed. "Someone told me you'd just remodeled the farmhouse on this property."

"That was my original plan, but the house was too far gone. I had it torn down and an architect friend helped me design this place. I was going for romantic country inn." Teresa finally smiled slightly. "I guess you approve."

Mac's gaze traveled over the airy room with its two sets of fanlight-topped French doors leading onto a veranda, and a beautiful French-style masonry fireplace. "It's gorgeous,

Teri. Really. You know, looking at this place and my club, I think you should have been an architect."

Teresa blushed. "Oh, I'm a fairly good *amateur* architect, but I as I said, I had the help of a real one. We had a couple of squabbles—I knew exactly what I wanted and he had some other ideas that he claimed would make the house more distinctive—but I stuck to my guns."

"You always do." Mac laughed, although he was already wondering if this architect was more than a casual friend. "Once Teresa Farr has her mind made up, there's no changing it."

"Some people call that being mule-headed and don't find it too attractive."

"I call it unfaltering and I find it damned attractive."

"Well . . . thank you." Teresa suddenly felt embarrassed and completely at a loss for something to do or say. At last she managed, "Do you want some iced tea?"

"Sounds good," he said, although he'd just had tea at his mother's apartment. "Will Sierra let me sit down?"

"Probably. Just move slowly and *very* cautiously."

Mac kept a stiff smile directed at the dog as he nearly crept over to a deep, cushiony chair. Once he was settled, Sierra must have decided he was no longer a threat, because she abandoned her guard duties and followed Teri out of the room into what Mac thought must be the kitchen. Mac took advantage of his time alone to study the room more closely. Beautiful pieces of Fenton Art Glass sat on the fireplace mantle, their gold, fern green, aqua, and ruby hues shimmering in the late-afternoon sun. On the middle of the shelf rested a tall black vase decorated with delicate hand-painted flowers. Mac was almost certain he remembered that vase from the Farr home. No doubt, it had been a choice of Marielle's, not Hugh's, he thought dryly.

Mac swiveled around and looked at the bookcase built into the wall between the French doors. Leather-bound editions of Thackeray, Austen, Dickens, Stendhal, Melville, Hemingway, and Bellow caught his eye. And of course there was an abundance of books by Fitzgerald. Mac remembered that Fitzgerald was Teri's favorite author and her eyes always became dreamy when she talked about the beauty of his prose. Until Mac met her, he'd never read a classic in his life. Now he, too, had a collection of Fitzgerald's works along with a couple of works by Hawthorne, and Tolstoy's *War and Peace,* a novel it had taken him an entire summer to read. Good heavens, he thought now. The woman had turned him into a literary giant!

He was still smiling at the image of himself as a master of literature when Teri walked back in the room carrying a tray bearing glasses of lemonade. She set the tray on the large cream-finished coffee table. "I brought chocolate-chip cookies, too. I baked them and Daniel says I didn't burn them as bad as I usually do, but I won't be insulted if you take a pass on them."

"Daniel's quite flattering, isn't he?" Mac grinned, immediately picking up a cookie.

"He's honest." Teri sat down on the couch across from him. "As you know, cooking isn't my forte."

"How would I know that? You've never cooked for me."

"Count your blessings." Teri grinned at him and Mac immediately felt more relaxed. Then she said, "So, you've obviously heard about Roscoe Lee Byrnes. Do you have an opinion about his veracity?"

"Do I have an opinion about the veracity of a serial killer dropping a bombshell the week he's to be executed?" Mac rolled his eyes. "I wouldn't believe him if he put his hand on a whole stack of Bibles, in spite of his newfound belief in Christianity."

"Then why is he claiming he didn't kill Dad and Wendy?"

"To get attention. He wants to go out with a bang—maybe have someone write a book about him, at the very least stir up a little excitement before the end. He's no Einstein, but he's smart enough to know he'll have people discussing him before he is executed. Hell, at the very least he'll make some headlines."

"That was one of Kent's theories, too." Teri took a sip of lemonade and looked beyond him listlessly. "I can't believe that after all these years, after all the mental and emotional effort I've put into leaving this tragedy in the past, it's come right up to slap me in the face again, right when I'm trying to start a new business."

"Teri, some people are going to grab on to this and gossip about it for weeks. But most people are going to see this for what it is—a ridiculous and cruel attempt to snatch a little excitement, a little fame. After all, even Byrnes must know that after all this time, people have lost interest in him, so he's simply fanning the flame of publicity."

"Do you really believe he's capable of that kind of thinking?"

"Yes, Teresa. He pulled off at least twenty murders without getting caught. He's definitely crazy, but he's not stupid. Most of Point Pleasant's population is going to realize that and not pull their business from Farr Fields."

"God, I hope not," Teri sighed. "I had such high hopes for this place."

"It's beautiful, Teresa. It's the only thing like it around here. You can't let yourself think everyone is going to come, mount their horses, and gallop to the hills. As for your students, I don't believe many parents want to put up with heartbroken children sobbing and throwing tantrums because they can't take their riding lessons anymore."

Teri thought of Daniel. After only one meeting with Caesar, the child had been crying because he thought his mother wasn't going to let him see the pony again before going home. "I hope you're right," Teri said, trying to make her voice sound more positive than she felt. Then she looked at him closely. "Is that why you came to see me today, Mac? To tell me to keep my chin up, think positive thoughts, pretend Roscoe Byrnes didn't decide to make himself a star the last week of his life?"

"Well, partly." Mac leaned forward, his hazel eyes intense. The sun shone on his wavy mahogany-colored hair and Teri couldn't help noticing his skin had turned that beautiful shade of golden tan so many women tried to get out of an instant-tanner bottle. She realized how closely she was studying his face and drew back, flustered. "I went to see my mother this afternoon and—"

"Really? How is she?" Teri asked quickly before taking another quick sip of lemonade and almost spilling it down her chin.

"Uh . . . she's fine. Working on a new recipe. It's top secret, so don't ask me for the ingredients," Mac joked while feeling puzzled by Teri's obvious discomfort. He wondered if it had been caused by his presence, then mentally told himself he was an egotistical idiot. "It's a muffin recipe," he blurted.

"Well, she won't have to worry about me trying to steal it," Teri said mournfully. "As you can tell by that tiny piece of chocolate-chip cookie you choked down, I'm the worst cook in the world."

"The cookies are delicious." Mac stuffed the rest of his cookie into his mouth and began chewing furiously. "Delicious," he sputtered.

Teri burst into laughter. "Geez, Mac, you didn't have to gobble down the whole thing in one bite just to reassure me! You and Sierra have the same table manners!"

He laughed, too, and choked. He ended up coughing loudly while Teri pounded him on the back. "Oh, *please* don't die here," she wailed. "My reputation in this town is bad enough without you dropping dead from eating a cookie I baked!"

Mac started laughing again, threw himself into another coughing fit, grabbed his lemonade, and drained the glass. When he'd gotten himself somewhat under control, he looked up at her with a red face and teary eyes. "I was just trying to show you I liked the cookies."

"That was very kind of you." Teresa's mouth quirked. "And quite brave."

"Gosh, Teri, I'd do anything for you."

Teresa knew he was kidding, but she suddenly felt her face growing uncomfortably warm. She wished Mac would stop smiling and looking into her eyes. Better yet, she wished he would leave. She hadn't been around him for four years, but both last night and today she had noticed how jumpy she felt in his presence, almost as badly as she had as a teenager. She returned to her chair and said with false lightness, "No more cookies for you. You can't handle them."

"Okay. Whatever you say." They exchanged strained smiles again before Mac cleared his throat and began talking, his tone turning serious again. "I came to see you because when I visited Mom earlier, she told me something I'd never heard before. Something about your mother."

Teresa immediately felt her expression grow stony. She didn't like to talk about her mother, not even with Kent and Carmen. She certainly didn't want to talk about Marielle with Mac MacKenzie.

Teri knew Mac was well aware of her reluctance to discuss her mother, which accounted for his rushing on before she could stop him. "Mom described the day your father fired her. You always told me that Wendy had been gunning for my mother for months and when Mom dropped a crystal bowl, Wendy took advantage of the situation to have Hugh fire Mom. But that's not what happened. At least it's not *all* that happened."

Mac paused. "Marielle came to the house that day. She was under court order not to come near you unsupervised, but she did anyway and Mom arranged for you two to meet at the side of the house, where she thought Wendy couldn't see you. But Wendy had seen Mom talking to Marielle at the door. Wendy watched you meet with your mother."

"Wendy didn't miss much of anything," Teresa said stiffly. "She seemed to have eyes in the back of her head."

"It's not Wendy seeing you that has me so dumb-founded. It's the fact that you *never* told me you saw your mother the day of the murders. You withheld the truth from me. Why?"

By this time, Teresa had grown rigid with a mixture of agitation and anger. "I didn't realize I was under an obliga-tion to tell you the truth, the whole truth, and nothing but the truth," she snapped.

Mac closed his eyes for a moment, then opened them and looked so deeply into hers she felt as if he could see to her very soul. "Teri, I know you were only seventeen, but I thought we were in love. *Real* love, not puppy love, not in-fatuation. People in love tell each other important things. I consider it fairly important that your mother actually came alone to the Farr home the day they were killed, something *you'd* consider important enough to tell me." Teri remained stubbornly silent. "You knew Beulah wasn't watching your mother's every move, didn't you?" Mac asked.

Teri looked at him defiantly, lifting her chin a bit. "Beu-lah could have done a better job, but it's not as if my mother was gadding around the state without supervision."

"But she wasn't supposed to go *anywhere* without su-pervision, especially not the home of her ex-husband and his pregnant new wife."

"All right!" Teri blazed at him. "My mother came to the house the day of the murders. So what?"

"So what?" Mac said incredulously. "So her coming caused a huge fight, that's so what. It caused Wendy to tat-tle to Hugh and Hugh to come home and start screaming at my mother. When he looked like he was going to get physical with her, you intervened. That day he smacked the hell out of you, not once but twice! No wonder you wouldn't see me that evening or the next day. You had a split lip you couldn't hide!"

"Yes, I did. I went for a very long walk by myself that night. No one believed I wasn't with you—no one except you—but I was alone. I didn't want anyone to see me. I didn't want anyone even to guess what my father had done to me. It was so disgraceful. Besides . . ."

"Besides what?"

"Besides, I didn't want people to know what had made him so mad at me. It wasn't just that I interrupted the tirade he was directing at *your* poor mother; it was also that *my* mother had come to the house. He was going to report her to the police. Wendy managed to keep him in check that day by telling him negative publicity about Mom would overshadow her party announcing the fact that she was pregnant. But I knew Dad would do it the next day—he couldn't control himself for long, even to please Wendy. He said he was going to report my mother for breaking her 'probation.' " She paused. "He also said he was going to report that you attacked me. He told me he'd claim *you* had given me that split lip, not him, and he said the police would take his word against yours any day, especially with Wendy backing up his story, which he knew she would."

Teresa took a long, shuddering breath. "But he didn't get a chance to report my mother's visit *or* make his accusation against you because he was murdered that night." She gave Mac a long look that both pleaded for his understanding and hinted at fury if he refused to give it. "Mac, don't you see why I couldn't tell anyone about Mom's visit? I also lied to the police about my lip—I said I tripped and fell, hitting it on the corner of my dresser. I didn't want them to know Dad had struck me. They would have thought his striking me gave me even more motive to kill him. Finally, I didn't want them to know about his threat against you. Any of those things could have given both me, my mother, *and* you even stronger motives for murdering him and Wendy right at that time. I was trying to protect all of us."

"You were also trying to protect someone else." Teresa's eyes flashed at him. "Teri, my mother was terribly upset over what happened that day." He fell silent and Teri sensed he was thinking about something his mother had said today—something he didn't intend to tell even Teresa. "Teri, did you ever see Mom between the time your father fired her and the time of the murders?"

"See her?" Teri asked in surprise. "No. She was a wreck. I'm sure she went straight home and wouldn't have dared come back. A few days after the murders, she came to Carmen's, where I was staying, but I had Carmen send her away."

"You had her sent away? God, you sound like Wendy."

"Don't you ever compare me to Wendy again!" Teresa flared, then, seeing the anger in his eyes, realized how haughty she'd sounded, especially to a man who'd had a lifetime of being sent away because he wasn't considered good enough to socialize with the town's "upper class." "I asked Carmen to send your mother away because I didn't think she should be associated with me at that time," Teri said softly. "Emma wasn't in good health and *I* was the prime suspect in a murder case. I didn't want to do anything that might draw her deeper into that horrible mess."

Mac's gaze softened; he sighed and finally leaned back in his chair as he slowly shook his head. "Poor little Teri," he said with what sounded like genuine compassion. "I knew you were suffering during that time, but I didn't realize how much. Good Lord, you weren't just protecting Marielle and yourself; you were also protecting Mom and especially me." He paused and said in a soft, warm voice, "You were quite a girl, Teresa Farr. You still are."

Teresa glanced down, unwilling to meet Mac's eyes, which had grown kind, grateful, admiring, even a bit intimate. She didn't want him to feel indebted to her. She didn't want him to think he could use compliments, warm gazes, and a deep, sonorous voice to win her back for what would just be another fling for him but much more for her. So much more for her. She could already feel the wall of ice she'd so arduously erected toward him melting within her. At this moment, Teresa wanted little more than to open her arms, to pull Mac close to her, to feel his skin against hers, his lips pressing upon her own—

Teresa jerked almost as if she'd been struck. What was she thinking? Was she about to let Mac insinuate himself into her life with a few kind words, a smoldering gaze, a nearly irresistible smile? Did Mac think that in spite of their past, she was so weak at this moment she couldn't stand up against his well-practiced charm? He once knew that for her he was like a flame is to a moth. But that was in the past. Now he was in for a surprise, she thought with almost frightening vehemence. She would *not* let Mac MacKenzie devastate her world again. She wouldn't even give him the slightest *hope* that he still meant anything to her, even if she had to be cruel.

Determination built of her old and new fear allowed Teresa to raise her gaze to meet Mac's and to let her own ebony eyes grow narrow, their expression harder. She leaned closer to him, her face grim, and said in a slow, definite voice, "I didn't lie just to protect you, Mac. I lied mostly because about an hour after the fight, your mother called me and *begged* me not to tell you what had happened. She was terrified of your reaction to her being mistreated by Dad and of him threatening to go to the police and accuse you of attacking me. She said she was terribly afraid of what you might do if you knew the whole truth about everything that had happened that day.

"I can tell by your expression that she left out that part of her confession today. But it's true and you should know I didn't keep quiet just for you. I kept quiet mainly for

Emma, because I loved her." Teresa leaned even closer to Mac and said with soft malevolence, "But I realized with a shock, Mac, that even your own mother thought you were capable of violence."

Mac stared at Teresa for almost a full minute after she'd told him about his mother's call to her the night of the murders. Then he stood up, said, "Thank you for the lemonade," and slammed out the front door. In a moment, she heard his car roar to life and speed down the road from her house to the highway.

"There's no way people can say we don't know how to treat guests well," Teri said cheerfully to Sierra, who had leaped up and barked when Mac slammed the front door. "Don't worry about him, girl. I don't think he'll be coming back for a visit, and dear God, am I glad."

Sierra sat on the floor, tilting her head and looking at Teri intently. She smiled at the dog again, started to say something else silly and jovial, and immediately burst into tears. Within a minute, she was sitting on the floor sobbing as Sierra clambered all over her, whining and burying her face against Teri's neck.

2

The hours after Mac left seemed interminable to Teresa. She was glad she'd sent him on his way. She hated herself for her brutal dismissal of him. She was glad he was gone, hopefully forever. She was bereft that he was gone and she might never see him again.

At last, exhausted by trying to analyze her feelings, Teri had decided to let the matter drop and busy her mind with something besides Mac MacKenzie. She tried to read but couldn't concentrate. She tried to watch television but kept finding channels running the Byrnes story. She couldn't think of one thing that sounded good for dinner, so she decided to skip it, although the rough day had not affected Sierra's appetite in the least. Finally, Teresa poured a glass of Chablis, put an Ivy CD on the stereo, and sat in near darkness, floating along with the music until nearly ten o'clock. Half-asleep and on her second glass of wine, she jumped when the phone rang. Teri reached for the handset on the end table beside her chair. "Hello?" she mumbled cautiously, expecting a prank call.

"I hear that old rascal Roscoe Lee Byrnes is back in the news."

Carmen. Teresa let out her breath, until that moment unaware she'd been holding it. "I wondered why I hadn't heard from you today."

"I've been running all over town spreading the word that Roscoe didn't really kill Wendy and Hugh. This seems like a small town until you've visited every house in the area."

"Carmen, this is not a joking matter," Teresa said sternly, although she couldn't stop the smile creeping to her lips. Maybe Sharon and Kent didn't appreciate Carmen's offbeat humor, but the woman usually managed to get a grin out of Teri by not acting like life was a minefield full of danger or, even worse, social disaster.

"Look, kiddo, I know this must seem like the end of the world to you, but it isn't." Carmen's voice was smooth and calm, as if she were discussing any everyday matter. "Roscoe has decided to make himself a star and he will get a couple of days of publicity, but that's it. I've seen the videotape of his heartrending confession that he didn't kill Wendy and Hugh. Believe me, he lacks the charisma of Ted Bundy. He looks like a murderer. He *sounds* like a murderer, and a dumb one at that. Nobody is going to believe him."

"Oh, I don't know about that, Carmen."

"Well, I do. People aren't buying it, Teri."

Teresa sat up straighter. "Carmen Norris, did you *really*

spend the whole day running around discussing Roscoe Lee Byrnes with anyone you could find?"

"Only a few people whose opinion I value."

"Oh no. If you mentioned it to *anyone,* Kent won't ever speak to you again."

Carmen laughed. "I'm not concerned with Kent's opinion of me, Teri. It couldn't be much worse than it already is, although I don't know what I ever did to offend him. Has he ever told you?"

Teresa had a hard time jerking her thoughts from Roscoe Byrnes to Kent's apparent distaste for Carmen. "I believe Kent just thinks all women, especially those over thirty, should be sitting home baking or something."

"Very tactful. And very evasive. But you're not one to pass along insults." For some reason, Carmen's voice sounded lighter. "How's Mac?"

"Mac? How did you know he'd been here?"

"I didn't. It was a guess you just confirmed." Teresa could have immediately bitten her tongue. "Did he offer sympathy and support?"

"Yes, at first, but I handled things all wrong."

"Oh, Teri," Carmen moaned. "Please tell me you didn't throw yourself into his arms and tell him you love him."

"Of course I didn't!" Teresa was indignant. "And I don't love him!"

"So you say." Carmen suddenly sounded serious. "Teri, I'm not your mother and you're an adult, but you can't leave yourself open to this man. You know what happened the last time—"

"Yes, I know what happened, Carmen. For heaven's sake, you're the one who dragged me to Club Rendezvous—"

"Only to see the club. Not to be with Mac."

"And I didn't invite him here today," Teresa plowed on. "I couldn't help it if he stopped by. What did you want me to do when he came to the door? Hide?"

Teresa took another sip of wine, waiting for Carmen to keep haranguing. Instead, Carmen said mildly, "Well, I don't hear that lilt in your voice you used to get every time you talked about him. You said you handled things wrong. What did you do?"

"You said I wasn't one to pass along insults. You were wrong. Can we just leave it at that?"

"I don't get any details?"

"Not tonight." Teri still couldn't bear to think of the merciless things she'd said to Mac, even if she felt she had good reason to discourage any further attempts of his to see her. "I'm too tired to talk about Mac's very short visit. It's been an incredibly long, depressing day what with Byrnes and all . . . ," she ended vaguely.

"I'm sure it has been. Hearing him trying to clear himself of the Farr murders must have been a surprising, not to mention crushing, blow just when you thought the mess was about over—finally. How are you holding up?"

"Okay, considering. I certainly hadn't expected him to put on a show so close to his execution. I guess he wanted to create a sensation before he leaves this life."

Teresa drained her wineglass, glanced up, and let out a small, choked cry when she saw a pale face staring at her through her living-room window. Her gaze locked for a second with that of the intruder's overly large, shadowed eyes. Then Teresa blinked and the face disappeared.

"Teri, are you all right?" Carmen's voice grew louder over the phone. "Teri, what the hell is wrong?"

Teresa's voice emerged scratchily around the wine that refused to make its way down her throat. "I saw a face at the front window."

"Was it one of those Gibbs men who work for you?"

"No."

"You said you only caught a glimpse. And you've been drinking."

"I've had two glasses of wine in the last two hours!" Teri replied hotly. "I forgot to turn on the porch lights. I'm going to the door and look outside."

"Teri, *no!*" Carmen almost shouted. "Have you taken leave of your senses? What if there's a killer outside? Are you just going to open the door and invite him in?"

"A killer? That's—" Teri broke off, realizing that opening the door was an impulsively stupid, dangerous idea. Maybe she *was* drunk, she thought. Carmen was still shouting on the phone. "Carmen, stop yelling at me. I'm not going to the door. I don't know what I was thinking. But I am going to look out the window."

"Teri, I'm going to call nine-one-one."

"Not yet! Hang on a minute."

Teresa usually closed the living-room drapes at night, but this evening she'd forgotten them. She'd remembered to lock the door. At least she hoped she had.

Panic seized her as she dashed across the room, twisted at an unmoving doorknob, meaning it was locked. "Thank God," she muttered as Sierra, alarmed by Teresa's obvious fear, stood behind her barking frantically.

"Be quiet!" Teri hissed at the dog nearly roaring at the front window. Teri dropped to her knees and crawled beneath the window—a trick she'd seen on television when a character didn't want to make a perfect target of himself—raised her head slightly, and peered into an indigo night lacking a moon and at least half of its stars.

Teresa thought she heard a man's voice. Suddenly, a blinding light flashed just above her head. She shrieked and fell backward, her heart pounding painfully, her breath gone, Sierra running in circles around her barking fiercely. The light continued to shine, bouncing around the semi-dark room, blazing over furniture, shining hardwood flooring, the telephone where even above Sierra's racket Teresa could hear Carmen screaming, "Teri! Teri!"

Still huddled on the floor, Teresa grabbed at the dog, which leaped repeatedly at the window, spattering saliva on the glass. Teresa had finally managed to get her arms around the dog's muscular body when again she heard a man's voice, this time loud enough to rise above the din in the house. "Miss Farr, are you all right?" Teresa huddled on the floor, shaken by an abrupt, profound panic. "Miss Farr, it's Josh Gibbs! It's Josh! Miss Farr!"

Teresa felt as if she was going to pass out in relief. No one was aiming at her with a gun. Joshua Gibbs stood on her porch sending the powerful beam of their large flashlight into her house. "Josh?" she yelled. She needed to hear his voice one more time to reassure herself of his identity. "Is it you and your dad?"

"Just me, ma'am," Josh shouted back. "You okay in there?"

"Yes, but there was someone at the window—"

"I was driving down the hill, comin' back from a friend's, and I saw him. Your porch lights aren't on, but I caught him in the headlights. I drove straight on up the knoll to your house, but he still got away from me. He took off for the woods. You want me to go after him?"

"No, don't bother." Teresa's voice cracked and she realized how ridiculous it was for her to stay huddled on the floor with the two of them shouting back and forth. "I'm sure he's long gone," she yelled, slowly getting up. "I'm coming to the door."

Sierra still yapped and growled, but her volume had lowered and she went completely quiet when Teresa flipped on the porch light, opened the door, and the dog saw a man she knew so well. Twenty-two-year-old Josh— tall and angular like his father with Gus's once-sharp-planed, handsome face—looked at her with his large, intensely blue eyes filled with as much excitement as she had ever seen in them. Always outwardly calm, Josh gave her a quick once-over as if to make sure she wasn't injured, then sent her a small, comforting smile. "I was going to break down the door when you didn't answer at first. I thought you might be lying in here hurt or unconscious. Are you sure you're all right, Miss Farr?"

No matter how many times she'd told both Gus and Josh to call her Teresa, they both clung to "Miss Farr." "Yes, I'm fine," she said, still slightly breathless. "Just scared. I looked up and there was this strange face at the window. . . ." She paused. "You said you saw him. Did you recognize him?"

"Well, no," Josh said slowly. He looked down and the porch light shone on the longish ash-blond hair his father always nagged him to cut. "This sounds crazy, but it didn't really look like a man. Or a woman."

"What?"

"I mean I couldn't tell because of the way it—*he,* probably—was dressed. From a distance, it looked like he was wearing some kind of long black coat with a hood pulled up. No need for a coat and hood on a warm night like this unless someone wants to hide himself."

A long black coat with a hood flashed in Teri's mind. A hooded figure that brushed against her in a hall and sliced her arm with a razor-edged knife. She felt slightly sick at the memory. "You sure you're okay, Miss Farr?" Josh asked.

"Yes," she said quickly. "I'm not hurt at all. I was just startled. I saw a face and then it seemed like an hour before you yelled at me."

"Sorry. I nearly floored the truck, but it took a few minutes for me to get up here."

"That's okay. I guess it was a Peeping Tom."

"Dressed like that?" Josh said, then looked as if he'd like to take back the words. "But it's warm and getting near Fourth of July and you know how teenagers are—always looking for trouble," Josh said as if he was far beyond his teenage years. Teri couldn't smother a smile, but Josh didn't see her. He had already bent down and was picking up something that lay on the porch directly in front of Teresa's door. "Well, huh," he mumbled, turning it over repeatedly, staring at it in the glow of the porch light. "Wonder what this is doing here? Do you think that person left it?"

Slowly, with dread washing through her like ice water, Teresa reached for the object and stared at it in astonishment. It was Snowflake, Celeste's horse-shaped night-light Teri hadn't seen since the night of the murders.

CHAPTER SEVEN

1

TERESA HAD BEEN SURPRISED and shaken when she'd found the note in her car and gotten the fax, but she'd calmed herself slightly by recognizing that at least one person couldn't resist harassing her the week of Byrnes's execution. After his latest confession, she'd braced herself for more of the same kind of cruel but cowardly pestering—the kind that came from someone who was content with sending written messages. She had not prepared herself for such bold torment, though.

Teresa had no doubt the night-light was the actual Snowflake. When she'd bought it, she thought it looked cold and expressionless, so she'd carefully painted the eyes rich brownish green with golden highlights and added long, curved black eyelashes. She remembered the sour looks on her father's and Wendy's faces when Celeste had squealed with delight over the night-light after merely muttering a polite, "Thank you," for their gift of an expensive ornate dollhouse.

"You know what that is, Miss Farr?" Josh asked.

"It's a night-light. A long time ago, I gave it to a little girl. She named it Snowflake." Teresa realized her voice sounded mechanical and she was saying more than she needed to, but she couldn't seem to stop. "I haven't seen it for years. . . ."

"I wonder who left it here. Could it have been the girl you gave it to?"

"What? Good heavens, *no*!" Teresa felt like the air had fled from her lungs at the very thought of Celeste Warner at the door, returning Snowflake. It was impossible yet somehow frightening. Teresa tried to calm her voice. "No, someone must have gotten hold of it and thought it would be funny to leave it, I guess . . . ," she trailed off, aware that Josh was peering closely at her. She knew she looked distressed.

"Want me to get rid of it for you?"

Teresa realized her hands trembled. "No! I mean, I'd like to know who left it here and report that I had a prowler, so I guess I'll give it to the police."

"You want to call the police now? I'll stay with you until they get here."

Teresa looked back at the phone. In the distance, she could hear Carmen nearly howling, "Teri! For God's sake, what's going on?"

"Oh, I was talking to my friend on the phone," Teresa said quickly. "She probably thinks I've been murdered. I don't think I'll call the police tonight—the guy is gone, anyway. I'll talk to them tomorrow." She was already pushing the door shut. "Thank you for the offer, but I'll be okay here alone. I'll just be sure to lock up tight. And would you look in on the horses? I don't think anyone would have broken into the barn, but I'd still feel more secure if I knew they were safe."

"Dad's home," Josh said, nodding at the small cottage he and his father occupied not far from the barn. "His hearing is still good enough to have picked up on them kicking and whinnying, but I'll make sure they're safe. Want me to call you after I've checked on them?"

"That's not necessary. I've imposed on you enough for one night. I'll take no call as a good sign."

"You didn't impose on me. I'm just mad at myself for not getting up here fast enough to catch that guy."

"Well, you gave it a good try. Thanks for looking out for me, Josh."

She closed the door before he could utter a word and immediately turned the lock and the dead bolt. No doubt Josh was puzzled by her abruptness, but she didn't want him to know how upset she was, both by the significance of finding Snowflake on her porch and by the thought of facing the police. After all these years they still terrified her.

She took a deep breath and hurried to the phone, cutting off Carmen in mid-shout. "I'm here! I'm okay!"

"Couldn't you tell me that earlier?" Carmen was still yelling. "You just left me hanging. Do you know what I was imagining?"

"That I was going deaf from your bellowing?"

"I do *not* bellow!" Carmen roared. Then, after a moment of silence, she started laughing. "I simply raise my voice."

"That's an understatement. I'm sorry I didn't let you know anything. Frankly, I forgot you were on the phone. Josh was on the porch."

"Was that young, handsome horse whisperer of yours peeping in the window?"

"No. Well, yes, because he was driving up the road when he saw someone else peeping in my window. He ran before Josh could get here, so we don't know who it was."

Carmen's voice took on a comforting tone. "You sound scared to death, Teri. It was probably just some teenager prowling around on a warm summer night and he couldn't resist looking in the window. I'm sure he's not a threat."

"I'm glad you're sure, because I'm not," Teresa said shakily. "Carmen, Josh said the person had on a long black coat and a hood. Does that remind you of anything?"

"Uh, well, it was no doubt just a disguise, someone having fun," Carmen floundered.

"Someone dressed like the person who murdered Dad and Wendy and almost killed Celeste just *happened* to come looking in my window tonight?"

Carmen hesitated. Then she said in a dispirited voice, "Teri, you had to know a few people in town were going to make something of Byrnes's claim that he didn't kill Hugh and Wendy. I mean, no sensible person would believe that horrible man, but not everyone is sensible. And even some fairly sensible people have a twisted sense of humor."

"I know, Carmen, but that's not all. Josh spotted something lying on the porch right in front of my door. It was Snowflake."

"Snowflake?" Carmen repeated blankly.

"The night-light I gave to Celeste for Christmas. Don't you remember me telling you how much she loved it and how mad Dad and Wendy were that she made such a big deal over a simple night-light and nearly ignored all their expensive gifts?"

After a moment, Carmen said, "Now that you mention it, I do remember. I didn't recall that Celeste had named the night-light."

"Well, she did. It was white, which is why she named it Snowflake." Teresa heard her voice growing louder. "She was always going on about how she wanted to have a horse just like Snowflake and now Snowflake has been delivered right to my door!"

"Take it easy, kid. Now *you're* the one who's shouting." After a moment, Carmen went on in a composed tone. "Now I do remember you telling me about the night-light,

Teri. In fact, I think you got it in Trinkets and Treasures just after I bought the store. But my God, there must have been three dozen of them. The former owner didn't believe in having much of a selection of merchandise—just about a hundred of the few items he did stock. That's why the store wasn't too successful before it fell into my capable hands. Anyway, I'm sure there isn't just one white horse-shaped night-light floating around town."

"This one was distinctive," Teresa argued. "I painted its eyes hazel and put little gold flecks in them—you know, like the flecks in Mac's eyes?" Teresa felt like kicking herself for mentioning Mac. "Celeste had seen Mac and she'd developed a little-girl crush on him and said something about him having dreamy eyes, some silliness." Teresa could have kissed Carmen for remaining silent. "Anyway, I gave it long, curling black eyelashes and a little smile, just like *this* night-light has. It *is* Snowflake, Carmen. I'm absolutely certain of it."

"Couldn't someone else—" Carmen halted. "I started to suggest that someone else had painted one of the night-lights exactly the same way, but that would be too much of a coincidence. So let's say it *is* Celeste's night-light. Because she loved it so much, couldn't someone have taken it out of your old house for her?"

"Like who? Kent? The police?"

"How about Celeste's father? What's his name? Jason?"

"Yes, it's Jason, but Celeste was taken to the hospital the night of the murders. She never returned to the house. I'm fairly certain Jason didn't, either."

"What about Celeste's clothes? Someone had to get those for her."

Teresa shook her head although Carmen couldn't see her. "Someone told me Jason didn't want anything from that house, including Celeste's toys and clothes. After Wendy married Dad, she bought everything new for Celeste, right down to her underwear. I remember Celeste telling me she liked her old clothes better, but Wendy had left them behind with Jason. Celeste said on the weekends she spent with her daddy, she got to wear her other clothes, so I know he didn't throw them away."

"Well, I'm not talking about clothes and toys that Wendy and Hugh bought for the child. I'm talking about that little night-light *you* got for her. I'm sure before the murders she'd told her father how much she loved it. When she was in the hospital, he might have thought it would cheer her up, make her speak."

Teresa sighed. "Sounds good, but I can't see Jason Warner entering a bedroom splashed with his daughter's blood to retrieve a night-light given to her by me, who everyone thought had nearly killed the child."

"I thought Jason was one of the people who didn't think you'd committed the murders. As I remember, it was his mother who was ready to send you straight to life in prison without parole." Teresa winced, and, almost as if Carmen could see her, she said, "Sorry, Teri. I shouldn't have mentioned Mrs. Warner. But the point I was trying to make is that Jason didn't seem to think you were guilty, and if Celeste wanted that night-light, he might have gotten it for her. You always said he nearly worshipped the child." After a moment of silence, Carmen added, "The only alternative I can think of is that after the police released it as a crime scene, someone broke into the house and stole the light. You did leave the house furnished, didn't you?"

"Yes."

"Did you have the locks changed?"

"Dad had them changed after he married Wendy. As far as I know, they only gave out one of the new keys—to Emma, so she could get in without waking Wendy. Dad didn't even give Kent and me keys. The police gave us the keys when the house was no longer a crime scene."

"I didn't know that!" Carmen sounded shocked. "I know the police let us in to get a few of your belongings right after the murders, but I didn't realize you didn't have a key."

"Well, I didn't and neither did Kent," Teresa said flatly. "Later the police turned over the keys to us, but neither of us had the stomach to go into that house and sort through everything. We both just wanted to shut the door and never look back."

"Well, no one could blame you for that. But if the house is fully furnished, Teri, it's even more likely that someone broke in, took things, and is using them to unnerve you."

"I know, but . . ."

"But what?"

"Carmen, when I heard Byrnes this morning saying he didn't kill Dad and Wendy, I knew the harassment would start up again and most of it would be directed at me." Teri paused. "But this couldn't be just the random act of some nut who wanted to spook me."

"Why not?"

Teresa's voice became high and tight. "Because the person who was on my porch, the person who left the night-light at my door, knew they were leaving something of significance to *me*. Somehow they knew *I* bought the night-light and I'd recognize it immediately because I'd painted the horse's face for Celeste."

2

"Kent, I don't think it's a good idea for Daniel to take riding lessons. He's too young. He's too timid."

Kent Farr lay against pillows propped against the head of the king-sized bed and watched his wife brush her gleaming strawberry blond hair. That hair was the first thing that had attracted him to her over a decade ago when he'd seen her standing in the sun wearing a cheerleader's outfit. The magnificent hair had hung nearly to her waist, then, and framed her lovely porcelain-skinned heart-shaped face with its freckles and big, soft eyes. She really didn't look much older than she had at sixteen, he thought in amazement as he looked at her now. But she acted as if she'd had twenty birthdays.

Kent took a breath, knowing they were headed for an argument they'd already had at least five times. "Sharon, Daniel is not too young to take lessons—you heard Teri say she has students even younger than he is—and the kid is *not* timid. Not by nature, anyway. After you've told him some story about a child who did the things he wants to do and met with disaster, *then* he gets nervous."

Sharon smacked the brush down on the dresser and whirled to face Kent, color high in her cheeks. "For one thing, Teresa is not a disinterested party. She's trying to start a riding school. She needs students."

"She needs paying students. Daniel's lessons are gratis, if you remember."

"And second," Sharon went on as if Kent hadn't said anything, "I do *not* try to keep Daniel from doing things little boys his age are supposed to do. I am *so* tired of you acting like I'm trying to turn him into some neurotic child afraid of the world—"

"That's exactly what you're doing. I just can't figure out why."

"I warn him about dangers because I want him to be *safe*. I am more interested in my son being *safe* than *macho*!"

Kent burst out laughing. "You think I want our little boy to be macho?"

"Yes, I do. You act like he's twelve or thirteen, not seven!"

"Sharon, that's ridiculous!" Some of the humor had left Kent's expression. "In what way do I encourage him to act thirteen?"

"Sex, for one!"

Kent's eyes widened and he sat straight up in bed. "Sex!

Are you saying I've been encouraging my seven-year-old son to have sex?"

"Not exactly, but when we were having dinner out last weekend and that pregnant woman walked by he said, 'Gosh, she's fat,' and you said, 'She's not fat, Son; she has a baby in her tummy. All babies come from their mommies' tummies.'"

Kent stared at her. "Was I wrong? Do they come from somewhere else?"

Sharon cocked her head and gave him a look of supreme annoyance. "Don't try to turn this into a joke. Daniel is far too young to learn all the ins and outs of sex."

"I'm not even going to touch that last phrase, Sharon." Kent tried unsuccessfully not to grin. "And I wasn't exactly explaining the sex act to him—just where babies come from."

"He's only *seven*!"

"Do you know how many times you've told me he's seven? I haven't forgotten my son's age, Sharon, and I don't encourage him to do daredevil things—"

"Like riding a horse!"

"Like taking riding lessons on a Shetland pony. Some of his friends do. Some of the kids who are younger than he is do. Six-year-olds. Think of it, Sharon. Some parents actually feel safe having their six-year-olds take riding lessons. It boggles the mind!"

A year ago, Sharon would have laughed at the exaggeration. Six months ago, she would have thrown back a sarcastic retort. Tonight she sat down on the edge of the bed and looked deep into his dark blue eyes—the same shade as his mother's eyes. "Kent, do you realize Daniel is almost exactly the same age Celeste Warner was when she was almost stabbed to death?"

Kent drew back slightly; then he frowned. "Is that what all of this overprotection is about? Because Daniel is nearing the age of Celeste when she was attacked? Do you think eight is some magical age when horrible things start happening to children?"

"Of course not! I'm not a ninny, Kent, although sometimes you treat me like I don't have any sense. But I can't help thinking about it. Celeste was eight. Daniel is almost eight. It's just . . . eerie."

"Eerie! What in the name of God is eerie about two children turning eight? Most children do, you know. Sharon, what's the matter with you lately? You're jumpy; you're suspicious; you fly off the handle over the least little thing. I know you're unhappy about my working so much, but I can't help it. I always expected to be head of Farr Coal Company one day, but I didn't expect it to be dropped in my lap when I was in my twenties. I've had to work twice as hard as anyone else would to prove myself. But it's work that keeps me away from you and Daniel. Not another woman." Sharon's eyes narrowed. "That's what you think, isn't it? That I'm a chip off the old block? That I have another woman on the side?"

"I am not even going to discuss that subject."

"Thanks for your trust in my fidelity," Kent snapped. "I feel so much better knowing my wife believes I'm faithful."

He knew from the look on her face she was about to come back with a scathing remark, but instead she drew herself up and gazed at him coolly, as if she were making all the sense in the world and he was being irrational. "Kent, how do you think this Roscoe Lee Byrnes business is going to affect Daniel?" Sharon asked softly.

"Roscoe Byrnes! Talk about changing the subject." Nevertheless, Kent stiffened. "Daniel doesn't know anything about Byrnes recanting his confession. Why should it affect him?"

"Daniel doesn't know anything about it, but other people do. If they don't mention it to him directly, they'll talk in front of their children and the kids will hit him with it."

"I guess that's true," Kent said thoughtfully, "but there's nothing we can do about it except leave town, and I can't take off from work right now. We'll just have to explain the situation to him before he hears it from anyone else."

"Explain what, Kent? That his grandfather and his stepgrandmother were murdered in their bed? That a girl just a few months older than Daniel was stabbed and could have died?" She paused, then added emphatically, "That everyone believed his aunt Teresa had committed the murders?"

"Not everyone believed that!" Kent sat up, threw off the sheet, and headed for the dresser. Sharon knew he was going for a cigarette. "You didn't believe it; I didn't believe it; your father didn't believe it—none of the people Daniel knows and trusts believed it. I think their opinion is going to mean more to him than that of a bunch of strangers."

"Or he'll be smart enough to know that no one who knew and cared about Teri *wanted* to believe it."

Kent had struck a match but let it burn almost to his fingertips without touching it to the cigarette between his lips. Finally, he said with an almost threatening quiet, "What I can't believe is what you just said." His tone frightened Sharon a bit and she sat still, hands folded, her eyes focused on Kent's chest, not his face. "Sharon, tell me the truth," Kent said coldly. "Were you just pretending to believe Teri was innocent back then?"

Sharon swallowed. "There was so much tension in that house. Even you can't deny that Teri hated her father and Wendy for what they'd done to Marielle. To make things worse, Teri had to live with Hugh and Wendy and she'd just found out they were going to have a baby." Kent stared at her stonily. "And finally," Sharon forged on, "in the afternoon, before the murders, no one saw Teri. She said she'd stayed in after she'd fallen and gotten that split lip. Yet she said she was out that night and she came in late."

"If you had a split lip, would you have gone out in the daylight? And you never came in past your curfew?"

"Well . . . I guess I wouldn't have wanted everyone to see the split lip, and yes, I guess I did stay out late a couple of times, but my circumstances were different. I had the ideal family. Mom adored Dad and Dad thought Mom walked on water. Even though she's been dead for four years, *he'll* never even look at another woman. Never!"

Kent looked stunned as her volume rose. "Sharon, if you're hinting that I'm involved with someone else—"

"Dad and Mom were perfect for each other—perfect—and the three of us got along wonderfully," Sharon went on. "I was a happy teenager from a happy home—"

"Sharon, we have a happy home—"

"You're gone nearly all the time and Daniel is away from me more and more. I don't like it! And Dad doesn't even come around as much as he used to, especially in the evenings—"

"Daniel is growing up, Sharon. You have to accept it that he's not going to cling to Mommy like he did when he was younger. As for your father, it's his month off the boat. Maybe he's visiting with friends or—"

"Or what?" Sharon glared at Kent. "Or *what*?"

Kent shrugged. "I don't know. Fishing?"

"Don't be foolish! And don't try to steer me away from the topic of Teri. When she was a teenager, she wasn't like me. Not that I blame her for being depressed and upset over your mother and Wendy and that whole mess, but Teri can be so volatile—"

"Volatile? More volatile than you lately, Sharon?"

"And she hated your father."

"If I remember, you weren't my father's biggest fan then, either. You detested him for trying to prevent us from getting married, especially because you were pregnant."

"Be quiet about the baby!" Sharon hissed. "And don't forget that you were furious with your father, too. You just weren't around. You were at school in Virginia. And I'm—I'm *me*," Sharon said as if this explained everything. "But

Teri is different. I've always thought Hugh gave her the split lip. You saw it. I saw it. She wouldn't tell me anything, of course, but I'm sure she confided in you."

"She has *never* told me Dad hit her. She said she fell."

"Which I'm sure you believed. I *know* you suspected your father hit her, and *I'm* certain of it." Sharon took a deep breath. "Considering how mad she was at him already, just how furious do you think Teri was the night of the murders?"

"She never said Dad hit her," Kent repeated mechanically.

Sharon looked exasperated. "Kent, have you forgotten the punch on the jaw your father gave you when he said you were *not* going to marry me and you said you *were*? It took five stitches to close the cut he left with that gaudy ring of his." She walked over to Kent and closed her cool hands around his arms. "Your father was a vicious, selfish, controlling man, honey. And you of all people know just what he was capable of driving someone to do, particularly someone who already had a huge amount of resentment and rage built up against him."

Kent ran a finger over the scar still visible along his jawline. His father had tried to knock him unconscious, and he'd hit Kent with that damned elaborate ruby ring Wendy had bought him on their honeymoon—bought for Hugh with Hugh's money.

Kent remembered the rage that flooded through him that night as he caught himself on the edge of his father's desk and managed to remain standing. He remembered the fury as well as the stony determination in his father's small, mean eyes. And Kent remembered realizing beyond a doubt that as long as Hugh Farr was alive he would never manage Farr Coal Company and have Sharon and their baby, too.

CHAPTER EIGHT

1

TERESA WOKE UP BEFORE the alarm went off and sat up in bed, swept by a feeling that something important was about to happen. She jumped up, ran to a window, parted the draperies, and threw open the window. Cool, crisp air hit her in the face. A lemon yellow sun shone in a cloud-studded cerulean blue sky. Josh and Gus were already exercising Eclipse and Caesar. Caesar. That's why Teresa had awakened with an air of expectancy. Daniel was to begin his riding lessons today.

Sierra lay on the bed, carefully watching her mistress, but too tired to rise after all the excitement last night over the night-light. Who could have left it? To her frustration, Teri had asked herself that question a hundred times after she'd gone to bed, keeping herself awake. She wanted to look bright-eyed and confident today, not red-eyed and tired. Or worried. Sharon could pick up on worry at a hundred feet, and Teri did not intend to mention the Peeping Tom or the night-light.

Teri stepped in front of the mirror and groaned. She'd put in another rough night and it showed. Astringent drops helped her sleep-deprived red eyes. Blush and concealer as well as peach-toned lip gloss also improved her looks. Twenty minutes later, wearing jeans, a turquoise blouse, and even a pair of shining silver and turquoise earrings, she decided she could pass for being well rested. If not well rested, at least colorful.

As she passed her office door, though, she caught herself looking almost fearfully at the fax machine. Its strident tone hadn't alerted her to any incoming faxes this morning, she thought thankfully. Still, she couldn't get the words of yesterday's fax out of her mind: "NO ESCAPE **NO ESCAPE.**" As she descended the stairs, she caught herself saying them aloud, wondering who had sent the fax, written the note she found in her car, and, worst of all, come right up on her porch to leave the night-light of a child who'd almost been murdered. Who would want to scare her so badly?

A lot of people, she thought. A lot of people had believed her a depraved murderess before Roscoe Lee Byrnes confessed. Now that he'd recanted that confession, those same people probably had snatched up their previous belief with a triumphant "I told you so" air and thought she was getting well-deserved torment she'd escaped for eight years because some mental case had decided he wanted attention.

But that didn't explain who had gotten possession of Snowflake. The house had been vacant for years. There had never been a break-in, but it was possible that anyone to whom the realtor had shown the house could have taken it. It didn't explain how that person would have known Teresa had given it to Celeste and decided to unnerve her completely by "giving" it back to her eight years later.

"Oh, for God's sake," she said aloud. "I'm like some little kid trying to scare herself." She looked at the dog standing beside her at the foot of the staircase. "We need some fresh air and sunshine, Sierra."

Without even bothering to fix her usual morning coffee, Teri hurried out of the house, which suddenly seemed small and almost airless. Sierra ran along beside her, joyous to be out romping on a beautiful summer morning, as Teresa walked to the ring where Gus brushed a docile Caesar. "Getting him all glamorous for Daniel?" she called, climbing up on the fence and sitting on the top rung.

Gus looked at her and smiled. His short ash-blond hair was heavily laced with gray and his skin was weathered, but he was as slim as his son, and his smile just as broad and welcoming. He must have looked just like Josh when he was younger, Teri thought. He would have been a heartbreaker. At fifty-six, he still was. His wife, Sarah, had died last year after a two-year battle with cancer, and to Teri's knowledge Gus had never seen another woman socially after Sarah's death. Teresa had no doubt that within the next few months Josh would leave the cottage he'd shared with his parents much longer than he'd wished, first because of Sarah's illness, then because Gus didn't want to be all alone.

"Mornin', Miss Farr," Gus said with a broad grin.

"I wish you'd call me Teresa. Or even Teri."

"It just doesn't seem right, what with you being my employer and a lady and all," he replied. "Josh said you had some unwelcome company last night."

"Yes." Teri's stomach tightened, but she managed a nonchalant, "Probably just a Peeping Tom."

"Maybe." Gus turned back to Caesar and began working gently with his fingers on a tangle in the pony's tail. "Josh said you recognized that little thing left on your porch, though. A night-light?"

"Yes, at least I thought I did. Then a friend of mine reminded me that a store in town had sold dozens of those night-lights the year I bought one. It probably wasn't the one I'd given as a present." Teri surprised herself at how easily the lie flowed from her. "So, does Caesar seem to be in a good mood this morning?"

"He's always in a good mood." Gus began brushing Caesar's tail with long, flowing strokes. "He'll be a good horse for little Daniel."

"I think so, too. Daniel's mother worries me, though. She's not in favor of him taking lessons. They were Kent's idea. Kent's and Daniel's."

"But when she sees how well the child does on the horse—and I'm sure he will—she'll change her tune."

"I'm not so sure, but I can always hope. Daniel is really excited about the lessons."

"Josh is going to give the lessons, and you know what a way with children he has. That boy is going to make a fine father someday."

"I agree." While Sierra sniffed assiduously at the grass, Teresa took a deep breath of the clean, warm air. She decided it couldn't be more than seventy-five degrees, although the sun was climbing in the sky, and the humidity was low. "I should take a ride on Eclipse today," she called to Gus. "I haven't exercised her for almost a week."

He nodded. "Fine day for it. You'd enjoy it. So would she." He turned and gave Teri a gentle smile. "You know, you're a born rider, Miss Farr. Just like your mother was. She never looked happier than when she was riding her horse."

Teri went stone still. "My mother?" Gus nodded. "You knew my mother?"

"Seems like a lifetime ago. It was back before she married Hugh Farr." Gus didn't look at her. He simply wet his brush in a bucket of water, then began to brush Caesar's mane to the right. "I worked at the Point Pleasant stables. That's where I met her. We went riding together a few times. Then to some movies, and had a dinner or two."

Teresa felt as if she had opened the door to an unexpected room. "You *dated* my mother?" She realized she sounded unflatteringly shocked. "I mean, I'm surprised because I've known you for years and you've never mentioned it."

"I know you still grieve for your mother—didn't want to bring up bad memories for you, but considering what that Byrnes guy pulled yesterday, she's been on my mind because of her disappearin' at the time of the murders. I figured she was on your mind, too."

"She has been." Teresa's eyes filled with tears and she blurted, "Oh, Gus, you're not one of those people who think my mother killed Dad and Wendy, are you?"

Gus almost dropped his brush and whirled to face her. "Marielle? Murder somebody? That's about as likely as the moon droppin' right on our heads some night. The Marielle I knew was just about the kindest, most gentle person I ever knew. I don't mean any disrespect to my wife, Sarah—she was a good woman—but she did have a short temper. I guess some people would've called her domineering. Not like Marielle."

Sarah—Gus's stern, whip-thin wife, whose dour face and harsh voice vanished only in the presence of her son, Josh, on whom she doted. Teri looked back at Gus, gently brushing Caesar's mane. She felt almost dizzy from Gus's revelation that he had once dated her mother, and as Teri sat on top of the fence, her mind teemed with a hundred questions. Finally, she picked one and tried to ask it casually. "You said *the Marielle I knew.* What was that Marielle like?"

"Well, beautiful, of course." Gus turned, looked at Teresa, and smiled. "Just like her daughter." Teri smiled back, but Gus had already turned away and was shaking the water from the brush before he placed it on the base of the pony's neck and ran it down the mane, smoothing the long hairs. "Marielle was real shy at first but amiable. After I got to know her better, I saw that sometimes, especially when her parents weren't around, she seemed content. Oh, not joking and buoyant, but sort of quietly happy, especially when she rode her horse."

"Good heavens, Gus, I didn't even know she had a horse."

He turned, surprise showing on his craggy face. "You didn't? It was a fine horse—an Arabian like yours. I thought that was why *you'd* gotten an Arabian for yourself."

"No," Teri said vaguely. "No, it was just a coincidence, I guess." She paused. "What did Mom name her horse?"

"Let's see . . . Cassandra! Like the woman in the Greek myth who could tell the future." Gus shook his head. "Too bad Cassandra couldn't tell Marielle what she had in store for her if she married Hugh Farr. But that's sour grapes talkin'. I shouldn't be sayin' things like that with Hugh bein' your father and all."

"You can't insult me about my father, Gus," Teri said dryly. "He was a complete jerk."

Gus burst out laughing so loud that Caesar started in surprise. Gus put a calming hand on the pony and began murmuring to him. She'd seen Josh do the same thing to skittish horses and they always immediately calmed. Carmen was wrong—Josh isn't the only horse whisperer, Teresa thought.

When Caesar had quieted and Gus began putting the finishing touches on his mane, just as if the pony were going to a competition, Teri spoke again. "May I just say one thing and ask one question about Mom before I stop bothering you?"

"Fire away," Gus returned.

"First of all, I think she would have been so much happier with you than with Dad."

Gus turned around. Even from a distance, Teri could see that he was touched. "Well, that's about the nicest thing anyone ever said to me."

"I mean it. Maybe you weren't in love with her. . . ."

Gus grinned. "You sure don't have the gift of second sight like Cassandra, Miss Farr, or you'd know I *was* in love with her. I just never had the nerve to tell her."

While Gus was looking at Teri, he seemed unaware of Josh leading the gray Connemara pony Cleopatra from the barn. Josh had clearly overheard his father, and although he never broke stride, he shot a narrow-eyed look at Gus, then at Teresa, his jaw so tight she could see the muscle flexing beneath his skin. He already knew, Teri thought in shock. Josh already knows his father once loved my mother and he resents it like hell.

Meanwhile, Gus went on talking loudly. "I thought Marielle had some fondness for me, too. She never said anything, but sometimes it seemed she gave me a certain kind of look, a sort of caring look, but maybe that was just wishful thinking on my part."

"I'm sure it wasn't." Teresa wasn't being polite or tactful. She could easily imagine her mother in love with this kind, placid, intelligent man—a man who would have treated her with warmth and gentleness, a man who must have been as handsome in his youth as his son was now, the son who was brushing Cleopatra with unusual vigor. Teresa could tell that the more Gus talked about Marielle, the angrier Josh grew, his face flushing to a deep red beneath the bright morning sun.

Teresa knew she should change the subject, but she couldn't hold back her next question. "Mom wouldn't have been interested in money, Gus, so how did she end up with Dad?"

Gus glanced away for a moment, looking thoughtfully over the rolling green acres of the farm. Teri thought he seemed to be deciding whether to answer. Then his gaze returned to her. "You're right, Teresa—your mother didn't give a whit about money—but her parents did, and they were a strong pair. Of course you'd know that, them being your grandparents and all."

"Actually, I was only around them a few times when I was little. Then they were killed in that train wreck. My grandfather always insisted trains were safer than planes."

"Yeah, I forgot how young you must have been when they died. Well, anyway, they ruled Marielle with an iron hand. They were always real pleasant to her in front of people, but I'm not so sure what they were like when there was no one around to see them. Anyway, your mother was timid with them."

Gus paused, frowning. Then he burst out, "Ah, hell, I've already called you Teresa, which I always vowed not to do, so I might as well come out with everything. You've got a right to know about your own mother. Marielle was downright scared of her parents. She'd never admit it, but when they were around I could see it in her eyes. And I remember how her parents' faces lit up one day when Hugh dropped by the stables to watch Marielle ride. I could tell she'd caught Farr's fancy and they were over the moon with joy.

"Not Marielle, though. She told me he'd been comin' by her house a lot, visitin', stayin' for dinner. She seemed troubled. One day we were riding and she was doin' a poor job of it, handlin' the horse all wrong, and finally she burst into tears and said she wished she never had to talk to Hugh Farr again. That's all she'd say. A week later, out of the blue, her father sold her horse she loved so much and she stopped comin' to the stables.

"About three months later, I read in the newspaper about her engagement to Hubert Farr. I tell you, Teresa, I just about cried. Me, a grown man. The paper ran their *betrothal* picture." Gus made a face as if he'd just swallowed something incredibly sour. "Hugh was smilin' all over the place and Marielle was tryin' to smile, but it wasn't workin'. I'd never seen her look like that, and I knew she was sad about the engagement, but she married him anyway."

Gus sighed. "I didn't see her again for years, not till she came to the stables with you a few times, but she never did more than say hello to me. At first that kind of stung, but then I realized she wouldn't want it gettin' back to your father that she was even comin' to the stables, much less talkin' up a storm with me."

"No, she wouldn't have," Teresa said vaguely, still surprised by all she'd learned in the last ten minutes. Although she had known Gus since she was an adolescent and he was working at the Point Pleasant stables, she'd never heard him talk so much. She sat stunned on the fence top, not knowing what to say after Gus's information about Marielle's "courtship" with Hugh Farr and Gus's own revelation that he'd been in love with her. Finally, Teresa blurted, "I wish she'd never married Dad."

"Then you wouldn't be here, Teresa, and you're just as nice as she was. You're just feistier, good for you. You've come through fire the last few years and I've felt real sorry about it, but you're just that much stronger for it." Gus, satisfied with Caesar's grooming, picked up his pail of water in his right hand and Caesar's lead rope with his left. Then he once again turned to Teri and said, "Your mother wasn't strong like you, Teresa. That's why I worry about her and I pray every night that poor Marielle finds her way home someday."

2

Sharon arrived promptly at ten o'clock for Daniel's first lesson, which was a near disaster. She pulled into the small gravel parking lot near the barn, where Teri, Josh, and Gus waited. Such a welcoming committee wasn't par for the Farr Fields staff, but Teri had warned Gus and Josh that they needed to give Sharon all the assurance they could.

Sharon popped out of the car, already looking worried,

even slightly frazzled. Daniel emerged more slowly. He wore a cowboy hat and boots, which Sharon told Teri had been bought by Kent at Daniel's insistence. The child looked ridiculous in the black hat too big for his little freckled face, and for some reason he was trying to walk bowlegged. A half-smothered snort of laughter emerged from Josh, who was promptly nudged in the ribs by his father. "Well, hello there, cowboy," Gus said heartily to Daniel.

"Hello, Mr. Gibbs." Daniel touched the rim of his hat first at Gus, then at Josh, and finally nodded to Teri. "I'm here to ride Caesar," Daniel stated with an air of sophisticated calm.

Aware that all three of them were about to burst out laughing, Teri quickly said, "Mr. Gibbs has him groomed and ready for you. His son, Josh, is going to give you your lesson this morning. Caesar can't wait to see you again."

At her last sentence, the child's face broke into a huge grin, showing a gap where his front tooth had fallen out, Teri hoped it had happened last night so the tooth fairy could come while he slept. "And I want to see Caesar!" Daniel said joyfully. "Mr. Josh, are we going to ride him downtown?"

Josh seemed to think over the matter for a moment, then said, "I think it would be better if we stayed here for your first lesson. But you'll have a good time; I promise. We'll go all around the ring and maybe even farther out into the fields."

Daniel beamed. Sharon's eyes widened. "Maybe he should just sit on the horse today."

"Just *sit* on him!" Daniel looked horrified. "Mommy, I came here to learn how to ride, not to sit. I know how to sit!"

"Not on a horse!" Sharon argued.

Annoyance flooded through Teri. Had Sharon brought Daniel only to forbid him to ride even with an experienced trainer standing right beside him? Teri was on the verge of snapping at Sharon when Josh intervened. He turned his boy-next-door smile on Sharon and stepped closer to Daniel, placing his hand protectively on the enraged child's shoulder. "Mrs. Farr, I start out children real slow." His voice was soft, reassuring, almost wooing. "We get to know the horse—Daniel has already met Caesar, but they need to talk man-to-man again today, and then I'll show him how the saddle fits; then I'll help him mount the horse and show him how to hold the reins just so. Today, we're going to concentrate on how to sit on Caesar. We'll walk around a little bit if Daniel's comfortable, but I'll be holding the lead rope the whole time. I'll take extra good care of him."

Daniel had taken Josh's hand and was holding on for dear life, looking at his mother with a mixture of pleading and determination. Sharon glanced at him, then back at Josh, still smiling, still maintaining an expression of confident reassurance. At last, Sharon relented. "All right, but don't turn your back on him for a second."

"I wouldn't dream of it, Mrs. Farr." Josh looked down at Daniel, whose hat had slipped sideways in his distress, showing his bright strawberry blond hair and one eye brimming with an unspilled tear. "Daniel, let's you and me go talk to Caesar for a few minutes. I've got a couple of apple slices you can give to him. He'll like that. But you'd better take off that hat, first. I know you two took to each other like milk and honey yesterday, but he's never seen you in a hat and he might not recognize you. He'd be real upset if he thought anybody except Dan Farr was comin' to ride him this mornin'. He's been lookin' forward to it."

Gus winked at Teri, who was amused by the drawl Josh had adopted clearly for Daniel's benefit. Meanwhile, Josh simply turned around and began leading Daniel to the barn, not waiting for another objection from Sharon. Josh kept up a steady stream of chatter, and in a moment Daniel was laughing, the incipient crying fit a thing of the past.

Teri took Sharon's arm. "I just made fresh coffee. Let's go up to the house. We can visit without Kent interrupting."

Sharon finally gave her a tight smile. "Okay, Teri. You don't have to get out the handcuffs. The overprotective mother will go quietly."

While Teri bustled around the kitchen pouring coffee, Sharon sat at the table—detached and clearly not in the least interested in anything her sister-in-law had to say. Teri chattered about a couple of her other students who were doing well on Caesar, the man who owned Captain Jack but rarely came to ride him, how she'd heard this year's fireworks display at Tu-Endie-Wei State Park was to be the biggest ever. She listened to her own voice, skimming over the surface of light topics while her mind churned with images of the fax and the note she'd found in her car, and finally Snowflake. Teri wished she had someone to talk with about it all—someone besides Carmen, who was busy at her store—but Sharon was not the person, particularly today. Today Teri wanted to keep things as placid as possible for Daniel's sake.

Thirty minutes later, Gus called Teri from the phone in the barn. "Miss Farr, I just wanted to let you know Mrs. Bailey called and said Polly wouldn't be coming to her lesson today," he said. "She said she'd call when Polly was ready to come back."

"She called the phone in the barn?" Teri asked. "When Polly has to miss a lesson, Mrs. Bailey always calls me at the house."

"Well, that's what I thought, but she said the line was busy."

"I haven't been on the phone. And she said she'd call when Polly was ready to come back? She didn't say Polly would be here for her regular lesson next week?"

"Well, yeah, that's what she said. I asked if Polly was sick, and Mrs. Bailey said no then she said yes real quick."

"Which means she was lying," Teresa said flatly. "She didn't want Polly taking lessons here anymore because of the Roscoe Byrnes business yesterday."

"Oh now, Miss Farr, don't get upset." Gus was making an unsuccessful attempt to sound cheerfully scornful. "Mrs. Bailey is kind of flighty sometimes. Maybe she just decided to send Polly to summer camp or the Baileys are gonna take a vacation."

"Then why couldn't she have said so?" Gus was obviously trying to soothe Teresa's nerves, but she could hear the insincerity in his voice. Lying didn't come easily to Gus Gibbs. "Mrs. Bailey is not in the least flighty and she told me back in early June that she wasn't sending Polly to camp and also that they wouldn't be taking a family vacation until August."

"Well, there could be another reason—"

"Yes, and I know what it is." Teri drew a deep breath, forcing herself not to fall apart because one student had canceled. "Oh well, at least Cleopatra gets the day off. How is Daniel doing?"

"Just fine. He's not timid around Caesar. He won't ride without his hat on, though."

Teri couldn't help smiling. "As long as Caesar doesn't mind the hat, we shouldn't, either. Sharon and I will be down to get Daniel in about half an hour."

As soon as Teri put down the receiver and turned around, though, Sharon was already rising from the kitchen table. "Daniel has been with the horse long enough for one day. I think I should take him home now. I don't want him so cranky he won't take his nap."

"Cranky! A *nap*!" Teri knew her voice was rising, but she couldn't stop objecting. "Sharon, he's almost eight. You can't tell me he still takes a nap! Good heavens, they don't have nap time in school!"

"When he was in nursery school—"

"Exactly. Nursery school. He was what—three, four?

You're just snatching him away because Polly Bailey's mother canceled!"

Sharon's color heightened in her tight face, but she kept her voice maddeningly calm. "Teri, please don't get so worked up about this. I couldn't care less about Polly Bailey. I simply think Daniel has been on that horse too long already. His legs will be sore or . . . or . . ."

"Or what?" Teri flashed. Then she noticed how stiffly Sharon stood, how she'd lifted her chin as if steeling herself for a verbal or perhaps even physical attack. She acts like she's *afraid* of me, Teresa thought, both shocked and hurt. "I'm sorry I snapped at you." The apology was genuine, but even Teri thought it sounded artificial. "I'm certainly not going to hold Daniel hostage here if you want to take him home." To Teri's horror, she felt her throat tightening as tears threatened. "I just hate knowing . . ."

"Knowing what?" Sharon asked cautiously.

"Knowing that my own sister-in-law wants to get her child away back to safety, and that means getting him away from *me* as soon as possible."

CHAPTER NINE

1

IT COULDN'T HAVE BEEN more than twenty minutes after Sharon had led a weeping Daniel to her car and driven away with unusual speed when Kent called. "Just wanted to let you know we have a buyer for the house," he said abruptly.

"The house?" Teresa repeated blankly, still ruffled by Sharon's hasty departure.

"Dad's house. You know, the one we've been trying to unload for nearly eight years? The realtor just called me and said someone offered to buy it for twenty thousand below our asking price. Considering how long it's been vacant, I think we can lower the price to get rid of it. At least I'm willing. How about you?"

"My God, yes." Teresa was stunned. For so long she'd thought no one would buy the house where two people had been murdered. Just a few months ago, she and Kent had talked about waiting another year and then tearing down the house and selling only the lot, which was in an excellent neighborhood. "Do you have any idea who's up for buying the local House of Death? That's what a lot of people call it, you know."

"Yes, I know. Especially teenagers. They think the house is cool because of its gory history. Anyway, the realtor didn't say much, but it seems the potential buyers are a young couple from California and they thought the house's history was intriguing—it seemed to be more of a selling point than a detraction, because the husband is a writer of horror novels. He's not famous, but he's sold a couple of books. I have no idea why the couple decided to move to West Virginia, and in my shock over being able to finally unload the place, I've already forgotten their name," Kent added dryly.

"Who cares?" Teresa asked, elated that the place was selling. So often she had overheard people referring to the house in which she'd grown up as "horrible" or "a house where no normal person would want to live." Yet she hadn't liked the idea of destroying the house, in spite of its tragic past, because her mother had loved it, appreciating its fine craftsmanship, cherishing its history that dated back to 1925, when it was built. Nothing bad had ever happened in that house—nothing bad until Hugh Farr had bought it and soon begun setting off a chain of events that would end in murder.

"So is it all right that I told the realtor we accept the offer?" Kent was asking.

"Thanks for waiting to ask me first," Teresa answered wryly. "But yes, it's all right. We still have to move out all the furniture. What will we do with it?"

"Taken care of," Kent said briskly. "You go to the house tomorrow and see if there's anything you want right now. I don't want anything and neither does Sharon. After all, Wendy got rid of most of the stuff that belonged to Mom.

Anyway, I'll let Jason know, too. Maybe there's something left in Celeste's room he wants."

"I doubt it and who could blame him? His daughter was almost murdered in there," Teresa said, feeling a shiver even in the heat of the afternoon. "But after all these years, he might feel different."

"Yeah, maybe." Kent sounded hurried and distracted. "Anyway, I've rented a storage space and arranged to have the furniture moved there in a couple of days."

"You don't waste any time, do you?"

"I just want to get this deal done. I thought you'd feel the same way, but if I've jumped the gun . . ."

"No. I want the deal done, too, as you put it. I'll check out the house tomorrow, and if I want anything, the movers you've hired can bring it here."

"Great." Kent paused, and Teresa had a feeling that for a minute he'd stopped shuffling papers, signing his name to letters and contracts, and given himself time to think. "Teri, I will be so glad to be rid of that place. For eight years, we've made sure it's well maintained. I know I should go by regularly to make certain it *is* being maintained properly, but frankly, I usually assign that task to a guy I trust who works for me because I don't even like to think about the house, much less look at it."

"I haven't even driven past it for over a year, and I haven't been inside since a couple of weeks after the murders. Now neither one of us has to worry about it anymore. It's finally become someone else's problem."

"Thank God." Kent sounded happier than she'd heard him for a long time. "This is shaping up to be a good day. By the way, how did my son do during his first riding lesson? Was he tired after the first whole hour?"

"Well . . ." Teresa hated to spoil Kent's mood, but there was no point in lying to him. He'd just find out the truth from Daniel. "He didn't stay for a whole hour."

"Why not?" Kent asked warily.

"Sharon got nervous and thought half an hour was long enough for his first lesson and she—"

"Made him leave." Kent's voice somehow sounded flat and angry at the same time.

Teresa immediately regretted having said anything to him except that the lesson had gone well. He *should* have heard what happened from either Daniel or Sharon, not from her. She wanted to smooth things over a bit. "Kent, we both know Sharon wasn't crazy about the idea of riding lessons. Then, after half an hour, I heard that the mother of one of my other students canceled—probably for good— and I made a ridiculously big deal over it. Anyway, I'm certain *I* gave Sharon a reason to think she should take Daniel home."

"And was he happy to be taken home early?" Kent asked sarcastically.

"Daniel had a good time while he was here, and as I said, maybe half an hour was enough time for him. You ride, so you know if you're not used to it and you stay on the horse too long, particularly if it's your first time on a horse, you can strain muscles and—"

"Don't evade my question, Teri. How did he act when Sharon took him home?"

"He wasn't happy."

"Define 'wasn't happy.' "

Teri felt cornered. "He cried," she admitted, and her brother swore under his breath. "But even if he'd stayed longer, he probably would have cried when it was time to go home. He just loves the pony, Kent. And he was all dressed up. I think he had plans to stay the whole day and thought he could charm Sharon into letting him. This is really nothing to get mad about, Kent. Sharon knows her child. She knows what's best for him," Teresa ended unconvincingly.

"You don't have to sugarcoat how Sharon acted, Teri. I'll be having a talk with her about this as soon as possible."

"Oh, Kent, don't overreact about today's lesson. I know she needs to lighten up about the riding lessons, but give her some time. Riding *can* be dangerous. Sharon just hasn't seen how particularly careful Josh and Gus are with children."

"I'm mad about more than her worrying over riding lessons. This hoopla she's creating over the lessons is part of a problem that's been brewing between Sharon and me for months, and it's time I finally had it out with her."

"What problem?" Teri couldn't help asking.

Kent hung up with a bang and Teresa's mood sank even lower. Certainly Kent needed to talk to Sharon about her possessiveness of Daniel, but not when he was angry. She knew they would have an argument tonight and it would be Teri's fault for stirring up his emotions. If there was one thing a couple having problems did *not* need, it was a meddling relative—

The phone rang again and when Teresa looked at Caller ID and saw the call was coming from the barn, she felt like not answering. More trouble with Sharon probably, she thought. Dread filling her mind like a dark cloud, Teresa picked up the phone and said, "What's the problem, Gus?"

"Oh, no problem!" Teri instantly recognized his falsely cheerful tone. "Just wanted to let you know you have a couple of unexpected visitors."

Teresa waited a moment, fully expecting him to say, *The sheriff and his deputy are here to question you about the night of the murders*. She heard voices, one sounding like a young woman's; then came the overly loud laugh Gus used to mask surprise or dismay. Finally, a notch below yelling, Teresa demanded, "Gus, who the hell is at the barn?"

"Well, you'll never guess," Gus boomed. "It's Jason Warner and his little girl. Miss Farr, Celeste Warner's come to see you!"

2

Celeste!

Teresa stood speechless, her mouth slightly open. Since the murders, not one day had gone by that she hadn't thought of the lovely child with large, sad blue eyes who Wendy had dragged into the Farr home after her triumphant marriage to Hugh.

At first, Teresa had decided to be nothing more than polite to the girl. Then Teresa had noticed how Celeste crept around the house as if she was trying to be as unobtrusive as possible, how she'd avoided her new stepfather, and how she often simply sat on the floor of her suffocatingly frilled and ruffled bedroom holding her large teddy bear and chanting childish rhymes of her own creation.

One day Teresa had heard Celeste pouring out her loneliness and unhappiness to the teddy bear, Yogi, who seemed to be her only friend. Touched, Teresa had entered Celeste's room and tried to talk to her, but the child had been too timid or too wary of her new stepsister to answer. After several more tries, though, Celeste had begun to talk more, and within a month she and Teresa regularly played and giggled together like contemporaries. Soon, Teri realized she'd come to love the child as much as if she'd been Marielle's child instead of Wendy's.

Then, after the murders, a seriously wounded Celeste had been wrenched away from Teri. She'd thought she'd never see the girl again, but at last, unbelievably, Celeste had come to see her. She was down in the barn as if she were a regular visitor, not the child so many people once thought Teresa had tried to murder.

After a moment of stunned silence, Teresa said, "Tell Celeste and her father to come up to the house. No! Celeste will want to see the horses, so I'll come down to the barn first."

"You're right," Gus said jovially. "She's near hypnotized

by Eclipse. She said she wanted to meet *your* horse before any of the others. Well, see you in a few minutes!"

Teresa dashed into the living room, glanced at herself in a mirror hanging above a long bookcase, smoothed her hair, and tucked her blouse into her jeans. Then she looked at Sierra waiting expectantly by the door. The dog was boisterous when meeting new people, but Celeste had loved dogs almost as much as she'd loved horses. Teresa decided to take a chance that Sierra wouldn't frighten the girl and clipped on the dog's leash.

They hurried down the slope from Teresa's house, and as they reached the open barn doors Teresa heard the murmur of voices. With her sharp hearing, Sierra immediately recognized that some were unfamiliar, and she barked loudly. "Hush," Teresa commanded. "Celeste doesn't know you. Don't scare her."

Actually, Teresa felt a tingle of uneasiness at seeing Celeste. They had been so close, but that closeness had been eight years ago when Celeste was just a child. She was a teenager now, and she'd been through hell. In the years since Teresa had come back from college, she'd never once seen Celeste. The small bits of reliable information Teresa had been able to glean about Celeste, though, let her know that in spite of the girl's silence, she did not suffer from any organic mental damage. The silence was merely the result of shock. Still, before the ambulance arrived to bear away the seriously injured child, one of the last people Celeste had seen eight years ago in that house of carnage had been Teresa.

As soon as she walked into the barn, though, a slender girl turned away from Eclipse, looked at Teresa and Sierra for a moment, then smiled and ran forward. "Teri! Oh, Teri, how much I've missed you!" Celeste exclaimed joyfully, flinging herself into Teresa's opened arms. They hugged fiercely for a moment. Then the girl stepped back. "You look just the same!"

"*You* certainly don't!" Teresa smiled as her gaze moved quickly over Celeste, whom she judged to be about five foot five. She had her mother's pale blond hair color, but otherwise she looked nothing like Wendy, who with youth, attractive clothes, and plenty of makeup still only achieved a sexy, piquant prettiness. Celeste was a true beauty with flawless ivory skin, large cornflower blue eyes with long, dark lashes, a narrow nose, and perfectly molded lips of a natural rosy hue. She wore a dated, almost childish pink dress, which Teresa immediately guessed had been made by Celeste's grandmother Fay. Celeste's long hair was held back with a pink velvet ribbon, and not a trace of makeup appeared on her face. "Celeste, you were a beautiful child," Teresa said sincerely, "but you're an even more beautiful young lady."

Celeste hugged her again. Sierra let out another strident bark and Teresa was glad for the diversion, because she felt tears rising in her eyes. "Celeste, this is Sierra," she said briskly. "She makes a lot of noise, but she's never bitten anyone. I hope you're not afraid—"

But Celeste was already kneeling, rubbing Sierra under her big pointed ears as the dog's tail flew back and forth in delight. "I'm not afraid of her. I could tell the minute I saw her she's a good dog," Celeste said happily, then bent and spoke directly into Sierra's face. "A good, friendly, *pretty* dog, isn't that right, Sierra?" The dog licked her on the nose and Celeste giggled.

"I hope you don't mind that we just dropped in unannounced." Jason Warner approached Teresa, holding out his hand. When Teri had last seen him, he'd been a youthful-looking thirty-two. Now, at forty, gray heavily laced his light brown hair and the wrinkles in his forehead looked as if they belonged to a man of fifty. He was still lean and looked strong, as if he'd worked at keeping himself in shape, and his smile was warm.

"After Celeste surprised us all when she started talking

again—" Jason broke off, his smile wavering as if emotion were about to overtake him. He swallowed and finished in a rush. "She was determined to come and see you as soon as possible. Her grandmother was . . . busy."

I'll bet, Teri thought. Fay Warner had been convinced Teresa had stabbed Celeste, and even after Byrnes's statement that he'd killed the Farrs, she'd still turned her head away whenever she'd passed Teresa downtown or in the grocery store.

"So Celeste called me at the office," Jason went on, "and I decided to take an early lunch. It was all very spur-of-the-moment. I did call, but your line was busy."

"I was on the phone," Teresa said unnecessarily, then added, "but it's fine. I'm thrilled to see Celeste. I'm glad to see both of you."

Jason smiled again, but he was saved from answering by Celeste, who'd darted over to the palomino. "What's his name?" she asked.

"Conquistador." Teresa joined Celeste and they both stroked the horse. "He belongs to my brother, Kent. I'm just boarding some of these horses, but the black Arabian, Eclipse, and the two ponies, Caesar and Cleopatra, are mine."

Celeste went to each stall, meeting and petting Captain Jack, Sir Lancelot, Bonaparte, and the most recent addition, another quarter horse named Fantasia. As she talked to both Teresa and the horses, Teri noticed that Celeste's speech sounded much younger than that of other teenagers who took lessons at Farr Fields. Teri guessed that during the last few years, Celeste had not interacted in a normal, social way with people her own age and therefore spoke and acted younger than sixteen.

"Gosh, you must be the happiest girl in the world to get to live with all these horses," Celeste told Teresa after she'd given ample attention to each horse. "I love horses. Teri, where's your horse you kept at the other stables? The one you let me ride a long time ago."

"I'm afraid he died a couple of years ago." Celeste's smile immediately faded. "But he was old, Celeste, and he'd had a very good life. Of course I miss him, but he died suddenly and the vet said probably without pain. I guess it was just his time to go."

"Oh," Celeste said tremulously. "Then he didn't get hurt or killed or anything."

He didn't get killed, Teresa thought. He didn't get killed like her mother and Hugh. "No, nothing like that," Teresa reassured the girl fervently. "He wasn't even sick before he died. He just acted tired. Then he lay down one day and didn't get up. He's buried here on my farm. There's a beautiful flowering crabapple tree overhanging his grave and he has a headstone. I put flowers on his grave every August seventh, his birthday."

Celeste still looked heartbroken. "I know everybody has to die sometime, but I don't like it. Still, it's nice that you to put flowers on his grave. Could I help you this year?"

Teresa glanced at Jason, who nodded. "Of course, Celeste. He'd appreciate that."

Celeste turned to Gus and to Josh, who were both trying to look busy while they watched the tenuous encounter between Teresa and Celeste. "Don't you wish horses could live forever?"

Gus looked startled but answered immediately, "Why, we sure do, don't we, Josh?"

Josh obediently nodded. "Yeah. Forever. But they have long lives compared to—" Teresa knew he was about to say "dogs," then caught himself and said, "Some other animals."

"I know." Celeste paused and stared into the distance for a moment. Abruptly she asked, "Teri, do you remember Snowflake?"

Teresa stiffened at the mention of the night-light left at her door by a hooded figure just last night. She tried to relax and smile casually. "Of course I do."

"I wish I still had Snowflake," Celeste said wistfully. "Snowflake and my teddy bear Yogi were full of good luck. Snowflake's light showed me where my toy chest was—the toy chest I hid in the night when Mommy got killed. Yogi helped, too. The doctor said I would've been killed if the knife hadn't gone into him first so it couldn't go all the way into me. But Yogi's gone for good. He got thrown in the trash."

A wave of sadness shadowed Celeste's face and Teresa said, "I'm sorry about Yogi, but he would have been glad he saved your life."

"That's what Daddy says." Suddenly, Celeste looked at Teresa fiercely. "I hope Snowflake isn't gone forever, though. We really need Snowflake for good luck *now*."

"Oh?" Teresa was taken aback by the girl's unexpected vehemence. "Why do we especially need good luck now?"

Celeste stepped closer to Teresa, her blue eyes huge in her pale face, and said intensely, "'Cause what killed Mommy wanted to kill me. It didn't because of you, but it still wants to kill me, and I know it wants to kill you, too."

CHAPTER TEN

1

EVERYONE IN THE BARN seemed to freeze at the sound of Celeste's pronouncement. Although Teresa merely stared at the girl, her mind churned with questions. Who? Why? How do you know? But she didn't trust herself to open her mouth. The questions would come out loud and shrill and terrified.

Jason finally broke the silence, walking toward his daughter and putting his arm around her tense, slender shoulders. "Sweetheart, that's a very dramatic and scary thing to say. Is it what you think?"

"It's what I *know*," Celeste said definitely.

Jason asked calmly, "And how do you know such a thing?"

"Death wanted to kill me before but didn't get me because of Yogi and Snowflake. And because of Teri. I know some people think Teri tried to kill me—people said all kinds of things around me because they thought I couldn't hear just because I didn't talk—but Teri didn't stab me. That's silly. Teri kept Death away from me. So now Death is mad and wants Teri to die, too. It just makes sense."

Finally Teresa spoke. "Honey, a *person* stabbed you and maybe the person isn't around anymore. Maybe it was just a stranger who got into the house that night or someone who was afraid of getting caught and ran away or . . ."

Teresa ran out of words as Celeste shook her head violently. "No, Death is still here. I know because of a smell and a sound and something about a face. It's still sort of jumbled, but I'll remember it better in a few days. I *know* I will.

"Anyway, I didn't talk for so long because I just didn't want to talk about that night. Everybody kept asking me about that night and I didn't want to think about it. But I started talking again when I knew Death was here. At first I was mad at myself for talking. Then I was glad because I had to warn you to be real careful and I had to tell everyone who wants us to stay alive so they can help us." Celeste looked at her father, then whirled and looked at Gus and Josh. "You have to protect Teri or Death's gonna kill her!"

Shaken to the depths of her being, Teresa tried to assure Celeste that she would be as careful as possible. Ten minutes later, she bade the girl and her father a pleasant goodbye when Jason—white-faced and taut—said he must get back to the office. After they left, Gus looked unsettled and asked Teresa if she was being threatened or had reason to be afraid. She lied, telling him everything was well with her, which she could tell he didn't believe. Before he could ask more questions, though, Teresa fled back to her house, Sierra running along beside her, then running circles around her, trying and failing to draw her mistress into an exciting game of chase.

When they got in the house, Teresa closed the front door firmly behind her, locked it, then went into the kitchen and gave Sierra a fresh bowl of water and fixed herself a tall glass of lemonade. She then meandered back into the living room, flopped down on the couch, and moaned, "Can this day get any worse?"

She quickly learned that it could.

Teresa hadn't even finished her lemonade when the phone rang again. Reluctantly, she rose from the couch and picked up the handset from the receiver next to a wing chair. Before she could say a word, Sharon asked caustically, "Well, proud of yourself?"

"What?" Teresa asked. "Proud of what?"

"Of tattling, of meddling, of generally causing as much trouble as you could between my husband and me?"

"But I didn't—"

"You didn't do what? Get right on the hot line to tell Kent I'd taken Daniel away from his lesson early? Whine and moan and make him mad that your half-crazy sister-in-law had hurt your feelings?"

"Sharon, I swear that is not what I meant to do. You know me better than that!"

"Oh, do I? Let's see what I know about you. I know that you've always leaned on your big brother, even when you were a teenager, causing trouble at home and then expecting Kent to take your side against Hugh for you, which he did, making Hugh hate Kent as much as he hated you."

A flame of anger was beginning to lick its way through Teresa. "I don't know that my father actually *hated* me *or* Kent, but if he did, it wasn't because Kent took up for me sometimes. It's because my father didn't know how to love anyone. He only knew coercion and intimidation."

"He loved Wendy."

"Oh, he did not and you know it! Sharon, what is wrong with you? Are you so mad at me for telling your husband you left the lesson early that you can't even look at the past with clear vision, now? Wendy was a sexy toy for Dad— someone to make him feel young and manly. And poor little Celeste meant nothing to him. My mother meant nothing to him."

"And *you* meant nothing to him, so you decided to make him feel the same way about Kent. That's why he gave us so much trouble about getting married. That's why Kent almost didn't . . . oh, never mind."

"No, finish your sentence." Teresa suddenly felt an icy calm wash over her. "That's why Kent almost didn't . . . what? Marry you? That's why he almost left you single and pregnant?"

"Teresa!"

"Oh, don't sound so appalled, Sharon. I don't know why you and Kent think no one knows you were pregnant with Daniel when you got married. People can count, for God's sake, and women aren't pregnant for six months and then deliver seven-pound babies."

Teresa felt that now was the time to cut this conversation off, but the stress of the morning seemed to have loosened the cap she usually kept tightly shut on her emotions, and she could not make herself stop talking. She closed her eyes as she heard herself going on in a quick, cutting voice.

"Kent standing up for me a few times against Dad had nothing to do with our father threatening to cut Kent out of his will to make Farr Coal Company completely mine," she continued. "Dad did that because he had this ridiculous idea you weren't good enough for Kent. And notice that I said *ridiculous*. Also, Wendy had plans for Farr Coal to eventually go to the child she was going to have with Dad. Anyway, I admit Kent dragged his feet about the marriage when Dad said he was going to change his will if Kent married you.

"I understand my brother," Teresa continued, unable to stop herself. "I know he'd worked most of his life to be the best at everything he did so he'd be worthy in my father's eyes of taking over the company. When he saw the carrot he'd been chasing most of his life about to be snatched away, he wavered."

"Teresa!" Sharon choked out again.

"Yes, he wavered. I didn't know why Kent was so jumpy that last month before Dad was killed, but the night after Daniel's birth, when Kent had drunk a little too much celebratory champagne, he admitted to me what Dad had been promising to do if Kent married you. Dad had pressured, and bullied and threatened, and in return, all Kent had done was falter slightly, but Kent couldn't forgive himself even for that. Good heavens, Sharon, Kent is human. He loved you but—"

"He loved Farr Coal Company more?"

"That is not what I said," Teri said in complete annoyance. "If you would just settle down and listen to me for a minute—"

"I have listened to you all I intend to for today. Maybe for a whole lifetime. You're just like your father, Teresa. You are bossy, interfering, and a troublemaker. You think everything and everyone is yours. You'd like nothing better than to tear my entire family apart. You have never liked me, and you'd connive with anyone to ruin my happiness. Well, let me warn you now that no one is going to take away from me the people I love. *No* one, no matter what I have to do to prevent it!"

Sharon slammed down the phone. Teresa held the receiver a moment, shocked and too shaken to move. She slowly hung up, thought about calling back, then decided Sharon needed time to cool down. Lots of time to cool down, because she wasn't just upset over Kent being angry with her for dragging Daniel away from his lesson. She was upset over things that had happened eight years ago, things that had happened right before the murders, when she'd been young, in love, and pregnant, and thought her dream of being Mrs. Kent Farr and proud mother of his beloved son was going up in smoke, all because of one irascible, selfish, downright cruel man the world would never miss.

Teresa couldn't say she blamed Sharon for feeling so resentful and angry when it came to Hugh. Teri felt the same way. The problem was that Sharon seemed to be attributing some of Hugh's awful personality faults and his worst manipulation tactics to Teresa. A year ago Sharon hadn't seemed to feel this way about her, Teri thought. But now, Teri believed Sharon was on her way to hating her almost as much as Sharon had hated Hugh Farr.

2

The afternoon was miserable for Teresa. First, she'd lost one of her best students, for she was under no delusion that Mrs. Bailey was ever going to let Polly resume her lessons. Next, Sharon had jerked a crushed Daniel away from the lesson he'd been looking forward to for weeks. Then Teri'd had a long upsetting talk with Kent. Next, Celeste had paid an unexpected visit to tell Teri someone still wanted both of them dead. Finally, she'd had a brief, fiery call from Sharon, to whom she'd said things that Sharon would probably hold against her forever.

"I had high hopes for today," Teri said aloud to her reflection in the mirror. "What the hell went wrong?"

Unable simply to brush bad encounters away, Teresa had a habit of dissecting scenes and conversations that had gone wrong, trying to find out where things had begun to deteriorate, determined to discover what she'd done to make things worse. In the past, Mac had teased her about the habit, telling her it was a useless form of self-flagellation, but she'd never been able to stop. She certainly wasn't able to stop on this chaotic day.

For the rest of the afternoon, Teresa wandered around the house, going over and over her conversation with Kent, then with Sharon, then picturing the trouble that would ensue between the two that evening. Teresa kept telling herself it wasn't her fault. Kent had asked her about the lesson. Was she supposed to lie to him? No. But she could have said he'd just have to wait and hear about it from Sharon and Daniel. The truth would have come out, but she wouldn't have had a hand in it.

And not only had she caused trouble between Kent and his wife; she'd also insulted Mac yesterday when all he'd done was come to offer his support. How presumptuous of her to suppose he'd wanted to do any more than tell her he was sorry about Byrnes's new bid for attention and that he still believed in her. Her face almost burned at the memory of how certain she'd been that he was trying to re-establish their old romance. She'd humiliated herself and she'd hurt him. My God, she thought, she'd told him his own mother believed her son might be capable of violence!

She felt bad for any trouble she'd caused between Kent and Sharon, but as much as Teresa hated to admit it, she was more miserable about the hurt she might have caused Mac. By eight o'clock, she was nearly writhing in shame over what she'd said to him last night. Just because she was going through a hard time didn't give her the right to lash out at him, she reprimanded herself. "I have to apologize to him," she told Sierra, who'd faithfully followed her mistress's constant pacing throughout the afternoon. "I'm going to his club tonight and I'm going to apologize!" She'd almost added, "And you're not going to stop me!"

Then Teri looked down at the loyal but tired and bewildered brown dog with her big, pointy ears and decided that in less than forty-eight hours, she had let this thing with Roscoe Byrnes turn her into a wreck. She could have ignored what he'd said. Carmen was right—Byrnes was probably only trying to get attention during the last days of his life. That and maybe, if he was smart enough, to cast doubt about who really murdered Wendy and Hugh Farr, to turn the original suspect's life into hell.

Well, if so, Byrnes had certainly gotten his wish, Teresa

thought, all because she had let him. She, not Byrnes, had lost control and already damaged feelings because she was shocked and frightened. What she had to do now, Teri told herself, was try to repair some of that damage.

She grabbed her beige tote bag, fished inside for her keys—swearing tomorrow she would clean out the deplorable amount of junk she'd stashed inside—and rushed for the door. She stopped when she noticed Sierra following, assuming her most plaintive look when the lack of a leash meant she wasn't going to be accompanying her mistress. "I'm sorry, but I can't take you tonight," Teri said. "But I promise to bring back some treats."

The moon shone silvery against a slate gray sky. Earlier, she'd heard that a thunderstorm was predicted for around ten o'clock, but she couldn't feel it in the air. She had no doubt the horses could sense it, though. They were extremely sensitive to weather changes.

Teresa drove straight to Club Rendezvous. The parking lot was a third full, quite good for this early hour on a weeknight when there was no band, indicating the club's popularity.

As Teri emerged from her car, she wished she'd taken time to change from the jeans and turquoise blouse she'd worn all day, but when she entered the club, she saw that at least half of its patrons also wore jeans. The mood was clearly more casual on a weeknight than the weekend, she thought as recorded sounds of John Mayer's "Waiting on the World to Change" washed over her. She went to the bar and asked for Mac.

"He's in his office," the young bartender told her. "Want me to call him and ask him to come out?"

"No, I'm Teresa Farr, a friend of his. I'll just go to his office."

"Mr. MacKenzie doesn't like for customers to come to his office—" Teresa turned and scanned the club, spotted the hallway near the door, and began walking toward it.

"Miss Farr," the bartender called. "You can't just go back there. Miss Farr—"

The bartender's protests followed her past the dance floor. Either he'd stopped talking or he was on the phone to Mac as she nearly ran to the back of the hall where long ago she and Mac had planned to place his office. And there it was. For some reason Teri couldn't identify, she was absurdly pleased to find that Mac hadn't changed their original layout of the club. Even if his office door did bear a brass plate engraved with the word PRIVATE beneath his name, she tapped twice and flung it open. Obviously surprised in spite of the phone in his hand—no doubt with the bartender on the other end warning him that a frantic woman was headed for his office—Mac stood up as Teri burst out with, "I'm sorry."

From behind his large mahogany desk, Mac stared at her for a moment. No smile of welcome warmed his strong features. He simply stood motionless, dressed casually in jeans and a green shirt with the long sleeves rolled halfway up his strong, tanned forearms. In an instant, she took in his dark hair gleaming beneath an overhead light, his greenish-brown eyes flecked with gold narrowing slightly, his jaw tightening. Finally, he muttered, "It's okay," into the phone and put it down on the handset. He continued to stand behind the desk and stare at her.

Teri closed the door behind her and began talking quickly, almost breathlessly. "I've been miserable all day. Well, I was last night, too, after you left. What I said to you was awful. Your mother did call me the day she was fired and begged me not to tell you about Dad hitting me or his threatening to go to the police about you, and she did say she was afraid of what you might do, but yesterday I implied she thought you were capable of violence—"

"You didn't imply it; you said it," Mac interrupted icily.

"Yes, I *said* it. But I know that's not what she meant. She was afraid there would be a physical fight, that's all—a fight that might end up with you being arrested for assault on Dad."

"And she was right. If I'd known what he'd done to you, I would have knocked the dickens out of him. He deserved it. But I didn't deserve what you dished out to me yesterday—implying my own mother thought I could be a murderer. That was below the belt, Teri, and I can't figure out the reason why, unless you were still paying me back for kissing another woman when we were engaged."

"I wasn't!" A mental sensor seemed to click in Teresa's mind, forcing her to tell the truth. "I mean, I was in a way, but not the way you think."

"Oh?" Mac raised an eyebrow. "Why don't you tell me what *I* think?"

"Mac, please don't make this so difficult." Teresa felt beads of perspiration popping out along her hairline, and she stepped closer to his desk, spreading her hands almost in supplication. "I can't explain exactly what was going on in my mind, but—"

"You mean you *won't* explain exactly what was going on in your mind."

"All right, dammit, I don't want to explain it right now. That's not what I came here to do. I came to apologize and to tell you I know now just as I knew eight years ago that your mother didn't think you'd kill anyone. My God, if I'd thought your own mother believed you capable of murder, would I have become engaged to you a year later?"

"Oh, I don't know," Mac said slowly, then leaned across his desk, his face and voice sardonic. "After all, I would have been killing two people you hated."

A short, flaming silence burned for a moment between them before Teri bent forward across the desk and slapped Mac's face. Given the angle at which it was delivered, the slap couldn't have done more than sting, but Mac's hazel eyes flew wide in surprise and his hand moved upward toward his cheek. Teresa turned and whipped out of his office. As she ran down the hall, she heard him calling, "Teri! Wait!" But she didn't stop.

In what felt like seconds she was in her car, careening out of the parking lot. Although she tried to keep her gaze straight ahead, it wavered for just a moment—a moment in which she saw Mac standing outside the doors of Club Rendezvous, his hand still at his cheek, his expression shocked and contrite.

3

Teresa drove blindly and furiously out of the parking lot and not until she was halfway through town did she realize that she was covered with a sheen of cold perspiration. She was also going fifteen miles over the speed limit. She abruptly slowed down, took a couple of deep breaths, and felt a tear run down her right cheek. She brushed it away with the back of her hand—a gesture that reminded her of a pathetic Daniel being led sobbing from her home and from the barn—while another tear slid down her left cheek.

She had slapped Mac. Slapped him across the face! She'd never done such a thing in her life and she was horrified. She had been furious and appalled when her father had struck her eight years ago and now she was behaving just like him! Was she no better than Hugh Farr? Was this inclination to strike and hurt hereditary?

"Oh, God," she moaned aloud, feeling shattered by what she had just done. She had gone to see Mac to apologize. "Some apology," she muttered again. "First you tell him his mother doesn't trust him; then you slap him. He's lucky you broke off the engagement before he suffered serious bodily harm."

Teresa turned on the radio in time to hear the weather forecast telling her of increasing wind speed because of the approaching thunderstorm. She jammed in a CD, then decided she needed quiet. She couldn't even concentrate on music, which usually calmed her nerves and diverted her mind from problems. As she drove along in silence, she gradually became aware that she'd driven most of the way home. On her left were a drugstore and a bank, and finally on the right was a cemetery. Across from the cemetery glared the lights of a convenience store. Glancing down at her gasoline gauge, she saw that she was dangerously low on fuel. Besides, she had promised to bring home a treat for Sierra.

Teri turned into the store's lot and pulled up to a pump. Her hands trembled as she removed her gas cap and inserted the gasoline pump nozzle. Across from her, two teenage girls in a beat-up sedan gestured flamboyantly while alternately grimacing and throwing back their heads in abandoned laughter. Finally, two teenage boys swaggered to the sedan, and, judging by the squeals produced when they immediately passed around cans of Coke, Teresa guessed someone had brought along liquor. A man at least thirty years older than Teri with a potbelly and sparse hair sauntered past her and drawled, "Lookin' good tonight, babe." "Thanks, sugar pie," she replied sweetly. "How're your wife and grandkids?" An aged SUV pulled up, driven by a harried-looking woman yelling at the five children squabbling in the car.

A stiff breeze suddenly blew Teresa's hair across her face, and she remembered the radio announcer's prediction of increasing wind speed. She tucked her hair behind her ears, feeling so tired, frayed, and upset she was tempted not to bother filling the car's gas tank. Then, as if someone above had read her thoughts, the pump finally automatically shut off. The tank was full at last.

Sighing in gratitude, she entered the store, picked up two cans of Sierra's favorite food along with a package of beef jerky, the dog's favorite treat, grabbed a container of fresh cream for her morning coffee, then took her place in an unusually long line. Tonight it seemed as if everyone in Point Pleasant who wasn't at Club Rendezvous had decided to stop at the Speedway convenience store. By the time she'd reached the register, she added a package of M&M's and a tabloid newspaper to her haul.

And now what? Teresa thought as she got back into her car. An evening of television? Reading? Listening to music and drinking wine? A rowdy game of fetch with Sierra?

As Teri turned onto the narrow road that led to her house, the wind picked up, sending the leafy limbs of sycamore trees swaying and a fat white cat skittering across the road in front of her. She braked for the cat, then looked up at the sky—black with a bank of billowy gray clouds moving in from the west.

Teresa knew the rustling of grass and leaves would make the horses restless. Gus and Josh were miracle workers when it came to calming her equine crew. Creeping ahead, she was peering at the cottage where Gus and Josh lived, looking for lights and their rugged SUV, when something dashed into the road.

Teresa slammed on the brake. The headlights seemed to have frozen a figure wearing a long, hooded black raincoat. The loose-fitting raincoat whirled as the figure turned and looked right at her. Teri caught a glimpse of a pale face and wide, startled eyes—blue eyes surrounded by heavy shadows—before long black hair blew across the ghostly features like a veil. Instantly, the figure ran for the mass of trees on the left side of the road and disappeared.

For an instant, Teresa sat mesmerized in her car. No, it couldn't be, she thought. It was the prowler. It was a teenager rushing for shelter before the storm hit. It wasn't; it couldn't be—

Teri nearly tore her seat belt loose and jumped out of the car. "Hey, who are you?" she yelled in a shaky voice.

As the tree limbs thrashed and she heard the first grumble of distant thunder, her gut feelings washed over her like a huge, cold wave and she called with desperate abandon, "Mom! Mommy, come back!"

CHAPTER ELEVEN

1

TERESA STOOD IN THE road, gazing at the mass of trees where the person had vanished, both desiring to and afraid of pursuing the figure she believed could be her mother. Teri's thoughts whirled. What if her mother had been alive all of this time? What could her reason be for returning after eight years? Had she heard about Roscoe Lee Byrnes's statement that he hadn't murdered Hugh and Wendy Farr and knew suspicion would once again fall on Teresa? If Marielle had committed the murders, had she gotten well enough, strong enough, to protect her daughter this time? Had she come home to confess?

No, Teresa thought vehemently. Her mother was dead. She *had* to be dead. She wouldn't have simply vanished off the face of the earth for eight years. It wasn't possible. Or was it? Just how hard would it be to assume another person's identity? As far as anyone knew, Marielle had no money or credit cards with her when she disappeared. She couldn't have used credit cards without being traced anyway. Could someone have given her enough cash to go far away from Point Pleasant? And what about identification? Eventually Marielle would have needed a birth certificate, a driver's license, a Social Security number. Given the state she was in when the murders occurred, she certainly couldn't have managed to acquire the documents by herself. Someone would have had to help her. But who? Obviously someone who cared deeply for her.

As the wind grew even stronger, whipping Teresa's hair into a tangled mess, raising chill bumps on her arms beneath the thin, cotton blouse, she realized she'd been standing outside her vehicle for at least five minutes. Her car headlights pierced the darkness straight ahead, throwing the road into sharp relief against the walls of trees on either side of the road. Even if the person who'd run into their shelter to hide was making the sound of a person running, Teri couldn't have heard it above the noise of leaves slapping together and the creaking of some slender branches. Cold, stinging raindrops finally began spattering her. With a mixture of reluctance and relief, Teresa climbed somewhat dazedly back into her car and headed for home.

She pulled her Buick into the garage and pressed the automatic-door remote control. The heavy garage door behind her car rolled down and shut with a reassuring thud. Still shuddering, Teresa opened the door leading from the garage into a small entrance hall beside the kitchen. Sierra had heard the garage door grinding down and waited for Teri, tail flying as she emitted the high squeaks that always signaled joy. Immediately sensing her mistress's mood, though, the dog backed off. "Good," Teresa praised. "I can't play right now, but I remembered your treats." She pulled the beef jerky out of the store bag, ripped open the package, and tossed a couple of strips onto the floor.

While Sierra began eating diligently, Teresa rushed to the front of the house and turned on the three bright lights lining the roof of the porch. The knoll leading from her house down to the field blazed to life. The sight of rain gleaming on grass wasn't overly cheerful, she thought, but at least the land in front of her home bore no human presence—no presence in a long, black, hooded raincoat.

Teri took a deep breath and after making sure the front door was locked and dead-bolted, walked as steadily as she could to the phone. In a moment, Kent barked, "Hello," in a sharp, angry voice.

"Kent," Teresa managed. "Kent—"

"Teri? If Sharon is there, put her on the phone this instant," he demanded.

His command took Teresa by surprise. For a moment, she went blank. Then her mind began to function again. "Sharon isn't here. What's wrong? Is Daniel all right?"

"No, Daniel is not all right." Kent took a deep breath. "Sharon and I had a disagreement—hell, who am I kidding?—Sharon and I had a loud fight about her ruining Daniel's riding lesson."

"Kent, I shouldn't have told you—"

"I would have known anyway. It turns out he's cried off and on all day because he's so disappointed about the lesson—he's cried until he's nauseated, and I am not going to have my son's health endangered because his mother is smothering him under the guise of protecting him."

"I'm so sorry," Teri said automatically.

Kent rushed on. "Sharon's turning him into a neurotic child. And to top it all off, she's furious with you for telling me she snatched Daniel from his lesson after only half an hour."

Teri was silent for a moment. She'd told herself all day

she shouldn't get further involved in this conflict between Kent and Sharon. She'd already made Sharon angry, and no matter what Kent said, Teri knew she'd been partially responsible for the obviously bad argument between her brother and sister-in-law. "Maybe you can solve this if you just talk about it instead of fighting," Teresa said cautiously.

"Sharon won't *talk*. She just *rants*!" Teri felt like telling Kent he, too, was doing a good job of ranting, but she knew now was not the time to point out flaws in his behavior. "She's probably run home to Daddy," Kent continued. "He's the root of our problems. If Gabe hadn't spoiled Sharon so badly her whole life, she wouldn't think everything should go *her* way. She wouldn't think I should have no say in the way Daniel is raised because she doesn't think of him as *our* son but only as *her* son!"

"I think this time her behavior has more to do with me than with her being spoiled," Teri finally ventured. "It's true that she's overprotective of Daniel, but frankly, I think she's scared to death of having him in my presence because she's never been sure I *didn't* kill Dad and Wendy, and Roscoe Byrnes's bombshell yesterday just made everything worse."

Kent inhaled sharply. "That's . . . ridiculous! Sharon would never think . . . that."

The sharply inhaled breath, the hollow, fumbling tone of his words, told Teri she'd hit the nail on the head. Sharon doubted her and she'd voiced those doubts to Kent, who was now trying in his inept way to comfort his sister.

"Well, maybe it is ridiculous," Teresa said for Kent's sake.

"It is," Kent answered promptly, a slight edge of relief in his voice. "Let's just forget Sharon for now. When you called, Teri, you sounded upset, not that I let you get out more than my name before I started in on my problems. Tell me—what's wrong at *your* home?"

"Well . . ." Teresa suddenly lost her nerve and regretted calling her brother because he was already wired and besides, he'd think she was crazy.

"Well *what*?" Kent's voice softened. "I know you're thinking you shouldn't have called me at all, and certainly not after I've had a fight with Sharon. But Sharon and I fight a lot and we always get through it, so stop feeling guilty or responsible. And Teri, although you're the strongest, most independent woman I've ever known, I'm still your big brother, so please do me the favor of turning to me now."

"Okay. That's sweet of you, Kent. But don't interrupt me. You interrupt all the time and it makes me—"

"I don't interrupt," Kent stated.

"I rest my case."

Kent sighed again. "You're right," he said in defeat. "I promise not to say a word until you tell me I can speak."

"That will be a first," Teri muttered dryly, "but here goes."

Teresa told Kent that she'd gone out earlier, leaving out the part about visiting Mac at Club Rendezvous, then about turning onto the road leading to her home just as the wind before the storm hit. "The trees were thrashing and I was driving slowly. Suddenly someone ran in front of me—a tall, slender person wearing a black raincoat with a hood. I only caught a glimpse of the face before wind blew hair across it. But there was a moment when I could see clearly—as clearly as possible considering the weather," Teresa said earnestly. "The person had a pale face, sort of sunken eyes—blue eyes, I'm fairly sure—and black hair, long black hair, thick and straight just like mine."

Teri paused. "The person looked right at me, then dashed into the woods beside the road. I got out of the car, but I didn't follow. I couldn't make myself. But, Kent, I *know* who I saw tonight. It was our mother!"

2

Teresa braced herself. Kent was going to either state positively that she did not see their mother or mock her as being silly and fanciful. For some reason, she could not take her eyes off the second hand of the clock on her mantle. Thirty seconds had passed before Kent said quietly, "Teri, where did you say you saw Mom?"

She closed her eyes. Her brother's voice had the quiet, careful tone people used with the mentally ill. "I said I saw her on the road to my house," she returned levelly. "She ran in front of my car. I almost hit her."

"And then she ran away."

"Yes. She darted into the stand of trees beside the road."

"And you didn't follow her."

"No."

"Why not, if you were convinced this person was Mom?"

Kent's question drew her up sharply. What could she say? That she was both afraid it was Marielle and afraid it wasn't Marielle and she couldn't bear the disappointment? No, Kent never dealt in subtleties or ambiguities. Teresa's reason for not following the figure would not make sense to him. "It all happened extremely fast," she said, trying to sound composed. "I was still nearly standing on the brake, afraid I'd hit the person, when I caught a glimpse of the face. The storm was coming. I got out of the car. I called, but she didn't answer. . . ."

More silence. Then Kent said, "Teri, you know that if you really thought you saw Mom, you would have followed her no matter how surprised you were or how hard it was raining. Now either you didn't see anybody—"

"I *did*!"

"Okay. Settle down." Teri clenched her teeth. "You saw someone, but no matter what you're telling yourself now, you instinctively knew it might not be Mom and you'd be putting yourself in danger by following . . . it . . . her . . . whatever."

"Mom," Teresa said stubbornly.

"No, Teri. It may have looked like Mom, although I don't see how someone who looked like Mom would just happen to run in front of your car and then vanish, but it *wasn't* Mom. Teenagers like to prowl around on these warm summer nights. Maybe your windshield was blurry. Or maybe you had Mom on your mind. Or . . . well . . . had you been drinking?"

His last question set Teresa seething. "I'd been drinking boilermakers all evening. I was drunk as a lord. I'm sure I hit at least four people on the way home. You'll read all about it in the newspaper tomorrow."

"Now, Teri," Kent said with the exaggerated patience he'd use on Daniel, "don't act like that. Don't get mad."

"I'll get mad if I want to!" Teri immediately realized she did sound like a child. No wonder Kent was talking to her as if she were the same age as his son. "Look, someone ran in front of the car—someone wearing a long black hooded raincoat, someone tall and slender like Mom, someone with a face like Mom's, someone with eyes like Mom's, someone with long black hair like Mom's. I saw all those details clearly in my headlights. Then the person dashed into the mass of trees. All I'm asking is what you think. You don't have to get sarcastic or act like I'm crazy."

"Teri, I don't think you're crazy, but when you called, you said you'd definitely seen Mom running in front of your car, not someone swathed in a black coat and hood you got a glimpse of before they ran away. And for the record, you did *not* ask me what I thought. You stated quite definitely that you saw Mom, whom we've not seen or heard from for over eight years, and neither have the police. Therefore, I don't think you have the right to get angry with me because I'm skeptical."

Everything Kent had said was true. And everything

Kent had said sounded as if he were reading it from a book about how to handle a hysteric. Teresa was furious, but she'd be damned if she'd continue to argue with her brother, to let him talk to her as if she were completely unreliable or prone to wild fantasies.

"Never mind." She was surprised by how cool her voice sounded, considering the thumping of her heart. "You're right. It probably was just a teenager." Just like the one who left Snowflake at my door last night, she thought, relieved that this morning she'd been more focused on calming down Sharon than telling her about someone leaving Celeste's night-light on the porch, a morsel Sharon would have immediately reported to Kent when he reprimanded her for dragging Daniel away from his lesson. "I guess I just had my mind on Mom and I let my imagination run away with me."

"Are you sure?"

"Oh yes. I feel much better now," she lied.

"I'm not so sure about that, Teri. You don't really sound—" Someone pounded on Teresa's front door and she nearly screamed. "What's *that*?" Kent demanded.

"The door . . ." Teresa's stomach knotted and her hand clamped the phone receiver in a death grip. "Someone's at the door. . . ."

"For God's sake, it sounds like they're trying to knock it down!" Kent shouted in her ear. "Is it those two guys you keep around there?"

"No . . . they wouldn't . . ."

Suddenly she heard Mac MacKenzie's familiar strong, deep tones that had always been like the sirens' call to her, no matter what the occasion. "Teri, come to the door! Teri, it's me—Mac."

"Did I hear Mac MacKenzie?" Kent demanded.

"Teri, open the door! One of your horses is loose. It's running like crazy. . . ."

One of the horses? Loose? *Running?* Teresa knew something had scared it, and abruptly all of her own fear vanished. "Something's wrong with one of the horses, Kent," she said in a rush. "I have to go."

Kent was still shouting questions when she slammed the phone back in the handset. Sierra beat her to the door. Later, Teresa thought they must have made a frightening couple—the dog barking deafeningly and jumping, Teri wild-eyed and panting—as she unlocked the door and flung it open to find Mac drenched in rain, raising his fist to give the door one more whack. Teresa darted back just in time to miss his fist and he stumbled into the room.

"God, I almost hit you!" Mac boomed.

"The horse!" Teri yelled above Sierra's excited barking. "Which horse is running loose?"

"I only got one good look. I think it's solid black—"

"Eclipse!" Teresa gasped.

"It was running around those rinks or rings—whatever you call them. It acted wild."

"She's my horse." Teri reached for her windbreaker hanging on the coat tree beside the door. "Was Gus or Josh chasing her?"

"Gus or Josh?"

"My hired hands."

"No one was out there. Just the horse." Teri pushed past Mac and stumbled on the rain-slicked porch. "You're not going to try to catch that horse alone!" Mac exploded.

"No, I'm not. You're going to help me."

"Help you! I don't know how to—"

Mac's car sat in her driveway, the engine running, the headlights slicing through the darkness. "Drive down to the barn," Teresa called to him as he followed her to the car. "Go slowly, but leave the lights on when you stop."

Teresa's gaze swept the fields spreading away from the barn. Lights shone in the windows of the Gibbses' cottage, but the barn sat in complete darkness. She couldn't understand it. If Eclipse had managed to get away from Gus or Josh, why weren't they trying to retrieve her? And why would she have bolted away from either of them anyway? Eclipse was not docile, but she certainly wasn't skittish, either. In fact, Teri could never remember the horse being frightened into an uncontrolled run—

Until tonight. Teri's eyes widened when she saw the black Arabian tearing across the wet grass, veering dangerously close to the sides of the riding rings, tossing her ebony head in the slanting rain. "My God," Teri groaned. "There she is, Mac. What on earth has gotten into her?"

"You're asking me?" His question could have sounded flippant, but it didn't. Suddenly Teri realized that although Mac didn't share her knowledge or love of horses, he was almost as shaken as she was by the sight of the beautiful horse running in a panic—a panic that could end with a broken leg or worse if she crashed into a fence. "What should we do?"

"Stay calm," Teresa said as they pulled slowly up to the barn. "Don't yell at her to stop. I'm going into the barn to get a bridle."

They ran to the wide barn doors, one of which stood partially open. Fear fluttered in Teri's stomach. Neither Gus nor Josh would leave the doors open on a stormy night when the horses tended to be nervous. In fact, Teri knew that when storms lasted through the night, one of them usually slept in the barn, quieting any horse that became frightened or skittish. But not tonight. Tonight the barn was completely dark and the only sounds were those of horses stamping and snorting.

Teri looked at Mac. "I know you're not crazy about horses. You can wait for me out here beneath the overhang."

Mac looked at her and shook his head, sending raindrops flying from his wavy hair. "I'm not letting you into that dark barn by yourself." Secretly, Teresa was relieved, although she'd never show it. Mac's strong male presence made her feel stronger and calmer, even if he didn't know a thing about how to corral a runaway horse. "Besides," he continued. "I don't dislike horses. I just don't know anything about them."

Mac took her arm firmly in his hand. The act seemed as natural as if he did it every day, and she could feel her fear ratchet down a notch. Then Teresa stepped inside the big barn with its sixteen-foot-high ceilings and went rigid. She could feel the tension in the air as the horses snorted, stomped, and kicked at their stalls. Be calm, Teri told herself as she began turning on the mercury-vapor lights. They were stronger than fluorescent lights, so she flipped on one at a time, not wanting to frighten the horses with a sudden blinding flash of all the lights.

"What should I do?" Mac hissed in her ear.

"You don't have to whisper, but keep your voice subdued," Teresa muttered. "And don't make eye contact with the horses. Staring into their eyes can make them nervous."

"You're kidding."

"Don't sound so shocked—humans are the same way," Teresa said softly. "The horses are upset already, Mac. Don't make any loud noises; walk casually and keep your head down. Just act like nothing is wrong. There is a phone on the wall to your right. The Gibbses' SUV is gone, but their cottage lights are on. I'm going to call. We need Gus or Josh to help us."

But the phone rang four times until the answering machine clicked on to inform her that no one was home, but her call would be returned as soon as possible. Teresa felt hope pop like a bubble within her. The Gibbses only left one small lamp burning when they were both gone. Lights glowing in more than one room always meant that at least one of them was home. Except for tonight.

She hung up and turned to Mac. "No luck. I don't know where they could be in weather like this."

"The storm blew up fairly fast," Mac reminded her. "Maybe they haven't had time to get back yet."

"If that's true, I hope they arrive soon. We need the cavalry. Until then, it's just us."

With Mac trailing carefully behind her, Teri moved forward toward the tack room. The smell of horseflesh and fresh hay washed over her, along with the smell of fear—the fear of the horses snorting, stomping, kicking, and whinnying.

"It's all right, Conquistador. Good girl, Cleopatra. You're safe now, Sir Lancelot. Teri and Mac are here to take good, good care of you," she crooned. The soft, lulling tone she'd learned from Gus and Josh usually calmed the horses, but tonight it had no effect. Teresa understood why. Deep within her, she felt that awful, intangible sense of *wrongness* she'd felt once before. She knew without a doubt that there was something menacing in this barn, just like something menacing had been in her home eight years ago when she'd awakened to find death in the house.

Teresa tried to force the memory from her mind. The barn glowed with lights now. She'd turned on every one. No one was lurking around, slinking through a dark hallway carrying a bloodied knife. But someone had let out Eclipse—*her* horse. Had that been a coincidence?

She looked toward her horse's stall. The stall door stood half-open but undamaged. Every good horseman knew a horse could kick open a door hooked shut by a latch fastened with screws. That's why Teresa had insisted sturdy bolts be attached to the stall doors. Gus had taught Josh never to be careless about making sure every bolt had been slid solidly into place after a horse was placed in its stall. Checking the bolts had become second nature with them, and a quick glance around assured Teri that all the stall doors remained bolted shut—all except for one.

"Do horses get loose often?" Mac asked close to her ear.

Teresa looked up and saw the crease between his eyebrows, the concern in his hazel eyes. "It never happens here. Gus and Josh are utterly dependable. I just don't understand . . ."

The sorrel Morgan, Bonaparte, let out a loud whinny and kicked forcefully against his stall. Both Teri and Mac jumped. "Oh, God, Bonaparte is always the most fretful of all the horses," Teri said. "That's why I keep him beside Conquistador, who's one of the calmest. Horses pick up on each other's moods, you know."

"No, I didn't. All I know about horses is that they have four legs and they're big," Mac muttered.

Teresa checked the bolt on Bonaparte's stall door, and went back to Mac. "I think he'll settle down as long as Conquistador stays cool."

They walked to the back of the barn until Teresa reached for a doorknob. "The tack room," she said, opening the door. Before them stretched a long room containing horse equipment arranged with almost military precision on shelves and racks. The floor was spotless, the two large windows so clean they looked transparent except for raindrops hitting them like a steady stream of bullets. "Gus keeps this place as clean as an operating room," Teri said as she quickly lifted a bridle from a rack. She looked at Mac. "Ready to corral a panicked horse?"

They hurried through the barn and stepped out into the hard, sweeping rain, closing the barn doors behind them. Eclipse still ran, splashing through rapidly forming puddles, once coming dangerously close to the fence surrounding a ring. Teri drew in a frightened breath and almost called the horse's name. She caught herself. The key was to remain calm. She knew if she got upset and started yelling, Eclipse would only run faster and farther away from her.

"What do we do?" Mac asked, standing beside her and wiping rain from his forehead.

"The most important thing is to not chase her. Eclipse is still running, but she seems to be slowing down. Maybe if she was spooked badly, the sight of me has reassured her a bit."

"Is that why you're not putting up your hood?"

"Exactly. She's not used to seeing me wearing a hood. I want her to recognize me. In the meantime, we'll just stand here and not try to approach her as long as she still seems jumpy."

Teresa knew she shouldn't take her gaze off Eclipse, but she was so afraid the beautiful horse was going to meet with disaster, Teri closed her eyes. She began slowly counting to twenty. She'd reached eighteen when Mac nudged her. "She's stopped running," he murmured.

Teresa opened her eyes to see that the horse had settled down to a trot. Then, as if someone had flipped a switch, Eclipse finally came to a complete halt. She stood almost motionless in the rain except for her head, which she dipped twice before turning toward Teri and Mac.

"Okay, let's approach her *very* slowly," Teri said. "You go to her right side and I'll go to her left. Still keep your eyes down."

As they walked casually toward the horse, Teri mentally begged Eclipse not to panic and begin running again. Luckily, the horse stood still, even when Mac and Teri surrounded her. Teri talked softly to her horse as she quickly slipped on the bridle. Eclipse snorted once and tossed her head. When Teri began walking calmly toward the barn, though, the horse followed peaceably.

Inside the barn, the other horses had relaxed considerably. They looked with interest at Eclipse, and Bonaparte whinnied, but the black Arabian did not react. Teri, congratulating herself on how well she was managing her horse, tossed a confident smile at Mac, who walked slightly behind her.

When they reached Eclipse's stall, Eclipse bucked and whinnied, her eyes rolling. Startled, Teri almost dropped the bridle straps. The horse had been docile from exhaustion just a moment ago. Now she seemed ready for another nightmare race through the field. Mac grabbed the bridle straps and helped hold the horse in place while murmuring the way Teri had done earlier. If not for him, Teresa would have lost control again. After a few seconds, Eclipse stopped bucking. Teresa knew something was very wrong—Eclipse had never been so out of control. With a shaking hand, Teresa pushed the stall door completely open.

And there lay Gus propped against the wall in the corner, his head tilted back, his jaw gaping, his blank blue eyes wide open, and the long, rigid, razor-sharp metal tongs of a stable fork buried deep within his blood-soaked chest.

CHAPTER TWELVE

1

AFTER THE FIRST BLUDGEONING shock of seeing Gus, Teresa became vaguely aware of Mac asking, "Teri? What's wrong? Teri!"

"Put Eclipse in the empty stall near the barn doors," Teri said woodenly, not turning around. "Don't rush her. Just be casual. Make sure the stall door is bolted."

"Teri, what *is* it?"

"Mac, just do as I say right now. You'll know soon enough."

You'll get to see brutal death up close and personal, Teresa thought as she heard Mac leading Eclipse to the vacant stall. You'll get to see what murder looks like—violent, bloody murder. It's a sight you'll never forget.

Teresa suddenly felt burning hot when just a moment ago she'd been cold from the rain. Gus's head seemed to lower;

his eyes seemed to fix on hers with a deep, pathetic plea. And now his mouth was moving—he was trying to say something, to tell her he was in agony, to beg her to help him. . . .

Teresa heard the other stall door bolt shoot into place; then Mac stood beside her. He peered into Eclipse's stall, then muttered a horrified, "Good God!"

His oath brought Teri savagely back to reality. Gus was not moving. His head was still tilted back, his jaw hanging open and still. He wasn't trying to speak to her. The thought that he could had been manufactured by shock and nerves, because Gus would never say anything again.

"Who is that?" Mac muttered as he stared at Gus's limp, violated body.

"It's Gus Gibbs, my stable manager," Teri explained with remarkable equanimity. She felt as if she were standing outside herself, cold and analytical and oddly unaffected. "That thing in his chest is a stable fork. It's used to muck out stalls. Some people use plastic forks. I use wooden-handled forks with metal tines. Extremely sharp, sturdy metal tines."

They both stood transfixed, staring at Gus's bloody body for what seemed to Teri an endless time. Soon, though, Teri began to shudder. Even her head bobbed slightly. Still she took a step forward.

Before she'd taken a second step, Mac wrapped his arm tightly around her waist. "We shouldn't touch him, Teri."

"But maybe we can do something." Teresa was surprised by her own voice, high and thin like a frightened child's. "Maybe . . ."

"We can't do anything for him, Teri," Mac said firmly, turning her away from the body and leading her toward the front of the barn. "I'm going to call nine-one-one. We can't touch anything. This is a crime scene."

"A crime scene . . . ," Teresa repeated hollowly.

"Unless you think Gus just fell on that fork, it is. Someone came into this barn, let your horse loose, and killed Gus. I don't know why; I don't know who. This is a matter for the police. Now come away from the stall and go with me to the phone."

"I don't want to leave him, Mac. He's all alone and hurt. . . ."

"Teri, he doesn't feel alone and he's not hurting," Mac said gently. He firmly pulled her away from the stall, then turned her and began walking her to the front doors of the barn. Just to the right sat a narrow, padded bench, and on the wall hung a phone. "I want you to sit down here." Mac's voice was cool and businesslike. "I'm going to call nine-one-one."

Teresa nearly dropped onto the bench, hitting with enough force to jar her teeth. She hadn't been sure of exactly what Mac was saying, only that he sounded calm, forceful, and in control. Thank God, she said mentally. Thank God I'm not alone.

She was vaguely aware of him speaking into the receiver, then sitting down beside her. A wave of sick dizziness overcame her. She closed her eyes and leaned forward, certain she was going to vomit. Teresa felt Mac's hand on her back, rubbing it as if to comfort her. She concentrated on a point of light behind her closed eyelids, a point of light that became bigger and bigger until that was all she could see. After a moment, she leaned back and took a deep breath.

"Better now?" Mac asked softly. She nodded and he put his arms around her shoulders again, this time drawing her close to him. "I know you're cold, but we have to wait here for the police."

"I thought you called nine-one-one. Isn't that just the emergency squad?"

"It's central dispatching. I told them what we found. They'll send the emergency squad *and* the police. I'm sorry you're so cold and wet, and we have to just sit here."

"You're even wetter than I am," Teresa mumbled, her gaze briefly skimming his soggy jeans and the drenched green shirt. She leaned even closer to him and laid her head on his shoulder. He took her hand in his and rested his cheek on her head. They used to sit the same way at night in the park when she was a teenager, and she slipped into the old position as if she'd been doing it constantly since those faraway, innocent years. "You'll catch a cold in these wet clothes, Mac."

"I'm okay," Mac said. "It's a warm evening. I'm not going to catch a cold. I never catch colds."

"I remember now. Your mother used to brag about that."

Mac chuckled. "Oh, God, that was noteworthy, wasn't it? Any mother would be proud of a son impervious to the cold virus."

"She had other reasons to be proud of you. Many, many reasons." Teresa lifted her head and looked into his eyes. "I'm so embarrassed, Mac. After hearing Byrnes say he didn't kill Dad and Wendy, you came to me to offer support. And what did I do? I told you your mother thought you were capable of murder. Then I came to apologize to you, and I ended up slapping you."

"And I was coming to your house to apologize for the way I so graciously accepted *your* apology in my office, and we end up chasing down a runaway horse and finding a dead body." Mac shook his head. "No one can say we're a boring couple, Teri."

Their faces were so close together, Teresa could feel Mac's warm breath on her cheek. The world seemed to fill with his gold-flecked hazel eyes with their laugh lines and that irrepressible twinkle that had always made her feel as if she were drowning in his gaze. She'd felt that way at sixteen. She realized she still felt that way at twenty-six. Quickly, she lowered her eyelids and put her head on his shoulder again, afraid that if he didn't kiss her, she would kiss him.

They sat quietly for a moment, listening to the horses breathe loudly, still excited, still uneasy because they could smell blood. Gus's blood, Teresa thought. Dear Gus, who would never smile at her and call her Miss Farr again.

After what seemed an endless time, Teresa said softly, "Gus used to be in love with my mother."

"What?" Mac blurted.

"He told me just this morning." She sighed. "This morning. It seems like a month ago. Anyway, he used to work at the town stables and Mom had a horse boarded there. A black Arabian just like Eclipse. Isn't that odd? Gus thought I'd bought Eclipse because she was like Mom's horse, Cassandra, but I didn't even know Mom ever had a horse. She never mentioned it. I never saw any pictures of her with a horse."

"So Gus got to know your mother at the stables," Mac said, his arm tightening around her shivering body. "Did he tell her he loved her?"

"No, but she probably guessed."

"Did he say if your mother returned the feeling?"

"He said something vague about her looking at him a certain way. I guess about that time Dad appeared in her life—"

"And she fell head over heels in love with the charming devil."

"Let's just say the devil. Afterward, her parents sold the horse and Mom stopped coming to the stables. Then Gus saw her engagement picture in the paper." Teri paused. "There was tenderness in his voice when he talked about Mom. I know he was always loyal to his wife, Sarah—who definitely disliked me, by the way—but I don't think he ever stopped loving his Marielle."

"She was like her daughter," Mac murmured. "Of course he didn't stop loving her. He couldn't."

Teresa was glad Mac couldn't see her flush, knowing Mac was saying he couldn't stop loving Teri any more than Gus could stop loving Marielle. But Teri was still afraid of

Mac's ability to hurt her, the emotional power he held over her, and she didn't want to betray her weakness now, just because she felt weak and frightened and lost.

Suddenly, in the distance, Teri heard sirens. The police were coming. The emergency squad was coming. None of them could do anything for Gus. They would just pull that awful rake from his chest, put him on a gurney, and take him away. Or rather, take away the lifeless shell that had once held the warm, gentle spirit of Gus Gibbs.

As the ambulance pulled up to the barn, Teresa remembered talking to Gus about her mother. The last thing he'd said about her was, "I worry about her and I pray every night that poor Marielle finds her way home someday."

Well, Gus, at least you don't have to worry about my mother anymore, Teresa thought wretchedly. And you don't have to pray every night that she'll find her way home again because she won't in your lifetime.

The police arrived about two minutes after the ambulance, and Mac gently told Teri to sit—he'd take care of the situation. She could have kissed him then, because she already felt her throat closing off and the hot, relentless tears of grief beginning to course down her cheeks. She was fumbling uselessly in her windbreaker pocket for a tissue when abruptly a new idea hit her with the force of an electric shock.

What if the person who had darted in front of her car earlier actually had been her mother? In that case, Marielle *had* come home again and with her, she'd brought death.

2

Half an hour later, Mac pushed Teresa through her doorway, where Sierra greeted her ecstatically, turning in circles, barking and squeaking. Teri kneeled and hugged the exuberant dog. "I need some of your joy, girl. It's been a rough night."

"That's for sure." Mac stood above Teri, looking through the open doorway at the red lights disappearing up the hill, bearing away police, emergency medical technicians, and Gus. He firmly shut the door.

"You need to get out of those wet clothes, Teri," he said authoritatively. "Your jeans are soaked."

"So are yours."

"I'm not the one shivering. Go change. I'll put on some coffee."

Teresa wasn't sure whether her shivering was because of wet clothes or shock. In either case, changing into something warm and dry and having a cup of hot coffee sounded wonderful. "The coffee is in a container in the cabinet above the coffeemaker," she said.

"I'll find everything." Mac held out his hand. Teresa took it and he helped her to a standing position. Their bodies were almost touching. Their gazes met and held, and for a moment Teri thought he was going to pull her against him. Then he gave her a gentle shove toward the stairs. "Go change clothes and use a blow-dryer on your hair. It's dripping."

Teresa followed his orders like a child, marching upstairs, stripping off her wet clothes, then impulsively turning on the shower, making the water as hot as she could stand it. Under the pounding water, Teri closed her eyes, trying to erase the last hour from her mind, but it was useless. Every detail flooded back with blinding clarity.

Although the sheriff knew the horse farm belonged to Teresa, when he'd first arrived, he'd directed most of his questions to Mac. It must be a guy thing, Teri had thought vaguely. Men always assumed other men could answer questions more accurately and coherently than women could. But eventually the sheriff had turned to her, asking why Gus had been in the barn, who had been in the barn with him, who could have wanted to kill him—questions Teresa couldn't possibly answer.

While the sheriff was questioning her, Josh Gibbs had arrived. His reaction to his father's murder had been stunned horror, followed by almost frightening fury. Finally, he'd taken a swing at Mac, the stranger Josh's roiling, baffled mind thought somehow must be responsible for Gus's death. Mac had seen the swing coming and dodged it. Police restrained Josh when he tried taking a second shot, but by then the shred of composure Teri had clung to snapped. To her humiliation, she burst into uncontrollable sobs.

"I'm taking Miss Farr back to her house," Mac had told the sheriff in a tone that brooked no argument. "She's had all she can take for one day."

The sheriff, not to be outdone, gave his permission, although Mac had not asked for it. Mac led Teresa out of the barn. Numbly she'd climbed in his car, and he drove slowly back to the house.

Now, as she stepped out of the shower, she realized she'd finally stopped shivering, but she felt cold deep inside. She slipped into underwear and then a heavy terry cloth robe she usually wore only in winter. She turned the blow-dryer on her hair for five minutes, then in a fit of impatience turned it off while her hair still streamed damply below her shoulders.

When Teri reached the foot of the stairs, Mac appeared holding two thermal cups of steaming coffee. He held one out to her and she took a sip, then smiled. "Just a tad of cream, a pinch of cinnamon, and no sugar. You remembered."

Mac grinned. "The only person I've ever known who takes cinnamon in their coffee is Teresa Farr. You're unique, Teri, in more ways than one."

"I'm not sure whether that's good or bad." Teresa felt her cheeks grow warm and she quickly looked down at her coffee. Mac's gaze seemed too familiar, too intimate, for her to return casually. "Your clothes are as wet as mine were," she said. I'll put them in the dryer if you take them off."

Mac raised an eyebrow and one side of his mouth quirked in an insinuating smile. "Upstairs on the right is the guest bedroom. In the top drawer of the dresser is a pair of jeans and a couple of shirts. I think they'll fit you," Teri said. "And quit smirking. The clothes are Kent's. Once in a while he stops by for a short ride on Conquistador after he leaves work."

"Convenient explanation, Teri," Mac said lightly.

"I don't need an explanation, but if the clothes belonged to a lover, I don't think they'd be in the guest room." Teresa stepped aside and motioned at the stairs. "Go change before you sit down and ruin my furniture with your wet jeans."

"So it's the furniture you're worried about, not my health."

"You don't catch colds, remember?"

As Mac disappeared up the stairs, Teresa walked through the living room sipping her coffee and musing at how strange it felt to be here with him, letting him fix coffee for her, telling him to change into Kent's jeans so his own clothes could dry. It felt strange, but it also felt familiar. And so it would, she reasoned. They'd known each other for years. They'd been in love. They'd once been engaged.

And that's what she had to remember, Teresa told herself. The love and the engagement were in the past. She couldn't put faith in the reassurance she felt with Mac tonight. She had to consider the circumstances. She'd just suffered the second-biggest shock of her life and Mac had been with her. Unlike the night when her father and Wendy had been murdered, she'd had someone to stand by her, actually to take over and to shield her from the barrage of questions and the suspicious looks, and then to whisk her away when she'd had as much as she could endure. Mac had shared this awful experience with her and he had been protective and comforting, but to comfort wasn't to love. Teresa had no idea how Mac really felt about her. And at the moment she had no idea how she really felt about him.

Mac came downstairs wearing Kent's jeans, which hit at least an inch above his ankles, and a polo shirt stretched tightly across his chest. He grinned and said, "I guess I'm bigger than Kent—I hope I'm not ruining his shirt." Then Mac had insisted on putting his own clothes in the dryer rather than letting Teresa do it. Finally, they sat down at the kitchen table, each with a second cup of coffee. Sierra was rewarded for her earlier good behavior with another piece of beef jerky.

"I guess I shouldn't be having all this coffee, considering how nervous I already am," Teri said.

"It's decaf. I hope you don't mind—I rummaged through your cabinets until I found some."

"I don't mind at all. It was very thoughtful of you."

Teresa realized how stiff she sounded, and when Mac reached over and covered her hand with his, she nearly jerked it away. Mac held it firmly and gave her an unflinching stare. "I know this situation must be uncomfortable for you, but you shouldn't be alone right now and I'm the only game in town," Mac said evenly. "I know you could call Carmen or Sharon and Kent, but then you'd have to replay the whole evening for them, and you don't need that to-night. Just put up with me for a little while. After all, you might need me. The sheriff said he wasn't through talking to you. He'd call the talk an interview, but it would be an interrogation and it's not happening while I'm here."

"No wonder he wants to interrogate me," Teri said drearily. "Who else would be the number-one suspect in this murder case? The notorious Teresa Farr."

"I'm not going to tell you you're being silly. I'm sure the cops do consider you a suspect, although I don't know what your motive would be for killing your hired hand."

"Gus," Teresa said. "His name is Gus Gibbs and I thought the world of him. He was kind and honest and funny and caring and . . ." Her eyes began to fill with tears.

Mac gave her a sympathetic smile. "Of course you would always call him by his name. Your jerk of a father always referred to 'the help,' not you or your mother. Both of you took a genuine interest in the people who worked for you. I know my mother thinks your mother was the best friend she ever had. She's never stopped missing Marielle."

Teresa flushed at the mention of her mother. Dear God, please let Kent be right, she thought. Please let my imagination be running wild, thinking it was Mom I saw running in front of my car. Let it be a teenager out for fun.

"Teri, what are you thinking?" Mac asked.

"Nothing important, just about tonight and . . ." She floundered mentally for a moment, then said, "I don't know why I didn't see Eclipse running loose when I came back from the club. She must have been outside by then."

"Did I arrive immediately after you did?"

"No. There was at least a twenty-minute lag."

"Then the horse could have gotten loose during that time. Or maybe it was loose when you got home, but you just didn't see it because it was behind the barn or something."

"I guess so," Teresa said unhappily. "But if I'd stopped at the barn instead of coming straight home, maybe I could have prevented Gus's death."

"And maybe you could have gotten yourself murdered, too. Besides, it's better that I can testify that you were here in your house, I took you back to the barn, and I was with you when you found Gus. You weren't alone . . . again."

"Not like the first time I found someone murdered," Teresa said bitterly. "I don't think the police would have believed that was a coincidence. Even I would have trouble believing it if I weren't the one who keeps finding mutilated bodies."

Mac was silent while she swallowed hard, then lifted her cup with a shaking hand and took a sip of coffee. Finally he asked, "Teri, why did you decide to come back here to live? Was it just because Byrnes had been caught and you thought everything would be the same as it was before the murders?"

"You think my life was great before the murders? My mother was deeply unhappy even when I was a little girl. I never liked my father, and the stricter he got with me, the more I rebelled, so that by the time he was killed, I already had a reputation for being wild, a troublemaker, an embarrassment to my whole family. I wasn't half as unruly as people thought I was, but I never tried to set the record straight. I enjoyed being a thorn in my father's side."

"I think a lot of people knew that, Teri. I certainly did. Anyone who got close to you knew you weren't some uncontrollable, wayward girl."

"Don't forget 'immoral.' "

"I thought 'wayward' covered 'immoral.' " Mac grinned. "And your relationship with me was to blame for getting you labeled immoral and me a pervert for dating a seventeen-year-old girl. But I'm not a pervert and you certainly aren't immoral when it comes to sex or life in general. You're actually one of the most honorable people I've ever known, and I've met a lot of people since I met you."

Teresa felt her cheeks coloring. "Honorable. No one has ever applied that word to me."

"That's because no one has ever known you like I do," Mac said softly. Then he smiled. "Remember when we met—you hung out your bedroom window and talked to me about Billy Idol's 'Sweet Sixteen.' You were flirting like crazy that day."

"And I was scared silly to be acting so 'brazen,' as your mother would say." Teresa grinned. "I did it partly because I knew my dad was upstairs and he'd hear me. I wanted to make him mad. But mostly I came on so strong because I had such a crush on you. I wanted you to think I was bold when it came to men. A real woman of the world." Teri suddenly burst into giggles. "Some woman of the world. I'd never even been kissed!"

"That's what made you so appealing—you trying to act like you flirted outrageously with men every day when I knew from my mother and my friends that you were really shy around guys." She blushed more, remembering how she'd deepened her voice to what she'd considered irresistible sexiness, batted her eyelashes, and flipped her long black hair over bare shoulders. "I think if I'd started to climb up that trellis leading to your room, you would have fainted, Miss Teri."

Teresa laughed. "Oh, I absolutely would have! I'd been practicing my seduction of you for about fifteen minutes before I got the nerve to call out to you. And even though you acted just the way I wanted you to—interested, faintly attracted—my heart was still pounding and my stomach was in a knot from nerves. For once I was relieved when I heard my father stomping down the hall and I had an excuse to flee from that window. What a femme fatale!"

"You were, even if you didn't realize it."

They smiled at each other. Teresa absently dropped another jerky strip to Sierra, who would no doubt suffer some stomach discomfort tomorrow for overindulging. Then Teri got up, filled her and Mac's cups with all the coffee left in the pot, and sat down again, suddenly feeling as tired as she could ever remember.

"Why don't you go on up to bed, Teri?" Mac said. "You look like you've just about had it. I'll linger awhile in case the sheriff gets really ambitious and comes up here. You need rest."

"I know I need rest, but I also need to answer the question you asked earlier. Why did I come back here?" Teresa took a breath and spoke slowly. "I came back because my brother and my nephew live here—they are my only living relatives, Mac, and I didn't want to keep them at a distance just because I was afraid of public opinion. I also wanted to show the people in this town I had nothing to hide, no reason to run from Point Pleasant." She hesitated, then decided to tell Mac the complete truth. "And I thought if my mother was still alive, she might come back here and . . ."

"And she couldn't turn to Kent?"

"Kent loved her, but I loved her more. And he's married and has a family, whereas I'm alone and I could concentrate just on her. I wanted her to come to *me* . . . at least, I thought I wanted her to come to me. But now . . ."

Mac frowned and leaned closer to her. "But now *what*?"

Teresa stiffened. Because of her shock over Gus's murder and because Mac was being so kind to her, she'd let her guard down; she'd talked too much. But she was going to stop talking. She wasn't going to tell Mac that earlier in the evening she'd seen a frantic-eyed woman she thought was her mother running across the road, perhaps running from the barn where she'd turned loose the horse that looked just like the horse Cassandra she'd had so long ago. Maybe Gus had walked in and caught Marielle turning Eclipse loose. Maybe he'd recognized her, wanted to help her, tried to keep her, to "capture" her—the last thing an unbalanced Marielle would have wanted. So rather than be trapped, to perhaps be held accountable for the murders eight years ago, Marielle had . . .

Teresa closed her eyes. Marielle had stabbed Gus to death.

CHAPTER THIRTEEN

1

A BELL. IN THE distance a bell. Her mother was ringing a bell, beckoning her—but beckoning her to where? To whom? A sad, lonely mother who loved her child dearly and desperately needed her, or a mother who had turned into a killer and wanted to use her daughter as a shield or even worse—

Teresa jerked awake, drenched with sweat. The bell rang again and she realized it hadn't been part of her dream. It was her doorbell. She glanced at the bedside clock. Seven thirty. She hadn't gone to bed until three.

Sierra had already sprinted down the stairs barking furiously at the closed front door as Teri clambered out of bed and slipped on a robe. She went to the front door hesitantly, expecting to see the sheriff. Instead, Josh Gibbs stood red-eyed and haggard on her porch.

"Oh, Josh, come in," Teresa said with a rush of emotion, opening the door, reaching out to take his arm and draw him inside. "I didn't get a chance to talk to you last night. I'm *so* sorry about your father. I can't begin to tell you how awful I feel. I can't believe anyone would hurt Gus—"

Teresa broke off immediately, realizing she was babbling while Josh's face remained like stone. Her hand dropped from his arm. "Would you like a cup of coffee?" she asked.

"I want to talk to you," he said without emotion.

"Yes, of course." Teresa suddenly felt absurdly guilty, as if she'd killed Gus. "I'm sorry we couldn't talk last night, but everything was such a mess and we were all so shocked. . . ."

Josh nodded as if he was supposed to respond, not as if the movement came naturally. "Shocked, yes." He swallowed. "I guess I could drink a cup of coffee."

"It'll just take ten minutes for me to put on a pot. Do you want to come in the kitchen?"

"I'll stay out here, ma'am, in the living room with the dog."

"Ma'am." "The dog." Not "Miss Farr" or "Sierra." Teresa realized Josh's world had been rocked last night. Still, the stiffness of his manner unnerved her. She fumbled with the coffeemaker and spilled grounds on the counter. She knew she should go back and talk to Josh while the coffee dripped, but instead she paced around the kitchen until the last drop of coffee hissed into the pot. Three minutes later, she carried a tray with full cups of coffee, sugar, and cream into the living room and made a great fuss of preparing each cup. Afterward, though, she was forced to sit down and face Josh.

"You said you wanted to talk to me," she dived in. "I suppose you want to know how I found your father—the circumstances, I mean." Josh nodded and Teresa started with Mac banging on her door to tell her about the panicked Eclipse, their capture of the horse, then the discovery of Gus's body in the stall. "I have no idea who let out

Eclipse or who could have . . . hurt your father," Teresa ended weakly, thinking she sounded as if she were more coldly self-concerned with conveying her innocence than with trying to comfort Josh.

He stared into his coffee cup as if he could see an answer in its depths. Finally, he began to talk, almost more to himself than to her. "One of my friends got a new stereo system and I went to his house to see it. He picked me up because Dad said he might need the car later."

"For what?" Teri asked sharply.

"He didn't say. In fact, I didn't even notice that he said he might *need* the car. It was the sheriff last night who jumped on the word. I don't think it's important. Dad probably just said that because he didn't like for me to argue with him, and he wanted me to realize that if I moved out like I planned, I wouldn't have it as easy as I did living with him." Josh half-smiled. "He didn't want to live alone after being with me and my mother for so long, although he and Ma didn't really get along. I guess you know all about them, though."

"No, Josh, I don't know anything about your parents' relationship," Teresa said carefully, remembering how Josh had looked when Gus had been talking to her about his feelings for young Marielle.

"Well, he wasn't happy with her and he tried to hide it, but he couldn't. Ma was real resentful. Bitter. Hurt." Josh looked directly into Teresa's eyes. "I don't blame her."

Teresa felt acutely embarrassed, as if she were overhearing an argument between Gus and his wife, Sarah. She didn't understand why Josh was telling her this. Maybe there was no purpose, she thought. Maybe Josh, still shocked, was simply rambling.

Then Josh suddenly leaned forward. "Do you think the person who was on your porch night before last and left the night-light murdered my father?"

Teri had the impression Josh was trying to startle an admission from her—if not a verbal response, then a physical one that would betray her knowledge about what had happened to Gus. But she had no actual knowledge—only doubt and fear.

At that moment, while Josh still leaned toward her intently, Sierra leaped up and started barking, making both Josh and Teri jump. A few moments later, the doorbell rang again. Teresa tossed Josh a nervous smile. "Sierra is my early alarm system." She stood up and headed toward the door, thinking distractedly, Dear God, I hope this isn't the sheriff. I can't face him.

But Kent stood on her porch, his face tense and strained. He plunged into the house, pushing Teresa aside as he demanded, "What the hell is going on around here? Why didn't you call me? Gus Gibbs has been *murdered*? Here? In your *barn*?"

Teresa felt her face blanch. She motioned at Josh sitting rigidly on the couch. "Kent, Gus's son is here. Please calm down—you're upsetting both of us."

"I'm upsetting *you*?" Kent blasted. "What about *me*?"

"What about you?" Teresa shot back. "This didn't happen to you. You're just throwing a fit because I didn't call you last night, and now is not the time to be worrying about yourself! Didn't you just hear me say this is Gus's son, for God's sake?"

Kent immediately seemed to shrink within his own skin. His face turned from white to red; he lowered his eyes, obviously trying to compose himself; then he moved toward Josh, hand extended. "Josh, I'm so very sorry about your father. I didn't mean to come in here like . . . like I don't know what. I was just stunned about your dad and worried about Teri. And about you, of course."

Kent could have left that last part off, Teresa cringed mentally, because he obviously hadn't given Josh a thought. Nevertheless, he thanked Kent for his false concern with the aplomb Teresa was certain she couldn't have managed in the same situation.

"I suppose you're busy making funeral arrangements," Kent said.

"The medical examiner probably won't release my father's body for at least a couple of days," Josh returned coolly.

"Oh, God. Of course." Kent's face turned redder. "I just thought maybe you were making arrangements for your father with Teri."

"I can make arrangements for my father by myself," Josh went on in the cool, composed tone. "I'm here because I wanted to ask Miss Farr about the person who was on her porch the other night." He stared at Kent, who looked blank. "The person who left that horse-shaped night-light."

Oh no, Teresa thought as Kent's gaze flashed to her. She purposely hadn't told him about her night visitor or the return of Snowflake. He was volatile enough after Roscoe Byrnes's announcement that he hadn't killed Hugh and Wendy. "What is he talking about?" Kent demanded of Teri.

"I had a prowler." Teresa tried to make her voice as nonchalant as possible. "Josh scared him away."

"A *prowler*?" Kent repeated as if she'd just said "a rapist."

"Yes. Well, probably just a Peeping Tom."

"Who was dressed in a black hooded coat and left a night-light at her door," Josh added.

Kent gaped at Teresa. "Just like the person you thought you saw last night? The one you thought was *Mom*?"

Josh stared at her accusingly. "Did you see someone hanging around here last night? The same person who was on your porch, who left that light?"

"What the hell light are you talking about?" Kent nearly yelled. "Teri, what is going on?"

Sierra began barking at the uproar and Teresa held up her hands, desperate to quiet the three of them. "Stop it!

All of you!" Sierra abruptly shut up, but Kent opened his mouth, ready to fire more questions at her. "Kent, I mean you, too!" Teri took a deep breath. "I saw someone on the porch night before last. He left something. Some kind of toy," she said vaguely. "And Josh, I did see someone last night as I was driving home. They ran across the road and into the woods. Maybe it was the same person; maybe it wasn't. I couldn't really see—"

"You saw someone with a pale face and big eyes and long black hair," Kent intervened. "You told me. You said it was *Mom*!"

"Okay, for a minute I thought it was Mom," Teresa admitted. "But as you pointed out, Kent, I was upset, I was thinking about Mom, I only caught a glimpse—"

"But you *saw* someone." Josh was on his feet now, his body trembling. "You didn't say anything about that to the sheriff last night! What are you hiding?"

"I'm not hiding anything, Josh. Last night I was just so exhausted and upset, I wasn't thinking clearly."

Josh's fists clenched in rage. "You weren't too exhausted and upset to spend half the night with that guy you were with in the barn!"

Kent whirled on her. "What guy?"

"M-Mac."

"Mac MacKenzie?" Kent shouted. "You spent the night with Mac MacKenzie?"

For a moment, Teresa almost cowered from the two furious men standing in her living room glaring at her. Then, slowly, she felt the heat of ire build within her. How dare these two males come into *her* home and start firing questions at her, putting her on the defensive, *yelling* at her, for heaven's sake? She had done nothing wrong. In fact, she'd had a much bigger shock than Kent, and one almost as bad as Josh's, yet they both seemed determined to make her feel guilty and embarrassed. It was outrageous and she wouldn't stand for it another minute.

Teresa drew a deep breath and looked squarely first at Josh, then at Kent. "I really resent the way both of you are acting," she said in a firm voice. "Josh, I am devastated about your father, and I did see someone running from this property last night, which I didn't mention in the barn, but I have every intention of telling the sheriff today.

"And, Kent, as for Mac, he came by here because we'd had an argument at his club. I left in a hurry and he decided to follow me to settle things. On his way to the house, he saw Eclipse running loose. He was banging on the door while I was on the phone to you. We caught Eclipse and then we found Gus. I was shattered. He stayed with me until I thought I could sleep, which wasn't for some time. I don't owe you an explanation for Mac being here, but I gave you one anyway and I will thank you to back off and stop acting like Dad!"

Teresa's last verbal jab at Kent hit home. He looked startled, then slightly ashamed as he silently acknowledged the truth of her comparison. He said nothing, however. He just stared at her.

Josh, on the other hand, seemed to go almost limp. His fist unclenched, the anger drained from his face, and his shoulders slumped. "I'm sorry, Miss Farr," he said wanly, as if he hadn't any energy left. "I hardly know what I'm saying, but that's no excuse. Dad would be ready to kick me right now and I'd deserve it."

"It's all right, Josh." Teresa gave him a small smile. "I understand that you're upset."

"Yeah, well . . ." Josh trailed off uncomfortably. "I gotta go. Like I said, I can't make any funeral arrangements until the police tell me it's okay. They have to do an autopsy. . . ." He suddenly looked almost sick. "I've gotta take care of the horses and I wanted to remind you that Bobby Loomis and Susan Woodward are scheduled for lessons, but the barn is a crime scene. We can't give lessons until the cops release it."

"Of course," Teresa said, remembering when the Farr home had been a crime scene and she'd had to wait two days before she could retrieve any clothes or toiletries. "I'll cancel those lessons and all the others for the rest of the week. And thank you for taking care of the horses today."

"I can't just sit around thinking about this. Dad always told me that you've gotta keep busy during bad times, so that's what I'll do. The cops said I can only do what's necessary for the horses—they don't want me in the barn any more than I have to be—but I'll be around if you need anything."

With that, he nearly fled out the front door. Teresa looked through the window to see him racing over the knoll to the barn, where she knew he'd throw the little energy he had left into feeding and grooming the horses before he faced the cottage where less than twenty-four hours ago he'd probably been having breakfast with his father.

Teresa turned to Kent. "Well, do you have any more questions for me? Any more accusations, complaints—"

"Teri, I'm sorry, too," Kent interrupted in his usual manner. "You just have to understand how shocked I was when someone called this morning and started asking about the murder and I hadn't heard anything from you. Then I came here and found out you'd been with Mac."

"You acted more upset about Mac than about Gus, Kent."

"I don't trust him, Teri. You've never told me why you broke off your engagement, but I know he did something to hurt you. And ever since, he's gone through women like they were candy, just tossing them away like they weren't worth anything—"

"It's my turn to interrupt," Teri said sharply. "Just how do you know so much about Mac MacKenzie's love life?"

"I hear things. Everybody knows about him."

"From whom do you hear these things? And why does *everybody* except me know about all of these women he supposedly treats so cavalierly? I talk to Carmen and she *does* hear everything, but she's never said anything about Mac treating women badly."

"She wouldn't to you. She cares about you. She doesn't want to hurt you."

"But I thought you didn't approve of her or my friendship with her and thought she was simply a gossip who'd repeat anything she heard."

"Well, I never said she was totally devoid of tact. If she were, she wouldn't have been such good friends with Mom. I mean, Mom thought the world of her, so I guess there had to be something worthy about Carmen."

"Yes, there is. And I think the reason you don't like her is because Sharon doesn't like her. I don't know what Sharon's problem with Carmen is, but the animosity is becoming unbearable." Teresa paused. "The subject wasn't Carmen, though. The subject was Mac. All I want to say is that I'm not involved with Mac, but if I were, that would be *my* business. I don't take orders from my big brother, orders based on a lot of rumors he claims to have heard."

Kent's eyes narrowed slightly. Teri knew he was bristling at her tone. At Farr Coal Company, he'd gotten used to being the boss, having people do what he told them to do. He didn't like Teresa's rebelliousness. Nevertheless, he knew that rebelliousness was an intrinsic part of her, that she was not easily intimidated.

Kent's manner almost instantly changed. "Teri, I think Mac wants you back. Maybe he genuinely cares for you. Most likely, though, he can't stand having you be the one that got away, the one who threw *him* over, and don't tell me the breaking of the engagement was a mutual decision. It was yours. Anyway, let me ask you something. You said you had an argument at his club and he came here to straighten out things between the two of you. Did you come straight home from the club and did he arrive immediately after you did?"

"I don't see what this has to do with anything."

"Just answer these two questions for me and I'll leave you alone."

"All right. No, I didn't come straight home. I stopped at the convenience store on the corner. I was there about fifteen minutes. And Mac didn't arrive here immediately, which you already know because I'd been talking to you for about ten minutes when he started banging on my door."

"Then think about this, Teri," Kent said slowly, almost grimly. "Mac had time both before and after you got home to go to your barn and let out Eclipse. Maybe he only meant to create some situation that would throw the two of you together, some way that he could *help* you and get back in your good graces, but something went wrong. Gus caught him. Maybe they struggled and in the heat of the moment . . ." He lifted his hands while her imagination created a picture of Mac plunging the stable fork into Gus's chest. "Mac has a temper, Teri. That's one thing everyone does know for certain—maybe everyone except Gus, who didn't know what could happen to him if he got in Mac MacKenzie's way."

2

After Teresa had showered, drunk two more cups of coffee, and forced down some toast, she remembered that the Farr house had finally been sold and Kent had ordered the furniture to be moved out tomorrow, which meant she was supposed to look at the place today and claim any pieces she wanted. The thought of visiting the house gave her the creeps, especially today after Gus's death. For a full hour, she told herself she wouldn't bother touring the house. She didn't want anything.

Then she remembered the grandfather clock. Her mother's grandfather had bought it for his bride. Marielle had inherited it after her parents' death, and she'd treasured it, planning to remove it from the house as soon as she'd completely recovered and set up a home of her own. Marielle had never gotten the chance to claim her clock, though, and it had stood in the Farr house all these years as if waiting. Marielle had loved the clock and Teresa knew her mother would have wanted her to place it in her home here at Farr Fields.

For a few minutes, Teresa considered simply calling Kent and telling him she wanted the moving men to bring the clock to her house, but remembering the clock had made her think of other things of her mother's that might still be in the house. Marielle had left quickly, then been shuffled off to a mental institution. Her clothes and necessary items had been sent to her aunt Beulah's upon Marielle's release, but Teresa couldn't remember anyone actually sorting through all of her mother's belongings. Some things of Marielle's might be in that house, and whatever was left, Teresa wanted the chance to see it and decide if there was anything of sentimental value. She would have to go, she told herself. It would only take an hour. She'd just dash through the house and get out as soon as possible. No big deal.

Still, Teresa took her time gathering four boxes for any small items she might want to take from her childhood home, then made a leisurely search for the house key. When she found it, she stuck it in her purse and started for the door, her dread growing. She nearly cried out in relief when the phone rang, delaying her trip.

"Hello!" she almost chirped.

"Teri? Is that you?"

"Of course it's me, Mac."

"You sound so cheerful. You took me by surprise after last night."

"Oh, I'm not as lighthearted as I sounded," she said, her voice falling to its normal timbre. "I was just going to our old house. It's finally sold and Kent arranged for everything to be moved out and stored tomorrow. I'm supposed to make a tour today and pick out what I'd like to have moved to my house."

"Do you want some company?"

Teresa longed to say yes, but she was afraid things were moving too fast between her and Mac. He'd been wonderful to her last night—kind, comforting, warm but not aggressive. She'd felt that maybe, just maybe, she and Mac could have a chance, but only if they took their relationship slowly and carefully.

"I think this is something I should do alone," Teresa said simply.

"Why?"

"I just . . ." She floundered for something tactful to say, then gave in to honesty. "I *want* to go alone, Mac. I don't relish the idea of seeing the house again, but I haven't been inside for eight years and I don't plan on ever being inside again. I *need* to go by myself for a final good-bye to the place where I had the worst experience of my life."

"Okay," Mac said amiably. "I don't quite understand your reasoning, but I know that once your mind is made up, arguing is useless. Just be careful."

"Be careful? What do you think is going to happen to me?"

"Considering the things you told me about last night— the note in your car, the fax, the night-light—someone might want to give you another scare."

"Well, no one except you and Kent knows I'm going, so I don't expect any pranks."

"I wouldn't call what happened to Gus Gibbs a prank."

Teresa felt as if she'd been slapped. "I certainly wasn't comparing Gus's murder to me getting a nasty note!"

"Now I've made you mad. I didn't mean you were demeaning the importance of his murder. Just don't stay in that house too long. I don't like the idea of you even being there."

"Thanks for your concern, but I'll be fine," Teresa said coolly, determined to act composed as she made a thorough search of the house for her mother's belongings. *Alone.* "I'll talk to you later, Mac."

Teresa hung up before he could say a word. She knew she was being childish—she probably shouldn't visit the house alone even though she didn't feel she would be in any physical danger—but she'd been offended by Mac's implied criticism. She didn't want his help. She didn't need his help. She could take care of herself.

Teresa tossed the boxes in her car and fifteen minutes later, she pulled into the driveway of her former home on Mourning Dove Lane. She sat for a moment staring at the graceful Georgian lines of the big brick house. Neatly trimmed hedges ran along the front, and a bright July sun bounced off clean windows set in neat white frames. Whoever Kent had hired to keep the house maintained was certainly doing a good job. Even the lawn had been recently mown and raked. Any stranger passing by would think a family was lucky to live in such a large, lovely home.

Teresa stepped out of her car, then pulled her boxes from the backseat. She stacked them awkwardly and was almost stumbling to the front door when she heard someone let out a shrill, "Yoo-hoo! Hello there!"

Teresa tilted her head and looked at a small, birdlike woman coming at her with a tiptoeing run. Teri half-expected the woman to look over her shoulder as if she were being pursued.

"Are you from the realty company or are you the new owner?" the woman asked.

"Neither. I'm Teresa Farr. My family owned this house."

"Farr," the woman repeated. Her smile froze. "Oh, *Teresa* Farr. I didn't realize. Obviously." She let out a loud nervous giggle that sounded remarkably like a horse whinny. "I live next door. My husband and I bought our house seven years ago. Our two kids were young then. Now they're in college."

Teresa remembered that the next-door neighbors—the ones who'd made the 911 call the night of the murders—had put up their house for sale two months after the murders. Unlike the Farr house, theirs had sold in less than a year.

"My husband told me to mind my own business, but I thought I should tell someone I've seen lights on in this house the last two nights in a row. Not bright lights—soft, glowing lights. Really just one light moving from room to room upstairs. It doesn't go fast like someone is carrying a flashlight and looking for something. It stays in a room for up to an hour. But I never see a car come or go and I don't see anyone come into the house or leave. Last night I stayed up until three o'clock watching. My husband said if it happened again tonight, then I could call the realty company and let them handle it. He's a great believer in me not getting involved."

Fear whispered at the back of Teri's mind. A soft light glowing through the upstairs windows? The last *two* nights? A real estate agent wouldn't be showing the house in the wee hours, and people wouldn't linger for nearly an hour in each room. This was beyond odd—it was definitely a sign of trouble, even if someone was just prowling around inside the house out of curiosity. No one should have a key to the house except Kent, Teresa, and the realty company.

"You probably think I'm exaggerating or I just imagined something, but I know what I saw," the woman said defensively, as if Teri had argued with her. "I have insomnia and I'm up almost every night until three or four in the morning. My husband says I'll just die from getting so little sleep, but I can't help it.

"Anyway, while I'm up at night, I spend most of my

time looking out of my windows," the woman said confidentially. "I have to say most people would be shocked if they saw all the peculiar things that happen on this whole street! I've seen the strangest comings and goings, midnight assignations, people carrying odd things into their houses under the cover of darkness. It's true! Oh, the stories I could tell! But I'm not going to tell you *everything*. I just want you to know about *your* house. The rest I'll keep to myself for a while—for the sake of safety, you understand."

Abruptly, Teri felt her fear dissolving as the woman turned and skittered back across the lawn, then stealthily opened her front door and darted inside as if she were in imminent danger. She was sleep-deprived and paranoid at the very least, Teresa thought. The poor thing sat up nights thinking she saw all kinds of suspicious activities on this street that to Teresa's knowledge had only seen violence once. The woman had certainly heard about the Farr murders—she definitely knew who Teresa was—and no doubt spent many nights creating fantasies about the house next door.

Teri shook her head as if clearing it of the uneasiness the woman had generated and walked purposefully up the two porch steps. She set down her boxes, put her key in the lock, swung open the front door, and stepped inside.

For a moment, Teresa felt overwhelmed by a sense of intrusion, as if she were violating the house's solitude. She had a flashing thought that if it could, the house would physically eject her, sending her sprawling back onto the lawn. She knew the idea was ludicrous, but the sensation lingered, causing her to stand rigid and breathless just inside the doorway, fighting the instinct to run to her car, drive away as fast as she could, and never look back.

She closed her eyes and took a deep breath, telling herself to calm down, to think rationally and get control of herself. This was just a house—an inanimate structure of wood and brick with no soul and no memory. She was the one who felt she didn't belong here, not the house. The house felt nothing, and the memory of what happened that awful night eight years ago was hers.

But as Teresa took two more steps into the house, she was sure that even after eight years the aura of fear, violence, and death lingered. She stood in the foyer beneath the sparkling crystal chandelier and looked at the big grandfather clock with its raised brass numerals, image of the moon phase, and beveled glass front. She remembered it tolling three times as she crept through the house that awful night, finding the bodies of Hugh and Wendy, and luckily interrupting the killer before he got a chance to finish off Celeste. Perhaps it would be natural if for her the clock symbolized everything terrible that had happened that night, but she'd loved it too long not to want it now. She definitely wanted it moved to her house tomorrow.

Teresa's gaze traveled to her left. Beyond the arched doorway, the living room stretched large and cool with its dove gray carpet, soft gold and rose tapestry-covered antique sofa and wing chairs, shining walnut tables, and the big fireplace topped by a wide marble mantle. Wendy had wanted to refurnish this room as well as the master bedroom, but Hugh had forbidden it, insisting that the room looked "classy" even if Marielle had been its decorator. If they had lived, Wendy would have eventually gotten her way, Teresa thought.

Teri looked away from the living room. If anything of Marielle's was left in the house, Teresa knew she wouldn't find it on the first floor. Resolutely, she picked up her boxes from the porch and carried them inside. She couldn't force herself to close the front door, though, and shut out the warmth and comfort of an ordinary sunny July day. It would be like shutting herself into a family crypt, she thought, and shivered. The door would stay open a couple of feet, she decided, even if a few flies made their way into the house. She wouldn't have to worry about them—she would be leaving as soon as possible.

Teresa began climbing the stairs to the bedrooms. When she was halfway up the staircase, her mind filled with the image of a figure dressed in black gliding down the stairs. Roscoe Lee Byrnes didn't look like he was capable of gliding. Thinking of his bulky frame, overly large head, and fat hands, she could only picture him clumping his way through life.

But Byrnes couldn't be as slow and clumsy as he looked, she reminded herself. He'd committed all of his murders in houses he'd entered so quietly and swiftly he'd been able to take at least twenty people by surprise. Twenty-two people if he truly had killed her father and Wendy.

When Teresa reached the top of the stairs, she once again stood still, not certain which bedroom she could bear to enter first. Her own, she decided. No one had been murdered or injured there. For some unknown reason, she had been spared—spared to be suspected of attacking everyone else in the house.

She walked into the bedroom she'd abandoned eight years ago. The day after the murders, she had come back with Carmen to gather up some clothes and toiletries. She'd felt dazed and had blundered around the room, not sure what she needed, opening and closing drawers, staring blindly into her closet, until Carmen had taken over and packed enough to get her through the next couple of weeks.

After the arrest of Byrnes, when Carmen had invited her to stay with her until she left for college in September, she and Carmen had visited the house once more to collect the rest of Teresa's belongings. She had not been in the house since then, and her room looked almost the same with its cherrywood dresser, chest of drawers, and nightstand, light green bedspread, and a couple of rock band posters that clashed badly with the framed Degas prints her mother had chosen. Teri couldn't imagine herself ever having loved this room or found it a safe haven after her father had married Wendy. It now seemed like a room she'd merely seen in a magazine—a place she remembered but that aroused no emotion in her.

Her father and Wendy's bedroom was another matter. Teresa stood in the doorway and stared at the bed where the couple had been stabbed so many times that not only the bedding and mattress had to be thrown away, but even the carpet—that horrible hot pink carpet—had to be removed and destroyed. After the house had been released as a crime scene and Aunt Beulah had claimed she wanted nothing to do with a house where murders had been committed, both Teresa and Kent had asked Carmen to help them, and the first thing she had done was hire a cleaning company and order them to "pull out all the stops" when it came to washing away traces of that horrible night. No detergents or special cleaning solutions could remove all the bloodstains, though. The wallpaper had been stripped and the walls painted an innocuous eggshell white.

But Teresa imagined she could still detect the coppery scent of blood—so much blood—that she'd smelled the night she'd slowly entered this room and put her hand on what was left of Wendy's abdomen. Police had wondered how two people could have been stabbed so many times and apparently made no sounds. They believed that when one was being stabbed, the other would have awakened.

At the time, Teresa had thought that although she was pregnant, Wendy had taken at least one of the sleeping pills to which she was addicted. The killer must have first slit Hugh's throat, so he couldn't scream, then stabbed him seven more times in the neck and torso. Teresa thought the killer had moved on to Wendy, who no doubt slept the sleep of the drugged, and proceeded to slash repeatedly the area of her uterus, where a fetus grew, her chest, and finally mutilated her pretty, vacuous face.

Teresa had not volunteered her theory about the order of the killings because she thought it made her sound too familiar with the mechanics of the crime, as if she'd known Wendy would be sleeping more deeply than was natural, so Teri's father should be eliminated first. Later, toxicology reports showed that Wendy had taken two of her pills. When the police announced that Hugh Farr had been murdered first, while his drugged wife slept, Teresa was relieved she'd said nothing.

Although Teresa had disliked both of them—detested them, actually—the natural humaneness in her cringed at the image of two people, lying oblivious and vulnerable in sleep, being viciously ripped and torn until their life blood soaked the carpet and splattered across the walls. Her father had hurt and humiliated her mother just as Wendy had hurt Jason by taking his daughter, but neither of them had deserved to be murdered, Teresa thought, surprised by the tears now rising in her eyes. What kind of monster could have enjoyed killing two people with such savage rage?

Teresa darted out of the room, glancing at her mother's Tiffany-style lamp still standing on the small table near the bathroom, and made a mental note to collect it before she left the house. Then she moved on to Celeste's room at the end of the hall, facing the front of the house. Here, too, the bedding and carpet had been removed, as well as the toy chest in which the child had hidden from the killer.

Teresa's gaze flew to the place where the night-light Snowflake had been plugged into a wall socket. No Snowflake. She would have considered the possibility that Jason had retrieved it for the child or that someone else had taken it as a harmless souvenir, but she was certain the person who'd left the night-light on her porch had meant it to stir up painful memories and instill fear in Teresa.

She told herself to stop wasting time in these rooms that held nothing for her. Also, the house had an unpleasant, deserted smell she found almost noxious. Teresa wanted to open windows and let clean, sun-warmed air into this monument of tragedy. But the house wouldn't like that, she thought. Eight years ago, the house had closed in on itself, clutching its memory of terror and carnage, and it did not want to be disturbed.

Teresa jerked as if awaking from one of her nightmares. "You sound as crazy as the woman next door, Teri Farr," she said aloud, somewhat reassured by the sound of a human voice even if it was her own. "I have work to do."

After Hugh married Wendy, Kent had refused to stay in the house when he came home from college every three weeks to see Sharon. He'd stayed in the home of a friend, and Wendy had unofficially turned his bedroom into a storage room. Even now, the door was kept closed. Teresa opened it and a musty smell washed over her. The door should have been left open and the house aired out more frequently, she thought in annoyance, almost stomping into the room. The real estate people had to know the mustiness would not make the house more appealing to prospective buyers. Apparently, the smell hadn't bothered the new owner who wrote horror novels, though. She was glad he'd bought the house but almost repulsed that part of the house's "charm" for him lay in its grim history.

Teresa was surprised by the number of boxes in the room. After Wendy had commandeered it for storage, Teri had never opened the door to Kent's bedroom and she'd had no idea how much had been stashed in here. She now walked purposefully to the first stack of boxes and saw that every one of them bore a label. She instantly recognized Wendy's rounded, almost childish handwriting on one reading: CURRENT EVENTS. Teresa couldn't resist looking in to find a collection of tabloids and popular magazines full of gossip about celebrities and pictures of movie stars' magnificent homes. So this is what Wendy considered to be worth cherishing, Teresa thought with a mixture of ridicule and pity. Another box labeled: CLOTHING held a collection of midriff-baring tops and low-slung jeans—clothes Wendy must have worn before she married Hugh and could not part with although she then wore clothing more suitable to her new station in life.

Teresa had glanced at nearly twenty boxes before she found one labeled simply: *M.* Marielle, she thought. "Well, Mom, Wendy reduced you to *M,*" Teresa said. "How petty and how like her."

The box held books. Marielle had been an avid reader. Her constant reading had annoyed Teri's father. He'd always asked his wife if she didn't have anything better to do than stick her nose in a book. Teresa glanced over the hardcover copies of works from Jane Austen to a couple of murder mysteries only nine or ten years old. Teresa set the box in the hall to take home.

She expected to find at least one more box full of books. When she found none, she was furious. Wendy had thrown them away or delivered them to Goodwill, probably playing grande dame to the hilt and pretending the books were hers.

The next box labeled *M* held newspaper clippings and photocopied articles about local events. As she riffled through them, she realized they were research for a book her mother had wanted to write. Her doctor had thought the project would be good for her, and she'd dived into it with an almost manic fervor that had lasted for nearly six months. Teresa remembered both worrying about her mother's abnormal fervor and being relieved because for the first time in years Marielle had seemed happy. Then Hugh had announced that he wanted a divorce, and Marielle's project and her happiness had crashed to a halt.

Teresa's mother had always wanted to write and she'd been fascinated by Point Pleasant history—all of the strange events that had happened as well as the eerie sites in the area that had given Point Pleasant a reputation for being "haunted." She had decided to write her book about the town and its history.

Teresa picked up an article about the Shawnee leader Chief Cornstalk, who had tried to prevent the invasion of Virginians into his tribe's hunting grounds by leading a group of Shawnee and Mingo warriors at the Battle of Point Pleasant in present-day West Virginia. Later, in 1777, Cornstalk visited Fort Randolph in Point Pleasant. The fort commander detained him and when an American militiaman from the fort was killed by Indians, soldiers executed Cornstalk and his son Elinipsico. Supposedly, Cornstalk cursed the area, and many people believed the curse was responsible for tragedies that later happened around Point Pleasant.

More clippings covered the collapse of the Silver Bridge in 1967, a disaster that claimed the lives of forty-six people. But most of the clippings and articles covered "Mothman," the creature many local people claimed to have seen in 1966. The creature, described as being about seven feet tall and shaped like a man with wings and large, burning eyes, was said to have taken refuge in one of the boiler houses in the vast deserted area where, during World War II, TNT—trinitrotoluene—had been manufactured and other explosives stored in concrete "igloos." The place stood on a web of underground tunnels people believed the creature used to travel without being seen.

Teresa remembered that her mother had been amused by the stories of Mothman, and thought about how much she would have enjoyed the movie *The Mothman Prophecies* starring Richard Gere. Marielle had been fascinated by the history of the entire Point Pleasant area, though. She had often talked Carmen into visiting what was commonly known as the TNT Area, actually now the McClintic Wildlife Preserve. Teresa even remembered several photographs Carmen had taken of Marielle standing by one of the unsealed igloos, an igloo Marielle had loved to explore and had even insisted Teresa, Kent, and Sharon come with her to inspect. Marielle had been so disappointed in Kent's and Sharon's reaction to the place that later Teri and Mac had nearly begged her to show them the igloo, and when they'd explored it, they'd acted as thrilled as if they were seeing the Tomb of Tutankhamen. They'd even taken an entire roll of film of the three of them feigning awe and fear inside and around the igloo.

Teresa now opened the third box labeled *M*. It contained picture albums and videotapes her mother had made. Even when she was depressed, Marielle had rallied enough to drag out the video camera to tape important events in her children's lives. Every tape was labeled in Marielle's elegant, sloping handwriting: Kent learning to ride a bicycle; Kent's high school graduation; Teresa and Kent going on rides at Disneyland on one of their rare family vacations; Teresa's dancing school recital; every birthday party Hugh had allowed Marielle to hold for the children.

Teresa looked for the tape of her sixteenth birthday party, her favorite because Hugh had been out of town, so Teresa had been able to invite more people than usual. They'd danced out on the patio until evening, and both Emma and Marielle had seemed relaxed and happy, having almost as much fun as the teenagers, while Hugh was gone. Unfortunately, that tape seemed to be missing. Teresa went through the collection a second time. "Damn," she muttered. "Of course my very favorite would be the one to go missing."

Teresa wanted the contents of all three boxes. She could carry the box of tapes and albums and the box of newspaper clippings at the same time, she decided. She'd take them down to the car right now, Teri told herself, spacing out her trips so she wouldn't find the task of loading this stuff so tiresome. It had nothing to do with her uncanny feeling that the house was holding its breath, waiting for *something*.

Teresa picked up both boxes and was almost to the bedroom door when she caught a blaze of color from the corner of her right eye. She took a step back and looked at a scarf of vivid yellow and burnt orange beside Kent's dresser. With a jolt, Teresa remembered giving it to her mother on her last birthday. Teresa could almost see her mother wearing the scarf one day when Teresa had a supervised visit with Marielle at Aunt Beulah's shortly before the murders.

Slowly, Teresa set down the boxes, walked over, and picked up the scarf. She'd paid a lot for it because it was a designer scarf. The designer's name was on the label sewn into the hem of the scarf. It was soft, not stiff, as it would be if the scarf had been lying on the floor for years collecting dust. With trembling hands, Teresa lifted the scarf to her nose.

The scent of sandalwood, warm and fresh, wafted from the scarf's silken folds.

CHAPTER FOURTEEN

1

TERESA ROCKETED OUT THE front door, missed one of the porch steps, and lurched into Mac's open arms. "Oh, my God!" she shrieked in fear and shock.

"No, just me." Mac hugged her for a moment, then held her out from him. His hazel eyes studied her intently as a frown line formed between his eyebrows. "You are white as snow," he said. "What's wrong? What happened?"

"My mother's scarf; I f-found my mother's scarf!"

"Well, she used to live in this house. You said she didn't take everything with her when she left."

"No, you don't understand." Teresa gulped for breath. "It's clean and it smells like my mother's perfume. And it's *fresh*, Mac. One of the last times I saw my mother she was wearing that scarf. Now it's lying on the floor in Kent's room where some of my mother's belongings were stored in boxes. But the scarf hasn't been lying on that floor for eight years, Mac. It *hasn't*!"

"Okay, okay," he said soothingly, pulling her against him again. She unashamedly clung to his warm, sturdy body. "You're trembling, Teri."

"Of course I'm trembling! The *scarf*—"

"I want to see this scarf."

Teresa pulled away from him. "You want to go into the house?"

"That's where the scarf is. You don't have it with you, do you?"

"No. I dropped it and . . . and ran like a scared rabbit." She was beginning to feel embarrassed. "It was just such a shock. And when I arrived, the woman next door told me she'd seen a light in the upstairs windows the last two nights."

Mac's eyebrows went up. "Did she call the police?"

"No. She said her husband didn't want her to get involved. And she seemed a little strange," Teri added reluctantly. "She said she sees all kinds of suspicious things happening on this street at night."

"Oh." Mac grinned at Teri. "Well, it's broad daylight, so let's go inside and check out this house."

"Wait." Teresa drew back and looked at him. "Why is it that lately every time there's an emergency in my life, you happen to be around?"

Mac's grin faded. "Are you accusing me of something?"

"No. I'm just curious about your fortuitous appearances. What are you doing here?"

"I told you I didn't like the idea of you coming to this house alone. I couldn't stop worrying about you, so I decided I had to make sure you were all right." Mac's voice was sharp-edged. "Does that suit you or are you still suspicious and mad?"

"I'm not mad at you," Teri said in defeat. "You were right—I shouldn't have come here alone. I didn't really feel as if I had to say good-bye to the house, as if that would be like saying good-bye to the past. I just wanted to prove I wasn't afraid. But I didn't prove I wasn't afraid—just the opposite. I'm sorry if I offended you. I'm also not sure we should go back inside."

The anger had faded from Mac's expression. "I don't think anyone would be brazen enough to lurk around inside the house during the day when the real estate agent might be showing the house. Besides, you must have found things you wanted."

"I did. Three boxes. I was carrying out two when I spotted the scarf."

Teresa insisted they leave the front door open when they went inside the house. Mac took her hand and she felt more secure than when she'd first entered the house alone. Had she really thought the house wanted her out? That she was violating it, that it was holding its breath? Really, how absurd. Just plain crazy. She held Mac's hand tighter.

"So far so good," Mac said lightly when they reached the stairs. Just then, the grandfather clock chimed twice—two loud, reverberating sounds Teresa thought she could feel in her stomach—and she gasped. "I see someone has been keeping the clock wound," Mac said. "I know the real estate people want the place to look its best, but that seems like going above and beyond the call of duty."

"It sure does," Teresa said faintly. "Kent has someone who looks after the place. I see that the lawn has been mown recently. Maybe the guy he hires wound the clock."

"Yeah, maybe." Mac looked thoughtful. "Although there's a layer of dust on the furniture in the living room. He's careful to wind the clock, but he doesn't dust. Odd." He turned to her and smiled. "Oh well, forget the clock. Ready to visit the second floor again?"

Teresa tried for a light laugh and managed a squeak. She cleared her throat. "Lead on."

But when they reached the top of the stairs, Teri took

the lead, sailing past the master bedroom without looking in and stopping so abruptly at the doorway to Kent's room that Mac bumped into her. "You need brake lights, lady." Mac laughed.

Teresa barely heard him. "It's right there," she said, pointing to the scarf she'd dropped as if it were a poisonous snake.

Mac picked up the scarf by its edge and looked at the bright, supple folds. "It looks almost new, Teri."

"But it *isn't*," she insisted. "That *is* the scarf I gave Mom. Look in the corner. I'm not all that handy with a needle, but I did manage to embroider an *M* in the corner. Look."

Mack held up each corner, and on the third one he found *M* embroidered with golden brown thread. "*See!*" Teresa said triumphantly. "Now smell it."

Mac put the scarf to his nose. "Sandalwood," he said promptly.

"I told you. Sandalwood is an ingredient of the perfume Mom wore. And the scent is not old, stale perfume, Mac. It smells like someone wore that scarf a day or two ago."

"Yes, it does," he said absently, staring in the direction of the windows.

"What's wrong?" Teresa asked.

Mac hesitated, then said, "I'm trying to remember where I've smelled that exact scent in the last two weeks."

2

Emma MacKenzie muttered, moaned, then snapped awake. For a moment, she felt utterly lost. She sat up on her couch and looked around at a small, neat living room decorated with good pieces of furniture upholstered in burgundy and navy blue. She also looked at the television. She didn't remember turning it on today, but she now saw a woman with long, dark hair sobbing stormily as a man flung himself through a door, saying, "It's *over*!"

"Mr. Farr?" Emma asked the man on the television. "Where have you taken me? I want to go home. Marielle? You're crying. Marielle? He's hurt you again." Emma squinted. "No, it's Teresa. Teresa dear?" Emma squinted until her eyes watered. "No, it's Mrs. Norris. Mrs. Norris? No, you can't be Mrs. Norris. What's wrong with me? What's wrong? I want to go home, do all of you hear me? My boy will take me home. Where's Jedediah Abraham?"

Slowly the image of her son, who insisted on calling himself Mac, brought her back to the day they had toured this apartment and she'd declared it just right, although Jedediah had said it was too small. She'd been adamant, though. She didn't want anything expensive, because her son was paying for it.

"I'm home," Emma said in relief. "I'm in my very own home just taking a little nap." She looked balefully at the television, which was not turned on. "And while I slept, I dreamed about one of those trashy soap operas Mrs. Beemer in Apartment Five was talking to me about out at the trash Dumpster this morning! Honestly, that woman!"

Emma stood up and stretched. She'd been so tired lately. She had trouble going to sleep at night, but she'd always had trouble sleeping. As soon as her head hit the pillow, her mind filled with fierce anxieties about the future and sad, dark memories of the past.

Lately, the past had occupied most of Emma's thoughts—the past when she'd worked in the Farr house for dear Marielle, who'd treated Emma like a friend, not a housekeeper; sweet Marielle who had been tossed away by that devil Hugh; who'd broken under the strain and had to go off to an insane asylum. Oh, they didn't call the place an asylum, but it was and Marielle had been humiliated.

But worst of all were Emma's memories of that appalling day when Marielle—thin, weak, and exhausted—

had shown up at the house to see Teresa and *she,* Emma, had set up the secret meeting between mother and daughter in the thick, blooming rhododendron and forsythia bushes at the side of the house. Emma had thought mother and daughter were safe, but that tramp Wendy had seen everything and sneaked a call to Hugh, who'd come home in a fury and fired Emma, struck Teresa, threatened Mac, and sent Marielle running into that melancholy mauve spring dusk from which she'd never returned.

Emma would never forget Hugh Farr—red-faced and raging, while that painted harlot Wendy had sat laughing . . . *laughing!* They were an unholy pair, blights on the earth, the vessels of destruction for their families.

Emma's breath was coming faster and she felt as if she had a weight on her chest. She concentrated on slowing her breath and relaxing, reminding herself that her tragic final day in the Farr home had been a long time ago. God had used a human instrument to administer divine justice. God had wanted Hugh and Wendy to be annihilated. At the time Emma thought it would have been best if the child of Wendy had died, too, but maybe God had not wanted to rid the world of Celeste—that was why Teresa had been able to save her.

But after the girl had started talking again, chanting terrible things in public about death and Teresa—linking them together, as if Teresa had been a bringer of death into the home, Emma knew Celeste *should* have died that night. God's plan had simply been interrupted. Celeste was like her mother just as Teresa was like Marielle. Yes, Celeste had cheated death that night with well-meaning Teresa's help, but she should have died, just as her mother had died.

"Maybe that mistake should be corrected," Emma said as she moved dreamily to her bedroom, where a framed photo of Marielle stood among the photos of her own three children. She gazed into Marielle's eyes, sad although the younger woman smiled. Yes, Marielle should be completely avenged and her daughter protected. It was *right* and Emma knew she was the only person who completely understood God's will in this matter.

She looked at herself in the mirror, noticing that her dress was looser on her than it had been two weeks ago and that her eyes looked as if they'd sunken and were almost lost in dark shadows. And no wonder. She'd lost so much sleep this week. And right now, she felt as if she might just drop into a heap on the floor.

Reluctantly, Emma lay down on her bed and once again drifted into a restless nightmare-haunted sleep filled with Hugh and Wendy and Celeste and Teresa and the lost Marielle.

3

Mac had helped Teresa collect all of the boxes and put them in her car. When they finished, he asked if he could take her to dinner tonight, and she'd promptly said yes. After today, she was done fencing with him. As she'd stumbled out of the house in terror, she could have cried with relief when his arms closed around her, and it wasn't just because she was glad to see another person. Instantly, she'd known only Mac could have made her feel secure enough to go back into that house. Only Mac could have given her the courage to hold that scarf again. Mac was her safe haven in what seemed to be a crumbling world. He was her safe haven because she was in love with him, and all she had to do was look into his eyes to know that he loved her, too.

After she returned home, Teri took time with her shower, picked out a navy blue sleeveless sheath with a simple gold chain and gold hoop earrings. After all, Gus had died only last night. She hadn't seen the Gibbses' SUV when she came in. Josh had been determined to look after the horses and give lessons this morning in spite of his grief and Teresa had felt maybe taking care of them helped him take his mind off his father. Now she hoped he'd gone to be with friends.

She intended to cancel all lessons for the rest of the week—she could only ask so much of Josh—but she was grateful to him for taking over today, because unless the situation was absolutely necessary, she didn't think she could enter the barn for a while, not after last night. Teri hoped she'd feel different about the place tomorrow.

As for now, all of the horses were wandering peacefully in the field. None of them had seemed skittish or had gone off their feed. They looked calm as they pulled up pieces of lush grass and chewed it interminably. "If only I felt so serene," Teri sighed.

While Teresa waited for Mac, she noticed the light blinking on her answering machine. The first message was from Josh:

"Miss Farr, you weren't around, so I couldn't tell you that I don't think I can hang around here for the next day or two. Don't worry about the horses. I've got two friends who know almost as much about horses as Dad and me, and they're going to look after them for you. They know horses, but I showed them how you want everything done anyway and how they have to be careful not to disturb anything to preserve the crime scene. They won't be staying in the cottage. I hope you don't mind and I'm sorry I couldn't ask you first, but I've just gotta get out of here. I'll be back no later than July 6. If you want to fire me, I'll understand."

"Oh no," Teri groaned. She didn't trust the horses to anyone except Gus and Josh, but she could understand Josh's desire to get away. She really didn't know how he'd been able to go back into the barn this morning to feed the horses, not after seeing his father impaled with the rake. The image made *her* shiver. She could imagine what it had done to Josh, and she chided herself for her flash of selfishness. It was certainly best for him to escape from the scene of his father's murder. Besides, the guys who were going to take over for Josh were his friends. He wouldn't turn over the horses he loved to a couple of goof-offs who knew nothing about proper horse care. They were probably going to arrive within an hour to do the evening feeding and maintenance. By tomorrow morning she'd know whether she could trust the horses to them.

Still, Teresa sensed this was the beginning of the end for Josh at Farr Fields. He would no longer want to work here where his father had been murdered, and she didn't blame Josh. She would have to hire other hands, but it would be hard to find a situation as convenient as the one with the Gibbs family had been.

The second message had been left by the county sheriff, who said he'd been to her house twice today and found her gone. He reminded her that he wanted to question her further about the murder of Gus Gibbs and expected to be in touch with her tomorrow. The idea of a police interview filled her with unreasonable terror—after all, she hadn't done anything and had no idea who would have wanted to kill Gus—but she'd been innocent when her father and Wendy had been murdered, too, and the police had grilled her until she'd become so frightened she could hardly speak. Certainly she wouldn't be subject to that kind of interrogation again, she thought. Such a thing just *couldn't* happen to her twice.

Except that it could, she thought dismally.

Just as she turned away from the answering machine, the telephone rang. "Hi, Teri," Carmen said. "How are you holding up today?"

"After Gus's death? All right."

"My God, Teri, I can't believe someone murdered that poor man. The evening newspaper says the police *suspect* foul play; I've heard from at least eight people today that he'd been stabbed with some kind of rake."

"That's true. A metal rake with thick, razor-sharp tines

that's used to clean out stalls. It was awful, Carmen. Naturally I was the one to find him."

"Of course. You seem to have been granted a dubious blessing—the ability to find bodies. Is there any chance it was an accident?"

"I don't think so. He wasn't lying facedown on the rake. He was sitting in the corner of a stall with the rake sticking out of his chest." She could hear Carmen's gasp of horror. "The police sent his body to the medical examiner's in Charleston for an autopsy, although the cause of death is evident."

"But it's procedure. They did the same thing with Hugh and Wendy." Carmen caught her breath. "Sorry to remind you. Why didn't you call me last night? Was it because Mac was there? His name is in the paper, too, as one of the people who found Gus."

"Yes. I'd gone to the club to tell him something and we ended up having an argument and I slapped him—"

"You *slapped* him!"

"Yes. I was furious. I stormed out of the club and he came after me. When he got to my door, he told me Eclipse was out running wild in the rain. He helped me capture her and get her back in the barn. That's when we found Gus."

"Oh, that's dreadful. Is the horse all right, at least?"

"Yes, she's fine. I can't imagine who let her out, but my theory is that Gus surprised whoever it was and they stabbed him. I don't think anyone came here to murder Gus Gibbs. The man didn't have an enemy in the world."

"At least that you know of, Teri. You were fairly close to Gus, but we never know anyone completely."

She's right, Teresa thought. She hadn't known until yesterday that Gus and her mother had once been involved. Teresa would never have thought of the two having a relationship. But apparently, after all those years, Gus still thought of Marielle.

"Do the police have any idea who killed Gus?" Carmen asked.

"If they do, they haven't let me in on it," Teresa said dryly. "I had a message on my machine from the sheriff, though. He wants to *talk* to me about the murder. He didn't get enough information last night. Mac cut him short when he saw that I was about to faint from exhaustion and shock."

"I guess I have to be glad Mac was with you, then."

"He helped me so much, Carmen. I don't think I could have held up without him. He was extremely protective."

"Good for him! Did he spend the rest of the night with you?"

"Only a few hours until I got sleepy."

"Oh." Carmen sounded relieved. "Well, at least he was there when you needed him. I tried to call you around noon to see if you wanted to be with someone, but I got no answer."

"I'd gone to our old house. It's been sold and Kent told me to get out anything I wanted before he had people come to put everything else in storage tomorrow."

"How wonderful that it's finally sold! And how nice of Kent to give you so much notice. She paused. "Teri, you should have called me, not gone to the house by yourself."

"Trinkets and Treasures was open today. I couldn't take you away from your store."

"I'm sure they could have muddled along without me for a couple of hours." Carmen paused. "How did you feel being in that house again?"

"Creepy," Teri answered honestly. "I only found three boxes full of Mom's stuff. Some books, some videos she'd made of birthday parties and special occasions, and her research on the book she wanted to write about all the spooky things that have happened around Point Pleasant, like Cornstalk's Curse and Mothman."

"Oh, Mothman!" Carmen laughed gently. "My goodness, I'd forgotten about that project of hers. I went up to the TNT Area—Mothman Central—and tramped around with her a couple of times. She thought the place was fascinating. I stepped on a snake once and almost fainted. I wasn't much of a research assistant. And of course, Hugh didn't approve of the whole endeavor."

"I was happy that she had something she was excited about, but I didn't take as much interest as I should have, and I could kick myself for that now. She was happy when she worked on that book. Anyway, I guess the house sort of got to me today. I felt uneasy." Teresa had no idea why she was reluctant to tell Carmen about the scarf. Was it because she knew Carmen would ask a hundred questions about it or because she didn't want to admit she feared a mentally unbalanced Marielle had come back to Point Pleasant? "I came out of the house in a hurry and there was Mac," she rushed on. "I'd told him I was going to the house. He'd dropped by to help me carry boxes."

"Oh? He came by to help you carry *boxes*. Well, now, wasn't that sweet of him."

Teresa rolled her eyes. "You can take that salacious nuance out of your voice. He carried boxes."

"And?"

"And what?"

"Teri, I know you too well."

"Oh, all right," Teresa said, only mildly exasperated. "We're going out to dinner tonight. Just dinner."

"Since when does Mac MacKenzie have *just dinner* with any female?"

"Well, I hope that's all he does if the girl is a minor," Teresa said lightly. "Dinner is not a commitment, Carmen. It's . . . it's dinner!"

"Very well put, Teresa. I'd been wondering what dinner was." Carmen paused for a moment and Teri braced herself for a lecture. Instead, Carmen said in a light voice, "You're a big girl, Teri. If you feel that having dinner is something you want to do, something that's right for you now, then I'm not going to rain on your parade."

Stunned, Teri muttered, "Well, thank you."

"But I am going to ask a favor of you."

"I knew there was a catch," Teresa said drolly.

"Tomorrow is the Fourth of July. Don't you always go to the park to the concert and the fireworks display with Kent and Sharon?"

"Yes."

"Good. This year Sharon's father, Gabe, is going with them, too, and he's asked me to come along. Will that be all right?"

Teresa blinked twice before she asked, "Gabe asked you to come? Not Sharon?"

"Sharon wouldn't ask me to do anything except to perhaps lie down on the road so she could run over me."

"Oh, you're exaggerating." Slightly, Teresa thought. "Of course *I* don't mind. Does Gabe know she considers going to the fireworks display a family thing? I can't remember a time when someone who wasn't part of the family came with us."

Silence thrummed on the phone for a moment. Then Carmen asked, "Teri, can you keep a very important secret?"

"A secret? Yes, I suppose, if it's for you," she said carefully.

"Gabe has asked me to marry him!"

"What!" Teresa nearly shouted. "Gabriel asked *you* to be his wife?"

"Teri, your complete shock is rather unflattering," Carmen said dryly.

"Oh, I didn't mean there's anything wrong with *you*. You're wonderful, Carmen. You're beautiful and smart and fun and . . . I just didn't know you'd been seeing Gabe O'Brien. When did your relationship start?"

"Almost a year ago, so don't think I'm jumping into anything."

"But why didn't you say something?"

"You know how Sharon is. She wants her father to act like he died right along with her mother."

Teresa had to admit Sharon was as possessive of her

father as she was of her son. "I understand why you didn't tell Sharon, but why didn't you tell me?"

"I didn't want you to have to hide anything from her. After all, she is your sister-in-law. I hope she accepts this with a modicum of good grace, but if she doesn't, I wanted you to have plausible deniability."

"My goodness, you should be advising the President." Teresa laughed. "I appreciate your concern for my relationship with Sharon, though. It's on shaky ground lately."

"So I've heard. She goes to Gabe with all her troubles and you ruffled her feathers over the riding lessons."

"Don't I know it! And Kent really resents the fact that when things go wrong for her, she runs to Daddy. Maybe when the two of you are married Sharon will realize she's not Gabe's sole focus and start acting more mature." Teresa paused. "So when are you getting married and when are you going to tell Sharon?"

"That concerns the favor I wanted to ask of you. We want to get married the middle of September—Gabe has some time off then and we'd like to honeymoon in New England before it gets cold. That means we need to tell the families soon. I don't want to do it as if we're ashamed of it or afraid of anyone's reaction. I want to make an intimate little party of it, so I wondered if after the fireworks show you could invite everyone back to your house. I'll supply the cake and other pastries and champagne and then we'll make the announcement."

Teresa felt a moment of rebellion. Carmen wasn't tossing around ideas with her. She had this announcement gathering planned and expected Teri to go along with her.

"Carmen, I'm not sure this is a good idea," Teri said evenly. "I know Sharon is going to be upset. Maybe it isn't fair to make her hear the news when she's in a group of people."

"But that's the point, Teri. I know she won't be happy, but she won't throw a temper tantrum in front of people."

"I don't think she'd throw a tantrum in any situation."

"Then you don't know her as well as you think you do," Carmen said sharply. "She doesn't care about what will make Gabe happy, only what will make *her* happy. She's always been that way. I wouldn't be surprised if she didn't let herself get pregnant on purpose to hook Kent."

"Carmen, Kent loved her!"

"But Hugh didn't approve of her. I'm sure he might have tried to talk Kent into giving her up, but Kent would have been less likely to do that if Sharon was pregnant with his child. Sharon knew that."

Actually, the idea had occurred to Teresa in the past, but she'd never voiced it and didn't like herself for thinking it, and she didn't like hearing it from someone else. "Carmen, maybe Sharon's pregnancy moved up the marriage a year or two—but he would have married her."

"Now I've offended you," Carmen said contritely. "I'm sorry. Sharon and Kent's relationship is none of my business. I'm just thinking of Gabe now. Gabe and me. Oh, Teri, I love him *so* much. I loved my first husband, but not like I love Gabe. It's like my world used to be black-and-white. After I fell in love with Gabe, it turned to the most beautiful color—and three-dimensional to boot!"

Teresa's flare of temper flickered and died. Carmen sounded like a teenager and it was both charming and touching. She'd also sounded completely sincere. She truly loves this man, Teresa thought. She's been alone so long, and before her husband's death he was sick for years. The woman deserves a wonderful, genuine romance.

"All right," Teri relented. "I'm still afraid this will back-fire—"

"If it does, it does, but at least I'll have tried to make this easier on Gabe. If he had to face Sharon alone and deliver the news . . . well, I don't even like to think about it. Besides, I want to make a celebration of the announcement. It deserves a celebration!"

"Okay, I understand. But why do you want to have the shindig at my house?"

"Sharon will refuse to come to my house after the fireworks. And your place is so much prettier than mine, up on that knoll with the landscape lights. At night it looks like something out of a fairy tale."

"That might be a slight exaggeration, but thanks. What about the food? Do you want me to bake pastries and a cake?"

"No!" Carmen sounded horrified and Teri grinned. "I mean, I wouldn't dream of having you miss any holiday activities so you can stay in and cook," Carmen said more calmly, seeming not to realize that Teri had been joking. "I'll bring the food in the late afternoon and we'll put it in your kitchen—most of it can go in the refrigerator—but if you'll meet Kent and Sharon at their house, then there won't be a chance of Sharon seeing it. Later in the evening, I'll come to the park and join you. And it has to look as if I'm joining *you*, Teri, not Gabe. We don't want to tip off Sharon."

Teresa couldn't help bursting into laughter. "Carmen, I feel like we're CIA agents planning a secret mission."

"Well, we might as well be," Carmen said. "The only difference is that Sharon is tougher than anyone the CIA has ever faced!"

CHAPTER FIFTEEN

1

TERESA HAD JUST HUNG up when Mac arrived at her door. She greeted him almost shyly, feeling like a girl going on her first date with someone she'd just met. Teresa knew she was being ridiculous—she'd known Mac since she was a teenager—but they'd grown so far apart since she'd broken their engagement, they really seemed to be starting over from scratch.

"You look beautiful," Mac said with an appreciative smile.

"I've had this dress for years. It's nothing special," Teresa said in a rush, not wanting him to think she'd really *tried* to look exceptional. "I hardly ever wear dresses nowadays."

"Well, you should. You have great legs," Mac said, his audacity tempered by his boyish smile. "I'm starving. How about you?"

"I haven't eaten all day. I forgot—me with the appetite

of a lumberjack. I want to go someplace where you get *large* servings."

Fifteen minutes later, they pulled up in front of a house-turned-restaurant nestled in the shadow of a rolling, green hill.

"Gloria's Lighthouse Café," Mac said.

"I've heard about this place, but I've never been here," Teresa said.

"Then you're in for a treat."

They walked inside to face a long bar, turned left, and went up two steps into a cozy dining room. A gleaming dark hardwood floor led to a tall enclosed brick fireplace with a wood stove sitting in front. On the mellow muted green walls hung paintings, some done by the restaurant's owner. Ceiling fans with lights hung above the diners. Teresa chose a table facing long windows through which she could watch the sky turn from cornflower blue, to orchid and coral, and finally to heliotrope.

Teresa and Mac both ordered steaks with baked potatoes, salad, and rolls. Teresa was glad the restaurant wasn't crowded yet. In fact, only two other couples occupied the dining room and they sat far away from Teri and Mac, talking quietly.

Teri fumbled with her napkin and gratefully reached for her glass when their drinks arrived. She felt as if she'd never been on a date and was certain she acted like it, too.

"Do you remember the last time we had dinner together?" Mac asked in a low, romantic voice.

"No."

"Oh. Neither do I." Teresa looked at Mac, then laughed. He grinned at her. "You were expecting some long, seductive description of that dinner, weren't you?"

"Well, yes."

"Sorry, but if anything significant happened over a last dinner together, I don't recall it. So much for softening you up with sentimental memories."

In spite of Mac's joking, Teresa still felt awkward and wished she could think of a pleasant, interesting topic that would take both their minds off of what seemed dangerously like a date. She took a drink of water, then cast around her mind and finally came up with, "Won't your club be opening in about an hour? Who takes care of things while you're away?"

"I have an excellent assistant manager. He's very ambitious, but he can't have designs on my job unless he wants to buy the place. I expect in about a year he'll want to move on and get a position in a big-city club."

"Will there be any franchises of Club Rendezvous?"

"Maybe in two or three years. It all depends on the economy."

"Doesn't just about everything?" Teresa's attempt at a gay little laugh sounded wooden. "I'd hoped to expand Farr Fields—buy more land, build a second barn—but I'm not sure I'll be able to keep what I already have afloat after all of this trouble." She immediately realized how self-concerned she seemed. "I wasn't referring to Gus's . . . death. That was a tragedy. I'll never forgive myself for putting him in danger."

"How did you put him in danger?"

Teresa looked at Mac in surprise. "Have you forgotten what happened eight years ago? Half of the town hasn't forgotten, even when Roscoe Lee Byrnes was holding firm on his confession. But now that he's recanted—well, you know all of the old suspicions of me have surfaced again. And I told you about the note, the fax, the night-light—I'm being stalked, so anyone who associates with me is in danger. Sharon was probably right to drag away Daniel from his lesson yesterday."

"So you think you're Typhoid Mary, a peril to anyone who comes near you."

"It seems that way."

"And this curse you embody went on an eight-year

hiatus? First there was Wendy and your father and Celeste, then nothing for years, and now Gus."

"You're forgetting about my mother," Teresa said quietly. "My mother . . . disappeared."

"Disappeared because she was murdered? Or disappeared and died?" Mac paused, then said with emphasis, "Or just disappeared for a while?" Teresa's gaze jerked away from him. "Teri, do you really think your mother is alive and in town?"

The question he'd wanted to ask since this afternoon was one Teri didn't want to answer. For a moment, she stared at Mac's earnest face—a face she'd once loved— and knew she couldn't lie to him. "I can't imagine that if my mother were still alive, she would have stayed away for so long. She knew how much Kent and I loved her. She wouldn't be so cruel."

Teresa paused. "At least, if she were herself, she wouldn't be so cruel. But she wasn't well, physically or mentally. She'd been released from the mental hospital, but maybe she shouldn't have been. That last day I saw her at the house—the day when Dad caught us—she was so thin and desperate. Frankly, she wasn't even making a lot of sense. She asked me to run away with her."

"She did?" Mac looked shocked. "You never told me."

Their salad arrived and Teresa was glad she didn't have to answer Mac for a moment. He repeated his question, though, as soon as the waitress left.

"I didn't tell you anything about seeing her that day," Teri said. "Your mother begged me not to, remember? Anyway, Mom kept saying, 'I can't get well here in this town. I can't get well without you, and you need to get away from your father and Wendy. I'm afraid of what they might do to you.' "

"What did she think Hugh and Wendy would do to you?"

"I don't know. After all, I was going to be leaving for college in September—I just had to get through the rest of spring and the summer—and both of them couldn't wait for me to leave. Dad only fought for custody of me to hurt Mom." Teresa sighed. "Maybe she was afraid Dad would beat me. Looking back, I'm sure he struck her more than once. And he slapped me twice the day Mom came to the house."

"So she was afraid for you as well as being devastated at having you taken away from her," Mac said thoughtfully. "Do you know how strong a motive that is for her killing Hugh and Wendy?"

"Yes." Teresa spoke barely above a whisper. "I've known it ever since the night of the murders. But it doesn't explain her attacking Celeste."

"You said she wasn't well. Maybe she just went into some kind of frenzy."

"The person I bumped into in the hall—the person who cut my arm—was definitely not in a frenzy. That person was almost frighteningly calm."

Mac raised his eyebrows. "You never told me that, either."

"Well, I've held back quite a lot over the years. I believe I've told you everything now." Mac said nothing and Teresa went on. "The point is that I've never been sure my mother didn't kill Dad and Wendy. Mom disappeared after the murders, but if she died, her body was never found. No Jane Doe bodies the authorities thought might be my mother have surfaced, either. Now Roscoe Byrnes has recanted his confession, suspicion has fallen on me again, and suddenly I thought I saw my mother on the road leading from my place—running away from the barn where Gus Gibbs was murdered. And today, I found Mom's recently worn scarf in our old house."

Mac frowned. "I want you to think about two points. One, that scarf is probably your mother's and it has been worn recently, but there's no proof that *she* wore it. Two, I understand why your mother would keep her presence a secret if she committed the murders eight years ago, but why would she kill Gus?"

"Maybe she was in the barn with Eclipse, who looks exactly like the horse she had when she was young, and Gus walked in. He recognized her. She still didn't intend to reveal herself unless she saw that I was in danger of being arrested and tried for the murders of Dad and Wendy, so she grabbed the rake and struck at Gus, then she ran. I'm sure she didn't mean to kill him."

"Well, if she wanted to keep her presence a secret, she would *have* to kill him. And don't forget that he was posed, Teri." Her eyes widened. "The hay in the stall had two tracks where Gus's heels had scraped as he was pulled to the corner of the stall. You didn't seem to notice, so I didn't say anything last night, but you should know now."

"Oh, God. How could I not notice?"

"Don't get upset, Teri. You were so shocked when you saw him, then I took you away. You were sitting over on the bench when the police mentioned it. The whole thing was terrible enough without you imagining someone dragging Gus over to a corner where he was hidden unless you completely opened the horse stall."

"Then Mom didn't want him to be seen immediately. Maybe she thought if he was found later, someone else would be blamed. Someone like Josh, who she probably knew wasn't home right then but would be later."

Mac closed his eyes for a moment, then looked at her sympathetically. "Teri, are you listening to yourself? One minute you're saying your mother isn't well, she's acting crazy, and then you credit her with extremely calculated behavior. It doesn't make sense."

Teresa dropped her gaze and sighed. "You're right, Mac. None of this makes sense. I'm just grasping at answers, no matter how illogical, because I feel like I'm under siege. I'm so scared, both for myself and for my mother."

"I know." Mac's voice was tender and understanding. "I also know how hard it is for you to admit you're so frightened. You've never wanted people to think you were afraid of anything. That's why I took the liberty of buying you what might be a valuable present."

"A present?" Teresa asked as Mac reached into his pocket. "Not a *gun!*"

"Hush!" Mac hissed. "Of course I'm not carrying a gun around in my pants pocket, although I don't think it would do you any harm to have a gun."

"Well, I don't own one. And as for buying one now—when I'm suspected of murdering three people—I don't think so."

"I'm one step ahead of you. I got this for you." Mac held out a shiny gold tube.

"Lipstick?" Teresa asked. "You think lipstick will help me?"

"It's a special kind of lipstick." Mac smiled. "It's lipstick pepper spray. It's perfectly legal—you don't need a permit to buy or carry it, and there isn't a problem with you keeping it concealed, like there is with a stun gun."

"Who would want to walk around *carrying* a stun gun?" Teri asked.

"I don't know. That's the problem with them. You have to tote it around in full view all the time or you could be arrested for carrying a concealed weapon. Anyway, pepper spray swells the mucous membranes and the veins in the eyes so your attacker can barely breathe or see, not to mention that it burns like hell. This little sprayer is good for up to six feet."

Teresa picked up the tube carefully and slipped off the top to see the small white pump. "All I have to do is squirt this once?"

"Well, I'd squirt it three or four times to be safe. And remember, you have to be close to your attacker. You can't disable him if you're clear across the room." Teresa looked at the tube doubtfully and Mac went on. "Look, Teri, I know this isn't the most dangerous weapon you could have, but as you've said, you don't already have a gun and now isn't the best time for you to buy one. Just keep this tube with you at all times. It's small—it will even fit into the pocket of jeans. Tight jeans, like you wear." She made a face at him and he grinned. "I want you to promise me you'll always carry it."

Teresa gave the tube one more dubious glance, then picked up her purse. "I'm afraid this dress has no pockets, so it has to go in the purse for now. But later, I'll wear nothing that doesn't have at least one pocket, and this will be in it."

"Promise?"

"I promise."

Just then their food arrived and Teri's eyes widened at the size of the steak, the baked potato, the ear of corn she hadn't expected, and the huge rolls. While the waitress finished organizing their food on the table and asking if they'd like anything else, Teresa tucked the tube of pepper spray in the top of her purse so she wouldn't forget it. She had every intention of keeping her promise to Mac to carry the little tube of spray all the time, and she already felt a tad safer.

2

"I won't be able to eat all day tomorrow to make up for what a glutton I made of myself tonight," Teresa groaned as they climbed the steps to her porch. "Still, it was absolutely delicious."

"I did notice that after declaring you couldn't possibly eat so much, you cleaned up your plate," Mac said dryly.

"No one has ever accused me of having a dainty appetite."

Mac gave her the slow, lazy grin she loved. "That's another one of the things I like about you, Teri Farr."

"That I eat so much?"

"That you don't pretend, even about how much you eat. Of course, with a slender body like yours, you don't have to worry. You're tall and slim like your mother. That's how she would have been if she'd eaten five full meals a day." He paused, then said slowly, close to her cheek, "You'll always be beautiful, Teri. Always."

When they reached Teresa's house after dinner, she had meant to kiss Mac good night at the door and then go to bed at a decent hour—*alone*. But after Mac had taken her in his arms and kissed her as if he hadn't kissed anyone for years, Teresa's resolve wavered. She wanted—desperately wanted—at least one more kiss. But not here with the porch lights blazing. Josh wasn't home, but her prowler might be lingering around. She didn't like feeling so exposed.

"Let's go inside," she murmured as Mac's lips touched her neck. "Mac, stop. I can't get my key in the lock."

He took the ring of keys from Teri, inserted the one she'd separated from the rest in the lock, and swung open the door. Sierra rushed at them, barking furiously. "Hey, girl, I'm glad to see you, too," Teresa said, bending to give the dog a "hello" pat.

But Sierra continued to huff, snort, bark, and growl, not settling down as she usually did when her mistress had returned home. Teresa suddenly became aware of more noise in the room. Noise coming from the television, which she definitely had not left on when she'd left the house with Mac.

"The TV," she said, moving closer to the television. "Mac, look at it."

She felt him standing behind her as she stared at the images on the screen. She wasn't seeing the regular Wednesday night programming. She was seeing herself wearing her best pair of jeans and a glittery top, laughing and clowning with a crowd of people, then leaning forward to blow out the candles on a cake.

Teresa was seeing the missing videotape of her six-teenth birthday party.

CHAPTER SIXTEEN

1

"MAYBE YOU JUST OVERLOOKED that tape this afternoon," Mac said with forced calm.

"I didn't!" Teresa snapped. "I looked especially for the tape of my sixteenth birthday because it was probably my happiest. I searched for it before I saw the scarf, so you can't say I was scared and overlooked it!"

"Okay, okay. Don't get so wound up," Mac said patiently. "The issue isn't so much the tape but that it's playing. You weren't watching it before I came, and even if you were, it would have ended by now. VCR tapes don't rewind themselves and play over and over. I'm going to check the doors. You stay here."

Mac went to the front door and carefully inspected the lock. "This is fine," he said almost to himself. When he went to the back door, Teresa watched herself on the tape—sixteen, happy, untouched by tragedy. She saw a young Teresa take the camera and turn it on her mother, who smiled with embarrassment and held her hands in front of her lovely face. Then Teresa had caught Emma, tall and spare, with her thick hair pulled back tightly. Emma, who'd always hated having her picture taken, had fled from the room as if Teri were pointing a flamethrower at her, sending Teri and her contemporaries into fits of teenage laughter as Teri had yelled, "I'm sorry, Emma. Don't be mad."

Mac walked into the living room, placed himself between Teresa and the tape playing on the television, took the remote control from her hand, and pressed STOP. Then he put his hands on her shoulders. "Maybe the lock on the back door has been picked, but I'm not sure. I'm not an expert. Just to be safe, you need to have your locks changed."

"Great," Teresa said in defeat. "Tomorrow is the Fourth of July. I'll never find anyone to do the work."

"Maybe not a professional locksmith, but I, my dear, can install new doorknobs with locks. The hardware store will be open tomorrow. I'll get the stuff in the morning and have you locked in safe and sound by noon. I need to go through the house now and make sure no one is still in here."

"This will be your second house tour for intruders today," Teresa said. "Maybe you should become a private detective."

"I think they have to follow people around, go on stakeouts, wade through bank records. Not for me," Mac said lightly. "I'd rather just hunt people down in houses and pummel them to death."

"I'll go with you, but I'm not pummeling anyone. I'm too depressed."

They looked in every room and every closet with Sierra trailing dutifully behind them. Nothing was missing or even disturbed and they found no one lurking in the house. They returned to the living room and Teresa removed the tape from the VCR, then thumped down disconsolately on the couch. She looked at the cassette label that read:

TERESA'S SWEET SIXTEEN BIRTHDAY PARTY

Her mother's handwriting on the tape she had made—a tape Teri had not watched since right after the party, a tape cartridge she hadn't seen for eight years, a tape cartridge that had not been in the box she'd found today in her former home.

"Where did this come from?" she almost wailed to Mac. "Who brought it here?"

"I don't know, but I do know we should call the police." She looked at him in alarm. "Teri, someone broke into your house. They didn't take anything—"

"No, they left something."

"It doesn't matter whether they took or gave. They broke in. You have to report this. You don't have to face the police alone. I won't leave you."

"*I won't leave you.*" The simple words shook Teresa. Did he mean just that he was not leaving her tonight to face the police, or did he mean he wasn't leaving her ever? Or did he mean both? Oh, she was too tired to analyze everything Mac said. Now she could only concentrate on the present situation and be glad he wasn't going to desert her.

A young deputy was sent to the scene. Teresa vaguely recognized him as one of the county deputies who had come the night before when they had found Gus's body. The deputy took copious notes and nodded his head a lot, agreed that someone breaking in just to leave a VHS tape was indeed strange, and checked both doors as Mac had done. Teri then told the deputy about the prowler who had left the night-light on the porch. He did not seem particularly impressed with that until she said she had seen someone who looked the same running across the road the night Gus Gibbs was murdered. The deputy asked for a full description, then narrowed his eyes and asked why she had said nothing about this person last night.

"I was very shaken and I just didn't think about it," she said lamely. "I didn't see the person come from the barn— just from my property. I intended to tell the sheriff about it today, but I haven't seen him. I'll be talking with him tomorrow, though."

Mac didn't give the deputy a chance to ask why she hadn't talked to the sheriff today. "In light of this person who's creeping around here wearing a black coat and hood, leaving things on Miss Farr's porch, coming from her property on the night of Mr. Gibbs's murder, don't you think she should have police protection?" Mac asked.

"We already have a city patrol car coming by here four times every twenty-four hours and a state police car come by twice," the deputy said. "I know it doesn't sound like much, but we're low on manpower right now—one deputy is out sick, and another's on vacation—so there's no way we can provide twenty-four-hour surveillance, but I'll see if we can't step up the patrols," the deputy said. "In the meantime, Miss Farr, it might be best if you stayed with a friend."

After he'd left, Teresa looked at Mac and said, "A patrol car coming by approximately every four hours will certainly scare off the hardiest of souls."

Mac laughed. "I know it's not much, but it's better than nothing. At least the break-in has been reported."

"And no one will dare do it again now that it has been officially reported."

"Don't be such a sourpuss," Mac teased. "Reporting it was the right thing to do."

"That will be a great comfort to me the next time someone breaks in here and kills me and Sierra."

"No one is going to get a chance to do that," Mac said, "because you are not going to be alone until this thing is over."

"Mac, I can't desert this place like the deputy suggested. Josh's friends are going to feed the horses, but the guys aren't staying here, and I'm not going to run off and leave the horses unprotected."

"Can't you pay Josh's friends to stay in the barn and watch over the horses?"

"The barn is a crime scene—it can't be disturbed except to feed the horses. Besides, I don't know who these guys are—I have no way to get in touch with them and I don't know where Josh is. I can't contact them."

Teresa took a deep breath. "I *can't* leave the horses, Mac. Some of them are mine. Most of them aren't, but they're being boarded here. Even if I weren't concerned about them because I love horses, it's taken me years to get my business going and I can't just toss everything aside. The safety of those horses is my responsibility and you can call me silly and childish and reckless and just plain stupid, but I *can't* leave them!"

"I hadn't intended to call you any of those things," Mac returned calmly. "I know you aren't going to leave the horses unprotected for long, especially after someone *did* go into the barn and turned loose your horse." Teresa noticed he'd carefully not mentioned the murder of Gus. "But tonight you *have* to get out of here until your locks can be replaced. That's why I want you two ladies to put together a travel kit, because you're coming to spend the night at my place."

"At *your* place!"

"Yes, Teresa. I have an apartment above the club and it's pretty nice."

Spend the night with Mac? Every bit of reason in Teresa told her to say no. Every bit of emotion desperately wanted to accept his offer.

"Mac, I don't know if that's such a good idea," she said, hearing the lack of conviction in her voice.

"Look, Teri, do you want to sleep in a house where

someone has picked your lock to come inside and leave a videotape?"

"No, of course I don't!"

"Well, I'm offering you an alternative. You could always go to a hotel, but they'll charge. I won't. Besides, the two nicest hotels in the area don't allow dogs."

"I can bring Sierra to your apartment? Because I'm not going to leave her here alone to face whoever, whatever—"

"I told the *two* of you ladies to put together your travel kit. I only see two ladies in the room—you and one with short brown hair and impressively large pointed ears." Teresa smiled. "Teri, I know you wouldn't run off and leave Sierra, either. I'm going to call a guy who's sort of an undercover bouncer at the club and ask him to spend the night *outside* of your barn. He can pitch a tent or something. It's a warm night. He'll guard your horses for you."

"You think he'll do it?" Teresa asked doubtfully.

"For some extra money, I know he'll do it. I'll also call the cops and tell them not to go berserk when they see him out there. Now go pack something. The sooner we get out of here, the better. Frankly, I feel a little creepy, too, knowing someone was here about ten minutes before we arrived. They had to be waiting until they saw my car coming toward the house, because the tape hadn't been playing for more than a few minutes." Teri hadn't thought of that. "Run along now," Mac said briskly. "And remember this is an overnight trip. You're not going on an ocean voyage."

"I wish we were going on an ocean voyage," Teresa muttered to Sierra, who followed her as she gathered up a nightgown, underwear, and some toiletries. "I'm beginning to feel about as comfortable in this house as I do in the house on Mourning Dove Lane."

2

"Beer, popcorn, and *The African Queen* on DVD," Gabriel said. "What more could a man want?"

"Me, I hope." Carmen sat down beside him on the couch, placing a fragrant bowl of buttery popcorn on her lap. "After tomorrow night, we won't always have to stay in the secrecy of our houses. We can actually go to the theater to see a movie."

"I like watching movies at home. You can always put them on hold if the mood overtakes you." Gabe leaned down and kissed Carmen's neck. "Get my meaning?"

"It was so subtle, I'm not sure I understood," Carmen giggled. "But even if you're in the mood, you will just have to wait, sir, because I made this popcorn just for you and it's perfect right this minute."

Gabe dipped a big hand into the bowl. "Smells delicious." He popped the handful of popcorn into his mouth. "Tastes delicious," he said around the fluffy kernels.

"Good. I also got your favorite brand of beer." Carmen sighed. "Gabe, do you know how fattening all of this stuff is?"

"Are you saying I need to lose weight?"

"Not at all. You're just right. But I can only have one beer and about one-eighth of this popcorn or I'll lose my girlish figure. Actually, I've already lost it, but I don't want to go any farther down the drain."

"You think you've lost your figure? With how you watch your diet and all of the exercise you do?"

"I used to be thinner when I modeled."

"Then you must have been too thin. You're on the verge of being too thin now. I mean, you have a beautiful figure, but am I imagining that you've lost a few pounds in the last couple of weeks?"

Carmen rubbed her slim waist and sighed. "No, you're not imagining it. I've lost five pounds. I've been worried."

"About what?"

"About us, silly. I've been afraid you'd keep stalling about announcing our engagement."

"I'm not stalling. We're telling everyone tomorrow night. Or is that off?"

"Oh no," Carmen said quickly. "I talked to Teri earlier. I'm going to take the food to her house in the afternoon—she offered to bake pastries, but she's just the worst cook in the world, poor sweetheart—and she's going to meet Kent and Sharon and Daniel at their house. I suppose you'll be there, as usual." Gabe nodded. "So the five of you will go to the concert first. I'll casually come up and join you. Then we'll all go back to Teri's and we'll make the announcement. How does that sound?"

"Good."

Carmen stared at him. "That wasn't very enthusiastic."

"Honey, you're going to wear yourself out constantly analyzing the tone of my voice. I'll be greatly relieved to make the announcement. Really."

"Well, I was hoping for more than *relieved.*" Disappointment edged Carmen's voice. "I'd hoped you'd be happy."

"I *will* be. Of course I'll be happy. I'm just not as expressive as you are, Carmen." He smiled at her, but she wasn't sure that smile quite reached his eyes. "Will you stop worrying? I don't believe I've ever met a person who worries as much as you do."

"What about the way Sharon obsesses over Daniel?"

As soon as the words were out of her mouth, as soon as she saw Gabe's smile disappear and the line form between his eyebrows, Carmen knew she'd made a mistake. Gabe would not brook any criticism of his daughter, even if the criticism were merely implied.

"Oh, what do I know about how a good mother should act?" Carmen said quickly, airily, desperately striving for self-deprecating humor. "My mother took off with another man when I was thirteen, and before that, she paid as little attention as possible to me. So did my father. Then I never had any children of my own, which was a great disappointment, but considering that if I'd had a child, he would have been young when my husband got sick, I guess it was for the best."

Carmen had been talking so fast, trying to compensate for her misstep, she ended on a breathless note. She was relieved when Gabe asked somewhat tersely, "You knew Marielle. Wasn't she a good mother?"

"Oh, she tried her very best, and considering her mental problems, she did an excellent job. The children adored her, especially Teri, but Marielle's depression and unhappiness affected them. It's wonderful that Sharon has such a healthy outlook on life—she can pass that on to Daniel," Carmen ended lamely.

"She's an excellent mother," Gabe said firmly. "Daniel is her world. Daniel and Kent."

And *you*, Carmen thought dismally. Sharon's world orbits around the three of you, and she's not going to let *you* go any easier than she would her husband or son.

"Let's watch the movie," Gabe said, reaching for his beer.

"Sure. *The African Queen* is one of my all-time favorites." Carmen pushed buttons on the remote control and the DVD started. She looked at Gabe's serious profile and took a gulp of her own beer, knowing she wouldn't be limiting herself to one glass after all.

3

After Teresa had gathered up dog treats and enough food for Sierra's breakfast, they were off to Club Rendezvous. Sierra, excited by all the goings-on in her usually quiet life, kept standing up on the backseat and thrusting her head beside Teri's, panting enthusiastically.

"You have to pardon Sierra's exuberance," Teri said. "We haven't had a sleepover for years."

"That's good to know."

Teresa realized she sounded as if she were reassuring Mac that she hadn't spent the night with a man for a long time. The implication was true, but she certainly didn't want Mac to know about the lack of romance in her life. "I don't take Sierra *everywhere* with me," she added almost defiantly.

The club's parking lot was over half-filled with cars. "Great for a weeknight!" Mac commented with a smile before he drove behind the big building in back to a private parking lot. "Do you ladies prefer to use the outside or inside entrance?"

"Outside," Teresa answered promptly, grabbing the paper bags holding her and Sierra's overnight gear. Sierra clambered into the front seat, afraid of being left behind, and Teresa grabbed her leash, dropping the bags. "Oh, hell!" she exclaimed.

Mac hurried around the car and picked up the bags. "Teri, have you thought of using luggage?"

"I didn't want to waste time digging it out from the back of the closet." Sierra, mad with joy over their nighttime adventure, jumped, spun, and pulled while Teresa held tightly on to the leash. "Besides, do you know how hard it is to get paper bags from the grocery store? You have to make a special request or they give you those flimsy plastic things that hold about three items."

"Then I'll be extremely careful with these two *paper* bags." Mac shifted them to one arm while he unlocked a door, beyond which rose a set of stairs. Sierra led the way, and when they reached the top, Mac unlocked a second door. "Enter my lair," he said with a flourish of his free hand.

Teresa and Sierra stepped into a service way leading to a narrow kitchen with white laminate cabinets and stainless-steel appliances. Beyond the kitchen lay a dining room and living room, both furnished in earthy colors that made them seem warm compared to the cold sterility of the kitchen. Tan and brown woven rugs decorated granite flooring, and light beige vertical blinds hung at all the windows.

"Wow," Teresa said, gazing around at the sharp-edged modern furniture, a mixture of glass, stainless steel, leather, and chocolate-colored suede. "We didn't design your living quarters all those years ago."

"That's because we thought we'd be married and living in a house suitable for at least two children." Teresa winced inwardly at the memory. When she was nineteen and engaged to Mac, she had expected to be Teri MacKenzie, wife and mother, at twenty-six. "You don't like it," Mac said flatly.

"As a rule I'm not fond of the stark modern look, but somehow it seems right for you."

"I don't know if that was a compliment or not," Mac said dryly. "Does 'stark' describe my intellectual state?"

"No. I just meant it seems like the perfect setting for a single man-about-town."

Mac emitted a short, sharp laugh. "A 'man-about-town' meaning a single guy in Point Pleasant?"

"For heaven's sake, Mac," Teresa said in exasperation. "Your apartment is extremely stylish and tasteful. Why do you care what I think anyway?"

Mac sighed. "You're tense. You always take that tone when you're tense." Teresa tried to shoot him a withering look, but he was already heading for another room. "I'll put your *luggage* in the bedroom."

"Mac—"

"Don't panic. I'll sleep in the living room. The couch is a daybed."

Teresa walked toward the suede-upholstered couch/ daybed. Sierra, always timid in an unfamiliar setting, followed so closely she kept stepping on Teri's heels. In a moment, Mac came back carrying Sierra's two metal bowls and the small bag of dog food Teresa had packed for the overnight visit. "How about Perrier water for Sierra and white wine for you and me?" he asked, going into the kitchen.

"She'll never drink regular water again, but it's fine. And I'd love a glass of wine."

Teresa picked up a copy of *Time* lying on the big glass coffee table, nervously flipped pages, tossed it down, and started rubbing Sierra under the ears. As soon as the dog heard dry food hitting her bowl, though, she shot to the kitchen. Traitor, Teresa thought, chiding herself for feeling so self-conscious she needed to occupy her unsteady hands by fondling the dog.

Mac returned with two wineglasses and a full bottle of white wine. "If I remember, you don't like dry white wine. You like it on the sweet side."

"Yes, but please don't give me a pompous lecture on wines," Teresa snapped.

"I wouldn't dream of it." Mac poured her glass and handed it to her. If he noticed that her hand trembled, he ignored it. Mac held up his glass. "To better times ahead," he said, not waiting for her to lift her glass. She knew instantly he *had* noticed her trembling hands.

He took a sip; she took two gulps and savored the taste of the cool wine flowing over the back of her tongue and down her throat, which felt dry as the desert. "Oh, that's good!" she exclaimed.

"So it seems." Mac's lips quirked slightly. "I thought you'd like it. It will help you relax."

"Whatever makes you think I need to relax?" Teresa asked wryly. "I thought the tape was a lovely welcome-home present." She frowned. "Mac, I hadn't thought of it before, but whoever broke into my home knew they'd have to get past Sierra. Even if they didn't know I had a dog, they would have heard her barking from outside."

"That's true."

Teresa pounced on his bland tone. "That's why you don't believe anyone *did* come into my home! Because there were no signs of her attacking anyone. You think I put that tape in myself!"

"Teri, stop being so defensive. We reported it to the police, and even if at first I thought you might have put in the tape yourself, that doesn't explain why it was still running when we got home. As for Sierra . . . well, I don't know why she didn't take a chunk out of an intruder."

Teresa sighed. "Well, I guess I do. It's because she never has. She barks and snarls and carries on like the most dangerous dog on earth when she's confronted with a stranger, but she has *never* bitten anyone. She's all noise."

"A stranger wouldn't have known that."

"No. And maybe whoever it was brought along something in case there was a truly vicious dog inside. Maybe some pepper spray, like you bought for me. But it became obvious fairly quickly that Sierra wasn't going to actually bite. She was unusually hyper when we came home, though. After all, she has met you before—you weren't a stranger. Something that happened earlier in the evening had her upset."

"The entrance of an intruder," Mac said flatly. "Teri, I believe that you weren't playing that tape in the afternoon. I believe you weren't even in possession of that tape. Do you think I would have invited you to spend the night if I thought you weren't safe in your own home?" Teresa raised an eyebrow at him. "All right, I deserve that look. Of course, I would have jumped at the chance to have you spend the night with me, but not in my bedroom with your dog while I'm on the couch. I know that's how it's going be and I still don't want you to leave. That should be a reassurance of my good intentions."

Teresa took another sip of wine and said softly, "Words come easily to you, Mac."

He stiffened and shot her an offended glance. "And what does that mean?"

"It means that you made a lot of promises to me when I was young. You made promises when we were engaged—promises always to love me and to be faithful. And you broke them."

"I did not break my promise to always love you. As for being faithful . . . well, I was." Teri raised her eyes and glared at him. "I *was*."

"Would the redhead I caught you kissing so passionately agree with you?"

"If she was being truthful, she'd tell you I never slept with her, Teri. Honestly, I didn't. But . . . I did come close."

Teresa felt tears rising in her eyes, quickly took a gulp of wine, and managed to ask with some control, "One month before our wedding. Mac, why did you do it? Why did you get involved with someone else when we were so close to really being together?"

"After you caught me with her, you yelled at me, you flung accusations at me, you broke off our engagement, but you never asked me *why*."

"I'm asking it now."

Mac suddenly stood and walked over to the windows, the blinds still open to the night. "I've thought a lot about it over the years. I'm not sure I entirely understand my own actions, but I believe I felt trapped."

Teresa flinched as if she'd been slapped. "Trapped? By me?"

"By my whole life. When my father left, I became the man of the family. I was eleven. I had a mother who was about to fall apart and two-year-old twin sisters. I started taking on every job I could, and Mom worked in a convenience store that made her a nervous wreck until your mother, God bless her, hired her as a housekeeper. I kept up my grades, looked after Mom and the girls, worked, and I fell in love with you when I was just shy of twenty. I'd dated other girls, but I didn't have time for anything other than a couple of movie dates with each one—something casual. When you were old enough, I began seeing you. When you were nineteen, we got engaged.

"Right before our wedding, I was just beginning to really earn some money, finding out what it was like to have free time, and . . . well . . . women who wanted to be with me. I was tempted. I thought, 'I can't tie myself down just when I've *finally* gotten freedom for the first time since I was a kid.' As for the redhead—Delores—she meant nothing to me. But you saw us together and you left. I didn't blame you. In one tiny, awful way I was relieved for nearly a year. By then I'd sown my wild oats, found out I didn't enjoy life without you, and would have given anything to have you back. But it was too late. I accepted it. I never stopped regretting it."

"You haven't acted as if you regretted it," Teresa said bitterly. "I'm always hearing stories about Mac MacKenzie, the local Don Juan."

"I haven't lived in solitude. I haven't been celibate. I'm a normal man, Teri. Did you expect me to sit in a tower and pine away for you all of these years? I didn't think I'd ever have a second chance with you. That doesn't mean I stopped loving you."

"Loving me?" Teresa murmured.

"Yes, *loving* you! Are you going to claim you didn't know it?"

"Yes, I'm claiming it because it's true. I didn't think you gave me a second thought. In the years since I came back to Point Pleasant, you've never come to see me, never called me. What was I supposed to think?"

"That I believed you didn't *want* to hear from me. That I thought I was respecting your wishes. We didn't exactly part amicably, you know. In fact, you said you never wanted to see me again."

"I was angry."

"When did you stop being angry?"

"About five minutes ago, when you explained to me how you felt at the time," Teresa admitted. "I'm not saying I would have taken it gracefully when I was twenty, or that even if I'd been older, it wouldn't have taken time for me to stop feeling completely deceived and rejected. But now . . ."

"But now?"

"But now I need another glass of wine." Teresa rose from the couch. "I'll get it."

Sierra trotted after her into the narrow, ultra-modern kitchen. Teri pressed her forehead against the cool stainless-steel door of the refrigerator for a moment, her emotions whirling. After finding them kissing as if the world were ending tomorrow, Teresa had believed Mac had been unfaithful for months, not just with Delores—the owner of the bar he worked at—but with other women, too.

Teresa had never questioned him about these supposed affairs. She wouldn't have believed any denials he made, anyway. Still, she now realized she hadn't given him a chance. And to hear Mac talk now, at the time, he hadn't wanted a chance. Only later had he realized that the kind of love they had was precious and often unobtainable—not something he could throw away and find again two or three years later. Maybe not even in a lifetime. When he'd made the realization, though, he hadn't pursued her again, honoring her wishes. All of these years, he'd kept his distance because he thought that's what she'd wanted. His respect for her feelings had to count for something, she thought.

She poured a glass of wine and walked slowly back into the living room. Mac stood by a window, looking out. He pulled the vertical blinds shut and turned to look at her in the soft light cast by incandescent bulbs in a tall, heavily shaded lamp. "That took a while," he said.

"I didn't rush," Teresa answered calmly. "I had to think."

"Think about what? Us?"

"What else?" Teresa set her wineglass on the coffee table. Before she could seat herself on the couch, Mac had crossed the room and taken her in his arms. "Mac, I—"

"You what?" he murmured, his breath warm in her ear, his arms pulling her closer to him.

"I'm not sure we should be doing this. We were engaged, but it was years ago. We've only been talking to each other again for less than a week. It's just so . . ."

"Right." Mac's warm lips trailed down her neck. "It's always been right for us, Teri."

"Sex, maybe. But I don't want just sex. I mean—"

"What do you mean, Teresa?"

Mac pushed the scooped neckline of her dress farther to the right and lightly, teasingly kissed her collarbone. A wave of heat flooded through Teri, but she still made herself say, "I want what we used to have—love."

"We can't have what we used to have." Mac stopped kissing her and looked penetratingly into her eyes, his own intense, seductive, and sincere. "We can have something better than we used to have, Teri. It can be better because we're both older, we've both experienced more of life, and we're both more certain of what we want."

"And what do we both want?" Teresa asked, clinging to him, feeling the warmth of perspiration beginning to cover her entire body, causing her arms to encircle Mac's neck and to hold on tightly. She felt like she wanted to cling to him forever, never to let go of his strength, his goodness, his charm, and his overpowering sensuality.

"We *both* want love, Teri," he said, barely above a whisper.

Teresa felt the last of her defenses crumbling away. No amount of effort could have made her lie to him now. Bending back her head to receive his deep kiss on her lips, she said softly, "Yes. Oh yes, Mac. I want love."

CHAPTER SEVENTEEN

1

THE NEXT DAY, MAC had returned Teresa and Sierra to their home and was installing new locks on the doors when Carmen arrived. Teresa braced herself, feeling that anyone who looked at her could tell she'd spent a passionate night with Mac. Carmen seemed distracted, though. Teresa was glad her friend had her engagement announcement to think about, instead of focusing her attention on Teri and Mac.

Together she and Carmen carried in a German chocolate cake, a pineapple upside-down cake, cupcakes, and a tray of petits fours. Carmen had also brought two bottles of a good champagne along with juice and soft drinks.

"Carmen, you've brought enough food to feed twenty people." Teresa laughed.

"I'm hoping everyone is in the mood for a real party."

Teresa studied Carmen closely. She looked trim and tailored in her slim jeans and a creamy knit top that played up her slim waist and beautiful shoulder-length brown hair, but her complexion was pale, and faint mauve shadows lay beneath her eyes. She probably hadn't slept well last night, and Teresa couldn't blame her. This upcoming marriage was terribly important to Carmen, and she would be facing an adversary wielding a weapon more powerful than a gun—the love and demands of a possessive daughter.

Teresa abruptly enclosed Carmen in her arms. "Calm down, Carmen," she said softly. "Don't expect Sharon to be whooping with joy tonight. At best, she'll say nothing. At worst, she'll say something nasty. But if Gabe truly loves you, which I'm sure he does, he'll insist Sharon accept you as his wife."

Some of the worry left Carmen's eyes for a moment and she smiled. "Could you give me that pep talk again before we make the announcement?"

"I'll give it to you all day long, with the exception of the time I have to spend talking to the sheriff."

"I forgot about that!" Carmen exclaimed. "Do you want me to go with you?"

"Thanks, but no. I want to face this on my own and not hide behind *anyone*."

Later in the afternoon, when Teresa returned from her meeting with the sheriff, she wished she hadn't pretended to be so strong and gone alone. The sheriff had made her repeat the sequence of events the night of Gus's murder three times. He'd demanded to know why she hadn't reported earlier the stranger who had left the night-light at her front door or what appeared to be the same person who had run in front of her car less than an hour before she'd found Gus in the horse's stall.

Although Teresa had answered all of the sheriff's questions truthfully, her answers sounded hollow and evasive to her own ears. She'd walked into his office confidently, with her shoulders back and her head held high. She left feeling like the frightened, slumping teenager he'd interrogated again and again eight years ago.

"I see the interview didn't go well," Mac said when she arrived home. "Did he get out the blinding light and the rubber hose?"

"Just short of it. If I'd made myself available for questioning yesterday, it wouldn't have been so bad. By avoiding him I made things worse."

Mac kissed her forehead. "Well, at least you faced him. It's over."

"For today. They still have no idea who killed Gus. If Roscoe Byrnes is telling the truth about not killing Dad and Wendy, they have no idea who murdered them, either, leaving me as the prime suspect. *Again,*" Teresa said in despair. "Now another person has been murdered right under my nose."

"What motive does the sheriff think you could have had for murdering Gus Gibbs?"

"I believe he just thinks I'm crazy. A homicidal maniac."

Mac frowned. "A homicidal maniac that waits eight years between murders? One that stays at the scene of her murders so she can be caught? Sorry, honey, but I'm not buying it."

"You're not the sheriff."

"And you're not under arrest, are you?" Teresa shook her head. "So stop looking so scared."

"I'm not sure I can."

"You have to for Daniel's sake. Tonight is the fireworks display, remember? What will he think if his aunt appears looking like she's facing the guillotine?"

Teresa groaned. "I forgot about that in the midst of my panic attack. You're right. I have to get hold of myself."

"Of course I'm right. I'm always right." Mac's eyes twinkled and he kissed her again, then wrapped his arm around her. "You didn't even notice when you came in. Kent's moving men arrived with the grandfather clock from your house and the lamp. I told them to put the lamp in your bedroom. I didn't know where you wanted the clock, so I had them place it right over there. If you don't like it, we can move it later."

Teresa rose and walked to the clock. It looked so much bigger in her house than in her former home—big but still beautiful with its intricate carving and the moon phase face. Mac had not wound the clock. It sat as if frozen in time, no hands moving, no pendulum swinging, no chimes ringing.

"Do you want to set it now?" Mac asked.

"No. I think I'll wait awhile. Maybe until tomorrow," Teresa said. Maybe tomorrow, when the memory of the sheriff's penetrating gray eyes and hard, relentless voice was not so fresh in her mind, when it had not stirred up painful recollections of this beautiful clock that had sat for years in the nightmare house on Mourning Dove Lane.

"Okay," Mac said offhandedly, although she was certain he understood her reluctance to get the clock going. "Josh's friends came and fed the horses, but I'm sure you'd like to go down and see for yourself that they're okay. I'll go with you. Then I have to pick up Mom—she wants to go to the concert and fireworks display—and you have to get ready to go to Kent's. I'll only be leaving you alone here for a couple of hours while it's still light outside."

"I will be *fine*," Teresa assured him. "I have a ferocious guard dog, a cordless phone I can carry around with me, pepper spray, and I'll stick a meat cleaver in my belt if you want."

Mac tilted his head and grinned. "I'll let you slide on the meat cleaver. If you bring it, I *guarantee* the sheriff will arrest you!"

2

"We didn't think you'd *ever* get here, Aunt Teri," Daniel cried as he stood in the doorway of his home. We've been waitin' and *waitin'*!"

"I think I'm right on time," Teresa answered, glancing at her watch.

Sharon appeared behind her son. "You are. He's been ready to go for an hour. We can't convince him the fireworks won't begin until after dark."

As Teresa stepped into the house, she remembered that the last time she'd spoken with her sister-in-law, Sharon had been full of anger with her for telling Kent she'd taken Daniel away early from his riding lesson. Sharon had seemed to think Teresa was deliberately trying to cause trouble between herself and her husband. Teri had almost dreaded coming to the house and enduring Sharon's residual ire, but instead the woman looked welcoming, her smile warm. Teresa wondered if she'd been forgiven or Sharon was merely acting, not wanting to incur further trouble with Kent by being cold to his sister.

"I saw your dad's car in the driveway," Teresa said.

"He's been here for twenty minutes," Sharon said, ushering Teresa into the house. "I think he's as anxious as Daniel to see the fireworks. Either that or something else has him nearly pacing the floor." Oh dear, Teresa thought. Gabriel O'Brien was as nervous about the wedding announcement as Carmen. "Dad, Teri's here!" Sharon called as if announcing that the life of the party had just arrived.

"Teri! Teresa! Well, don't you look fine!" Gabe boomed, enfolding her in a bear hug. In all the years Teresa had known him, Gabriel had never hugged her. "Pretty as a picture. You and Sharon will put every girl in Point Pleasant to shame. Yes, indeed!"

Kent and Sharon were both looking askance at the big, handsome man with the unusually high color and loud voice.

Teresa wished she could tell him to tone down, to act more naturally, but she didn't have a chance with two sets of eyes on her. Even Daniel gave his grandfather a puzzled glance.

"So nice to see you, Gabe," Teresa said. "It's been ages."

"Ages. Yes, *ages*! Let's see—was it Christmas?"

"Yes, right here at Kent and Sharon's party. We both drank too much eggnog and did that unforgettable duet of 'Good King Wenceslas.'" Dear God, Teri thought, someone please save us from this ridiculous display. "Were we too awful, Sharon?"

"I've heard worse." Sharon's smile seemed plastered into place. "You two seem in a very good mood."

"It's Fourth of July," Daniel piped up. "They're excited about fireworks."

"And the concert," Kent intervened. "We're going to hear the concert first."

Daniel's smile wavered and he looked worriedly at his grandfather and Teresa. "Are you two gonna sing 'King Wen'slas'?"

At that, everyone burst into laughter and the tension broke. Teresa could have kissed her nephew, although she dreaded the next few hours. By midnight, Sharon won't be laughing anymore, she thought dolefully. *Please* don't let this evening turn into a disaster, for Carmen's sake. Gabe seemed to have heard Teresa's silent plea, because when no one was looking, he moved closer to her, took her hand, and squeezed it.

Daniel did not allow any dawdling, and within ten minutes they headed downtown—Kent, Sharon, and Gabe in one car, Daniel insisting on riding with Aunt Teri. Teresa was perplexed by his insistence on being alone with her until the little boy asked anxiously, "How's Caesar? Does he miss me too much?"

"Oh, he misses you a lot," Teri said. "He had such a good time with you on Monday."

"Was he mad 'cause Mommy made me leave early?"

Teresa knew she had to phrase her answer carefully. "No, Daniel, he understood, because a lot of kids only stay for half an hour when it's their first lesson. You see, when you ride a horse, you use muscles in your legs that you don't use when you're just walking or running, so it's good to start out slowly so you don't get sore legs. Caesar certainly wouldn't want you to get sore legs from riding him. He'd be afraid you'd never come back."

"But I didn't get sore legs," Daniel told her fervently. "I didn't!"

"So it's a good thing your mommy took you home a little early."

"I guess, but I wanted to stay and Daddy got mad about it. They had a fight. I wasn't s'posed to be listenin', but I did anyway. They fight a lot."

Teri caught herself before she asked, *About what?* She mustn't question Daniel about his parents' marriage. It would be an intrusion. Also, Daniel would tell Kent and Sharon, and Sharon would blow up again. "All couples have arguments," Teresa said blithely. "It's nothing to worry about, Daniel. But back to Caesar, he's been spending a lot of time in the barn this week with his girlfriend Cleopatra. All the horses are getting a vacation for the Fourth of July, so he'll be extra glad to see you when you come back to ride him."

Teresa thought they'd gotten an early start, but when they reached downtown Point Pleasant, she saw streets already full of people wandering from one concession stand to another, standing in groups talking, eddying toward Riverfront Park, built on the West Virginia bank of the Ohio River. She was glad she and Kent had agreed that if they got separated, they would meet on the twelve graceful steps leading up to the post office.

After finally finding a parking spot, Teri took Daniel's hand firmly in her own and they made a game of rushing through the crowd to meet the family at the appointed spot. They arrived to find Kent lolling against the brass railings of the steps while Sharon paced the sidewalk. "Teri, for God's sake, where have you been!" she pounced as soon as Teresa and Daniel drew near her.

"I had trouble finding a parking place, Sharon." Teresa looked up two steps at her brother, who rolled his eyes. Gabe stood beside him anxiously scanning the crowd. Teri knew Gabe was looking for Carmen. "Daniel says he'd like a cup of Kool-Aid before we get our seats at the concert."

"Oh, I don't know about him drinking Kool-Aid from a concession stand," Sharon said fretfully. "You never know how sanitary these places are. Daniel, wouldn't you rather wait until we get home to drink something?"

"Mommy, that'll be hours and *hours*! This afternoon Daddy said I could get Kool-Aid."

Kent joined them and Daniel slipped his hand from Teri's to his father's. "I'm sure they don't serve poisoned Kool-Aid here," Kent said to Sharon.

"I didn't say it was poisoned; I just said it was unsanitary—" Sharon gave up when Kent turned his back on her and began marching Daniel over to a concession stand.

Gabe had joined them and Teri looked at him almost desperately. "Quite a crowd, isn't it, Gabriel?"

He nodded. "Beautiful weather. Not too hot, not too humid."

"So I win my bet," Teresa told Sharon. "You owe me ten dollars."

"What?" Sharon asked irritably.

"On Sunday I said we'd have great weather for the Fourth and you said we wouldn't. We bet on it. Remember?"

Sharon looked at her in surprise. "Oh! Oh, of course." She began fishing in her colorful straw tote bag. "I know my wallet's in here somewhere."

"Sharon, I was kidding," Teresa laughed. "Save all that money for Daniel's college fund!"

"College. Oh my, all too soon he'll be leaving us," Sharon said sadly. "I hope he doesn't choose somewhere *too* far away—"

"Sharon, the boy is seven," Gabe said lightly. "You've got lots of time before you have to worry about him going away to college!"

"Hi, everyone!" Carmen seemed to have appeared out of thin air, her smile wide, her voice a trifle high-pitched. But she looked beautiful and far younger than her years in well-cut designer jeans and a flowing top of intermingled pink and peach. Long gold earrings dangled gaily beneath her silky hair. "Is everybody having fun?"

"Oh, just tons of fun," Teresa said wryly. "We're mourning over Daniel leaving for college." Sharon shot her a murderous glance and Teri reminded herself she needed to keep everyone as calm and happy as possible. This certainly wasn't the time for sarcasm. "I'm teasing you, Sharon. I didn't mean to be offensive."

Sharon gave Teri a slightly placated look, which distracted her from noticing the furtive smile Gabe tossed Carmen. Honestly, Teri thought, Gabe and Carmen are acting like they're fourteen. I can't believe they're so afraid of what Sharon thinks.

But they were, Teresa told herself sternly. At least Gabe cared mightily what his daughter thought, and all of Carmen's future happiness seemed to rest with Gabe.

Carmen was attempting to make small talk with Sharon when Mac sauntered up with his mother, Emma, in tow. "Well, fancy meeting you here!" he said, tongue in cheek. "Mom, you remember Teresa, don't you?"

Emma MacKenzie looked at her son as if he'd lost his mind. "Jedediah Abraham, I told you she's come by to visit me. Don't you listen to me?"

"Yeah, Jedediah, don't you listen?" Teri asked, grinning as Mac's color heightened. "How are you, Emma?"

"Fine, just fine," the woman said enthusiastically, although she had shadows under her eyes and her smile was wan. "I've been looking forward to this. It was so nice of Jedediah to bring me instead of one of his young lady friends."

Teri raised her eyebrow at Mac and his color rose even more. "Mom, I don't have young lady friends anymore." Emma looked at him quizzically. "I'll explain later."

"Now she probably thinks you're gay," Teresa muttered to Mac as Emma continued to look at her son in bewilderment.

Kent approached them, scowling. "Oh great, the gang's all here. Mac," Kent said curtly.

"Kent," Mac returned. "How's business?"

"Fine. Yours?"

"Great."

"Good."

Teresa closed her eyes briefly. They sounded like two cavemen grunting at each other. This was going to be one long evening, she thought with a silent groan. "Well, let's get our seats for the concert before they're all gone," she said, heading determinedly for the entrance to Riverfront Park just past the post office. "I, for one, can't wait to hear the music."

Once they were all seated in the stadium-like arena, Teresa felt her tension begin to ebb. Evening was falling, turning the sky to beautiful shades of amethyst and cobalt streaked with the deep tangerine of a sinking sun. The Ohio River flowed calm and sparkling beyond the stadium.

Teresa felt her muscles begin to loosen as she listened to the sounds of soft rock performed by a local musician with a guitar he played beautifully and a voice she could listen to all night. Every year she looked forward to hearing him and she'd never understood why he didn't go professional.

Everyone seemed to relax—everyone except Carmen, who sat beside Teresa nervously drumming her fingers on her thigh. Once Teri reached over and covered the woman's hand. Carmen tossed her a fleeting smile, held still for nearly three minutes, then began drumming her fingers again.

Although Daniel seemed to enjoy the music, he was elated when the concert ended and it was time for the fireworks display. He reached for Teri's hand, then wisely gave the move a second thought and took his mother's as they eddied toward the four-acre Tu-Endie-Wei State Park, located on the point where the Ohio and Kanawha Rivers meet. The site of the Battle of Point Pleasant, fought in 1774 between the Virginia militia and Native Americans under the leadership of Chief Cornstalk—the same Shawnee chieftain who was said to have placed a curse on the area before he was killed in 1777—was commemorated by an eighty-four-foot granite obelisk. Children played on the steps leading to the obelisk, but Sharon held Daniel's hand tightly, preventing him from joining the crowd.

If Teresa had not been so concerned about how this evening was going to turn out for Carmen, she could have laughed at the elaborate casualness between her and Gabe. Carmen barely looked at her fiancé, sticking as close to Teri as possible, making inane conversation, laughing too loudly, while Gabe concentrated on Sharon, acting as if she were the only person he could see.

Suddenly Gabe boomed, "Hey, Daniel, see the Mansion House over there?"

Daniel looked in the direction his grandfather pointed and said, "It looks like a little old log cabin to me."

"Well, it's called the Mansion House," Gabe said insistently. "Walter Newman built it in 1796."

"Oh. Was Walter Newman a friend of yours?" Daniel asked.

Teresa heard Kent choke back laughter. Gabe's expression reflected a mixture of insult and amusement. "I'm not *that* old, Daniel." Gabe then adopted the tone used by adults when trying to make children interested in a subject. "The Mansion House is the oldest hewn-log house in the Kanawha Valley. Back in its day, the place was a tavern. Now it's a museum. I'll bring you down someday."

"Okay," Daniel answered vaguely, clearly not at all interested in visiting a museum. "Is it time for the fireworks?"

"They should start in a few minutes."

Everyone turned to look at Mac, who'd gotten separated from them and obviously had nearly run to catch up, dragging his mother along with him. Emma appeared winded and annoyed as she pulled her arm free of Mac's hand and said, "For heaven's sakes, Jedediah Abraham, what's gotten into you? I haven't seen you so excited over fireworks since you were ten."

"Sorry, Mom," Mac said contritely. "I'd just like for us to get near that low wall surrounding the park like we used to do. You could sit on it and catch your breath."

"I wouldn't have to catch my breath if you'd stop dragging me," Emma returned crossly. "If you're so anxious to be with Teresa, then go with her. I'll catch up."

When they finally reached a spot everyone deemed suitable, Teri felt as breathless as Emma. I won't have fond memories of this Fourth of July, Teri thought in despair. So far, every member of this unlikely group looked tired, slightly sweaty, irritable, and ill at ease. Everyone except Daniel, who paid no attention to the adults droning about a museum and griping about walking too fast.

Teresa had smacked at the third mosquito to bite her arm in the last two minutes when the first firework went off in a blaze of red, white, and brilliant blue. Everyone oohed and aahed and clapped raucously, as if they'd never seen fireworks before tonight. Daniel jumped up and down in excitement. Teresa breathed easier. At least everyone's attention would be diverted for a while, she thought in relief. She was already exhausted.

As the fireworks burst in gorgeous jewel-toned patterns in the night sky, Teresa's gaze wandered around the crowd. She was startled to see Josh Gibbs standing a few feet away, his arm draped over the shoulders of a slender blonde. He smiled at the fireworks, leaned down while the girl whispered something in his ear, then laughed and gave her a lingering kiss. He looked happy and carefree—not like a young man whose father had been brutally murdered just days earlier. Anger rushed through Teresa. Josh had no right to be having so much fun when poor Gus—

She immediately stopped her train of thought. People reacted to shock and grief in different ways. Just because she was frantic when Marielle disappeared, and inconsolable for months when the woman never came back, didn't mean that Josh had to behave the same way in order to prove his love for his father.

Teresa abruptly looked away from the young man, not liking the path her thoughts were taking. She'd been unfairly judged so often in the past, she had no right to judge anyone else, she told herself firmly. Josh had loved Gus, of that she was certain.

Another firecracker went off with such a resounding blast the ground shook and Carmen let out a loud, startled cry, then immediately clapped her hand over her mouth when people turned to look at her. Carmen was never softspoken, but tonight nerves had turned her voice up a notch. Teri gave her a reassuring smile as a second spectacular green and orange firework immediately followed. In its light, Teresa caught sight of Jason, Fay, and Celeste Warner.

Again, Teri was shocked. She hadn't seen any of the Warners at the Fourth of July celebration since the murders. Celeste—dressed more fashionably in jeans and a T-shirt—stood between Fay and Jason. In fact, they stood so close to the girl, Teresa had the fleeting image of two Rottweilers guarding their charge. No one was going to get near that girl, Teresa thought, and was glad. Celeste might be on her way to recovery, but she definitely needed to feel safe. After all, she still thought someone wanted to kill her. And me, Teri thought. And I'm not so sure she's wrong.

Abruptly, the sheriff loomed in front of Teresa. She blinked and took a step backward in surprise, a move for which she could have kicked herself. She didn't want the man to know he intimidated her. She mentally scrambled for composure and managed a casual, "Hello, Sheriff. Enjoying the show?"

"Very much," he said, glancing at Mac, who was almost imperceptibly moving closer to Teri, as if to protect her, just as Jason and Fay were protecting Celeste. "How about you, Miss Farr?"

"I love the fireworks. I come every year." She thought she sounded overly cheerful and almost childlike. "I'm sure you know my brother and his wife and their son," she said, motioning at Kent, who looked daggers at the sheriff. Sharon literally pulled Daniel against her as if the sheriff were going to whisk her child away from her. "And Sharon's father, Gabriel, is with us tonight."

"Gabe," the sheriff said, touching the brim of his hat. Gabe nodded and quickly looked away.

Carmen burst out with a hearty, "Hello, Sheriff. I haven't seen you in Trinkets and Treasures for ages!"

"Hello, Miz Norris," he said. "I don't do a lot of shopping except at Christmas. You already getting your stock for December?" he asked.

Carmen laughed stridently. "Well, not *this* early. It usually starts arriving in early November, though. I'll be putting it on display around Thanksgiving, if that makes any sense. The holidays are so close together, you see."

"Yes, I see." The sheriff's cool gray gaze returned to Teresa. "Any more trouble at your place today?"

"No. Thank goodness." Teresa told herself to stop being frightened. No matter how hard she tried to hide it, she knew the sheriff could nearly smell the fear emanating from her. "Can you tell me when the barn will be released as a crime scene? I board other people's horses, you know. They want to ride them. I haven't let anyone in the barn except the boys who feed the horses, though. I've been very careful."

The sheriff's mouth quirked in a half smile at her breathless assurances. "Tomorrow you can start conducting business as usual," he said. "But I'd appreciate it if you didn't leave town."

"I'm not leaving town," Teri said hastily. "I'm much too busy."

The sheriff nodded again and drifted away. Teresa felt a momentary wave of dizziness, wondering why she couldn't conquer her ridiculous fear of the police.

Then she glanced over at Celeste Warner, who stared in her direction with big, haunted eyes. Teresa had thought the girl was enjoying the fireworks show—just a couple of minutes earlier, she'd seen Celeste clapping and smiling—but now she looked positively terrified. Teresa couldn't tear her own gaze away from Celeste's eyes—the eyes that had seen the murderer of her mother, the eyes that had seen someone plunge a knife into her own abdomen. In spite of the warm evening, Teresa felt chilled as memories of walking down the dark hall and bumping into a murderer before she found the small, slashed body of Celeste washed over Teresa as if it had all happened yesterday.

And she knew she would never stop being afraid.

CHAPTER EIGHTEEN

1

CELESTE WARNER HUDDLED IN the backseat, trembling. Her grandmother had chattered all the way to the car, then asked her why she was so quiet. Celeste had merely shrugged her shoulders, too shaken to trust her voice, and Grandma had begun talking again, fast and steady, the way she always did when she was excited about something. She'd loved the fireworks display, which she hadn't attended since Celeste had stopped talking.

I shouldn't have started talking again, Celeste thought in agony. If I'd stayed quiet, I would have been safe. And I could have thought of some way to keep Teri safe, too. I'm smart—smarter than anyone knows. I could have come up with a plan to protect Teri *and* me. If only I hadn't started talking!

And now she'd seen Death. At the fireworks display, when she'd looked around, she'd seen *it*. No, she'd seen the *person* who killed her mother. All along, Celeste had known a *person* had killed her mother and tried to kill her. She had known, but she hadn't wanted to believe a person would do such a thing, so she'd turned the person into an *it*—Death. But she was a kid then. She was almost an adult now. Besides, she knew she couldn't pretend any longer, because she'd seen the killer—a person—in the park tonight.

Celeste had tried to look away and couldn't. She'd willed her gaze back to the fireworks, but she didn't seem to have any control over her own body. She could *not* turn away. She could *not* look away. And then her gaze had met another's. The gazes locked. Finally, the other set of eyes had narrowed slightly and Celeste had felt a cold wind wrapping itself around her heart. When she'd finally managed to tear away her gaze and stare up at the sky where the fireworks had turned into a garish blur, it was too late. Celeste could feel Death watching her.

"Honey, does the cat have your tongue?" Fay craned her neck and looked in concern at Celeste curled into a ball in the corner of the backseat. "Celeste, baby, what's wrong?" she demanded in alarm. "Dear God, what's *wrong*?"

"We have to leave here," Celeste ground out in a barely audible voice. "We have to leave town tonight."

Fay frowned. "What are you talking about?"

"We have to leave!" Celeste cried. "I saw the person who killed Mommy!"

Jason whipped the car to the side of the road, ignoring the blasting of a car horn behind him. Fay slammed against the door and cried out, but Jason paid no attention, turning to face his daughter. "You saw the person tonight?" Celeste nodded, tears running down her cheeks. "Who was it?"

Celeste shook her head violently. "No. I can't . . . can't . . ."

"You have to tell me," Jason said loudly. "Who *was* it?"

"No . . . no . . . can't . . ." Her voice faded even lower. "No . . . can't . . ."

"You can't what? Talk?" By now Jason was shouting, making Celeste cower. "I'm sorry. I didn't mean to scare you, sweetheart, but you have to tell me who you saw!"

"Leave . . . must leave."

"Celeste—"

"Leave!" Celeste whisper-screamed. "Have to leave!" Suddenly her eyes seemed to glaze, and she shrank into herself, her face beginning to go blank.

"Jason?" Fay asked fearfully. "Jason, what should we do?"

Jason looked at his horrified mother, then at Celeste, who once again seemed to be completely withdrawing from the real world, burying herself in the shelter of silence and total passivity. "All right, honey. Don't be afraid. We'll be out of town by morning," Jason said soothingly. "Just let me know one thing. Did the person who killed your mommy see you?" Celeste barely nodded. Jason hesitated. "Do you think the person knew you remembered?"

Celeste shuddered uncontrollably, thinking of those eyes—those knowing eyes—fixed on her, and nodded yes. Yes. *Yes!*

2

"Mom isn't feeling well," Mac murmured in Teri's ear. "I have to take her home before I can come to your house."

"Oh *no!*" Teresa felt complete despair. Carmen and Gabe wanted to make their big announcement, and Sharon was going to take it badly. Teri *knew* she would take it badly. There might be a scene. Teri had been counting on Mac to help her smooth things over if the situation got out of control. "Mac, I need you!" she hissed.

"I'll be there just as soon as I take Mom home," he said earnestly. "Have you looked at her? Something just came over her. I think she might pass out if I don't get her home."

Teresa covertly peeked at Emma, who indeed looked tall and bleached and rigid, as if she were using every ounce of her strength to hold herself together. "You're right. Get her home," Teresa said. "If you can't come tonight, I'll understand."

"I'll be there," Mac assured her. "Just try to keep Carmen and Gabe from saying anything until I arrive."

He took his mother's arm and led her gently away from the group. Sharon looked at them. "Emma isn't feeling well," Teresa explained, although Sharon hadn't asked for an explanation. "He's just going to take her home and then—" Teri realized she'd slipped and almost said, *And then come to my house for the party.* She still hadn't mentioned the get-together to her sister-in-law and now she couldn't put it off any longer. "Sharon, I bought some cakes and pastries and champagne. And juice for Daniel, of course. I thought it would be fun if we had a little after-fireworks party tonight."

When Sharon didn't answer, Teresa looked at her more closely. Sharon's face had turned pale as parchment, making her freckles stand out sharply, and her eyes seemed almost to jitter in their sockets. Teresa had never seen her sister-in-law look so strange, and alarm instantly flooded through her. "Sharon? Are you all right?"

Sharon's odd, nervous gaze fastened on Teresa and she almost hissed, "What is going on tonight?"

"I don't know what you mean." Teresa knew how unconvincing she sounded. "I just thought I'd like to put everything that's happened this week out of my mind. And I'm sure Kent wants to celebrate our finally selling the house. I thought it would be nice to have an impromptu little gala," Teresa ended lamely.

"A *gala*?" Sharon repeated.

"Well, yes. Just a kind of mini-party, our own Fourth of July celebration. Nothing special—"

"That is a damned lie," Sharon returned in a steely voice. "Something has been wrong all evening. I've felt it for hours. Now you come up with this absurd idea for a party that will keep Daniel up until midnight, which you *know* I won't allow!" Kent and Gabe had drawn closer to Sharon, Kent looking bewildered, Gabe looking apprehensive. "I know there's some kind of conspiracy going on."

"A conspiracy?" Teresa tried to laugh, but nothing came out. "I don't know what you mean."

"Yes, you do!" Sharon's face had turned from white to almost scarlet. "Teresa, you've never been a good liar. I want to know what's going on and if you don't tell me—"

"Carmen and I were going to announce our engagement," Gabe said.

Carmen gasped and muttered, "Gabe, don't."

But Gabriel rushed on. "We've been seeing each other for months. I proposed in the spring and we're getting married in September. We delayed telling you because we knew you wouldn't be happy about me getting married again. Anyway, Carmen and I put Teresa up to having this get-together at her house. We thought we'd tell you there, but I haven't been feeling right about the whole thing. It isn't fair to put Teresa on the spot like this. So I'll just say it plainly, Sharon. I'm marrying Carmen."

Sharon looked as if someone had dealt her a crashing physical blow. She literally staggered and swayed as if she might faint. Kent reached for her, but she jerked away from him. She pinned Carmen with an almost frightening slit-eyed look and said savagely, "You bitch!"

"Sharon!" Gabe said loudly, although Teri thought he sounded more concerned than angered.

Sharon rushed on. "I've suspected for months something was going on with Dad. He hasn't acted like himself. At first, I thought he was sick. That's why I've been so nervous, as all of you have so tactfully pointed out to me. Finally, I realized there was a woman. I told myself it was something extremely casual. But his behavior, his seeing less and less of Daniel and me—well, I knew there was something more serious going on with him.

"For about a week, I thought the woman might be you, Carmen, but then I told myself Dad couldn't be so stupid as to get involved with *you*! Years ago, one evening my mother attended a meeting in the conference room at a motel about ten miles from here. Afterward, when she got in her car, she saw you coming out of a room. She said your hair was mussed and you had this sickening lovey-dovey look on your face. You got in your car and drove off. Mom was curious, so she stayed and watched. Five minutes later, Hugh Farr came out of the same room. It was obvious you two were having an affair.

"She told me and I promised not to tell, not even Kent. But Mom would understand my not keeping the secret *now*, not when Dad is involved with you, Carmen. He's too good, too naive, to imagine what you really are, so it's up to me to protect him. Do you understand me, Carmen? I will do *anything* not to have my father involved with you!"

Gabe had lifted Daniel down from his shoulders and the child looked at his mother with wide, startled eyes. "Sharon, that is enough!" Gabriel's voice lashed at his daughter. "I won't tolerate this from you, especially here in public. My God! What would your mother think?"

"Yes, what *would* she think, Daddy?" Sharon was backing away from them, tears beginning to pour down her face. "What would she think of you sleeping with another woman? Planning to *marry* another woman, not to mention Carmen Norris! Carmen *Norris*! It's sickening! It's blasphemous!"

"Sharon, stop it!" Kent nearly begged. "You're acting like a maniac!"

"I hate you!" Sharon shouted at her father and Kent. "I hate *both* of you! And as for you, Carmen—"

Before any of them realized what was happening, Sharon turned and began running at top speed, pushing her way through the little crowd of people whose curiosity outweighed their good manners. The four adults stood stunned for a moment. Then Kent tried to pursue his wife, struggling to make his way through the gaggle of onlookers without knocking down anyone, tripping once and almost falling.

Gabe, slower to react, followed him by about fifteen seconds, leaving Daniel standing by himself. The little boy burst into frightened sobs and Teresa rushed to him, picking him up and holding him tightly. "It's okay, Daniel," she said. "Your mommy is just upset. Everything will be fine."

But Daniel was not to be comforted and neither was Carmen, who stood still as a statue looking stunned. All of her careful planning, Teresa thought in a flash. She loves Gabe so much and he pushed past her without a word, his entire being focused on his daughter. "Carmen," Teresa said, carrying the weeping Daniel toward Carmen and touching her arm. Carmen jumped and looked at Teri as if she didn't know her. "Carmen, we weren't expecting Sharon to take this news well. . . ."

"Take it well?" For a few moments, Carmen's shocked gaze rested on Teresa's face. Then the woman abruptly burst into loud laughter. "Well, that's an understatement. She sure as hell didn't take it well. Did you hear those lies she was spewing? She doesn't care who she hurts. She's horrible!"

"Oh, Carmen, please." Teresa felt helpless, her nephew sobbing onto her shoulder, her friend looking as if her world had just caved in on her. "Just give her some time, Carmen. She'll come around."

Carmen laughed for a few more moments, then stopped as suddenly as she'd begun. Tears welled in her eyes. "Time? Time won't change her mind, Teri. You know it won't change her mind. She's always hated me."

"I don't know that she hates you, Carmen, but Gabriel

loves you. He's going to marry you even if Sharon doesn't stop acting crazy. And she *is* acting crazy tonight. My God, she even ran off and deserted Daniel!"

"My mommy's crazy and she doesn't want me anymore!" At this, the little boy wailed even louder and Teresa wanted to swallow the words. She bounced him as if he were a baby, looked at Carmen, who was dissolving into a broken, weeping mess, and wished herself a thousand miles away from this almost farcically nightmarish scene. But wishing wasn't going to help anything, Teri told herself sternly. "Come on, Carmen. Let's get out of here. Maybe the guys have caught up with her."

Carmen was reluctant to go, but Teresa finally got the woman moving, although she had an odd, shuffling walk and slumped shoulders. Carmen—who always walked smartly and had excellent posture. At last, they found the men standing beside an empty parking space two blocks away. "She took our car," Kent said in amazement. "We saw her just tearing off like there's no speed limit. She was headed north."

"Toward home," Teresa said. "I'm sure she just went home."

"All right, here's what we're going to do," Gabe said. "Teri, I'd appreciate it if you'd drive Kent and me to his house. If Sharon isn't there, he can take his car and I'll take mine and we'll both look for her. After you drop us off, take Daniel to your house."

"I'll take Daniel *and* Carmen," Teri said with a significant look at Gabe. He hadn't even glanced at his alarmingly pale fiancée.

"Thank you, Teri, but I need to be alone," Carmen said in an odd, distant voice. "I want to go home." She gave Teresa a weak smile and took Gabe's hand, holding it up to her lips. "Please call me in a little while, Gabe."

"I will," he said absently.

"I mean it. *Please* call."

"Carmen, I said I *will*." He was curt and distracted, his mind obviously on one person—his daughter.

Carmen glanced at him, her eyes devoid of all joy, all hope. She dropped his hand and walked away from them, her shoulders sagging.

"Gabe, I think you could have been a little kinder to Carmen," Teresa couldn't stop herself from saying. "She's very shaken."

Gabe looked at Teresa in puzzlement, then in dismissal. "What? Oh, I'm sure Carmen understands."

Yes, I'm sure she does, Teri thought, suddenly almost as angry with Gabe as she was with Sharon. Meanwhile, Kent stood by looking like a little boy waiting to be told what to do next. "Kent, may Daniel spend the whole night with me?" Teresa asked sharply.

Kent seemed to snap back to semi-life. "Danny, do you want to go home with Aunt Teri?" he asked. The child sniffed mightily and nodded yes. "Okay." Daniel sniffed again, looking a tad less distraught as Kent went on, "Teri, would you mind having company tomorrow as well as tonight?"

"I'd love it!" Teresa said with more enthusiasm than she felt. She loved her nephew dearly, but she worried about how to handle him tomorrow if Sharon and Kent couldn't resolve things tonight. Oh well, she thought, she'd try to remember how she used to entertain Celeste when Wendy would vanish on one of her all-day shopping trips.

Teresa, Kent, Gabe, and Daniel reached Kent's house to find it deserted. Kent resolutely climbed into his SUV and Gabe into his dated sedan, and both set off in search of Sharon.

Sharon, Teresa thought with dread. Sharon who had headed wildly into the night, just as Marielle had eight years before.

3

Emma barely spoke in the car on the way back to her apartment. Mac kept looking at her anxiously. "Mom, what's wrong? Do you feel sick?"

"No, Jedediah," she said in a shaky voice. "I'm just tired. I've been doing too much lately, not sleeping well, and tonight was a strain—all that rushing around trying to keep up with Teresa. Honestly, Son, you should have just gone to the fireworks with her."

"I wanted to go with *you*." Mac's voice was sincere. "I just thought we could tag along with Teri and the group."

"Honey, that group didn't want us with them. No one except Teresa, that is. And maybe Carmen, although she was as jumpy as a scared rabbit. I've never seen her that way. She's always been so in control of herself, so calm, so confident. Just the opposite of poor Marielle."

Mac sighed. "I'll tell you a secret, Mom. Carmen and Gabriel O'Brien are engaged."

Emma looked at him with shocked green eyes. "Carmen and Mr. O'Brien? Good heavens, there's a match I would never have imagined!"

"I know. I was surprised, too. And so was Teri. Carmen didn't tell her until yesterday. Carmen and Gabe knew Sharon wouldn't be happy about it, to say the least, so they planned to tell the families at a little get-together at Teri's tonight. That's why Carmen and Gabe seemed nervous. And I think Sharon sensed that something was up. Anyway, we were invited to their 'coming out' party, too. I think Carmen believed the more people present, the better Sharon would behave, although I have my doubts. But that's why I was trying to keep up with Teri. She's almost as jumpy about this to-do tonight as Carmen is, and I told her we'd be there for moral support."

"You told her *you'd* be there. You're the one she'd look to for moral support. Besides, I just can't go."

"Why not?"

Emma looked at her lap. "I . . . I just don't feel up to it. I usually go to bed early. And Carmen . . ."

"What about Carmen?"

"Oh, I suppose I'm being terribly selfish, but I don't think I can bear seeing her preparing for a happy new life when poor Marielle could be dead."

"Mom, we don't know that Marielle is dead. But if you're not feeling well, I'll just skip tonight. They'll never miss me."

"You must go, Jedediah—Teresa is counting on you. All you have to do is drop me off at my apartment. I'll just go straight to bed and you go on to Teresa's."

Mac shook his head. "I don't want to just leave you, Mom. You don't look right."

"I *do* look right, just tired."

"I should stay with you for a while, at least."

"Jedediah, if you do that, I won't be able to go to sleep, and sleep is what I need." Emma reached over and patted him on the thigh. "If I get a good night's rest, I will be right as rain tomorrow," she said reassuringly. "I promise."

Mac had reluctantly agreed and walked her to her door, where she had given him a peck on the cheek like a shy young girl on her first date. Emma then refused to let him come into the apartment as she disappeared inside. When he saw a light come on in her living room, he went back to his car and slowly drove out of her parking lot.

Mac was halfway to Teresa's when he'd been overcome with a feeling that his mother was not all right, in spite of all of her protests. She had not looked well—not at all. And she hadn't even sounded like herself. Her voice had been thin and a bit labored, as if she was having trouble breathing.

I shouldn't have mentioned the shindig at Teri's tonight, he thought, furious with himself. Mom never wants to be a burden and I made her feel like she was keeping me away from my one true love. That is the last thing in the world she'd want to do, no matter how bad she felt. I should never have left her, no matter how insistent she was.

When he pulled back into the apartment complex parking lot, Mac immediately noticed that his mother's car was gone. He rushed to her door. It was locked. He beat on it anyway until the resident of the next unit opened his own door.

"Hey, what's the noise all about?" the elderly man asked crankily.

"My mother is Emma MacKenzie. I dropped her off here about fifteen minutes ago. I walked her to her apartment and she went inside, but she wasn't feeling well. I came back to check on her, but she isn't opening the door. She might be unconscious."

"Unconscious my foot!" the man snapped. "Emma took off about ten minutes ago. I had my curtains open and I saw her go flyin' past like she was sixteen. I peeked out the door and saw her get in the car." He grinned. "If you ask me, kid, your mama had a hot date she didn't want you knowin' anything about. Go on home and mind your own business. Just because some of us are over sixty doesn't mean we're dead!"

Mac stood, his mouth half-open in surprise, wondering where on earth his mother could have left for in such a hurry.

4

As soon as they reached home, the Warners launched into fevered activity. Fay had lunged for the phone to call the police, but when Celeste became hysterical, Jason held his thrashing daughter against his body and told his mother to put down the phone receiver. "Mom, I don't think Celeste can stand for us to sit around waiting for the police to come and ask dozens of questions. She can't answer anyway. We should just get some stuff together and get out of here as fast as possible. We'll call the police tomorrow"—he looked at Celeste—"when we're far, far away."

Celeste nodded emphatically and when Fay saw the relief in the girl's expression, she agreed. "All right. Sweetie, Grandma's going to get some clothes together for you first. Then I'll pack a few things for myself. We'll be ready to go in a jiffy." She'd suddenly looked anguished. "Jason, where will we go?"

"Maybe Charleston. Maybe Columbus. Let me think about it for a few minutes. In the meantime, I'll get some of my own stuff together." He looked at Celeste. "Will you be all right sitting here on the couch? Or would you rather go upstairs with your grandmother?"

Celeste dug herself into a corner of the couch and grabbed a pillow, clutching it against herself as she'd once clutched her teddy bear Yogi for protection. She didn't want to be alone, but she didn't want to take her gaze off the front and back doors, which she could see from the couch. She wished she could tell her father that he needed to watch the doors, but her throat was so tight she knew the words would not emerge. And he and Grandma were hurrying. Everything would be all right. Everything would be just fine, Celeste told herself as Fay raced up the stairs, muttering to herself. Daddy wasn't like Hugh. Daddy would take care of them.

Celeste watched the clock hanging above the television set. Ten minutes had gone by when she suddenly felt electrified. Teri! She had to warn Teri!

The girl turned to the phone on the table beside the couch. She picked up the receiver and dialed Teresa's number, which she'd memorized two days ago.

The phone rang once. Twice. Three times. Then a breathless Teresa answered. Celeste said scratchily, "Teri."

"Who is this?" Celeste decided Teri must have taken a

moment to look at the Caller ID. "Celeste? Is that you?" Celeste tried to speak and couldn't. "Celeste, what's wrong?"

One more try. Celeste managed, "Kill," or at least she thought it sounded like "kill." She could say nothing else.

"Kill? Is that what you said? Celeste?" Teri sounded almost frantic. "Celeste?"

Celeste hung up. A few moments later, the phone rang. Celeste saw that the call came from Teri. She picked up the phone and once again, she was mute. But Teri had to know something was wrong, Celeste thought. The call, the fact that Celeste couldn't speak, the mangled word "*kill*" . . .

Fay Warner rushed down the stairs carrying a tote bag and a suitcase and almost screamed, "Put down that phone!" Startled, Celeste slammed down the receiver. Fay closed her eyes. "I'm sorry, honey. I don't know why I said that. Who were you calling? Oh, you can't answer."

Fay opened her terrified eyes. Strands of hair trailed down from her French twist, and her face had lost every ounce of color. Celeste dug herself deeper into the couch corner, thinking her grandmother looked like some wild creature in a horror movie. "I know I forgot some things, honey, but we can always pick up whatever we need." Fay dropped the bags and shouted, "Jason! Jason, are you ready?"

Celeste's father emerged from his bedroom carrying a brown duffel bag with a piece of blue cotton sticking out of the side. A shirt, Celeste thought. "All ready," he said breathlessly. "Thank God I got gas and went to the automatic teller at the bank today."

Fay flew at him, nearly hitting him with the tote bag and suitcase. "Money! Do you have enough? You probably don't. Did you have your credit card?"

"I have two credit cards. We'll be fine for a few days. I'm going to put our stuff in the car," Jason said, heading for the kitchen door leading to their rear driveway facing an alley. "Get Celeste ready. She might need a jacket—I don't know." He opened the door and stepped out into the darkness. "And don't forget your blood pressure medicine, Mom."

"Oh! I *did* forget it!" Fay skittered to the kitchen cabinet beside the sink where she kept her medicine just as the phone began to ring again. "Jason Warner, you just saved my life. Where *is* that bottle of pills—"

Fay and Celeste both went rigid as they heard an exclamation, a shriek of pain cut short and followed by a sickening thud. Fay's wild eyes met Celeste's, then flew to the opened kitchen door. "Jason?" she wavered. "Ja—"

And *it* was there, dressed in a long, hooded black raincoat. It halted for a moment in the doorway, blinking against the bright kitchen light, focusing on Celeste. It surged forward, but Fay blocked its path, screaming shrilly, "No! Get out! Celeste, *run*! *No!*"

Celeste sat frozen on the couch for what seemed an interminable time, long enough to see the knife jab into her grandmother's neck. Fay grabbed at the wound, trying to stanch the burst of blood, still letting out strangled little shrieks, as the knife descended again. And again. And—

With a speed borne of pure white terror, Celeste leaped off the couch, streaked toward the front door, flipped the lock, and flung the door wide. She heard *it* let out an inhuman sound of fury that mingled with her grandmother's weakening bleats of shock and pain. Celeste ran into the night, veering away from the glow of the old-fashioned lamppost standing by the front walk, desperately seeking the safety of darkness. She dodged into the tall shrubbery surrounding the neighbors' house and hit the cool, shrouded ground as *it* pounded out of her own house, breathing so hard she could hear it this far away. At least, Celeste thought the breathing was not her own.

She lay on her abdomen and slithered between the shrubbery and the house, keeping her head down so she wouldn't rustle the shrubbery leaves, holding her breath until her lungs felt as if they would explode. She crawled to the front of the house, thinking that the killer would probably go toward the back, where the shrubbery was thicker.

Then, marshaling all of her courage, Celeste launched herself across the dark front lawn of the house next door, crossed the lightly traveled residential street, and skittered behind the shrubbery adorning the house directly opposite her grandmother's.

Peeking through thick, leafy spots in the bushes, Celeste saw someone come out of the front of her house—someone in a long, hooded coat—and glance up and down the street. When the porch lights next door flashed on and a man stepped out, the figure disappeared back into the house. Celeste knew, though, that as soon as the man retreated into his home, the figure would appear at the front door again, scanning the street for her, perhaps deducing that the most natural place for Celeste to go would be to the safety of the thick foliage across the street.

Celeste's mind worked frantically. Where should she go? To a neighbor's house? She couldn't speak. They would think she was pulling a prank and not let her inside, but the noise caused by her attempt to find safety would certainly draw the killer. The police? Police headquarters was clear downtown, Celeste thought, heart sinking.

Teri's house! Her father had taken her to Teri's new house this week. It was so close. "Too close," Grandma Fay had muttered when she thought Celeste couldn't hear her. Celeste knew Teri's house was near one end of the mysterious place called Defense Logistics Agency, where Grandma said heaven knew what kind of secret stuff went on—stuff no doubt connected with dark and scary government experiments. Daddy had always laughed at Grandma, then told Celeste it was where Santa Claus lived, like Celeste was five or something. Anyway, she remembered seeing the edge of the Defense place when she visited Teri—the north end, Daddy had said, and Celeste knew that you turned right from her house to go north. She had to go north. North meant Teri.

In moments, Celeste burst from the shelter of the shrubbery and, staying as close to the houses as possible, sprinted to the street running vertically from her own. She stayed low and close to the front of the houses, not wanting to alert any dogs that might be in their backyards, moving as quickly and quietly as she could.

At last Celeste crossed another street and darted down a narrow road lined with woods. She darted into the woods, then began navigating around the trees—shaking, sweating, mad with fear, yet still thinking clearly enough to watch her footing. She knew that just a few feet away from the street lay what her father often referred to as "the low ground," a sort of wooded ravine. I have to be careful, she told herself. I have to be careful to stay far enough in the woods so that I can't be seen, but not so far that I fall into the ravine.

Celeste wasn't certain exactly how far she had run when she crashed to the ground and rolled behind a bush, gasping for air, her chest burning, a knife-edged pain gouging mercilessly beneath her ribs. She held a hand to the pain, knowing it wasn't caused by a real knife, knowing she had temporarily escaped Death, and for the first time she realized she would never see her grandmother and her father again.

But Celeste had no tears. She had no voice and she had no tears. All she had was the will to survive.

CHAPTER NINETEEN

1

DANIEL HAD STOPPED CRYING by the time Teresa pulled into her driveway. She handed him the automatic garage door opener. "Push this button to make the door go up," she told him. Daniel, his forehead furrowed in concentration, pushed the button. Up went the door, on came the automatic light, and he smiled. When they'd pulled inside, Teresa told him to push the other button, and the door shut with a bang behind them.

"That was fun, Aunt Teri! Mommy never lets me touch the opener at our house."

"Well, this is a special occasion." Your mother is God-knows-where in God-knows-what condition, that's the occasion, Teresa thought sadly. But all she could do to help was calm down Daniel, whom his loving mother had scared half out of his mind. "Let's go in and see Sierra."

"Can we go see Caesar later?" Daniel asked.

Teresa pictured the expanse of dark land between her house and the dusk-to-dawn lights on the barn. She, too, had been shaken by Sharon's emotional display, not to mention that the memory of Gus lying murdered in Eclipse's stall still filled her mind. She'd checked on the horses before she left for the fireworks display, and they were fine. Now the last thing she wanted to do was go to the barn when all was so still and dark. "We'll visit Caesar in the morning," she said cheerfully. "Caesar is already asleep by now."

The answer seemed to satisfy Daniel, who climbed out of her car and hurried to the door. Sierra had heard them enter the garage and stood on the other side of the door, barking and jumping excitedly. Just as they entered, the phone began to ring and Teresa rushed for it, nearly falling over Sierra. Maybe someone had found Sharon.

Teresa picked up the receiver and managed a breathless, " 'Lo?"

Labored breathing. Then, "Teri?"

The voice was scratchy but definitely female. Teresa looked at the Caller ID and saw "Warner Jason." Jason Warner? "Who is this?" Nothing. "Celeste, is that you?" Teri asked, fear edging her voice. "Celeste, what's wrong?"

Silence for a moment. Then a grating, "Kill."

"Kill! Is that what you said? Celeste? *Celeste!*"

Someone put down the receiver. Daniel, who had dropped onto the floor to pet Sierra, looked up anxiously. "What is it?"

"I'm not sure," she said absently, dialing the numbers she'd seen on Caller ID. She could tell someone picked up the phone. Then she heard a woman's voice in the background screech, "Hang up that phone!" The connection went dead again. Teri dialed once more. This time, nothing.

Oh, God, first Sharon, now Celeste, Teresa thought, her heart pounding. What could be wrong with Celeste? Why was she calling, then barely speaking? Because, like one terrible time before, shock and terror stole her ability to talk?

Teresa's first impulse was to grab her keys and drive to the Warner home. Then she looked at Daniel, now standing, small, wide-eyed, and pale. He was so frightened already because of his mother that Teresa couldn't frighten him more over Celeste. She certainly couldn't leave him here alone or load him in the car and drag him to the Warner house, either.

Teresa took a deep breath. "I think someone is just playing a telephone game with me. It's not very nice but not something to scare us. What about something to drink?" Teresa tried to look untroubled. "I have apple juice and orange juice and Coke and milk—"

"I will have a Coca-Cola," Daniel returned promptly with great dignity. "I'm parched."

"Coke it is," Teri said, hiding a smile and glad that she'd bought caffeine-free cola. At least the drink wouldn't keep Daniel awake. If any child needed a long, calming night's sleep, it was her nephew. Sierra accompanied her and Daniel to the kitchen, staying close to Daniel, which pleased him immensely. Before Teresa fixed their drinks, she dug in a kitchen cabinet and found her police scanner. If there was trouble at the Warner house, she'd certainly hear about it over the scanner, she thought. Daniel laughed as they heard the cops talking with dispatch in crackly voices. Teresa was relieved that Daniel found the device entertaining.

As she poured Daniel's Coke, Teresa looked at all the food Carmen had brought earlier today. How she wished they'd had the party, the announcement had been made, and Sharon had found the grace not to make a scene. But she had made a scene. A *frightening* scene. Teresa now realized Sharon had been experiencing serious emotional problems for months—the mood swings, the tantrums, the extreme overpossessiveness. I should have recognized the signs of an oncoming breakdown, Teresa chided herself. *My mother went through the same thing. I've seen it all before. I just didn't* want *to see it again.*

"Want a cupcake, Daniel? *I* didn't bake it, so it should taste really good."

"Sure. What flavor?"

"Let's see—we have chocolate and strawberry."

"Okay."

"Which one?"

"Both," Daniel said firmly. "I'm real hungry, too."

Sharon would disapprove of her son having a cola and cupcakes right before bed, Teresa thought, but right now all Teri cared about was restoring the child's sense of well-being. If Coke and cupcakes would do it, she was happy to let him have what he wanted.

As soon as Teresa set out the food, Daniel made a dive for it, but Teri insisted he wash his hands and his tear-stained face first. Then she sat down with him, marveling at the resiliency of children as he wolfed down both cupcakes and drank his big glass of Coke dry. He looked at her with a satisfied smile. "I cleaned up my plate. You hardly ate anything, Aunt Teri."

Teresa glanced at her chocolate cupcake that looked like it had been nibbled on by a mouse. "I don't have much appetite."

Daniel's smile faded. "'Cause of Mommy?"

"Well . . ." She hesitated. "Yes, Daniel, I'm concerned about your mom. I'm sure your dad and your grandfather will find her, though."

Daniel's gaze dropped to his plate filled with crumbs. "Mommy's been different than she used to be," he said quietly. "She cries. She gets into fights with Daddy. I try to make her happier, but I can't."

How well Teri knew what Daniel was feeling. She'd tried so hard, wished so desperately, to ease Marielle's depression, to hear Marielle laugh, to see the unhappiness disappear from her beautiful face. But Teri had been successful for only fleeting moments—moments she'd cherished and moments she mourned because they were all too few.

"Sometimes we can't make other people feel happy no matter how hard we try," she told Daniel, speaking to him as if he were an adult. He seemed to appreciate her approach and listened intently. "You shouldn't blame yourself because *you* couldn't make your mommy feel happy. What's bothering her is beyond your power to fix, honey, but there's medicine that can help her."

"There is?" Daniel asked, his face brightening. "You mean Mommy might get better?"

"Yes, Daniel. I think your mommy is going to be just fine."

Teresa smiled and prayed she wasn't building false hopes, because she wasn't at all certain Sharon was going to be fine ever again.

2

When Gabriel and Kent separated at the house, they'd agreed that Kent would go north and Gabe south in search of Sharon. Kent had sped out of his driveway and shot up the highway, seeming to know exactly where he was going. Gabe had gotten into his own car, pulled to the end of the driveway, and merely sat with the engine running.

Why had he said he'd go south? Nerves, he thought. After all, Sharon had fled *from* the south end of town. Why would she drive back there, back into the mass of cars leaving the site of the fireworks display? Sharon wouldn't drive into a possible traffic jam.

At least Gabe didn't think she would. Judging by her earlier behavior, he didn't know what Sharon would do, and he didn't believe she knew, either. He'd never seen his daughter in such a state. It had been almost unbearable for him. He'd lost her mother, whom he'd loved dearly. Now he was in danger of losing his daughter, whom he loved more than anyone in the world, even Daniel. Even Carmen.

Gabriel felt the sting of guilt when he thought of Carmen. She'd seemed so dejected when she slumped away from the group after Sharon had fled. Even her usually animated face—her beautiful eyes—had looked blank. He knew he'd been short with her, but he'd been aghast at his daughter's behavior. Horrified. Sharon's reaction was not one of mere disapproval or displeasure—she'd been wild, fierce, full of hatred for Carmen and disgust for her father. She'd called his relationship with Carmen *blasphemous*. It wasn't normal.

Unless, of course, Carmen really had been involved with Hugh Farr as Sharon claimed. The idea of Carmen having sex with Hugh made Gabe feel nauseated. Sharon said her mother had told her about the affair. But her mother, Helen, could have been mistaken. Helen *had* to have been mistaken, because Sharon wouldn't make up such a hideous lie unless she was sick. But if she *was* sick, what was wrong and when had it started? When he'd begun seeing Carmen. He realized that now, although for months he'd tried damnably to never acknowledge it. And now look what his willed ignorance had wrought. Look what he had allowed to happen to Sharon, his darling, his life.

Almost without knowing it, Gabe had driven north, but unlike Kent, he'd made a right turn before he reached the road leading to Teresa's property. The turn he made was into a cemetery—the cemetery where his wife was buried. He stopped his car, retrieved a flashlight from his glove compartment, and made his way through the dark, quiet grounds to the headstone of Helen O'Brien, his wife, who had died of a cerebral aneurysm just before her fiftieth birthday. She should have lived to be at least eighty, Gabe thought in misery. She should have lived to see the grand-son she'd adored grow to manhood. Helen had been so gentle, so loving, quiet, and shy, a true lady, completely devoted to home and family.

She'd been so different from the outgoing, flippant, glamorous Carmen, who'd never had a child, who'd been a widow for so long it seemed as if she'd never been married, who'd never understood his sensitive, delicate Sharon who *needed* to be babied, Gabe told himself. Sharon wasn't strong like Teresa Farr. He didn't *want* Sharon to be like Teresa Farr.

Teresa had made no secret of her strained relations with Hugh. In fact, although Gabe couldn't stand the sight of Hugh Farr, he secretly thought Teresa had borne the murder of her father a bit too bravely, almost as if she didn't care that he'd been stabbed to death, which was downright unnatural, Gabe told himself, working up a case against the young woman Carmen seemed to admire so much while never quite successfully hiding her disdain for Sharon. Carmen hadn't appreciated or understood his Sharon, who loved and honored her father, who visited her mother's grave once a week and left fresh flowers even in the middle of winter.

Sharon, who so often came to her mother's grave when she was lonely or hurt or upset.

But not tonight, Gabe saw with a plunge of his heart when he looked at the quiet grave with its simple gray granite headstone, the fresh flowers left by Sharon on Sunday now drooping almost desolately in the moonlight. Tonight, Helen O'Brien's grave lay in peaceful solitude in the low, velvety folds of this beautiful July night.

3

Celeste had rolled into a ball in the deep grass and weeds a couple of feet from the road until her ragged breathing slowed and the pain beneath her ribs receded to a slight, dull throb. She thought she'd eluded her pursuer, but escape wasn't her only mission. I still have to get to Teri, the girl thought. I'm not the only person Death wants tonight.

Cold although the night was warm, Celeste ran her hands over her T-shirt to discover she was soaked with sweat. No wonder, the way she'd been running earlier, she thought, and what were wet clothes compared to getting killed? Still, the clamminess was uncomfortable. Celeste reached into the pocket of her jeans and withdrew a rubber band she'd slipped in before they went to see the fireworks. She pulled her long, damp hair into a ponytail, exposing her hot neck to the barest whisper of a breeze that had sprung up sometime during her flight. The air on her neck felt wonderful and she almost made a sound of relief before reminding herself to be as quiet as possible.

Celeste felt temporarily safe from the killer, but she knew she still had quite a way to go on foot before she reached Teri's. This time, she took off in a trot instead of a run. In the distance, she heard the occasional boom of fireworks put off by individuals at their houses. Daddy always complained, saying fireworks were dangerous and most of the people who put them off didn't have a permit, nor did they have police or emergency vehicles present in case of an emergency.

Daddy.

Celeste finally felt the press of tears behind her eyes, but she forced them down. She had to watch where she was going, where she was stepping. The moon and stars seemed to have abandoned this particular night when the only light came from the occasional flare of one of those illegal fireworks. Celeste knew she could *not* trip and maybe twist an ankle. She had to move as fast as possible but also with extreme caution. Grandma always said Celeste had to be *careful*. She'd said it so many times, Celeste had wanted to scream during her years of silence.

Now Grandma would never tell her to be careful again. Once more, the tears pressed. Once more, Celeste fought them. Not now, she told herself. Tears could come later, when there was time.

At least, Celeste hoped there would be time for tears.

4

"Gabe?"

"Carmen."

"Gabe, you said you'd call me. I've waited for two hours. Did you find Sharon?"

Gabriel sat down on his old, worn recliner, holding a can of beer in one hand and the phone receiver in the other. He felt hot and cold at the same time. He also felt overwhelmingly tired while at the same time thinking he'd never be able to sleep again—at least not unless he simply collapsed from either relief or sorrow.

"No. Kent sent Daniel home with Teri and he's still driving around looking for Sharon. He suggested that she might come to my house—her old home—so he told me to wait here for a while. I don't think she'll come here, but I'll wait a few more minutes. That's all I can stand. I *have* to go back out again and look for my girl."

"Oh, Gabe, I'm so sorry. You sound exhausted."

"I am."

"Then you shouldn't go out again now. Please stay home and rest," Carmen pleaded.

Gabriel felt a rush of irritation. Did Carmen think his getting enough sleep was more important than finding Sharon? Could Carmen possibly believe *anything* was more important to him than finding his daughter?

"Carmen, I can't rest until I locate Sharon," he said with strained patience. "I'm not going to collapse from losing sleep for one night. I'm not a doddering old man, you know."

"Of course you aren't! I didn't mean to imply—" Carmen started over, "I'm so sorry for how Sharon took our news."

"We didn't think she'd be happy about it."

"Not being happy and throwing a screaming fit are hardly the same," Carmen said tartly. Gabriel could almost see her eyelids flutter the way they did when she thought her natural outspokenness had taken her too far. "I mean, Sharon was so overwrought. I knew she wouldn't be happy, but I didn't expect her to be—"

"Out of control. Wild. A lunatic," Gabe snapped. "I know what you think of Sharon!"

"Gabe, I—"

"You've never liked Sharon," Gabriel rushed on. "You think she's a spoiled brat, or now, even worse. You probably think she's some kind of mental case like your good friend Marielle Farr!"

"What made you believe I think she's like Teri's mother?"

Because of the way she acted tonight, Gabe thought. Because she hasn't acted quite right for a few months. Because something *is* wrong with her.

But Gabe would not say any of this to Carmen. It was one thing to admit it to himself. It was quite another to admit it to an outsider. *Outsider?* The word drew him up short. He was supposed to marry Carmen in two months. Just this morning he'd told himself how very much he loved her, what a wonderful woman she was, how he couldn't wait until he could call her "wife." And now he was thinking of her as an outsider?

"Carmen, I have to ask you a question. What Sharon said about you and Hugh Farr—"

"Is a damned lie! She's crazy!" Carmen snarled. Gabe could hear her sharp intake of breath. "I mean, it isn't true and the *idea* is crazy, not Sharon."

After a moment of silence, Gabe said, "Of course."

"I didn't mean to snap about what Sharon said. Clearly she believes it. Helen must have seen Hugh with someone else and mistaken her for me. But now we know why Sharon has always disliked me."

"Yes, we do."

Silence spun out before Carmen asked, "Will you consider resting for at least another hour and let Kent take over the search now?"

"No. I'm going back out as soon as we get off the phone. It's my duty to find her, not Kent's."

"But he's her husband—her next of kin."

"Legally he's her next of kin, but she's much closer to me than *him*!"

"And that's what you want, isn't it?" Carmen burst out. "When she and Kent have had problems, you haven't encouraged her to work them out with him. You've encouraged her to come to you, and then you've always taken her side, always told her she's right, let her turn you against Kent. You told me you didn't like him anymore."

"You said you didn't, either!" Gabe flared.

"I said he'd changed. No wonder. First his father was murdered and suspicion fell not only on his sister but also on him, then he had a shotgun wedding to your daughter—" Gabe stiffened, his face suffusing with red. "And finally, you've never turned loose of her. You fanned the fires in their marriage—the fire of anger, not of passion. I think you did that so she'd eventually leave him, and she and Daniel would come home to you!"

By now, Gabe's annoyance had turned to fury. "That is the vilest lie I've ever heard! If I hadn't heard you say it, I wouldn't believe you *could* say it! Is this what you've always thought of my daughter?"

Carmen paused. He could hear her breathing heavily. He pictured her fighting for control over her emotions, for her usual self-possession—the self-possession he'd admired and loved. "Gabe, I went completely overboard a minute ago. Please forgive me. I'm concerned about Sharon, too. I'm worried—"

"You're worried that her behavior is going to change my mind about marrying you." Gabe felt as if he saw the whole situation clearly now. Sharon had known more than she said about Carmen, even if she'd been wrong about an affair between Carmen and Hugh. Sharon had acted so wildly tonight because she was afraid of the harm a marriage to Carmen would do to him, the father she loved so much. "I believe you said exactly how you felt, Carmen, even if you are completely wrong."

"Gabe, *please* listen to reason," Carmen begged desperately. "I'm just afraid her reaction will make you think twice about marrying me. I don't mean this as an insult, but she *can* be manipulative."

"Thank you, Dr. Norris. I thought I was the manipulative one, trying to break up her marriage so she'd come home to Daddy," Gabe returned icily.

"Oh, Gabe, I'm sorry. I'm so upset I hardly know what I'm saying tonight. I didn't mean to criticize either one of you—"

"But that's what you did. And you didn't just speak out of anger—you said what you *really* feel. After all this time, I finally know what you think. Well, listen closely, Carmen. You can say what you want about me, but I won't have you criticizing my daughter!" Gabe looked at the small oil portrait of his dead wife, Helen, hanging on the wall—Helen, with her kind eyes and gentle smile—and he made a quick, definite decision. "Carmen, I think we should forget about this wedding for now."

"Gabe, *no!*" Carmen cried in anguish.

"Yes," Gabe returned coolly. "I'm afraid that's the way things have to be until I take care of my daughter."

But as he hung up, Gabriel O'Brien knew his wedding to Carmen wasn't merely on hold.

It was canceled.

CHAPTER TWENTY

1

TERESA HAD BEEN SO preoccupied with reviewing the events of the evening, she hadn't noticed when Daniel stopped talking. She looked over at him to see his eyelids drooping as he began to sag in his chair. She glanced at the kitchen clock.

"Daniel, it's twelve o'clock! You have to go to bed!" The child jumped, then made an effort to open his eyes wide and sit up straight on his kitchen chair. Both attempts failed.

"I'm gonna stay up all night," Daniel said truculently. "You can't make me go to bed."

"Oh yes, I can."

"Cannot, cannot." Daniel's eyelids were beginning to droop again. "No!"

Teresa looked at the stubborn little boy planted firmly on his chair. She was *not* going to carry him upstairs and toss him onto a bed. Then inspiration struck.

"Daniel, if you go to bed now like a good boy, I'll let you ride Caesar tomorrow." Teresa hated to stoop to bribery—she was quite certain all the child psychologists would frown on it—but at this point, all Teresa cared about was that the exhausted little boy get some sleep. "How about it, Daniel? You can stay up all night, or you can go to sleep and when you wake up tomorrow, take a ride on Caesar. Which will it be?"

Daniel looked at her mutinously with his tired eyes, but his love for the horse outweighed his determination to show Teri who was boss. "Well, maybe I am a little bit sleepy." Teresa smothered a smile. The little boy wasn't going to wilt, but he was attempting to make going to bed his decision, not her command. "I'd prob'ly ride better tomorrow if I took a nap."

"I'm sure that's true."

"So I guess I'll go to sleep for a little while."

"I think you've made a wise decision," Teresa said gravely. "Would you like to take your nap in the guest room or in my room?"

Daniel pretended to think this over. Finally, he asked, "Does Sierra sleep with you?"

"Yes, but there would be plenty of room for the three of us. I have a queen-sized bed."

"Well, if Sierra's gonna be there, I guess I'll sleep in your bed. But it's not 'cause I'm scared to be alone. I'd just like to sleep with Sierra. Mommy won't let me have a dog, even though I've asked and asked. You won't tell her I slept in the same bed with Sierra, will you?"

"I absolutely will not." Teresa was sincere. She would do just about anything to make Daniel comfortable on this strange night. Besides, she didn't think Sharon would care what sleeping arrangements she made as long as Daniel was safe.

Ten minutes later, she had Daniel tucked into her bed. She'd motioned for Sierra to jump up, too, and the dog now lay beside Daniel, who flung his little arm lovingly across the dog. Daniel's eyes were already shut and his breathing becoming deeper and regular and she made another motion for Sierra to hold her position while Teresa tiptoed out of the room. Normally, Sierra wanted to be with her mistress at all times, but the dog was so enamored of Daniel, who never tired of giving her the ear rubs she loved so much, Sierra acquiesced and stayed with her new charge for the evening.

Teresa quietly closed the bedroom door so no noise would disturb the little boy who'd finally surrendered to sleep. She went downstairs and did what she had to do—

Pace and worry.

Mac had said he was just going to drop off his mother, then come to her house. "So where is he?" Teresa asked no one. Was Emma sick? Had it been necessary for him to stay with his mother? He would have called to tell me, Teresa thought.

Unless he'd been in a car wreck. Unless he were in an ambulance or even the hospital, maybe unconscious, maybe *dying*. Teresa's heart pounded as she rushed to the phone. Gory, tragic scenes flashed in her mind—Mac lying bloody and battered, perhaps mumbling her name, perhaps already drawing his last breath without her by his side, holding his hand, telling him again as she had last night that she loved him, that she'd never stopped loving him.

He'd given her his cell phone number last night and she'd already memorized it. Teresa dialed frantically. The phone rang twice and then sent her directly to voice mail. She'd left a message—somewhat garbled, laced with irritation and a couple of expletives simply because she'd frightened herself so badly—then the allotted time for her message abruptly ended.

Mac couldn't be deliberately dodging her, she thought. Not after last night. Not after promising not to desert her during what he'd thought was going to be an edgy, potentially disastrous engagement announcement at her house. He'd left before the scene downtown, before Sharon had stormed away. He didn't even know she was missing.

Teresa knew calling the club would be useless. She called his apartment and got his answering machine. Then, as a last resort, she'd looked up Emma's phone number and called her apartment. Nothing. Not even an answering machine. And Emma had supposedly wanted to go home because she didn't feel well. At least that's what Mac had told Teresa.

"And if it's what he told me, it's true," Teresa told herself severely. The only reason he might possibly want to lie to her was that he didn't want to attend the "party" at Teri's house, but Mac would have simply refused to come. He would have been nice, he would have been apologetic, but he would have refused. He wouldn't have just left her hanging, wondering where he could be after midnight when he was supposed to be with her.

Returning to her original scenario of the car wreck, Teresa called the emergency room at the hospital. Someone answered, then immediately put her on hold. She held. And held. And held until she had an urge to toss the receiver through her picture window. She knew the emergency room was always busy on the night of the Fourth of July—too many untrained people tried to set off their own fireworks and ended up being burned or even losing a finger. Worse. She remembered a boy she'd gone to high school with setting off a firecracker incorrectly and suffering third-degree burns to most of his face. He'd been such a handsome guy. Now people told her he was a complete recluse.

Teresa shook her head as if trying to shake free of the terrible image. She hadn't thought about that poor guy for years. But of course she had to remember him tonight, she thought with irrational resentment—a night when she was worried sick that Mac and Emma might be lying in a car being eaten away by voracious flames and excruciating heat.

Teresa decided she would try the hospital again in a few minutes. In the meantime, she'd see if Kent had found Sharon. She dialed his cell phone number and Kent nearly yelled, "Sharon! Where are you?"

"It's Teri, not Sharon, which you would have known if you'd looked at your Caller ID. But I can tell that you haven't found her."

"No, dammit."

"And neither has Gabe?"

"I just talked to him a few minutes ago. He's gone home to wait for a couple of hours. She might go there."

"Good idea. She certainly won't come here."

Kent began speaking in a guilty, defeated tone. "I've known for months things weren't right with Sharon. She thought Gabe was seeing someone and that didn't suit her. And I've been gone a lot—I've been working twelve hours a day including Saturdays, but I'm half-convinced Sharon believes I have a mistress. Also, we've found out she can't have any more children. She wanted three because she was an only child and lonely. Anyway, knowing she can't have more has made her cling even tighter to Daniel."

"Oh, Kent, I didn't know you couldn't have more children."

"Sharon didn't want anyone to know. I think she could have stood it if the problem was with me, but it's with her. It doesn't matter to me. Thousands of children in the world need a good home. But Sharon won't even talk about adoption. She considers it an announcement to the world that she's a failure." The energy left Kent's voice and Teresa could almost see him slumping behind the wheel of his big SUV. "Going to the cops won't do any good. She's only been gone a couple of hours. But I'm not going to stop looking for her, Teri, because I'm afraid this night could be the breaking point for my wife."

"It won't be," Teresa said fervently. "Sharon is not like our mother, Kent. She's much stronger than she seems."

"I hope so," Kent said doubtfully. "How's Daniel?"

"Sleeping soundly with Sierra lying right beside him."

"Oh great, Sharon would love that. A dog in bed with our son."

"Sierra had a bath less than a week ago. And Daniel adores her. *And* Sharon doesn't have to know."

"I guess she doesn't. Teri, I should get off the phone now. Sharon might be trying to reach me."

"All right. Good luck and call me as soon as it's convenient." Teresa added somewhat self-consciously, "I love you, big brother."

She couldn't see him, but she heard the slight smile in his voice. "Love you, Teri. And I'm sorry I set fire to your Barbie doll when I was eleven."

"Don't worry about it. I've bought a new one. Now go find your wife."

Teresa set down the phone and went into the kitchen for a glass of wine. A mixed drink or two glasses of wine a week were usually her limit, but she had to admit this had been an unusually stressful week. Alcohol didn't solve any problems, but it did make her feel slightly more relaxed. She took a sip of the sharp, cold white wine and jumped when the police scanner crackled to life.

Teresa barely listened as the dispatcher spoke. "Any available city unit in vicinity of Mount Vernon Avenue."

Mount Vernon, Teri thought. So near. She was listening more closely when a policeman answered. "City Three. What do you have?"

"Third-party call disturbance. Possibly a domestic at 4021 Mount Vernon. Caller heard screaming, saw what appeared to be a young woman running from front of the house. Caller also thinks they see a body lying near a car at the back of the house."

Teri dropped her glass of wine. Four-oh-two-one Mount Vernon was the address of Jason and Celeste Warner.

2

Hands trembling, Teri dug through a drawer until she found a phone directory. First she looked up the address of Jason Warner and her heart sank—4021 Mount Vernon. She'd correctly remembered the Warners' address. Next she looked at the phone number and dialed frantically. She let the phone ring ten times, her fear growing with every unanswered ring, then replaced her receiver in the handset.

There could be dozens of reasons that the Warners weren't answering tonight, she told herself. They hadn't gone directly home after the fireworks display. Fay had decided to make Celeste go to bed early and had turned the phones down low so no ringing would awaken the girl. The Warners just didn't feel like answering—

And their next-door neighbor had called the police about a disturbance, people screaming, and a body lying in the backyard. Maybe Celeste. She'd told Teri in the barn that someone still wanted her dead. Perhaps she'd been right.

Except the dispatcher had said that what appeared to be a young woman had been running from the front of the house. Oh, God, please let that be Celeste, Teri prayed. Celeste, who must have been trying to call her earlier when she and Daniel had just arrived. Celeste whose last word to Teri had been "kill."

Teresa took a deep breath, trying to calm herself. The voice on the phone had been so gravelly, maybe the word hadn't been "kill." And maybe the voice hadn't even belonged to Celeste, she thought. Maybe it all had just been another prank.

Except that Caller ID showed the earlier calls had come from the Warner house. Except that police had been summoned to the house because a "third party" had heard screaming. *Screaming!* "Sure, there's nothing to worry about," Teri muttered sarcastically to herself. "Those are all simply a bunch of coincidences. The Warner family is just fine."

Teresa tried the Warner phone number again, and again no one answered. She put down the receiver, feeling nervous perspiration popping out on her forehead. She could only remember one night of her life that had been worse than this one, and she certainly didn't want to think about what had happened *that* night.

Hardly thinking about what she was doing, Teri stooped and began picking up pieces of the wineglass she'd dropped on the floor. She didn't realize one had punctured two fingers until she saw a drop of blood hit the vinyl. She glanced at her finger, removed a splinter of glass, then mentally cursed as more blood dripped from a second minuscule hole. God, she'd been careless, she thought. She'd been careless *and* numb. She still felt no stinging pain— she just couldn't stand the sight of blood. Not tonight.

A roll of paper towels stood conveniently nearby and Teri tore off one, wrapping it tightly around the index and middle fingers of her right hand. She applied pressure for about a minute, then removed the towel, too impatient to coddle herself any more. She reached for the phone and dialed the Warner home again. No answer. She sighed in frustration. When she replaced the receiver, she saw her blood on the numbers. Blood on the floor, blood on the phone. Blood in the Warner house. She was certain of it.

Teri felt a sudden need to make sure her nephew, at least, was safe. She grabbed another paper towel in case her fingers were still bleeding, then nearly ran through the house and up the stairs to her bedroom. Teri opened the door and tiptoed inside the room. Sierra raised her head, but Teri held two fingers up to her lips and the dog seemed to understand the message. Someone once made that gesture to me in a dark hall, Teresa thought with a shiver, and I, too, went completely silent.

Daniel lay on his left side, his right hand touching Sierra's shoulder. The dog always slept at the foot of the bed when Teri was in residence, but tonight Sierra had obviously been trying to comfort the frightened child. Dogs could sense so many things for which humans often didn't give them credit. Sierra had known Daniel was scared and troubled. But now his face looked smooth and peaceful in sleep, his mouth open slightly, his strawberry blond hair skimmed back from his forehead and slightly damp although the room was comfortably cool.

As Teri stood watching him for a moment, he mumbled, "Mommy," then, "it's not a real dog," before kicking spasmodically and rolling onto his side. Even in his sleep, he was still worried about what *Mommy* would say, Teresa thought sympathetically. Well, maybe Kent had been so overwhelmed with managing a company thrust on him when he was young and inexperienced, he'd comforted himself with the idea that Sharon's problems would "just work out by themselves." After tonight, though, he couldn't abrogate his responsibility to his child any longer. Kent would know that in her current state of mind, Sharon was a damaging influence on the boy and do something about the problem—something sensible yet *kind*. Sharon would not be treated as Marielle had been because Kent, thank goodness, was no Hugh Farr.

Teri bent down and kissed Daniel lightly on the forehead, an informality Daniel granted no one except his daddy, mommy, and grandfather when he was awake. "Gotcha!" Teresa whispered, smiling. She then blew a kiss at Sierra, whose amber gaze ricocheted between Daniel and Teri, her two charges. Teri walked quietly out of the room, leaving the door open a couple of inches.

Descending the stairway, she still heard the pops and booms of fireworks in the distance. Normally she took her binoculars to the front porch and tried to spot the fireworks of those few lonely stragglers still trying to put on a show.

But tonight she wanted only to huddle in a chair and lose herself in a book. She went in the kitchen, glanced at the mess she and Daniel had made, finished cleaning up the broken glass, even running a miniature sweeper over the spot so Daniel wouldn't cut his foot if he came downstairs barefoot, and finally she turned off the police scanner. She'd heard just about all the bad news she could tolerate for one night.

Teri went back to the living room, feeling as if she should call and check on Carmen's state of mind, but she didn't need a phone call to let her know Carmen's emotions had gone through the wringer tonight. Also, she might have taken a pill and Teri would awaken her from the merciful oblivion of sleep.

Teresa paced around her living room, amused by how perfect it looked. She liked a neat house, but she certainly never kept every ashtray in place, every tabletop looking as if it dared a dust mote to land on its surface. She'd been expecting guests tonight. If things had gone well, china plates and champagne flutes would be sitting around the room and Teri would be dreading the cleanup job she'd have tomorrow morning. Now she felt as if cleaning would have been a joy if only Carmen and Gabe's announcement hadn't caused the storm of the century.

Teri passed over *The Grapes of Wrath* in favor of *People* magazine and leaned back in the big recliner that always felt soft and welcoming, as if caressing her tenderly. Except for tonight. The chair back felt too stiff and she thought she felt a lump in the seat cushion. She stood up to investigate, then heard a knock at the door.

She could have cried in pure relief. Mac, at last. Well, she'd just give him a piece of her mind! She'd ask why he hadn't called her. She'd ask why he hadn't answered his cell phone. She'd ask where the hell he'd been!

Angry and tired as she was, Teri nevertheless pulled a

wide-toothed comb from the small drawer of the table near the entrance and ran it through her hair, then tossed it back in the drawer. She didn't want him to catch her primping. He deserved to see her at her worst. He should *never* have just left her hanging for so long. But he was here now, she thought with a lightning change of mood. Daniel had Sierra for protection and Teri had Mac. Dear, handsome, funny, loving, sometimes absent-minded Mac.

But when she swung open the front door, she found Carmen standing on her porch. She wore old, ragged jeans, a gray T-shirt that looked wrinkled and sweaty, as if she'd worn it while doing heavy labor, and a loose navy blue windbreaker. Her brown hair hung tangled around a face white as parchment except for messy smears of black where tears had dragged mascara and eyeliner down to her high cheekbones.

Madeleine, Teri thought briefly. Carmen looks as otherworldly as Madeline in Poe's "The Fall of the House of Usher."

"Carmen?" she asked faintly. "What happened? Have they found Sharon?"

Carmen shook her head no.

"Where's Gabe?"

Carmen began to tremble, then flung herself into Teresa's arms. "Gabe has left me," she grated out. "Marriage to him was the last, best dream of my life, and he simply smashed it with one brief, devastating phone call."

3

Jason Warner slowly opened his eyes. For ten seconds he stared at the dark sky in complete confusion until pain like a red-hot poker stabbed somewhere in the region of his stomach. He put his hand to the pain, pressed—the act making him cry out in agony—and jerked away his hand, raising it to eye level. Even in the darkness, he could see the dark liquid floating down to his wrist, working its way between his fingers. Blood. Lots and lots of blood.

He tried to sit up, to see the extent of the damage to his body, but the slightest movement made him feel as if huge, hideous hands were digging out his insides. The image brought on the urge to throw up, but he used every ounce of his waning strength to control the urge. Instinctively, he felt the urge could kill him. It was possible to die of pain. He knew that wasn't just an expression.

Jason turned his head slightly to the right and saw the tire of his car—the car that would have offered protection and escape if they'd just gotten inside and away from this place five minutes sooner. He knew a suitcase, a tote bag, a duffel lay scattered around him, flung by his own startled hands when something, some*one,* wearing a long dark coat and a hood had flown at him, knife raised, long silver blade caught in the glow of the porch light, flashing wickedly before it plunged into him, driven by a strong hand and guided by someone emitting a low, animal-like cry of triumph as the knife pushed through skin and muscle, and sent blood gushing across his shirt.

The knife had twisted and Jason had uttered a stunned sound of shock and pain, before dropping to the ground. His attacker had turned him over, withdrawn the knife, causing Jason another nearly unbearable wave of agony, then dashed for the house and the open kitchen door.

Jason looked straight ahead again, took as deep a breath as possible, and lifted his chin, craning back his head. The kitchen door still stood open, bright light spilling from the small room his mother kept immaculate. Except she would keep it immaculate no longer. Jason moaned when he saw Fay, sprawled close to the door, her hand clutched to her neck, the left side of her face and her left hand, arm, and side bathed in a garish wash of fresh crimson blood. He could even see her blue eyes, open, staring at nothing.

And Celeste? He drew enough breath to utter her name,

but unless she'd been close to the door, she couldn't have heard him. Had she escaped? Or was she lying inside the house, dead? Or maybe, like years ago, close to death?

The doorway began to shift, then to whirl. Jason closed his eyes, knowing he was on the verge of passing out. He couldn't look at the spinning world any longer, but he could still hear—not the boom of fireworks but a sound like sirens. He tried to open his eyes, but the effort was too great. He took as deep a breath as he could manage, waiting for death to enfold him, when suddenly a white light shone through the veil of his eyelids. Jason wondered if this was the light everyone talked about seeing when you were dying.

His question was answered when he heard someone yell, "He's over here and he's alive." Then someone gently touched his shoulder and a deep male voice said, "Just be calm, fella. I'm a cop, and emergency services will be here any minute. You're going to be all right, now."

CHAPTER
TWENTY-ONE

1

CELESTE HAD RUN ALONG the chain-link fence surrounding Defense Logistics Agency until she'd come to a slope. Halfway down, her tennis shoe slipped on dew-laden weeds and she'd rolled all the way down into a field. At first terrified that she'd either broken her leg or sprained her ankle, she'd sat still, looking around, trying to catch her breath. Then she stood, feeling only minor pain in her ankle. Slowly, carefully, she crept across the back of the field where the undergrowth was high, crossed a narrow dirt road, drew a ragged breath, and almost burst into tears when she read the dark green writing on a large white sign:

FARR FIELDS

She was not Catholic, but she made the sign of the cross and mouthed a silent prayer to the dark sky. She'd made it.

She was hot, she was dirty, she was exhausted, but she'd made it to safety.

Celeste darted to the trees lining the edge of the road and skittered across the open fields where the beautiful horses whiled away their days eating grass, soaking up the sun, occasionally being taken for a walk or even a run. Crouching behind one of the ring posts, Celeste looked with longing at the big, luxurious barn. She ran for the corner and felt an almost overwhelming desire to enter, pet the horses she knew had not received enough attention since the murder of Gus Gibbs everyone kept trying to keep her from hearing about, then crawl onto a mound of hay and sleep peacefully the rest of the night. In the morning, there would be time to think about Daddy and Grandma. She would have the rest of her life to think about Daddy and Grandma.

But they're dead, Celeste told herself. As much as it hurts, I know they're dead. But Teri is still alive—I *know* it; I can *feel* it! And she'll stay alive if I can help her like she once helped me.

2

Teri led a weeping Carmen to the couch and sat down beside her. Suddenly Teri realized she'd never seen Carmen cry. Oh, a few controlled tears had stood in her eyes sometimes when she'd talked about Marielle after her disappearance, but generally Carmen always had been upbeat, optimistic. She'd always told Teri not to lose hope about *anything,* but Carmen's flowing tears let Teri know that Carmen now had completely lost hope for herself.

A lot of people in town thought Carmen's outer self-control indicated a lack of feeling anything for anyone. How wrong they'd been, Teresa thought. Carmen had cared about Marielle. And no one who saw Carmen now could say she wasn't crushed by Gabe's—Gabe's what? Teri realized she didn't know exactly what had happened between Carmen and Gabe, and now bluntly asked her, just as Carmen had bluntly asked Teri what had happened when she broke off her engagement to Mac.

"Are you asking if he 'jilted' me?" Carmen managed a tiny, sarcastic smile. "Not exactly. He said we had to put off the wedding until after he's taken care of his daughter."

Teri leaned back and looked at her friend with a smile. "Good heavens, Carmen, he hasn't dropped you. He just wants to postpone the wedding—"

"You don't know him as well as I do and you didn't hear him on the phone." Carmen made the pathetic sound of a dying animal. "He is not going to marry me, Teri. Gabe O'Brien simply doesn't want me anymore."

"That can't be true, Carmen. Now pull yourself together and think about this logically. A few hours ago, he loved you so deeply he wanted to spend the rest of his life with you. Do you think because his daughter had a temper fit about it, he's going to throw you away?"

"Honestly, yes. He doesn't think his daughter is just having a temper fit. He thinks she's having a nervous breakdown. He even compared her to your mother, Teri." Teresa winced. "Oh, God, I shouldn't have said that. I'm sorry. I said about five other things to Gabe on the phone I'm sorry for, but I said them, and he'll never forgive me."

"You don't know that, Carmen. Gabe was speaking in the heat of the moment just as you were. As soon as they find Sharon—and they will, very soon, I'm sure—he's going to think this through and realize what happened. He doesn't want to lose you, Carmen."

After a moment of silence, Carmen said harshly, "Sharon told him I had an affair with your father."

Teresa felt herself blushing like a child. She didn't know why she found Sharon's accusation of a sexual involvement between her father and Carmen so unsettling. It was ridiculous, Teri told herself. Preposterous! Absurd! At least four more synonyms popped into her mind with flashing speed. Yet she had the sensation of grasping at straws, at grabbing for easy, dismissive words that required no thought. Teri wondered why she felt so awkward.

Because something about the very suggestion of Carmen and Dad having sex, not once but many times, feels sickeningly possible, she thought in surprise. Because Carmen's betrayal of Mom, supposedly Carmen's best friend, suddenly doesn't seem at all unthinkable, Teri realized in surprise, remembering little glances, brief touches, small, intimate smiles between Hugh and Carmen, turned off like a light switch when they caught someone gazing at them.

Carmen looked at her piercingly. Unnerved, Teri said quickly, "Gabe doesn't believe you were involved with my father. If over the phone he sounded as if he did, it's just because he's flustered. When he calms down, Carmen, he'll realize you couldn't even stand to be around my father, much less to be his mistress. You just need patience. This rift between the two of you can be fixed."

"Oh, how I wish that were true." All of the life suddenly seemed to drain from Carmen. She slumped on the couch, clasping her hands, her gaze far away. She looked dead, and abruptly Teresa felt afraid for her. And *of* her, she admitted to herself. The Carmen Teresa had known and loved for years had suddenly become someone she felt she barely knew. But at least the woman was no longer giving her that probing, piercing look that seemed to reach her very soul, Teresa thought in relief. She'd never seen that look in Carmen's eyes before tonight.

"Carmen, I think you need a drink to calm you down," Teri said abruptly. "I'd offer a tranquilizer, but I don't have any."

"I'd rather have a drink," Carmen said in a toneless voice. "But not champagne. God, not champagne."

"I wasn't thinking of champagne. I have beer. I also have some tequila and margarita mix. How about a margarita? You've always loved margaritas."

"I have?" Carmen said vaguely. "It's so silly, but at the moment I can't seem to remember what I did and did not love." She glanced at Teri. "Yes, I would like a margarita."

"Good. So would I." Teresa stood. "You just relax on the couch and I'll bring out the drinks in a few minutes."

Carmen leaned forward slowly and shifted several times, as if she were trying to coordinate the parts of different bodies. "I'll go in the kitchen with you, if you don't mind. I don't want to sit out here by myself." She looked around. "Where's Sierra, by the way? You two are nearly inseparable."

"On a usual night, yes, but tonight's special," Teri said lightly as she dashed into the kitchen, Carmen shambling along behind her. "Daniel is staying with me and he wanted to sleep with Sierra."

"Sharon won't like that."

"Sharon won't know if I can help it. Anyway, my only fear was that Sierra wouldn't sleep with anyone except for me, but she snuggled right up to Daniel," Teri chattered, knowing she spoke louder and faster than usual, wondering if Carmen even noticed. "*I* never get snuggled, but I think she realized Daniel needed all the comfort he could get in spite of the Coke and cupcakes he'd had earlier. The poor little guy was completely thrown by his mother's scene downtown."

"No wonder. Sharon will be the talk of the town tomorrow. That should make her happy. She always wants to be the center of attention."

Carmen's words were bitter, but her voice sounded flat. She could have been talking about someone she didn't know.

"I don't think she wants the kind of attention she got tonight." Teresa stretched to reach a bottle of tequila on the top shelf of a kitchen cabinet. It sat beside a bottle of scotch and a bottle of bourbon. "I guarantee she'll regret it tomorrow."

"She probably loves that everyone is so worried and out

looking for her," Carmen went on in a distant voice as if she hadn't heard Teri. "Do you think she'll come here?"

"Oh, I doubt it. The only reason she would is if she thinks I have Daniel, and if she comes here to get him, I won't let her have him. Not if she's alone. If Kent is with her . . . well, Kent wouldn't want Daniel disturbed. I don't think you and I will be seeing Sharon tonight."

Teresa pulled a bottle of margarita mix from the refrigerator. She poured tequila and the well-chilled mix in the blender and turned it on, hoping the noise wouldn't awaken Daniel. She was pouring the drinks into big glasses when Carmen asked, "Where's Mac? Has he joined the search, too?"

"I can't find him, either. He said Emma wasn't feeling well and he was going to drop her off at her apartment, then come here, but he's never turned up. I've tried his cell phone, his home phone, and even Emma's phone, but I can't get an answer anywhere."

"So you and Daniel are all alone."

"Yes." Teri hesitated, suddenly hit by the strong scent of sandalwood. "Carmen, did you just put on cologne?" she asked, turning around.

"It's my favorite scent," Carmen returned calmly, steadily pointing a .22 revolver at Teresa's forehead.

3

Celeste was girding herself for a run across the field and up the knoll to Teri's front door when she saw someone climbing Teri's front porch steps. She instinctively hit the ground, flattening herself as much as possible in the well-trimmed grass. Celeste squinted furiously, but the person in long ragged jeans walked with head lowered and hands tucked inside a voluminous windbreaker. Teri's visitor didn't dress or walk like anyone with whom Celeste was familiar, and she couldn't get a good enough look at the face to be sure of the identity.

In fact, she wasn't even sure if the person was male or female. She *knew* it wasn't Mac—he was taller. She'd seen him one Saturday when Daddy had taken her to Bennigan's and he'd winked at her. Then she'd seen him tonight with Teri. When Celeste had lived in the Farr house, Teri and Mac had loved each other, although Teri had told her it was a huge secret that she must never tell, and she never did. Anyway, she knew the person dragging to Teri's door wasn't Mac. Maybe it was that guy Josh she'd met in the barn the other day, she thought anxiously. He was the son of Gus Gibbs, the man who got murdered. Some people said Josh had murdered his father, but Celeste *knew* he hadn't, and it wasn't just because he was cute. Everything would be okay if it was Josh.

If it wasn't Josh, it could be Kent, Celeste thought, desperately hoping she was right. She remembered him as being bigger than this person seemed to be, but she'd been little when she last saw him. Anyway, the important thing was that Kent wouldn't hurt Teri. Kent had loved Teri, although he'd always tried to act cool, like he didn't even notice his younger sister.

Or maybe it was Kent's wife! Celeste had met her a long time ago, before she and Kent got married. Hugh hadn't liked her. Hugh hadn't liked anyone except Mommy, Celeste thought bitterly. He'd been mean to Kent's girlfriend and one day made her run from the house crying. Celeste couldn't remember the girl's name. Besides, her name didn't matter. Celeste didn't care about names.

But she feared. She feared she knew who had come to see Teri and she feared she knew why. With a sinking heart, Celeste saw Teri open the door. The person flew into Teri's arms and Teri clasped the person, whom she immediately pulled inside, closing the door behind them.

Oh, please don't let that be who I think it is, Celeste begged no one in particular. *Please.*

Celeste waited until she'd regained her breath and her legs felt slightly rested before she stood and moved quickly toward the house. Her recent encounters with shrubbery reminded her that people often let it grow as high as first-floor windows. People like Teri. Celeste dodged behind the sturdy boxwood shrubs that surrounded most of Teri's house. Whenever Celeste came to a window, she rose just high enough to look inside, even if it was dark. At last, she came to a window from which spilled a warm, bright glow. Forcing herself to ascend until her eyes were just above the windowsill, she saw a kitchen. In the kitchen, Teri stood holding two large glasses of a greenish liquid.

And the woman Celeste had seen at the fireworks display—the woman who'd cried out in surprise when a loud firework startled her, just like she'd cried out eight years ago when she'd opened Mommy's bedroom door and seen an eight-year-old Celeste standing there. The woman in the park whose gaze had landed on Celeste, who had been unable to stop staring since she'd heard the woman's surprised yelp. Earlier this evening, after all these years, they'd seen each other and each had known—Celeste knew this was who had killed her mother and Hugh, and the woman knew that Celeste had finally recognized her.

And now that woman was sitting at a kitchen table pointing a gun at Teri's head.

4

Margarita mix slopped out of both glasses, but Teresa didn't drop them. "Carmen, what are you doing?" she asked in a calm voice that she thought sounded like it belonged to someone else.

Carmen said disdainfully, "What does it look like I'm doing?"

"It looks like—" Teresa closed her eyes for a moment, then looked sternly at Carmen. "Put down that gun before you hurt someone."

Carmen burst out laughing, a grating laugh Teresa thought must be ripping at Carmen's throat. "Oh, really? Well, I would never have guessed!" Her laughter abruptly stopped. "I have every intention of hurting someone."

Teresa stared at the woman she'd considered her friend. "Carmen, you've been under tremendous pressure with the store and Sharon and Gabe and . . ." Teri went blank, unable to think of any further pressures in Carmen's life. "I know you're terribly upset because Sharon humiliated you, but you have to remember that we're in Point Pleasant, West Virginia. People around here will gossip about it for a week, then find a new topic. By now, Gabe and Kent understand that Sharon needs professional help and they'll get it for her. As soon as his fright about his daughter is over, Gabe will be more than willing to plan a wedding if you'll still have him."

"You're never at a loss for words, Teri. Of course, most of what you said is completely wrong, but it sounded good. That's what counts. Sounding good and looking good. Strength, sincerity, devotion, and love—well, in the world outside of books and music, they really don't count for much. I learned that the hard way."

"When you were a child?"

Carmen's mouth pulled to a lopsided smile. "Nice stalling tactic, Teri. Yes, I started learning the truth about life in childhood. I've been learning ever since. Tonight endeth the lesson."

"My mother said there was a deep sadness in you—you just hid your sadness better than she did hers. But she thought that sadness must be what drew you together."

"Oh, wise Marielle." Carmen rolled her heavily shadowed eyes. "Teri, did you really think I would choose droopy, pathologically shy Marielle Farr to be my best friend? God!"

"You didn't . . ."

"I didn't what? Like her? Feel sorry for her? No to both. I wanted to get close to your *mother* so I could get close to your *father*. Hugh Farr—the man with more money than just about anyone in this whole state! And while the rest of the country might think all West Virginians are on the dole, they are sadly mistaken!"

"So Sharon was right. You were having an affair with my father." Teresa shook her head. "I don't know why I'm not surprised. I should be stunned, but maybe all along something I buried deep inside was that I sensed a connection between you and Dad."

"A connection. Quite a connection. Shortly after I became a regular visitor at your house, coming to dinner, dropping by in the evenings for a drink with Marielle and her restless husband, Hugh and I began what we joked was the relationship of the century! He couldn't get enough of me, and believe me, Hubert Farr was insatiable when it came to sex."

"I really don't care to hear the details," Teresa said with disgust. "And if you had no feelings for my mother, what about your own husband? I thought you loved John. You stayed home for years taking care of him."

"Exactly." Carmen nearly spat out the word. "Years when I was young and beautiful and should have been out having a good time. Instead, I was stuck with *him*. The first five years we were married, John was healthy, handsome, charming, and had a substantial bank account. And just like that"—she snapped her fingers—"my dear husband came down with carcinoid malignancy. Shall I describe it to you? Tumors develop in the appendix, the rectum, the small intestine, and the windpipe. The tumors are slow-growing and they produce severe abdominal pain, weight loss, constipation, diarrhea, and gastrointestinal tract bleeding, to name some of the more pleasant symptoms. And to top it all off, I discovered John had hardly any health insurance. He wasn't rich, but we lost what he did have in a very long effort to save him. And, of course, the louse had *no* life insurance."

"Oh. I . . . see."

"How could you?" Carmen snarled. "You've never been in a bad situation in your life." Teresa stared at her unflinchingly. "My mother left me without a backward glance. My father cared nothing about me. A modeling career passed me by because I was *two* inches too short—two inches that you have and don't appreciate. Then I married a man who became a disgusting invalid—and believe me, his illness *was* disgusting. None of that was fair, Teri, but I don't take things lying down. I *fix* them. That's all I tried to do—correct a destiny that had gone off track.

"But after nearly two years of being Hugh's mistress, I was getting desperate," Carmen went on, now speaking sociably, as if to a casual friend. "I felt a difference in Hugh—he was easily bored, you know. Still, my husband lingered. The oncologist said it was a miracle." Carmen let out a harsh, jarring laugh. "So one night I gave John a bit too much morphine—enough to shut down his respiratory system. Not even his doctor was skeptical about John's death. The authorities didn't even do a tox screen."

"We all felt so sorry for you," Teresa murmured. "You were probably laughing at us, gloating that you'd gotten away with murder."

"I did John a favor—I ended his suffering." Carmen smiled for a moment. Then she sighed. "I knew I couldn't have Hugh immediately. Things had to be done tastefully, which was easy because almost everyone in town knew Marielle had mental problems. For two years we'd talked about how simple it would be for Hugh to completely break her emotionally." Teresa tried not to let Carmen see her wince. "She took a lot of medication. He said sometimes she didn't even pay close attention to what she was taking, and he could mix up things, put her in a drugged state, and pretend she'd done something to hurt you—inflict an injury in the night to a sleeping victim. Ring a bell?"

"So Dad gave you the idea for how to commit his own murder," Teresa said in a bleak voice. "I wish I could think that was almost funny, but I can't."

"No? I can. I did for over eight years." Carmen took a deep breath. "We knew if Marielle appeared to have hurt you, no one would blame him for putting her in an institution and then realizing he had to divorce her—for the sake of his children, of course. To set you both free of the memory of your dangerous mother.

"In a while, Hugh could have married me with no one suspecting anything wrong. After all, by then I would have been friends with the family for years. Dammit, it would have been *perfect* if not for that empty-headed, overblown, stupid little whore Wendy Warner!" Carmen's voice turned loud and vicious. "God, I can hardly bear to say her name, even now! You don't know how good it felt to stab her over and over and—"

"Carmen!" Teri's voice emerged like a whip as she watched Carmen's hand wavering dangerously, her finger pressing slightly on the trigger of the gun. Her heart pounding, Teresa murmured, "Carmen, I hated Wendy, too. But she's gone. Neither one of us has to think about her anymore. Don't think about her. Just—"

"Settle down and quit yelling? Maybe lose control of this gun? You're right, Teri. I must stay in control." Carmen stood up. "I want you to turn around and put those glasses on the counter. Don't try anything, as they say in the movies, because I have the gun at your head. After you set down the glasses, turn back to me."

Teresa turned slowly and set down the glasses. Facing the window for an instant, she thought she caught a glimpse of blond hair, of a pale forehead and blue eyes, but then the image vanished. A reflection, she thought. But a reflection of whom? Not of her or Carmen.

"I told you to put down the glasses and then turn back to me," Carmen said impatiently. "Are you going to gaze out the window all night? Are you wishing on a star, perhaps?" Carmen giggled, and for a moment Teresa thought the woman might be losing concentration and she'd have a chance to dive for the gun. But as abruptly as Carmen's giggling had begun, it stopped.

Teri turned and faced the woman who looked as if she'd aged twenty years since early in the evening. She'd looked lovely at the fireworks display—younger than her age, bright-eyed, her cheeks bearing the same natural blush as a teenage girl. Now she was a shrunken, wild-eyed, grayish-skinned parody of that lovely woman.

"What now?" Teri asked.

Carmen smiled. "Now you go upstairs and get Daniel."

CHAPTER
TWENTY-TWO

1

CELESTE DIDN'T KNOW THE woman pointing a gun at Teri. She didn't remember her from the days when her mother had been married to Hugh. Celeste was fairly certain she'd seen her in Bennigan's the day she smelled the perfume that had made her start talking again, and of course she'd seen her at the park tonight. The woman was older than Teri but younger than Grandma—at least she'd looked younger at the fireworks display. Now she looked even older than Grandma—tired and so weird she could go out on Halloween without a costume. Someone had said the woman's name. What was it? Carla? Carlene? Cameron?
Carmen!
Celeste let out a silent *Yes!* Then she clapped a hand over her mouth, thinking that for now, at least, it was good that she'd lost her voice. Otherwise, they would have heard her. She already thought Teri had seen her when Teri

turned around and put the glasses on the counter. She'd looked right at the window and Celeste had seen her frown slightly before Celeste had time to duck. Then Teri turned around again. Celeste had raised her head high enough to see that *Carmen* was talking. She also still had the gun pointed at Teri.

Perspiration ran in thin rivulets down Celeste's arms. A fourth mosquito bit tenaciously on her neck, and the bites on her hands and arms itched unbearably. She thought longingly of the insect repellant Grandma had tried to douse her with before they went to see the fireworks. She'd dodged the spray then. Now she'd gladly put it on every inch of her exposed body, but it was too late. Besides, mosquitoes were the least of her troubles.

Celeste knew most girls her age had cell phones. Daddy would have bought her one, but there was no need for a girl who couldn't speak to have a cell phone. He'd mentioned getting her one just a couple of days ago. She wished she had one now, but they hadn't had time to pick out one. Besides, once again she could not speak. Who would she call? She knew her own home phone number, Teri's number, and 911. She certainly wouldn't call 911. She'd seen the sheriff laughing with Carmen. They were friends. He would never believe his friend was holding a gun on Teresa Farr, even if Celeste were capable of telling him what was happening. He'd think she was playing a trick.

Mac. Mac could help Teri. Ever since Celeste was eight years old, she'd thought Mac MacKenzie could probably do anything. She never told Teri she had a crush on Mac, but she figured Teri knew. Teri wouldn't have been jealous, though, and even at eight, Celeste had known guys didn't usually fall in mad, romantic love with little girls. Her mommy had told her about creepy guys who liked little girls, but Mac was anything except creepy.

Yes, Mac could save the day, Celeste thought. But Mac wasn't here. If only she could send him some kind of mental message, he'd come. It sounded silly, even to her, but she didn't care about being silly right now. She cared about saving Teri's life.

Celeste reverentially closed her eyes and pictured her beautiful night-light Snowflake. You're magical and mystical and all that stuff, she told the absent Snowflake. You helped me once. Help me again. Wherever you are, help me and help Teri.

Celeste opened her eyes, blushing in the darkness because she knew regular sixteen-year-old girls didn't beg night-lights for miracles. If she'd spoken that message aloud and anyone heard her, they'd put her in some place for crazy people and never let her out.

But Teri would understand. And maybe, if Celeste wasn't actually as crazy as she knew her thoughts made her seem, Snowflake would once again come to Celeste and Teri's aid.

2

Suddenly Teresa's legs felt like water. Go get Daniel? "Carmen, you don't intend to kill a child, do you?"

Carmen looked at Teri as if she were stupid. "Well, it isn't the first time, now is it? Don't you remember Celeste? Hugh dumped me and your mother and married Wendy in record time, leaving me with a consolation prize—he bought me Trinkets and Treasures, where I could work until I died. But I bided my time. And then I read in the paper that Wendy was pregnant—they'd even given a party to make the announcement—and I couldn't stand it any longer. So I came into that house and I killed him and I killed Wendy and I left you with barely more than a scratch on your arm."

"To point suspicion at me."

"Exactly. My only disappointment was that I didn't get to kill Wendy's spawn, Celeste. *You* ruined that."

"And I'm so glad I did."

"Yes, aren't you?" Carmen gave her a bone-chilling smile. "But unlike cats, girls don't have nine lives."

"Celeste?" Teresa's voice shook. "On the scanner I heard a call to come to the Warner house. A neighbor reported an attack. You went there, didn't you? You *killed* Celeste!"

"Well, not quite. I got her father and her grandmother, but that slippery little girl got away. At least for the time being."

"You killed Jason and Fay Warner?" Teri asked in horror. "Why?"

"All I really wanted was the girl. She recognized me in the park tonight. I don't know how after all these years, but she knew I was the person who'd killed her mother. I knew at the park I had to shut her up before she could tell anyone—at least anyone who would believe her. But it turns out that as far as Gabe was concerned, I didn't have anything to fear from Celeste. My real nemesis turned out to be Sharon."

Carmen tilted her head, and her eyes took on a faraway, musing look. "I really did *love* Gabe. I didn't love your father—he was basically a brute. I wanted what he could give me. But my feelings for Gabe had nothing to do with money or position. I just wanted him. But once again, I lost out. Sharon didn't want me to have him, and with him, Sharon came first, not me. So, odd as it seems, Celeste didn't ruin my life with Gabe—Sharon did. Gabriel gave up *me* for that spoiled, self-centered brat."

Carmen paused, looking slightly beyond Teri as if her consciousness were temporarily leaving her body. Then she snapped back to attention. "You know by now I don't lose well. At first I thought of killing Sharon, but I don't know where she is. Then I thought of killing Gabe, but he's out looking for Sharon. So I came up with a much better plan—a much more hurtful plan. I will take away the only thing they love as much as each other—Daniel." Carmen tilted her head and smiled girlishly. "Now let's go get the child. Together."

3

Carmen flipped on the upstairs hall light so Teresa could clearly see the way to her room, but she ordered Teri not to turn on the bedroom light and startle both the boy and the dog. "Tell him to get dressed or you dress him if he can't do it himself."

"Why does he have to be dressed?"

"Because we're leaving. Anyone could come here at any time."

"So you're not just going to shoot us here?" Teri asked.

"That would be simpler, but not so much fun for me. And not so frightening for the kid. And as for you . . . well, I have another reason for not wanting to kill you here. Now go wake him up and remember that I'm standing right here with a gun pointed at the boy. Don't let him see me, though. I don't want him throwing a fit."

Awash with chills that her jeans and long-sleeved blouse did nothing to help, Teresa quietly opened the bedroom door. In the light from the hall, she saw Sierra immediately raise her head, big ears standing alert and tall. Teresa held her finger up to her lips, a sign Sierra knew meant "quiet," and crept toward the bed. Daniel lay curled in a fetal position, his strawberry blond hair rumpled, his little face round and vulnerable.

Teresa felt as if someone were squeezing her heart. She was supposed to wake up this innocent child and lead him into the night at gunpoint. How could she do it? But what else *could* she do? If she refused, Carmen would simply shoot both her and Daniel in the bedroom. Carmen was fond of killing people in bedrooms, Teresa thought in dry contempt. The bitch. Besides, if Carmen was determined to make this execution more complicated than it had to be, she might be giving Teri a chance to do something, to save Daniel, she thought. Please let me come up with some brilliant idea, she begged silently.

"Daniel?" Teresa whispered. She reached out and softly placed her hand on his arm. "Daniel, honey, you have to wake up now."

The child muttered fretfully and tightened his grip on Sierra. The dog's amber eyes searched the doorway. She knew someone lurked there, Teresa thought. Sierra didn't bark because beneath the perfume, she picked up a familiar scent—Carmen's scent—but she knew something was wrong.

Teresa tried again. "Daniel, you must wake up." She tugged on him. "I need for you to wake up *now*."

Daniel rubbed his eyes. Then they immediately snapped open. "Is Mommy home?"

"Not yet, I'm afraid, but we have to go somewhere."

"Where?"

"Well, that's a secret. We're going to play a game, Daniel."

"A game? I'm too sleepy to play a game."

"I know it's late, but this game is going to be worth waking up to play. You'll need to get dressed and then we'll be on our way."

"On our way where?"

"That's part of the secret. Do you want me to help you dress?"

"No," Daniel replied promptly. "I'm a big boy. You wait outside," he said with prim dignity.

Teresa retreated. Before Carmen had a chance to protest, Teresa said, "He's not going to use the phone because he doesn't think anything is wrong. If I insist on staying in the room, he'll get cranky and move more slowly. Certainly you can contain yourself for five minutes,

Carmen. After all, you have the rest of the night to do away with Daniel and me."

As the two women stood in the hall, listening to Daniel chatter fussily to Sierra about people making you go to sleep, then waking you up and telling you to get dressed and go outside when it was still *dark,* for gosh sakes, Teresa felt a sudden red-hot rage when she thought of Sharon. If it hadn't been for her, there wouldn't have been the terrible scene downtown, Carmen probably wouldn't have cracked at this moment, Daniel would not be staying in this house, and he would be in no danger from Carmen, whose anger Teresa believed was directed at her as well as the child. Being able to get both of them at once was a bonus for Carmen.

"Carmen, just take me," Teresa said desperately. "Daniel hasn't even seen you. He's no danger to you."

"I want him to die."

"To hurt Gabriel, the man you say you *truly* love. That's not love, Carmen."

"Shut up," Carmen snapped. "You don't know anything about love."

"Apparently I don't know anything about what *you* call love." Teresa peeked into the bedroom to see Daniel struggling to pull his socks right side out and put them back on his feet. "You say you want to kill Daniel to get back at Gabe and Sharon. Why do you want to kill me? Certainly not to get back at *my* father."

"No, I took care of him directly. Besides, getting rid of you would have been doing him a favor."

"Thanks," Teresa said flatly.

"You know it's true." Carmen sighed. "My reasons for wanting to kill you are more complex than my reason for wanting to kill Daniel. They have to do mostly with who you are and what you are."

"How fascinating. Would you like to explain?"

Carmen's pale, black-smudged face turned querulous. "How much longer is it going to take for that kid to dress?"

"Just a minute. Tell me why you want to kill me."

"Oh, Teri, you can be so tiresome." Carmen paused. "You grew up with all the things I didn't have—money, position, a doting mother."

"But you must have seen that having a family with money and an inherited *position,* as you put it, in the community isn't necessarily a recipe for happiness. I was miserable. So was Mom."

"Oh yes, dear Marielle. Beautiful, wealthy, showered with so many blessings and completely oblivious to all of them except her two overprivileged, ungrateful children. She had everything, but all she could do was drift around being frail and sad. I would have detested her even if she hadn't stood between me and Hugh."

"My mother was a wonderful woman, a gentle and loving woman," Teresa returned through clenched teeth, knowing how ridiculous it was to argue with this crazy woman who saw the world through the funhouse mirror of her mind. "I want to know if you hurt my mother—"

"I'm ready, Aunt Teri." Daniel's voice sounded tired and put-upon. "Can Sierra come with us on this secret mission?"

"No, honey." Teresa tried to sound light. "She'll make too much noise. Just slip out of the bedroom and close the door behind you. She'll whine for a few minutes, then settle down and go back to sleep. Hurry!"

In a moment, Daniel sped through the doorway, and closed the door just a second before Sierra reached it. She immediately began to bark. Daniel looked up at Teresa, flashing his grin with the missing front tooth. Then he caught sight of Carmen looming in her dirty clothes and grotesquely smeared makeup, and he let out a shriek. At that point, Sierra went wild, throwing herself against the door.

"Go," Carmen ordered, pointing the gun at Teresa. Daniel let out a whimper.

"Daniel, we have to do just what the lady says," Teri

said calmly. "I know it seems strange, but you'll understand later."

Carmen let out a burst of scratchy laughter and Teresa would have loved to slap her, gun or no gun. But Teresa held on to her composure and firmly held Daniel's hand as they dutifully trooped downstairs to the living room, Carmen following close behind. Carmen then directed them to the kitchen and out the back door. "And now what?" Teresa asked as they walked the narrow stone path next to the tall shrubbery at the rear of the house.

"I parked my car on that little isolated road to the north of your property," Carmen said. "We're going out the back door to avoid all those damned lights on your porch, walk to my car, and drive to one of your mother's favorite spots—McClintic Wildlife Preserve, better known as the TNT Area. You remember it, don't you, Teri?"

"TNT Area?" Daniel repeated with a catch in his voice. He turned to look at Carmen. "It's creepy there! I'm scared of that place!"

"I know you're scared of it. Your grandfather told me. We're going, though."

Daniel's voice had already begun to quiver with fear. "But there's a monster named Mothman up there and hidden tunnels and little huts that hold things that explode and Timmy Rollins says there's even places for vampires to live and—"

Carmen cut him off with a harsh laugh. "That's right, Daniel. The TNT Area has *all* of those awful things. Every single one of them." She flashed him a bizarre, lopsided, shadow-eyed smile. "We sure are going to have a really good time up there tonight."

CHAPTER
TWENTY-THREE

1

CELESTE WAITED UNTIL CARMEN'S and Teri's voices had faded in the darkness—at least five minutes, she thought—and crawled out from behind the shrubbery at the back of Teri's house. She kept low in case anyone looking back could see her in the light still glowing through the kitchen window, and scuttled to the door, fiercely hoping it had not locked when Carmen slammed it behind her. The knob turned easily in Celeste's hand. She opened the door no more than absolutely necessary, slipped in, shut the door behind her, and locked it. Only then did she realize she'd been holding her breath.

Once inside the kitchen, though, she stayed quiet so she could better hear if anything else was going on in the house. When chatter burst from the police scanner, she involuntarily opened her mouth in a silent scream. She was still mute, she thought in despair. She was still unable to call anyone for help.

And that awful Carmen—that *murderer*—had said she was taking Teri and Daniel to the TNT Area. Celeste knew about the TNT Area. Grandma had never taken her there, and when she'd once let Daddy know she wanted to go, he'd explained that it was a really big, scary place where even *he* didn't want to go. That had settled the matter for Celeste. Grandma had tried to convince her that everywhere except home was scary, but if Daddy thought this place was scary and he didn't want to go, either, she'd known it must be true.

And yet Carmen with her gun was making Teri and Daniel go to a place where even Daddy would have been scared to go. Celeste knew what Carmen was going to do to them. The same thing she'd done to Mommy and Hugh so long ago, the same thing she'd done to Grandma and Daddy just a little while ago.

Celeste suddenly felt dizzy and sat down on a kitchen chair, trying to control her breathing, trying to stop the tears running down her face for what seemed like a lifetime. Finally, she couldn't stand it anymore and stood.

After two steps, Celeste paused and lifted her face, her nose twitching like some night animal's trying to pick up the scent of danger. But she smelled only one thing—*the* smell, the scent she'd detected in Bennigan's less than a week ago, the scent Carmen Norris had worn when she'd killed Mommy.

Gathering her courage, Celeste eased out of the kitchen, through the dining room, and into the living room, where only one lamp near a recliner remained shining. From upstairs came the sound of a dog alternately barking and whining while frantically scratching at a door. Sierra, Celeste thought. Teri's cute brown dog that made so much noise but wouldn't bite was trapped in a bedroom and

probably scared silly, wondering what had happened to
Teri and the little boy. Celeste couldn't allow Teri's dog to
be upset.

Celeste barely hesitated before darting up the stairs and
running to the room at the end of the hall. She opened the
door and the brown dog flung herself forward, barking and
snarling as if she were going to kill Celeste. In a moment
of panic, Celeste backed away from the dog, then opened
her arms rather than taking a defensive posture. If only I
could talk, Celeste thought. If only I could calm the dog
with gentle tones. Instead, Celeste kneeled and smiled,
then held out her hand. The dog snarled some more, eyed
her warily, then slunk forward and sniffed her hand. In a
moment, Sierra was burrowing against Celeste, who
rubbed her comfortingly behind the ears.

Celeste didn't like staying upstairs and feeling cut off
from the rest of the house. When she stood and began descending the stairs, she was glad Sierra followed her
closely. Both stopped when they reached the living room.
Celeste's gaze darted to every shadowy corner, then at
Sierra, who stood rock-still, the hair along her backbone
raised. She feels okay with me, Celeste thought, but she's
ready for danger.

Danger that seemed to descend immediately when someone pounded on the door. Celeste instinctively dropped to
the floor. Sierra ran to the door in another frenzy of barking
and snarling.

Another strike on the door with a fist. Then a man
yelled, "Teri! Are you awake?" Sierra continued to raise
the roof, sounding like a hundred-pound Doberman.
"Sierra?" the man shouted. "Sierra, it's me—Mac. Teri?
Sierra, get Teri!"

Mac? Celeste frowned. The Mac who loved Teri? Could
Mac MacKenzie actually have turned up at just the right
time? Had her wish to Snowflake *really* had any effect on
this situation?

"Teri!" he yelled again, now ringing the doorbell along with knocking. "Teri, I'm sorry I didn't call. Let me explain—"

When Celeste threw open the door, he jumped. He squinted at the girl standing in the dim light of the living room. Finally he asked, "Celeste?" She nodded. "Celeste, what are you doing here?"

Celeste pointed at her throat and shook her head. Mac frowned. She tapped her mouth and shook her head again. Mac frowned. Meanwhile, Sierra jumped around, barking, whining, squeaking, as if trying to explain the problem. At last, Celeste opened her mouth, pointed to it, then raised her hands in helplessness.

"My God, you can't speak!" Mac shouted as if she were deaf. She nodded. "What's wrong? Why are you here? Where's Teri?"

Celeste shook her head again. She motioned for him to come in, then ran to the end table beside the recliner. She picked up a notepad and began to write.

2

Carmen walked behind Teresa and Daniel as they tramped across the back of Teri's property until they came to the narrow, rutted lane where Carmen had left her car. She ordered Teresa to drive while she sat in the backseat, clutching Daniel against her until he cried out in protest. "Be quiet, little boy," Carmen hissed. Then to Teri, "I'm holding the gun. If you try *anything*, Teresa, and I mean *anything*, I will shoot you and then the kid. Do you understand me?"

"I understand," Teri said evenly. "I'll do exactly as you say. Just don't hurt Daniel."

"Don't *make* me hurt Daniel. If I have to blow off his head in this car, it will be your fault."

Daniel whimpered, and Teresa briefly closed her eyes. How could this be happening? How could Carmen—her friend—have so quickly turned into such a monster?

But the woman hadn't abruptly changed character tonight. For years, something dark, ugly, and deadly had coiled beneath her lovely face, her beautiful eyes, her warm and protective manner. Teri asked herself why she hadn't seen it. Why hadn't her mother seen it? Why hadn't Gabe seen it?

Daniel made small mewling sounds and twice Carmen had told him to shut up, the second time with an intensity that frightened Teri. If Daniel didn't be quiet, the woman was going to lose control and kill him, Teri thought. She had to do something to distract Carmen. "I suppose this is going to be my last night on earth," Teresa said almost casually, "so would you mind answering a few questions for me? It seems only sporting."

Carmen let out a bray of laughter. "*Sporting*. How quaint! All right, as long as you concentrate on your driving. You haven't forgotten your way to the TNT Area, have you?"

"Not a chance." Teresa had reached the end of the rutted lane. Unnecessarily, she put on her blinker, and turned onto the highway. "First of all, I'd like to know how you got into our house that night eight years ago. Dad had the locks changed after the divorce."

"And he had to give the housekeeper one of the new keys because she came in so early. I dropped by every few weeks to see you—usually when Wendy was out. Emma always left her purse in the laundry room. One morning I simply removed the house key from Emma's key ring, had a copy made, and stopped in again that afternoon. I had an excuse ready for visiting a second time the same day, but I didn't need one. The back door was usually left unlocked during the day, so I came in quietly and replaced Emma's key with no one the wiser. No harm done."

"Except the police suspected Emma because she had a key to the house—a key that either she *or* Mac could have used."

"Yes, well, the more red herrings the merrier. Nothing happened to either of them."

"Not that you would have cared if it did."

"No, I didn't care. As your father always said, they were just the hired help, and no one cares what happens to the hired help."

Teresa glanced at the speedometer. The last thing she wanted was to be stopped by the police. Carmen would shoot both of her hostages before the cop even made it to the car door. "I know on the night of my birthday you made an excuse to go to the restroom at Club Rendezvous, then slipped out and left that note in my car. It wasn't a spontaneous move. You'd even brought a newspaper clipping along, which means you'd planned on leaving the note. That's probably why you insisted we go to the club in the first place. I also know you must have sent the fax the next morning, the one supposedly from my father. Why did you feel it necessary to start tormenting me after eight years?"

"If you're smart enough to figure out that I lured you to Mac's club so I could leave the note and clipping for you, you should be smart enough to figure out the reason. But I guess not. Try Celeste. Celeste, after eight years of glorious silence, started blabbing her head off in Bennigan's right after I'd passed her table. I was afraid she'd recognized me *then*. I thought if she hadn't definitely recognized me, she at least had the glimmer of an idea I'd been the one who'd killed her mother. She looked right at me before I stabbed her. I've been trying to get at her for ages, but Fay and Jason kept her so well protected I never got a chance.

"After a few years, I didn't think I needed a chance. But then she started talking. Most people thought she was nuts, so I didn't believe she'd be considered a reliable witness, but just in case *anyone* took her halfway seriously, I needed to throw suspicion back onto you, just as I'd originally planned. The first step was to have you start acting jittery, scared, right after Celeste began to talk. You had to act as if her talking really shook you because it put you in danger. After all, not *everyone* believed Roscoe Lee Byrnes killed Hugh and Wendy."

Carmen suddenly laughed again. "And then lo and behold, the very next morning the son of a bitch recanted his confession! Talk about a stroke of luck! I knew then there was no such thing as justice in the world. I've always known it, but I never had *proof*. That was my proof. If justice existed, Roscoe would have gone quietly into that good night called death and you would have been forever exonerated of killing Hugh and Wendy. But there *is* no justice. Don't you see, Teri? There . . . is . . . no . . . justice!"

"It would seem you're right." Teresa kept her voice neutral. She knew showing contempt for Carmen might be a fatal mistake. "What about the night someone in a long black coat with a hood like yours left Snowflake on my porch? That couldn't have been you, Carmen—I was on the phone with you."

Teresa glanced in the rearview mirror long enough to see Carmen smile. "I had a key to the Farr house. I've gone in and out dozens of times. I took that night-light years ago. I don't know why—maybe because it came from Trinkets and Treasures, which the munificent Hugh so generously gave me as a parting gift.

"A couple of months ago, I caught a teenage boy shoplifting in the store. He was terrified. He begged. It was his third offense. I finally said I wouldn't tell the police as long as he promised to do me a favor someday. I made certain he knew I was serious—he did *not* have a free pass. Well, I finally demanded my due. I lent him this coat, gave him the night-light, and told him exactly what time to leave it on your porch, making sure you caught a glimpse of him—hood, makeup, wig, and all—just to give you even more of a scare. And I knew he wouldn't dare tell anyone—they might go to the police and if so, I had a surveillance tape showing him shoplifting. If I went down, so did he."

"It was a good plan," Carmen said with satisfaction. "I called you at the time I'd told him to arrive. Even if you'd had the slightest doubt about me being involved in your recent harassment, you couldn't suspect *me* of leaving the night-light—I can't be in two places at once. So, everything worked perfectly."

"And it never occurred to me that if you'd been as frantic as you'd seemed, you would have called the police to come check on me, not hung on the phone screaming," Teresa said. "I was stupid."

"Yes," Carmen answered with mild amusement. "Stupid."

"You also took that videotape of my sixteenth birthday from Dad's house, picked the lock to my house, and put on the tape just before I got home with Mac."

"You told me you were going out to dinner with him. Sierra didn't react too badly when I came in—she knows me. But you were so slow. I waited until I saw the headlights of Mac's car coming toward your house before I stuck in the tape and went out the back."

"Clever. You also left Mom's scarf in Dad's house, didn't you? The woman next door is definitely paranoid, but she was right about seeing lights upstairs."

"I knew the very day the house sold. The real estate agent dropped into Trinkets and Treasures just brimming with the news. I took a chance that you couldn't resist going in the house one last time and rummaging through Marielle's junk. I still had the copy of Emm's key to the house. I left the scarf that night. I went back the next night to make sure the scarf still had that distinctive, deceptively fresh scent."

"Oh, it did. You'll be glad to know that finding it scared the hell out of me." Teresa paused. "But I saw Mom wearing that scarf just days before she disappeared. She didn't leave it behind in the house for you to pick up on one of your secret tours. When did you take the scarf from Mom, Carmen?"

Their gazes met in the rearview mirror. "On the day she came to see you, Teri. On the last day of her life." Carmen gave Teri that odd, tilted smile again. "Well, we're finally at the TNT Area. Let's see what it has in store for you and Daniel."

3

While Celeste wrote, Mac hung over her shoulder, nervously jingling change in his pocket and yelling, "Carmen did *what*?" and, "She made them go *where*?" until Celeste would have screamed, if she could have. When she finished, she held out the paper and he jerked it from her trembling hand, read it again, and burst out with, "Oh, my God!" Then he rushed to the phone.

His anxiety had communicated itself to Sierra, sparking another barking fit. Celeste knew Mac was trying to talk to the police, so she dragged the dog into the kitchen and grabbed one of the strawberry cupcakes arranged on a platter, crumbling it up and tossing it into a dog dish. Sierra promptly stopped barking and began eating as if she hadn't tasted food for a week. When she finished, they returned to the living room just as Mac hung up the phone.

"The police are headed for the TNT Area, but they don't know where to go when they get there. The place covers hundreds of acres. Do you have any idea where Carmen was taking Teri and Daniel?" Mac was still shouting at her and Celeste clapped her hands over her ears and grimaced while shaking her head. "No idea at all?" Mac yelled.

Celeste gave up trying to make him understand that her hearing was fine. She shook her head sadly. Mac muttered, "Damn." Then he boomed, "Celeste, I have good news for you. The police just told me that your father is alive!"

Celeste's blue eyes flew wide. "That's right. Your father was stabbed, but the wound wasn't fatal. A neighbor called nine-one-one and the paramedics came immediately. Your dad is in surgery, but they think he's going to be all right." Celeste beamed. Then Mac said more softly, "I'm afraid your grandmother didn't make it, though. I'm very sorry."

Celeste's head drooped. Mac leaned down, took her face in his hands, tilted it upward, and kissed her lightly on the forehead. "Everyone has been looking for you, honey. I told the police where you are and they're coming to get you." Celeste shook her head and pointed at Sierra. "They'll take her, too. You run and find one of her leashes. I think Teri keeps them on a hook in the kitchen."

When Celeste returned with a leash firmly attached to Sierra's collar, Mac looked out the window. "I see a police car coming up the road now. Everything is going to be fine, kiddo."

Five minutes later, a patrolman gently escorted Celeste and an exuberant Sierra to a police car. Mac leaned in before the policeman closed the door. "I'm sorry I have to leave you, Celeste, but I want to help the police find Teri. You've been an incredibly brave girl. I'm so proud of you. Teri would be, too. And I want you to remember something, Celeste. Teri loves you very much and she has tremendous faith in you. She'd want you to know how she feels about you, no matter what happens."

As Mac shut the door, Celeste smiled tremulously, tears spilling over her cheeks. She hadn't been able to save Grandma, but Daddy was alive, and maybe, just maybe, Teri would survive this horrible night, too.

4

At 2:30 a.m., the highway was nearly deserted. Mac knew the police were ahead of him although he couldn't see any police cars. He remembered that Marielle's parents had owned a building near the entrance to what was now the McClintic Wildlife Preserve and had willed the building to her. Maybe Carmen had taken Teri and Daniel to the building. At least Mac hoped she had because it was easy to find and he could think of nowhere else to look. He'd directed the police to the building.

As he drove, Mac finally tried to absorb the fact that Carmen, of all people, had killed Hugh and Wendy Farr, stabbed Celeste, pretended to be Teri's friend for years, killed Fay Warner and injured Jason, and now taken Teri and Daniel hostage. Mac had known the woman since he used to mow lawns for the Farrs and she'd been friends with Marielle. *He'd* had only a speaking acquaintance with her, but she'd always been nice to him. She'd been so kind to Teri and she'd always seemed so *normal* that he still couldn't completely believe Celeste's story. Oh, he was certain someone had kidnapped Teri and Daniel, but perhaps Celeste had made a mistake about *who* had kidnapped them. She'd been a traumatized girl for so long. She was traumatized again. Maybe she was basing her accusations on old, tangled stories and misunderstandings. She *had* to be wrong.

Except that for some reason Mac couldn't quite identify, he didn't believe Celeste was mistaken. Attractive, hardworking, funny, charming Carmen Norris was a cold-blooded killer.

Four miles north of Point Pleasant, Mac turned in at the wide Y-shaped entrance to the wildlife preserve. His headlights pierced the unusually dark night, revealing a paved road edged by well-cultivated corn and soybean fields. Just beyond the fields, he saw the outline of the building owned by Marielle and the flashing of lights atop patrol cars. He pulled into the parking lot, jumped out of his Lexus, and without switching off the engine dashed to the nearest policeman.

"Anybody here?" he asked nervously.

The young patrolman shook his head. "The building is locked up tight, Mr. MacKenzie. We've searched all around it and we can't find any recent signs of people being here—not even fresh car tracks. I'm afraid no one is here."

"I'm not surprised," Mac said hopelessly. "This place is too open—too close to the road, too visible to anyone passing by. Carmen would have taken—" Mac broke off, unable to say "Teri." "Her and the boy somewhere more isolated."

"Do you have *any* idea where that might be? After all, this place covers over two thousand acres."

Over two thousand acres. Mac knew the area was huge, but hearing someone actually announce an approximation of the acreage caused his hopes to sink. How could he possibly find Teri in such a big place, especially when time was so important?

Mac closed his eyes, trying to recall everything he knew about the area. He remembered that during World War II, two power plants had been constructed to supply energy for the manufacture of explosives. One of the plants—located across from the building Marielle had owned—had been destroyed. He knew a maze of tunnels lay beneath the ground of the complex. He remembered that after the war, parts of the complex had been sold off to chemical companies for storage of their materials.

Storage. The word echoed in Mac's mind. Not only chemicals were stored in the TNT Area. During the war, manufacturers had stored explosives in "igloos," steel and concrete domes covered with dirt and grass so they would be invisible to reconnaissance planes. Marielle had been intrigued by the history of the area. Many times his mother had mentioned that Marielle had tried to talk Emma into visiting the site with her when she did research for the book she hoped to write, but the area had terrified Emma. "You couldn't get me up there for love or money," Emma always said. "I'm afraid the only people who will go with Marielle are Teresa and Carmen. Mostly Carmen. She loves that place almost as much as Marielle does."

But Teresa and Carmen weren't the only people who'd accompanied Marielle to the TNT Area. *He* and Teri had gone one day because Teri thought it would please her mother. They'd gone to one particular igloo—one Marielle favored because it was not sealed shut. She'd told them she'd come to it with Carmen and that Carmen had taken one photograph of her by the igloo, but she wanted more. So they'd made an adventure of exploring the place and of taking pictures. Many pictures, because Marielle had been so taken with the structure, even the inside where the walls bore graffiti, names of supposedly "easy" girls and their phone numbers, highly creative commands for some unpopular town figures to "go to hell," a few inverted pentagrams. Mac now frowned, feeling desperate. If only he could remember the location of that igloo . . .

5

Teresa hadn't gone far into the TNT Area when Carmen instructed her to take a left turn. They drove a few feet before reaching a low iron bar blocking the road. Carmen told her to shut off the car and get out. "And remember, I have Daniel tight in my grip," she added.

While Carmen slid from the backseat of the car, Teresa stood in the warm darkness, listening to frogs croaking around nearby ponds and the occasional hoot of an owl. She'd never liked this place, not because it was said to have been the home of "Mothman," the creature she'd always thought to be the ridiculous invention of idle minds, but because the area had been the site where death was manufactured—death in the form of explosives. Some of those explosives remained here, hidden, waiting. The thought gave her a chill.

"You're shivering," Carmen said right behind her. "It's not at all cold. Are you frightened?"

"Yes. Who wouldn't be?"

"Good! No false bravado. I hate when people try to act brave in the face of death. Unless they don't care about dying."

"Gus cared about dying," Teresa said stonily. "Did he try to act brave?"

"Gus made the mistake of walking into the barn when I was letting Eclipse loose." Carmen laughed again. "He thought I was Marielle. He was overjoyed! Did you know he and your mother used to have a little bit of a relationship? Nothing that went very far. I never could understand it—your mother had Hugh Farr, but the man she wanted was Gus Gibbs! Anyway, when he got a good look at me, it was all over for him. The rake was there, just waiting for me, and I put Gus out of his misery."

"And turned Eclipse loose, then ran out of the barn right in front of my car."

"Running in front of your car wasn't planned, but you should have seen your face! Then you jumped out in the rain and started wailing, 'Mommy!' Oh, my God, it was priceless!"

"I'm glad you thought so." Teresa started to turn around, but Carmen gave her a sharp, "No!" Teri obeyed, standing still on the dirt road, letting the night sounds of the deserted area wash over her, knowing that soon she would hear nothing. "May I ask one last question?" she ventured.

"I suppose." Carmen had begun to sound tired. She'd had a rough evening, Teresa thought with gallows humor.

"What happened to my mother?"

"Oh dear, I thought you would have guessed by now. After the big scene at your house, when Hugh caught her and she managed to escape, she came running to me. To *me*! She cried and moaned and carried on in that damned hopeless, helpless way of hers that had always driven me wild. I snapped. I just couldn't take it anymore, especially after just finding out that Wendy was pregnant.

"I put on a good show. I comforted her for a while, then I told her I'd drive her back to her aunt Beulah's house. Only we never went to Beulah's. I drove her straight up here, right to the igloo ahead of us. It was evening by then. I didn't have to worry about anyone seeing us. Tired as she was, she couldn't resist getting out to look at that old igloo she'd loved. While she was wandering around, mumbling to herself, I stabbed her. Quite a number of times, actually. And it felt *so* good to finally end her mewling self-pity. So very, *very* good!"

Teresa's stomach clenched. For a moment the dark, lonely landscape spun and she thought she was going to throw up. Then she drew a deep breath. "What did you do with her body?"

"I buried her up here."

"Where?"

"It doesn't matter. Just take my word for it that you'd never find her, even if you got the chance to look. There's probably not much left of her anyway. Still, you'll be with her. That's why I wanted to kill you up here, Teri. You're like her—the woman with everything, even love. You have everything I *should* have had, just like your mother. But I didn't allow her to keep everything and I won't allow you to, either. I hate you just as much as I always hated her. And don't tell me I won't get away with this. I've been prepared for years. I have money hidden and false identification documents. I'll leave this godforsaken place and get a new start just after I've killed you and Sharon's little, sniveling spawn."

Teresa almost whirled on the woman, wanting to claw out her eyes, wanting to knock her to the ground and beat her head against a rock, wanting to do *something* violent to avenge her mother. If Teresa had been alone, she would have, knowing she had nothing to lose. But Carmen still held Daniel, who cried softly, steadily, hopelessly. Poor little Daniel, who would die because he'd been sent to spend the night at Aunt Teri's house. Teresa closed her eyes again, thinking that she simply could not bear what was happening. She almost wished Carmen would just raise the gun and shoot her in the head.

Almost. She could *not* give up on Daniel.

Teresa opened her eyes and said in a shockingly steady voice, "What do you want us to do now, Carmen?"

"I want you to walk straight ahead to that igloo. You can skirt around the bar blocking the road. I've done it a hundred times. So did your mother."

So did Mom, Teri thought as she began to walk slowly through the grass damp with dew at the edge of the road, hearing Carmen and Daniel trailing behind her. Her mother had walked to that igloo with Carmen. Teresa remembered the photo Carmen had taken of Marielle laughing as she'd stood beside the igloo. She had no idea this was where she'd die.

Teresa reached the door of the igloo. She didn't ask what to do next. She grabbed the bar holding the door closed and tugged. It began a slow, grinding movement, then opened.

A wave of musty air washed over her. The total darkness inside seemed to reach for her, luring her seductively into oblivion. It would be so easy to just walk in, to let the darkness swallow her, to let Carmen fire the gun. Teresa took a step inward, feeling drawn, pulled into oblivion—

Then a light flashed on. Carmen had brought along a flashlight. Of course. She'd had this whole thing planned, Teri thought. She wouldn't forget a flashlight, especially since this wasn't her first time—she'd performed this scene eight years ago with Marielle Farr as her victim.

Marielle, Teri thought. Not Marielle *and* another hostage, one whom Carmen held tight while she also aimed a flashlight, not a gun. She couldn't do both at once. She couldn't clutch Daniel, a flashlight, *and* a gun. For just an instant, Carmen was vulnerable.

Teresa stealthily reached into her pocket, closed her hand around the lipstick pepper spray, and plunged toward Carmen. As she charged the woman, Teri flicked off the top of the spray tube. Their bodies met and, Teri sprayed the liquid into Carmen's big blue eyes. Once. Twice. Three times.

The woman let out one short, sharp cry before she and Teri crashed to the ground. Daniel backed away, screaming shrilly, but Teri barely heard him. "Go!" she yelled at him. "Run!" She wasn't sure if he obeyed. She was too intent on finding the gun. Carmen fought and cursed as Teresa's hands raked over her, digging, searching, but the woman's eyes were streaming with tears and she couldn't keep her hands away from them, couldn't get a good grip on Teresa. After what seemed an eternity, Teri grabbed at cold metal, then realized she'd captured the flashlight. She dropped it, desperately seeking the gun. The gun, dammit. Where was the gun?

Suddenly, the world around them burst into brilliant light. Vaguely aware of noise amid the struggle, Teri looked up. Cars. Headlights. Red lights flashing garishly in the soft darkness of undisturbed wilderness. She was dreaming. Teri knew she was dreaming. Carmen let out an animal-like cry of frustration before pain pierced Teri's temple. She shot me, Teri thought vaguely as the world began to fade. Carmen got me after all, just like she did Mom.

EPILOGUE

TERI STOOD IN THE bright sunlight just outside the barn. She drew in a deep breath of fresh, sun-warmed air and watched as Sierra capered after a butterfly. Had it only been a week since Carmen had arrived with food for her engagement party? Had it only been a week since Teri and Daniel had almost died at Carmen's hands?

For two days after Carmen had delivered that furious blow to Teri's temple with her own gun—the .22 she'd finally found—Teresa's thoughts had been muddled, her recollections sketchy. She'd realized Mac was worried—Kent was worried—but she couldn't focus. Then, on the third morning, she'd awakened with her mind sharp, the events of that awful night sharp-edged and so clear they hurt. She wanted to forget, but she knew she'd never be able to wipe that night from her memory.

Worst of all, she'd never be able to wipe Carmen Norris

from her memory—worst because just as Carmen struck Teri in the head with her gun and, half-unconscious, Teri had rolled off Carmen's body, one of the policemen had shot Carmen. Teri had felt something warm and wet and clinging splattering all over her face before she'd slipped into darkness. All Mac would tell Teri was that the cop had gotten Carmen in the head and that it had been bad. Carmen couldn't have felt much pain, though, Mac always added. She must have died almost instantly.

Teri now watched as Mac's Lexus started over the hill. He stopped the car beside the barn. Celeste popped out of the car and ran to Teri, her blond hair flying, her smile wide. She hugged Teri ecstatically, bent to pet an excited Sierra, then flung herself back into Teresa's arms. "Oh, Teri, everybody said you were okay, but I had to see for myself. You look great! Well, you have a little bit of a bruise, but you're still the most beautiful woman in the world!"

"I agree," Mac said, striding toward Teri. His wavy hair glistened in the sunlight and his gaze sought hers, warm, protective, and loving. Teresa tore herself away from Celeste and went to Mac, melting into his strong embrace. "Hey, you've still got quite a grip there, Teri!" He laughed. "I'm not going anywhere."

"I guess I can't stop thinking about Fourth of July night when you left with your mother and you never came back."

Mac looked shamefaced, although he jumped to his own defense. "I've apologized. I've *explained*."

"That when you went back to your mother's apartment and she wasn't there, you went to the emergency room at the hospital. That she'd gone there because she thought she was having a heart attack and she didn't want you to know. False alarm, thank God. That when you got out of the car, your cell phone fell out of your pocket and you must have kicked it under the next car. That you tried and tried to call from the pay phones in the hospital, but either they were tied up or when you got one and dialed my number *I* was on the phone."

"Did you forget that those awful women behind the hospital receiving desk wouldn't let me use one of their *official* phones meant only for hospital use?"

"You did indeed. It's a highly unlikely story—so unlikely that I believe it and you're forgiven. Although if you'd been here—"

"You might not have come so close to . . . well, I don't even want to say it." He looked over at Celeste. "But even if I let you down, Teri, you did have a guardian angel."

Teri smiled at the girl. "You saved my life, Celeste. Mine *and* Daniel's."

"Well, barely," Celeste said, blushing. "I couldn't even talk. I thought it was going to be like last time when I *couldn't* talk for a couple of years. But when I found out Daddy was still alive . . . well, my voice just came back." Some of the joy left her eyes. "But I feel so bad about Grandma. If it wasn't for me, she'd still be alive."

"She died protecting you, Celeste," Teri said. "I didn't know your grandmother well, but I know how important you were to her, and if she had to die now, not twenty years from now, she would have wanted to die taking care of the girl she loved most in the world." Celeste's eyes filled with tears and Teri said quickly, "I asked Mac to bring you here for a reason. Let's go into the barn. I have a surprise for you."

"Are you going to let me ride Eclipse?" Celeste asked excitedly.

"Just wait and see," Teri answered cryptically.

The inside of the barn was bright with sunlight glowing through the skylights. Still, Teresa flipped on a couple of the artificial lights so that every horse stood out clearly. Celeste wandered past the stalls, greeting Bonaparte, Conquistador, Fantasia, and Sir Lancelot. Just before she reached Eclipse, she stopped abruptly and gasped. A cream-colored Morgan with a graceful neck, a narrow, elegant head, and melting dark eyes whinnied, then pushed her muzzle into Celeste's outstretched hand. "Meet Snowflake," Teri said. "She's all yours."

Celeste's mouth parted slightly. Her eyes met Teri's. Then, in a tiny voice, she asked, "She's mine? Really mine?"

"Yes, honey," Teresa said. "I know she's not white, like the original Snowflake, but she's a very light cream with only a couple of dark markings. I hope you're not disappointed."

"Dis . . . disappointed?" Celeste ran from the horse, threw herself into Teri's arms again, and cried, "Oh, thank you, Teri! Thank you, thank you—"

"Okay!" Teresa laughed. "I guess she meets with your approval?"

"I never thought in my whole life I'd have a horse like her! I can't believe it! Daddy won't believe it! Daddy will pay you—"

"No, he won't," Teresa said firmly. "Snowflake is *my* gift to you." She looked down into the girl's brimming eyes. "Now go pay attention to your horse. She misses you already."

In a moment, Celeste stood in front of Snowflake, stroking her, talking to her, dripping tears onto the horse's muzzle, which Snowflake did not seem to mind at all. Sierra, unable to contain herself in moments of joy, stood beside Celeste, twisting, turning, and frantically wagging her tail.

"Buying that horse for Celeste was wonderful of you," Mac said. "I know it cost a fortune."

"I am a wildly successful woman. I'll have you know I gained two new students this week, now that everyone knows I did *not* kill anyone." She sobered. "Not even Carmen."

"She deserved what she got, just like Byrnes did," Mac said.

"And how's your mother?" Teri asked.

"She'd been going downhill the last week because Celeste's talking and Byrnes's recanting his confession upset her. She wasn't sleeping much, and when she did, she had nightmares. She kept mixing up your mother and Hugh with Carmen and Hugh. In her subconscious, she knew about the affair—I think she even saw Hugh and Carmen having some breakup scene at your house, but she wasn't sure of what she was seeing. Down deep she's always known about them, though, and it's been eating her alive for years. She'll be all right now that we know what was troubling her. My mother is a survivor."

"I wish mine had been. I can't even give her a proper funeral. We have no idea where Carmen buried her. The police dug all around the igloo and found nothing, and no one is going to let us dig up half of TNT looking for her."

"But you said you're going to put up a monument for her here at Farr Fields—something small and pretty, just like she'd want. We'll have a service. You and Mom and I will be here. Kent and Daniel and Sharon."

"Sharon only if she's out of the 'convalescent' home, as Kent insists on calling it," Teri said. "I don't think it's a bad thing that this nervous breakdown happened. Sharon has needed help for a long time. Kent was just terrified she was going down the same road as my mother."

"And he didn't want it to affect his public image," Mac said sourly. Teresa shot him a stern look. "All right. I promised I'd try to resurrect my friendship with Kent." Mac paused. "Especially since he's going to be my brother-in-law."

Teresa raised an eyebrow. "Oh, is he?"

"Isn't he?"

"I don't know. Is this your way of proposing, Mac? If it is, I can't say much for your style."

Mac immediately dropped to his knee, pulled a ring case from his pocket, snapped open the lid, and held up a sparkling solitaire set in platinum. "Teresa Lynn Farr, will you do me the honor of marrying me?"

While Teresa pretended to think about it, Celeste dashed to her side, her eyes twinkling. Teri put her left arm around the girl's shoulder and said, "The answer is yes on one condition."

"And what's that?" Mac asked.

"That Celeste will agree to be my maid of honor."

"Oh, Teri, really?" Celeste cried. "This day just gets better and better. Yes, I'll be your maid of honor! Oh, *please* marry Mac! You have to, Teri; you really do!"

Teresa looked deep into Mac's eyes—the eyes she'd loved since she was sixteen. "Yes, I guess I really do."